THE EMPEROR CODE

ORDER OF THADDEUS • BOOK 9

J. A. BOUMA

Copyright © 2020 by J. A. Bouma

All rights reserved.

EmmausWay Press

An Imprint of EmmausWay Media Group

PO Box 1180 • Grand Rapids, MI 49501

www.emmauswaypress.com

No part of this book may be reproduced in any form or by any electronic or mechanical means, including information storage and retrieval systems, without written permission from the author, except for the use of brief quotations in a book review.

This book is a work of fiction. The characters, organizations, products, incidents, and dialogue are drawn from the author's imagination and experience, and are not to be construed as real. Any reference to historical events, real organizations, real people, or real places are used fictitiously. Any resemblance to actual products, organizations, events, or persons, living or dead, is entirely coincidental.

Scripture quotations are from New Revised Standard Version Bible, copyright © 1989 National Council of the Churches of Christ in the United States of America. Used by permission. All rights reserved.

PROLOGUE
NICOMEDIA. AD 337.

The patron of Christ's Church was dying.

And apparently, the man had a secret to tell.

Theophilus groaned as the imperial *carpentum* weaved through rough streets laid in uneven bricks, a privilege usually reserved for wealthy Romans not men of humble positions such as himself. Yet there he was, cloistered in the rickety wooden box, its arched rooftop bearing the stale, stuffy, staid air that had travelled with him from Edessa the past several days, a miasma that threatened to slay him before he reached his destination, a curious call that still made no sense.

It had come in the dead of night a week heretofore. He had been awakened by the master of his brotherhood himself, bearing an imperial messenger and an urgent plea to race posthaste to Nicomedia–before it was too late. For what, he hadn't a clue. Only that a dying man had something that needed to be entrusted, and only to a man from the brotherhood.

Taking nothing for the journey as his brotherhood required —no staff, no bag, no bread, no money, no extra shirt even— Theophilus set out at once. He was told neither the name of the individual nor the location. However, he figured it was someone of great import for all the trouble.

Now he neared a certain seaside town that housed such a guest.

And he dreaded what it meant—what he would find, and hear.

He groaned as the four wheels trundled over another uneven patch of road, each wheel bouncing and thudding and bumping until he thought every bone would fall out of their sockets. All roads may lead to Rome, but not all roads were created equal, even in the city that had become an interim capital for the Emperor until nearby Byzantium had been given the honors, being christened Constantinople after the Emperor's namesake.

Emperor Caesar Flavius Constantinus, the Greatest, Pius, Felix, Augustus.

Suddenly, the view opened up, the *carpentum* having emerged beyond the modest city toward its final stop. The sky was ablaze with the setting sun, and white-capped waves journeyed lazily toward the shoreline a few stadia beyond the road. Three or four boats remained moored at sea buttressing the ancient Greek town, perhaps hoping for one final catch before the day was through.

One end of Theophilus' mouth curled upward at the sight. How life would have been different had he not joined the brotherhood those many years ago. Surely Father would have passed along his own boat upon death, and he would have carried on the family trade with sons of his own, his wife and daughters caring for a modest home perched on a bluff, a handful of cypress trees casting tired shadows across their property as night neared.

The smile was quickly turned upside down at a hot breeze gusting off the sea, carrying the putrid scent of salted fish and rotting garbage and decaying humanity inside his carriage with menacing invasion.

He shielded his face with one arm, the thick wool habit sleeve offering some relief, but his mouth filled with the sour taste of bile. He swallowed hard and closed his eyes, turning from the scene as a memory surfaced from the ancient town's history.

Although not experiencing it firsthand, he had heard reports from the brotherhood that Nicomedia had been the center of persecuting efforts under Emperor Diocletian and his Caesar Galerius. Near the end of February thirty-four years ago now, during the pagan festival of the Terminalia, the Emperor ordered that the newly built church at Nicomedia be razed, its precious scrolls containing the Holy Scriptures burnt, and its modest wealth seized. But that wasn't all, for the next day he issued his first of many edicts against the Christians, ordering similar measures rendered against their places of worship across the Empire.

As one could imagine, the destruction of the Nicomedian church incited panic across the city and beyond. At the end of the month, a fire destroyed part of Diocletian's palace and then another several days later. Although no judgment had been rendered against a particular party for its cause, Galerius blamed the Christians. And he enacted his vengeance without mercy.

The man oversaw the execution of two palace eunuchs with brutality, claiming they had conspired with the Christians to start the fire. He followed this by executing six more members of the Church through the end of April that year. Soon after, Galerius declared Nicomedia to be unsafe and ostentatiously departed the city for Rome, followed by the Emperor himself. So it was ironic another Emperor had taken up residence, given its sordid imperial past.

Why Constantine ever made the seaside village his home

was a mystery. Perhaps, in some small way, it was to redeem this memory. After all, it was he who was responsible for freeing the Christians and liberating the Church to begin with, raising it to a plateau of power they could never have envisioned mere decades ago.

A fresh sage, woodsy scent suddenly washed over his *carpentum*, followed by the spicy scent of burning wood and roasting meat and baking bread. He sat straighter as neat rows of cypress trees began trotting by the carriage window, his stomach rumbling in protest at the scent of blessed food even as it roiled with nervous energy at the task set before him.

They had arrived. The villa of the Emperor, Constantine the Great—and by some accounts, the savior of Christianity.

It didn't take long for the carriage to reach the stately homestead of cut stone and cedar wood, capped by a sloping roof of burnt-red roof tiles. Flapping flames on mounted torches cast an orange glow across the circular drive as they pulled up. A dispatch of Roman soldiers milled about, their swords clanging against their armor, two of them coming up fast to investigate their arrival.

The driver exchanged words with the men, one of them popping his head inside the carriage for inspection.

Theophilus steeled his face and swallowed, a ripeness wafting from the man threatening to turn his stomach again.

When all was confirmed, the driver climbed down and opened the door.

Theophilus stepped out just as a man appeared through the shadowy entrance. He had to catch himself at the sight. For the man who greeted him was not the man he was expecting.

"Brother Theophilus," he said, voice high and heady, a mop of gray hair falling to thin shoulders.

"Bishop Eusebius…" Theophilus said with a bow, his mind racing with the possibilities of the famed Arian priest of the

Christian sect deemed heretical by the Council of Nicaea just over a decade ago.

But why was he there? What business did he have?

More importantly: Did the ecclesiastical leader know of Theophilus' business?

"Come," Eusebius said. "We haven't much time."

The man spun around and disappeared through an arched doorway and back into the shadows. Theophilus quickly followed.

The pair walked past an expansive walled garden of lilies and jasmine, a fountain bubbling at the center and a flock of exotic birds of dimmed fluorescent colors cawing about the grounds. At the center of the compound a set of stairs took them to the second floor, ceiling vaulted high and torches lining the wall. Another detachment of soldiers were awaiting them, two of which were standing guard outside a massive wooden door, darkly stained and polished to a shiny sheen.

As Eusebius approached, the men opened the doors. He led them inside, a sight that was truly to behold.

The space was vast, and hot. Sweltering, actually, and permeated by the stench of rot and decay.

Of death.

The ceiling was vaulted higher yet than the hallway outside, strong cedar beams above supporting the room of cut stone and mortar, lit by a few dozen oil lamps. The scent of olives from the burned oil mixed with the fetid stench and—

A wracking, hacking cough suddenly refocused Theophilus' attention to a massive bed at the end of the chamber. A canopy of fabric draped over top, providing a modicum of privacy from a retinue of nurses and physicians keeping watch over the man darkening Death's door.

Eusebius motioned for Theophilus toward the bedside of the Emperor who continued his sickly episode.

He nodded and approached the man with hesitation, but

shuffled up through the parted curtain of fabric next to the Emperor's bedside.

The man was staring blankly at the ceiling, a shell of his former self, face sunken with thinning hair and eyes bulging behind deep sockets accented by jutting cheekbones. Hard to imagine the same person lying prone, rail-thin from malnourishment and soaked with sweat, unshaven face and exposed arms blotchy with sores and burst blood vessels—to think this was the mighty Constantine the Great...

A hand suddenly grasped his own resting on the bed. Clammy and boiling with fever, yet firm and commanding.

"You've come..." the Emperor wheezed.

Theophilus caught his breath and cleared his throat, then bowed. "Emperor Caesar Flavius Constantinus, the Greatest, Pius, Felix, Augustus. I am at your service, my liege."

"Leave us..."

The room immediately hastened to oblige the Emperor's order. All except one attendant who stayed near Constantine's bedside, opposite Theophilus, and Eusebius.

As if sensing the bishop's continued presence, the Emperor slowly pivoted his head, eyes black voids yet bearing a certain spark of life. He would not go before he imparted to Theophilus his final words.

"You too..." was all he could muster, yet clearly directed toward the remaining priest.

Theophilus dared not look, instead standing statue still with bowed head.

He heard a muffled gasp from behind before the quiet whisper of the man's sandals across the stone floor. Then the door's tired hinges before thudding closed with an echo that evinced the man's indignation.

Silence flooded the space, punctuated by the Emperor's shallow breaths and the lamps' gently flapping flames.

"I have a confession to make..." Constantine said, getting down to business.

A confession? He wasn't a priest or bishop. The request unnerved him, even more than standing in the man's presence to begin with.

He took a cautious breath. "Emperor, wouldn't you rather like it if I called Eusebius back? Perhaps he could—"

Constantine launched into another wretched cough, the hacking and wracking returning, as if the man would die then and there.

Theophilus turned toward the door, expecting help to come rushing inside. None came. Even the attendant was slow to move, busying himself with gathering a long sheet of parchment, almost like a scroll, and stuffing gleaming metal objects inside a satchel.

Eventually, the coughing ceased, and a voice more powerful than Theophilus expected emerged.

Then the Emperor began confessing. Something wholly unexpected. Beyond what he could have imagined the so-called savior of Christianity confessing.

The attendant took down every word, the Emperor careful to enunciate each syllable so as not to confuse his meaning.

Soon he was finished, and the attendant brought the satchel and the confession around for Theophilus' viewing.

"Go on, take it..." Constantine said.

The man hesitated, searching the attendant for clues but finding none. He took the satchel and the long parchment, finding something curious inside the sack.

Six golden cylinders.

What on earth...

"Go on, open one..." the Emperor instructed.

Fearing he had little time left with the man, Theophilus took one. An end bore a small knob. He grasped it and began twisting, the end of the cylinder coming out with ease.

Inside was another piece of parchment, rolled and curiously bearing Greek marks in black ink. He shook the golden object, the parchment sliding out.

Heart hammering now and head swirling with possibilities, he unrolled it.

Nearly dropping it at first sight.

He read it. Every line, every word, every Greek character.

One end of his mouth curled upward. How fortuitous....

His brotherhood had wondered if copies of the famed document had survived. However, no one had made mention of six such documents in existence. But it was more than that.

Never in his wildest dreams did he imagine the Emperor himself had been harboring them. What was the meaning of this? His palms were growing moist at pondering all it could mean—for his brotherhood, for the Church.

The Emperor was wheezing now, his lungs grasping for breath even as his soul grasped for life.

"Breathe not a word of this, do you hear me?" Constantine managed. "Secret it away for safekeeping."

Theophilus quickly nodded, stuffing the scroll back into the cylinder, then the golden cylinder back into the satchel bearing the others, pondering all that was being asked of him.

There was a knock at the door. Eusebius, accompanied by the Emperor's physician, entered with an acknowledging word. Theophilus folded the parchment and slipped it inside his tunic, setting his garment back in place.

The doctor hustled to Constantine's bedside, leaning down for a listen, intuiting the man's state of health.

"It is time for you to retire," he told the men.

By then, Constantine's eyes had closed and he had faded, nearing Death's door.

"Not until the final rite," Eusebius protested. He nodded at the attendant, who left and returned with a basin filled with water.

The bishop took it and began praying over it, uttering an ecclesiastical incantation that commandeered the liquid for the Church's sacred purposes.

He then gave the basin to the attendant and shuffled to the Emperor's bedside.

Theophilus withdrew, making room for the man and the Church's familiar rite of death and clenching the satchel he had been entrusted as he looked on.

Easing a hand behind the Emperor's head, the bishop dipped his hand inside the basin to baptize him.

"*In nomine patris*," Eusebius said as he poured a handful of water over Constantine's forehead, the holy water cascading down the dying Emperor's face.

He continued, "*et filii*," then scooped another handful before letting it fall upon his head again.

Dipping for one more handful of holy water, Eusebius of Nicomedia intoned, "*et spiritus sancti. Amen*," letting it fall with finality upon Constantine's head.

The bishop eased the Emperor's head back down.

And the man immediately snapped open his eyes, startling Theophilus and the bishop. The men looked at one another, wide-eyed and cautious.

Then he heaved a breath and sighed, his mouth grinning as he sank into the bed before slumping in death.

The pair stood in silence, along with the attendant. Constantine the Great was dead. No telling what that would mean for the Empire.

Or the Church.

Theophilus eased the satchel still clenched in his hand around his shoulders. "I suppose I shall be going, Bishop Eusebius." He went to leave when a hand grasped his arm, firm and unyielding.

For a moment he thought it was Constantine, coming back

from the dead to recant his confession. A ratcheting tremor up his spine confirmed his fear.

It was the bishop, fixing him with determined eyes. The man stood still—still grasping, still fixing.

Theophilus opened his mouth but could not speak. He was paralyzed with wonderment.

The man finally let go, placing the hand instead on Theophilus' back and guiding him to a balcony just past the bed, offering a reassuring smile that accomplished everything but.

"Let us talk," Eusebius said as they walked outside, waves crashing in the distance under a sea of stars shimmering like diamonds strewn across the sky, a sweet smell of lilies and jasmine rising from the gardens below, offering a modicum of comfort.

"Alright," Theophilus said, voice faltering. He recovered, adding: "What is it you would like to discuss?"

The bishop folded his arms and chuckled. "Really? Must I spell it out for you?"

No, he didn't.

The confession.

Theophilus took a breath but said not a word, instead reveling in the heady scent of honey that reminded him of home.

The bishop stepped toward him. "What did he say in my absence?"

He swallowed. "He said...well, he offered his confession."

"Confession?"

"That's right. Before his death."

It wasn't a lie, per se. A misdirection of the truth, yes. But not a lie.

"To you, not even an elder of the Church?" Eusebius spat with revulsion.

Theophilus let it go. Not only because he couldn't care less what the man thought of him, but because he had to act. There was an urgency about what the man offered. And others aside from the Arian bishop would surely be after the information he now held.

Wanting to use it for their powerful ends to change Christianity's course.

He knew which side he was playing for. The Bishop was a different story…

He felt a sudden line of sweat begin to bead at his forehead, even though it was a cool night. And the confessional letter the Emperor had him secret away seemed to pulse at the inner lining of his tunic.

He adjusted it and raised his head with stature. "I am sorry, bishop, but my lips are sealed, bound by the seal of confession. You would not have me divulge such things, would you, particularly the words of the Empire's titular head?"

The man frowned and narrowed his eyes. "No, I suppose not…" He eyed the bag Theophilus was clutching. "Then what is in the sack?"

"A gift," he simply said. "From the Emperor."

The bishop furrowed his brow. "For whom?"

"For me, actually."

The man went to say something more but stayed his tongue and retired.

Standing still, the waves continuing to lap on cue, one after another, Eusebius finally broke away, turning back toward the room and retiring.

He simply said, "Come along. We mustn't keep you any longer."

Theophilus followed and soon they were back at the front, the driver of the imperial *carpentum* standing stiffly to oblige his transportation needs.

Climbing back inside the darkened tomb that could very well service those deathly needs, Theophilus shifted to find

Eusebius whispering into his driver's ear. Neither man made eye contact.

Then the driver nodded and swung the door closed, the bishop sauntering back into the shadows without a word.

Soon the orange glow of the villa torches faded and the succulent smells of roasting meat and baking bread were replaced by the twin terrors of dead salted fish and human waste—from rotting cabbage to the carcass of some mangy dog to excrements cast aside without care.

Theophilus' thoughts immediately turned to next steps. How best to preserve Constantine's confession while also preserving his own life.

Because he knew without a shadow of a doubt what lay in store for his kind when one catches a glimpse of the back of a doubting bishop.

It wasn't long before the familiar crashing waves grew closer, followed by the faint calls of city life, even in the dead of night.

Resolve flooded him as they neared. He knew what he needed to do.

They came up fast to a string of shops and houses made of stone and mud. If he were to do it, it would have to be—

Now!

Theophilus threw open the door and leaped from the carriage, his tunic nearly coming undone in the flight.

He stumbled hard to the road of uneven bricks before rolling down into the dirt beyond—nearly smacking into the wall of some shop and barely missing a pile of something that stank to high heaven.

Theophilus gathered himself quickly as he heard the driver yell a string of Greek curses in the night, the *carpentum* coming to a halt and the man easing down from his perch. His knees were bruised and hands torn from the gravel, but he stumbled as fast as he could toward the shore where he spotted a lone tree bearing witness to the night.

He slid behind it, lungs burning for air and body aching from the tumble. But he was alive, and from what he could see, the driver was none the wiser as to his movements.

Several beats later, the *carpentum* was heard clamoring away from sight and sound.

He had to act before it was too late.

For him, for the confession.

Stealing himself further down the shoreline, he spotted a moored boat. Perhaps one of the night-time raiders fishing for food and fortune. He wasn't sure. What mattered was the gifted lifeline that could prove useful.

It was larger than he understood at first sight, made of heavy, durable wood and flipped onto its stomach until morning. He grasped one side and began heaving it upright, tipping it until it slipped from his grip and crashed to the stony shore.

He let a curse slip but didn't wait for repercussions. Pushing it out to sea, he tossed the satchel inside and hopped in himself, grabbing the oars.

The current was strong, and it tugged him back to shore with a vengeance. But he wouldn't let it, putting to good use the skills he learned as a lad to draw him farther out to sea.

When he was confident of his security, he let the oars rest, winded and worried from the night's events. He leaned back and stared up at the blanket of stars overhead, out of breath and out of options.

Then it hit him. He knew what he had to do.

He reached inside his tunic for the letter. He unfolded and read it, marveling again at what the Emperor had spoken.

Then he tore it. Tore the letter filled with Constantine's dying thoughts into six pieces, rolling each of them around the copy of the Church's code, now bearing the Emperor's own creed. He stuffed each of them into the gilded cradles gifted him by Caesar Flavius Constantinus. His brotherhood would never believe it even if he could tell them, not a word.

But one thing more was needed.

Reaching into his cloak, he withdrew a medallion and eased it from around his neck. Snapping the thin leather strap looped through the object passed down through the ages, he set the medallion on the boat's floor and struck it with a hidden blade, its point piercing the center and splintering into three jagged pieces. He struck it again into a larger piece, splitting it in half, then again for a final splinter.

Six pieces to mark the Emperor's code as authentic.

Perhaps one day it would surface again.

Just when the world needed it.

He dropped a piece of the seal inside each of the six golden cylinders.

Then he grasped the oars and began paddling, launching himself and Constantine's confession on a long journey he prayed would pay off.

One way or another.

CHAPTER 1
APOLLONIA, LIBYA. PRESENT DAY. JUNE 16.

Silas Grey forgot how uncomfortable a dig-site cot could be. Especially after a ten-hour flight, and especially after being put through the wringer just two months ago dismantling a major conspiracy that nearly debunked the Bible and broke the Church.

But he wasn't complaining. Not in the slightest. He was back out in the field getting his hands dirty with an archaeological dig that could shed light on one of the earliest community of believers in Jesus Christ in one of the most neglected parts of the world.

He rolled onto his back and raised his arms above his head, grunting as he stretched the sore out of his limbs, the sound of waves crashing against the shore beyond his tent music to his ears and the rising sun casting hopeful beams filtering through the thick canvas a blessed sight that promised good things to come.

Silas smiled. It was going to be a fabulous day.

Several months ago, Naomi Torres, one of his agents from the Order of Thaddeus and lead archaeologist with Project SEPIO, had led a team of researchers to the shores of North Africa with the hope of better understanding the seedbed of

Christianity. Little did most Christians know, but the faith many detractors and conspiracy theories and doubters claim was cobbled together by dead white guys from Rome and the outer reaches of Europe was actually birthed through the efforts of very non-white midwives.

Of course, the Twelve Apostles are the most well-known of such men: Peter, John, James, Andrew, Philip, Thomas, Bartholomew, Matthew, James son of Alphaeus, Simon the Zealot, Jude Thaddeus, and then Matthias who replaced the disgraced Judas Iscariot. All very non-white Jews who had recognized Jesus of Nazareth was the long-promised Messiah. They neither converted nor conspired to craft a new religion. Instead, they trusted Yahweh—the God of Abraham, Isaac, and Jacob—had made good on his promise to rescue the world through the Suffering Servant Messiah and put it back together again, fulfilling his promises in Jesus' life, death, and resurrection.

But then the faith exploded out from Jerusalem into Judea and Samaria and on to the utter parts of the earth, just as Jesus Christ had instructed his disciples before he ascended into heaven. Moving out into Syria and Persia, even beyond into modern India. The Apostle Paul took the faith throughout Asia Minor and on to Rome, which could arguably—and anachronistically—be called southern Europe. But an unknown player in the formation of Christian culture was south of the Mediterranean Sea: Africa.

Reality is, Christianity has a far greater history in the continent, especially in the north, than its Western or European expressions. From Egypt to Sudan and Ethiopia to Eritrea, from Libya to Tunisia and Algeria to Morocco—early African Christianity played a decisive role in the formation of the Church, both its culture and practices, but also its doctrine and teachings. What was later taught throughout Europe was originally shaped in Africa by such names as Tertullian, Cyprian, Athanasius, Augustine, and Cyril.

And the Order of Thaddeus aimed to explore more of that history and those personalities, exploiting them in the interest of preserving and protecting the once-for-all-faith entrusted to God's holy people by Jesus Christ himself. After all, it was their mission, given to members of the Order by Jude Thaddeus himself, an apostle of Christ.

The smell of frying salted bacon and strong brewing coffee and spicy burning wood wafted inside Silas's tent on a warm current, one flap of his canvas entrance having come undone during the night. It was waving lazily in the morning breeze, the heavenly scent carried along up the bluff laced with salted fish and the traces of early morning conversations and laughter.

Silas's stomach was rumbling now at the invitation to taste and see the goodness of the Lord for a new day. Literally, in the form of a hearty Order-issued breakfast. No doubt with Gapinski at the griddle. He rolled out of the cot, his bare feet hitting the packed earth. He closed his eyes and sighed, that blessed feeling of all the potential that lay beneath the ground clearing his head and allaying any anxiety he held for what the day might bring.

Several weeks ago, SEPIO had been warned about a potential—*something* in the works targeting Western workers in the area. Vague and undefined, but something that could derail their archaeological endeavors, not to mention threaten their lives. He'd been unable to shake the worm of worry working through him during the flight and then barely slept a wink because of it.

Victor Zarruq had brought news from one of their field operatives who had heard internet chatter surrounding the dig, along with a warning. The man was a trustee of the Order's board of directors who had been sent to help smooth Silas's transition into Order Master after Rowen Radcliffe's death. And as the former bishop of Libya, he knew all too well the dangers that the region posed, a hotbed for religious and political zealotry and terrorism. A follow-up conversation with the agent stationed in their Rome office bore little concrete information. Only that the Order's activity in North Africa seemed to have generated chatter on the dark web, along with a curious reference to an emperor code that bloomed into wide-ranging conspiracy theories involving the Church.

Which was even more concerning.

Because the day before they got the intel tip, Markus Braun, the social-media titan and founder of the WeNet platforms who had architected the conspiracy that had threatened to discredit the Bible and its message, had made mention of such a code during his take-down attempt of the central element of the Christian faith. Whatever it was sounded more like a bargain-bin Kindle conspiracy thriller than anything remotely connected to the Church. But the fact others were parlaying the language on anonymous, black-hole sectors of the internet was most alarming.

Especially since Silas had no clue what either the specific threat posed or what the cryptic reference meant. Because there were over seventy emperors during the first few centuries of the Church's early life who could fit the bill. Nothing had come of the intel after he arrived the first time, so he had made trips back and forth every so often to check on Torres's progress and keep an eye on the threat. A flurry of chatter across the dark web a day ago sent him and his SEPIO agents flying to North Africa again.

And back into the fray again, though he was beginning to have his doubts.

Silas pushed through his tent flap, the smells and sights and sounds washing over him like a warm blanket, a balm for his mind-numbing worries and bone-weary body. He smiled at what lay before him.

A burnt orange glow hovered on the eastern horizon, a fission explosion splitting the emerging indigo day sky from the waning night time, stars and a full moon fading fast. Seagulls called out to one another high in the sky down to a flock of them nesting on an outcropping of boulders and ancient stone, all that remained of the ancient city poking up from the seawater after sinking beneath the surface a millennium ago.

The Order of Thaddeus camp of seven canvas tents housed the coterie of researchers as well as his SEPIO crew. Torres was overseeing the dig, supplemented by Zoe Corbino's technological know-how from their headquarters back in Washington, DC, security muscle from Matt Gapinski and Celeste Bourne, and his own leadership—however modest and meager it might be, given the talent stuffed inside those tents.

The encampment was arrayed in an arch on a bluff overlooking the sea, the rising sun paving the waters with gold, capped by lazily rolling white specs that promised reasonable seas and enough of a breeze to keep the bugs away and keep from overheating. The worst things you could get on an archaeological dig were pesky bugs and suffocating heat while you were knee deep in a hole trying to unearth the past. Dirt clung to you even worse than the pesky bugs, made all the worse by the red welts they left behind. And that wasn't even touching on the diseases they bore, much less sunburn. The breeze and modest early summer temperatures should keep both at bay.

Oh, yes, it was going to be a fabulous day! Especially with the view on the western front of the encampment: the East Basilica of Apollonia, with all of its pale-white pillars still standing and all the secrets it held beneath its sand.

At the center of the encampment was a goodly fire, wood stacked and going white from flickering flames inside a makeshift fire pit made from stones from the shore. It was draped by two iron griddles, and now Silas smelled baking batter.

"Pancakes?" he muttered, his mouth slackening and watering with delight. He slipped into a pair of sandals and was instantly drawn toward the makeshift kitchen like a tractor beam, eager to fill his belly with the morning goodness as much as to join the others who had already been roused from their sleep for breakfast.

Silas walked across the rocky ground, nodding to a pair of researchers. Couldn't recall for the life of him who they were, but he was sure they were top-notch. The Order hired only the best when it came to defending and protecting the faith—whether brains or brawn.

And then he saw her. Celeste Bourne. His bride-to-be. Long brown hair askew, her braid having been undone for sleep and falling across her shoulders with wavy delight. Wearing light-weight grey hiking pants and a dark-blue T-shirt, a cream-colored wrap-around keeping her warm. He figured she wasn't wearing any make-up either, given the conditions, but it didn't matter. Natural was the way to go for her. He stopped a few paces from the center of camp to admire his love.

What a beut...

"I hear you are to be married soon," a familiar voice said from behind. Buttery and bassy and accented with the tongue of the land.

Silas turned to find Bishop Victor Zarruq smiling at him and nodding toward Celeste. The man's bushy salt-and-pepper beard was a bit matted from sleep. He was wearing his trademark long linen cassock with an interweaving pattern of blues and greens and blacks running down both sides, a cap of the same pattern crowning his bald head. The man had served most of his life in the very soils that hid the traces of early Christianity, faithfully shepherding Christ's flock in the midst of severe religious persecution. A few years ago, over twenty believers had been kidnapped by radical Islamic terrorists in the Libyan city of Sirte. While they were Egyptian Coptic Christians, the man still felt responsible for the events that had sent a ripple of persecuting worry throughout the Libyan churches. He retired shortly thereafter, but his steady hand had helped strengthen believers facing the prospect of martyrdom. Now, he was offering the same helping hand to Silas and SEPIO in the face of prospective persecution—in all its forms.

Silas nodded and turned back toward the woman who was now helping Gapinski with the pair of griddles. "That I am. We tie the knot this fall. That's the plan, anyway."

Zarruq folded his arms across his generous belly and began stroking his beard. "You are being a very lucky fellow, Master Grey. Very lucky, indeed. Her beauty is only outmatched by her intellect and strength of character. A godly woman, she is."

He laughed. "Indeed, I am a lucky man. And you don't know the half of it, buddy!"

The bishop turned to him with a chuckle, grin widening. "I am certain you are correct. But I am very happy for you both."

"Thank you, bishop."

"Good morning, sleepyhead," Celeste said in perfectly polished Queen's English, walking over with a plate piled high with Gapinski's breakfast goods.

Silas's mouth salivated at the sight. "Good morning, yourself." He took the plate. "You certainly understand the way into my heart."

"Oh, I've definitely figured out not to stand between you and your favorite meal of the day. Although, best get it straight before we tie the knot that I've got two left hands when it comes to cooking." She nodded to the bishop. "Good morning, Victor."

"Good morning, my dear," Zarruq replied with a bow.

Silas crunched into a piece of bacon—heaven!—and frowned. "What do you mean? I thought you loved to cook."

She scoffed. "What are you playing at? You know the kitchen isn't my thing."

"No, I didn't."

She crunched into a piece of bacon herself. "Well, you do now, love."

Zarruq giggled, then threw his hand against his mouth. "I believe I will see Matthew now for my own plate." Walking away, he added with a whisper: "I would mind my Ps and Qs if I were you, Silas."

Quickly changing the subject before things got dicey, Silas asked his director of SEPIO operations, "Have you heard anything more from our agent in Rome about our little project here in Libya?"

Celeste smirked. "You're a smooth one, Master Grey." She led him to the center of camp, explaining, "Nothing more. Seems the dark web has gone radio silence."

"That doesn't sound good."

"I reckon you're right."

"What about the emperor code reference? Anything more come of that, from the agent in Rome or analysts back at DC HQ?"

She crunched into her bacon and shook her head.

"Oh for two?"

"Sorry, love. Wish I had more. But have a bite of pancake. It will do you a world of good."

They reached the center of camp, a gust of wind fanning the fire and whirling smoke combined with the smell of bacon and pancakes. Gapinski was serving a group of researchers stacks of flapjacks, wearing a white apron and oversized chef hat.

Silas chose not to worry about the troubling news and take Celeste's advice. He stuffed a bite of syrup-soaked pancakes into his mouth and hummed with pleasure. "Is this real maple syrup?"

Gapinski spun around, armed with a spatula and bearing it like a sword. "For your FYI, it is. But I don't want to hear nothin' about pinchin' pennies this or pinchin' pennies that."

Silas held up a hand of surrender. "I didn't say anything!"

"Because two months ago, you were crabbing about spending bank on our ride and then you went around and booked us a flea-bag hostel in Miami. I swear we got lead poisoning from the walls. And herpes or something."

Silas frowned at Celeste. She shrugged and ate a bite of pancakes herself.

"And then you dragged my fat hinny halfway across the world to boondocks it up with nothing but canvas and cots, so the least SEPIO can do is spring for a bottle of sugar-shack delights! Besides, it ain't pancakes without the genuine syrup, anyway."

Silas stuffed another bit in his mouth. "We're in agreement on that. But only one question."

Gapinski folded his arms and glared at him with suspicion, chef's hat wilting to the side now. "Yeah, what's that?"

"Canadian or Vermont?"

Gapinski scoffed and spun back to the griddle. "Is it really a choice?"

"Vermont," the pair said as one.

Silas shook his head and took another bite. "Say, where's Torres?"

Celeste nodded toward a grouping of pale pillars poking up from the rocky land. "Already at work."

He nodded, crunching into his bacon. He finished the last of his pancakes and grabbed another plate stacked with flapjacks and soaked in the Vermont candy.

"Dude! Lay off the goods," Gapinski said, reaching to snatch back the plate.

Silas held it out of reach just in time. "Chill, Gordon

Ramsay. It's for Torres. Want to make sure she's fueled up for the day."

Celeste finished her plate. "I'll join. You wouldn't happen to have a proper cuppa around here, would you?"

Gapinski raised a brow. "Uhh, come again?"

"She means a cup of tea. Earl Grey, if you have it."

"Ahh, another one of those Britishism." He cleared his throat, then replied in his best British accent, "Sorry, mate. How 'bout I throw another shrimp on the barbie?"

Celeste frowned. "You're about nine thousand miles off from anything close, mate. Now why don't you be a good lad and grab the pot of joe and follow us down to the dig, ehh?"

Gapinski watched her leave for the East Basilica, a laugh escaping her while she shook her head. "Was it something I said?"

"Not if you're in Australia."

"My bad. I didn't offend her, did I?"

"No. She loves being confused with blokes from down under. I'll grab the pancakes, you grab the coffee."

"I would like to join you, Master Grey," Zarruq said, setting down his own finished plate of breakfast. "That is, if it is alright with you."

Silas shrugged. "The more the merrier. Besides, I hear the dig was sort of your idea to begin with."

"I suppose that is true, it was."

The three men began the trek down toward the dig site, a plate of pancakes and a carafe of coffee with accompanying tin mugs in hand.

The sun was higher in the sky now, the site of the former basilica up ahead shining brilliantly in the morning light. Boasting five Christian basilicas, their remains looking like the picked-over bones of some ancient carcass, Apollonia offers one of the best glimpses of life and ecclesiastical architecture of the early Church. Each Christian house of teaching and worship was built before the 7th century, exemplifying the height of Byzantine design. But the crown jewel, the largest of the churches in the Pentapolis of ancient Cyrenaica, was smiling at them in the rising sun now. In fact, the original foundation goes back to the period of Constantine from the early 4th century—making it one of the earliest African Christian churches.

"So what's the deal with Libya, anyhow?" Gapinski said as they neared. "It's not like they were any hub of Christianity."

Zarruq gasped and stopped along the path, planting his hands on his hips and shaking his head, mouth agape.

"Was it something I said?"

Silas chuckled. "Pretty much, but don't feel so bad. Most Christians are ignorant about how important the land is to the faith, even Libya specifically."

Recovering, Zarruq put a hand on Gapinski's shoulder. "Forgive me, Matthew. I did not mean to offend."

"Naw, it's all good," Gapinski demurred as they resumed their trek to the site.

"It is just that my homeland is near and dear to my heart. Especially its very special place within the history of the Church."

"Tell us about that history, Victor," Silas said.

Before he could answer, a scream pierced the morning air.

CHAPTER 2

A second cry rose above the din of waves crashing in the near distance now.

Confirming the first one wasn't a mirage of sound, a trick of the shore and ruins bouncing sound waves around from the fishing boats anchored at sea or those seagulls calling out to one another.

Which sent a surge of fight-or-flight adrenaline coursing through Silas's body, both activating him to take option one and also reminding him of the rumors that had been circulating in one corner of the dark web about Western activity in Libya.

Now all signs were pointing to *their* activity.

He wished he would have paid more attention to the warnings, trying to suss out the source and target.

Because it was go time.

Again.

Silas and Gapinski looked at one another, setting down their breakfast goods and drawing their weapons, readying them for action.

"Always something," Gapinski growled.

"You heard it, too?"

"Roger that."

Silas turned to Zarruq and put out a staying hand. "Return to camp, bishop, and put it on lockdown."

Before the man could protest, the pair of SEPIO agents took off toward the columns a quarter of a mile ahead, their bony fingers reaching up from the earth like possessed corpses, as if lying in wait to curl in on the pair of SEPIO women trapped down below.

The pair hiked it on the double, tearing across the uneven ground and kicking up rocks and dirt that made Silas's feet burn through his open sandals. He nearly lost one of them cresting over a hump in the path, but he kept going. Kept tearing after Celeste, the memory of her crying out in that godforsaken cemetery last year at the hand of his brother pushing him forward—with zero concern for his feet.

His step faltered on a piece of ruin jutting up from the path, sending him stumbling to the rocky ground.

And Gapinski plowing into him from behind.

The pair tumbled and cursed before springing back to the chase. Knees bruised, hands scraped and bearing blood.

But they pressed on, desperate to answer the cries that had gone silent. Soon they came up fast to a waist-high wall, part of the basilica's original apse.

Silas climbed over it with ease. Gapinski, not so much, struggling to lift a leg and ally-oop over the barrier, flopping hard on the other side with a cry.

"Sonofa—"

"No time for cussing now!" Silas interrupted. "Pick yourself up and get to it!"

He left his partner behind, heart hammering in his head for him to save his bride-to-be and—

Another scream sounded. Toward the sea and over another wall facing north.

But this one was not like the first.

Different tone, different timbre.

Less frightened and frazzled. More joyful and jubilant.

Which was odd.

Then another one was thrown up into the morning sky, followed by laughter and whoops of victory. One he recognized instantly above the chaos.

Celeste.

Confused, he ignored his aching legs and hustled faster toward the new sounds, weapon drawn on taut arms and leading the way as Gapinski came limping up to his side.

They crested the north wall just as Celeste and Torres popped up.

Throwing up frightened screams along with their arms in surrender.

"Oy! Bloody—"

Torres cut off her surprise with a string of Spanish.

"Sorry!" Silas exclaimed, throwing up his own hands with acknowledgment before stuffing his Beretta at his back. "We heard the screams and thought the worst."

Gapinski shoved his SIG Sauer at his side as well. "Yeah. Thought you were being overrun by terrorist whack jobs and facing no uncertain doom."

"No uncertain doom?" Torres said, raising a brow and flashing Celeste a frown.

"And overrun by terrorist whack jobs?" Celeste said, echoing Torres's feigned offense. "Who do you think we are? A bunch of SoCal bimbos who can't take care of themselves?"

Silas put up a hand of surrender. "Duly noted. And for the record, I do know you can take care of yourselves. But the jury is still out on the SoCal bimbo part."

Celeste punched his shoulder. "Cheeky."

"If you weren't facing no uncertain doom at the hands of terrorist whack jobs, why all the hysterics?" Gapinski asked.

Now Torres threw a punch into his shoulder.

"Ouch!"

She grinned. "The *hysterics*, as you put it, were because of what I just uncovered. You're never going to believe it!"

"Believe what?" Silas asked.

"Just—well, see for yourself..."

The women scampered back over the north wall. The two men looked at one another and shrugged.

Silas went first, following after them with Torres leading the way. She was heading toward a square hole that had been carefully excavated from the soil several yards away. The full measure of it was obscured by four crumbled columns turned on their sides, crisscrossing the path leading down to the main excavation site.

Soon they reached the X-marks-the spot, a plot about the size of a modest garage with ropes tied around wood stakes anchored around the perimeter. Plastic sheeting was draped across the edges to mitigate water runoff and falling debris. Shovels and hoes and rakes were scattered about, along with buckets filled with sand and gravel and pieces of the broken basilica. A wood ladder lay propped against the side leading down into the maw and electric cables attached to a silent, rusted generator went with it.

Torres switched the equipment on before mounting the ladder and descending, followed by Celeste. It rumbled to life, coughing black smoke and an annoying buzz-saw growl that sounded like it was on its last leg.

Silas leaned over the side for a look. A tent was spread above the opening, offering relief from the sun but making it difficult to make anything out in the early morning. But what he saw made the ends of his mouth curl with interest.

Cut stones, carefully placed on one another and sealed with mortar formed sturdy walls on all four sides, the layers of sand and dirt and gravel having been carefully removed by Torres and her team of experts. Below the ladder was a floor paved with tile and patterned with an intricate viney weave of faded white and black. A wood table sat off to the side against one wall, a smattering of tools and papers spread across its surface. Torres flipped on a pair of yellow tripod lights aimed at the center of the space.

"Isn't it remarkable?" Torres asked before waving her arms.

Silas was grinning now and folding his arms. "Sure is. An expertly managed dig, Torres."

She smiled. "Thanks. I think we've managed alright."

"How long have you been at this?"

"The better part of four months, since before I was called back for the last SEPIO mission. Flew back once that was wrapped up and got back to the grind. Couldn't sleep last night and wanted to finish the floor. So I've been down here since two or three this morning."

"Jeez Louise, sister!" Gapinski said. "That's dedication."

Torres shrugged. "What can I say? I'm a shovelbum at heart."

He scrunched up his face and leaned forward. "What is this place, anyhow?"

"A baptismal," Silas said. "By my count, one of the earliest known established architectural features of a church in North Africa."

Torres nodded. "That's right. We're not sure if it was original to the basilica or added after the fact, but it may have been the center of the African Rite here in Cyrene."

"Really?" Silas whistled. "Nice work, Naomi. I can't wait—"

Something caught his attention down below. At the center of the floor.

He leaned forward into the rope barrier, putting his hands on his knees. "What the heck?"

Torres glanced at Celeste before eyeing the space.

"Something caught your attention, love?" Celeste said, joining in the search.

He ignored her, mounting the ladder and scrambling down to the floor.

"Dude, where's the five-alarm fire?" Gapinski called after him.

Silas headed toward the center of the baptismal where he had glimpsed the symbol in the bright tripod lighting.

There it was.

An *X* and *P*, one on top of the other.

The women gathered at his side as he stood staring at the tile bearing a symbol that was all at once remarkable and intriguing and confusing. Soon Gapinski had made his way down the ladder and sauntered up for a look as well.

He whistled. "Wow, what a find."

Silas said nothing, continuing to take it in.

"What is it?"

"I'm with Hoss here," Torres said. "Not sure what has you so enraptured."

"Agree," Celeste added. "What are you playing at, Silas?"

Silas knelt and swished away earth packed into the symbol etched into a tile the size of a paperback anchoring the center of the baptismal. A symbol that had garnered its fair share of controversy—inside and outside the Church. And correction: It wasn't so much etched as it was inlaid with some sort of metal alloy, pairs of smaller tiles lined next to one another radiating from the center in neat lines toward the walls, right and left, up and down.

What did it mean?

"Alright, Indy," Gapinski said. "You've had your fun."

"He's right, love," Celeste agreed. "How about you fill us in on your revelation?"

Silas took a breath and stood, folding his arms and taking a step back. "It's the Chi-Rho."

"The whatchamacallit?" Gapinski asked.

"The symbol of Emperor Constantine?" Celeste said.

"Emperor who?" Torres asked.

"The savior of the Church, and some would say the *founder* of the Church."

Silas scoffed. "The latter sentiment is definitely bunk, shared by the likes of Dan Brown and Noland Rotberg, our intrepid New Testament scholar, if you can call him that, from the last mission. And the idea Constantine saved the Church is debatable. But he did put it on a better footing after ending centuries of on-again, off-again persecution."

"Converting the Empire to the faith also helped matters."

"Again, debatable," Silas added with a wink. "No offense."

She folded her arms and winked back. "None taken. So what's with the symbol do you suppose? Why here?"

Silas shook his head, bringing a hand to his chin as he contemplated its meaning.

"Alright, can I ask a basic knuckleheaded question?" Gapinski said. "What's the Chee-Chee Woo-Woo, or whatever it is."

"Chi-Rho," Silas corrected. "It's one of the earliest forms of christograms formed by combining the first two letters for Christ in Greek. *Christos.*"

"Chi and Rho?"

"That's right. The X and P you see there, superimposed on top of one another."

Torres asked, "Then what's the connection with this Constantine character?"

"Glad I'm not the only one not in the know..." Gapinski muttered.

Celeste chuckled. "No worries, mate. Most Christians aren't in the know when it comes to the earliest days of the Church. Especially the emperor responsible for saving Christianity."

"Again, debatable," Silas said with a wry grin.

"So what's the deal then?" Torres asked.

"The Chi-Rho was used by Emperor Constantine as part of a military standard, mounting the symbol on flags for his Roman army. The Labarum, as Constantine's standard was known, cast the symbol of Christ in gold and was paraded at the head of military battalions."

Gapinski smirked. "Gives a whole new meaning to the whole 'I'm in the Lord's Army' song I sang as a kid."

Silas turned to him, brow raised. "The what?"

"You know," he said before singing, "*I may never march in the infantry. Ride in the cavalry. Shoot the artillery.*'"

Crickets and stares from the other three.

"Oh, come on," he said, continuing to sing, "*I may never shoot for the enemy. But I'm in the Lord's army! I'm in the Lord's army! Yessir!*"

Celeste laughed. "Sorry, mate. I haven't a clue what you're playing at."

"Don't quit your day job, pal," Torres said.

"Was this one of your Southern Baptist traditions?" Silas asked.

"Maybe," Gapinski muttered. "But y'all missed out, that's for sure."

"Apparently..."

"Oy, look there!" Celeste exclaimed. She knelt down and ran a finger across one side of the symbol, picking away mortar and dirt, working more of it loose until a deep groove was evident along one side.

"Nice work, darlin'!" Silas exclaimed, bending beside her and trying to repeat her work around the rest of the perimeter, but making less progress.

"Do you suppose the tile is removable?" Torres asked, bending in for a look.

"Don't know. Hey, you got a pickaxe or trowel handy? Hammer would be nice, too."

She nodded. "Coming right up." She grabbed all three lying on the wood table at one end of the baptismal.

"Thanks," he said, taking the tools and putting the pickaxe and hammer to work, gently scraping the pickaxe along one side of the tile and tapping it with the hammer to help loosen the mortar. It began chipping off before cracking and breaking up. A surge of excitement suddenly rushed over him from being behind the reins of a pair of archaeological tools he hadn't touched in far too long.

Smiling at his success, he set the tools down and cleared away the debris.

Torres picked them back up. "May I?"

"Be my guest."

She smiled as well and set about continuing the work on a third side while Celeste and Silas finished up with the fourth. Soon, they had removed all the mortar surrounding the center tile, the symbol of Constantine beginning to create an uneasiness within Silas.

Torres turned the pickaxe around, then began to wedge the flat end into one of the sides.

"No, wait!" Silas exclaimed, grabbing back the tool.

"Oh, I see how it is," Torres said. "Want the glory of the reveal without the hard work getting there."

Silas frowned. "It's not like that, and you know it."

She giggled and nodded.

"What are you playing at, Silas?" Celeste asked. "What's the matter?"

"Paranoid, are we?" Gapinski chuckled. "Afraid a big, bad boulder is gonna come crashing out of some hiding place if you pop the top?"

He ignored the man, smacking the pickaxe against his palm in contemplation. "It's just...this is unusual. To find the Chi-Rho like this."

"But not unheard of, right?" Torres asked.

"True. But there haven't been many places where it's been discovered. Especially at the bottom of a baptismal."

"Until now..."

He considered this, continuing to slap the pickaxe against his open hand.

"Then what are you thinking?" Celeste asked. "What do you think it means?"

Silas took a breath and shook his head. "Not sure. But it seems like some sort of seal. Perhaps of Constantine himself."

"Only one way to find out," Torres said from the floor, one end of her mouth curling upward as if in a dare.

Now he joined her in the grin, that feeling of being on the cusp of unearthing some hidden gem from long-lost history fueling him forward. In this case, the gem was the Church's history.

But what?

Like she said. Only one way to find out. The rising euphoria overrode any warning from the back of his lizard brain.

He handed the pickaxe back to Torres. "It's your dig. You do the honors."

Her wry grin widened into a delighted smile. Torres took it and got to work, carefully inserting the flat head into the groove Celeste had first made. Taking a breath, she glanced at Silas for confirmation; he gave it.

Then she gently began to press down on the handle, carefully applying pressure and working it up and down.

Until it suddenly popped loose, one end jumping above the lip of the floor and a sigh of air from the compartment below throwing up the scent of dry earth and plaster.

The four gasped at the unexpected success, holding their collective breaths and waiting for that big, bad boulder Gapinski warned about.

The seconds ticked by, crashing waves and calling seagulls and that growly generator above the only soundtrack for their wait of the inevitable.

Nothing else came.

Silas reached for the tile, then looked at Torres for confirmation; she gave it.

He threw her a delighted smile of his own and removed the cover.

Literally holding his breath for what he might find inside.

All four craned toward the opening as one, still holding their breaths before emitting the same startled gasp at what they saw.

Inside was the round mouth for some sort of compartment. About the size of a coffee mug, seemingly drilled down into the earth.

But that wasn't the end of it.

Staring back at them the full circumference of the compartment was what looked like pure gold. A cylinder filled the space partway inside made of the precious metal.

Most unusual.

Without a word, Silas reached inside to pull it out.

When Gapinski slapped a massive paw over his hand. "What if a big, bad boulder really is gonna come crashing out of some hiding place if you remove—whatever the hey-ho day that is?"

Silas raised a brow. "Now who's paranoid?"

Gapinski frowned and pulled back "Just saying...Steven Spielberg had to have known a thing or two about these sorts of things. How else did he craft such believable stories?"

Ignoring the man, he grabbed for a small knob attached at the end of the gold cylinder—almost as if whoever put it there anticipated someone pulling it out again—and began sliding it from the shaft. It was heavy, as expected, and came easily. Soon he was cradling the magical object in both hands, all at once marveling and confused at what he was holding.

"Blimey..." Celeste said.

"*Dios mío...*" Torres echoed.

"Amazing..." Silas managed.

"All of the above..." Gapinski said.

The cylinder was a long tube the size of his arm, smooth and shimmering and perfectly preserved. Which made sense, as every metal except gold is susceptible to oxidation and corrosion. But still...

What the heck was this doing buried under hundreds of pounds of dirt in North Africa, hidden in a secret compartment at the bottom of an early Church baptismal—and sealed by a tile bearing the imprimatur of Constantine?

"I say we take this solid bar of gold to the nearest Libyan bank and buy ourselves an island in the Virgin Islands!" Gapinski said. "Because this SEPIO gig is for the birds after what we went through two months ago."

"You can't buy an island with a bar of gold, dingbat," Torres said.

"If Richard Branson can, why can't we? Besides, surely this rod of gold will fetch a pretty penny."

Silas turned the cylinder over in his hand. Not a mark on it, not a stitch of writing or symbols or characters. Smooth as glass. Or gold, as the case may be. But while heavy, it wasn't as heavy as it should be.

He held it to his ear and shook it.

Torres asked, "What are you—"

He held up a hand to cut her off. Listening, discerning, intuiting what might be inside.

Then he heard it. A faint clanging of something inside the hollow cylinder.

Silas grinned. "There's something inside."

"What?" she exclaimed, reaching for it as if to take it from him.

"Oy, look there," Celeste said, pointing to the one end of the object bearing the knob.

He furrowed his brow and spun the object around, eyeing it before finding confirmation of his original deduction. A small indentation ran around just inside the edge.

Like a cap, to seal whatever was inside.

Silas glanced at his partners and took a breath. "Here goes nothing..."

Grabbing the knob between his thumb and index finger, he pulled.

It didn't give.

He frowned, pulling harder.

More nothing.

"Here, let me try," Torres said, reaching for the gold cylinder again.

He handed it over. "Be my guest."

She pushed a lock of stray dark curls behind an ear and took it, holding the object in one hand and the knob in the other. She twisted it, gritting her teeth when it didn't give and bearing up her face in a scrunch before laying into it again.

Then it moved.

Not by much, but enough that the sliding offered a faint echo in the chamber.

A startled cry rose from the other three, then cheers for her to continue.

Torres did, twisting it back and forth, little by little, centuries of settle pushing back hard.

Suddenly, it popped. She gave a startled cry at her own power and was soon holding the cover in her hand. And wearing pride on her face.

"Nice!" Silas said.

She shrugged. "A woman's touch."

"I guess so." He reached for the object, then stopped short. "May I?"

She held it out. "As you wish, Master Grey."

Silas grabbed the object back, the earthy yet tangy scent of aged pulp and ink wafting out from the opening.

Peering in for a look, he muttered, "What the heck…"

CHAPTER 3

Silas rushed over to one of the tripod lights and held the golden cylinder aloft for a better look.

Yep. There it was.

Nestled down inside was what looked like some sort of scroll. And curiously a piece of parchment rolled up around the entirety of the thing.

And something else, glinting from the bottom.

He eased the object on its side, the faint clang he heard earlier falling out first into his palm.

It was some sort of coin. Not round, mind you, but jagged. Misshapen, like a puzzle piece. He handed it to Torres, who began speaking in hushed Spanish.

Silas angled the gold cylinder toward the ground and shook it to retrieve what remained.

A rolled-up parchment slid out, brown and smelling of freshly pressed paper.

Adrenaline coursed through him at the sight, sending his heart racing and head swimming with delightful possibilities.

Celeste came up to his side. "What is it?"

"Some sort of manuscript..." Silas muttered with a mixture

of awe and confusion. Absentmindedly, he handed her the gold cylinder, still in awe of what he held.

Gapinski groaned. "Not another one of those..."

He carefully unrolled the parchment, its fibers surprisingly spry for being centuries old.

Scrawled across its surface were the distinct characters of ancient Greek, from top to bottom. Not the Egyptian variant of Coptic, like the forged Muratorian Fragment from the last mission. This was Koine, the style used to write the New Testament and in the writings of the early Church fathers, in addition to the Church's ecclesiastical edicts and letters during those earliest centuries.

Silas began translating it from memory.

And instantly recognized what it was.

He sucked in a breath of surprise. "Can't be..."

A sudden tremor ratcheted through Silas's hands as the significance and weight of what he was holding took hold of him. His hands grew moist from the adrenaline surge and oddly the opposite reaction gripped his mouth, dry as the sand above.

He swallowed hard, going back over the Greek characters strung together in words and sentences and stanzas of the ancient code that had guided the Church for generations.

The world around—the bright yellow lights from the tripod lighting beginning to flicker slightly now under the exhausted generator still rumbling above; the smell of earth and pulp and ink and generator exhaust; the sound of crashing of waves against the rocky shore and those seagulls still calling out to one another beyond the lip of the excavated hole—the entirety of existence shrunk down to that moment in that hole in the ground holding that document.

Bearing those words. And with those signatures at the bottom.

"Can't be..." he muttered again, not understanding or comprehending or believing what they had discovered.

"Silas, what is it?" Celeste asked.

"Yeah, you're killing us with anticipation, Smalls!" Gapinski complained. "Should we anticipate a coterie of box-men whack jobs or Nousati crazies, or what?"

Torres raised a brow. "Coterie? Big word, Hoss."

Silas let the parchment roll back into form and grabbed the golden cylinder from Celeste. He turned it and shook it.

Out fell the other parchment that had remained stuck inside. Not as large. About the size of half a page from a paperback, and thicker. Must have been wedged in there around the larger, lighter parchment rolled up like a scroll inside.

This time written in Latin.

On closer look, there was a curious feature: Both the top and bottom of the parchment was jagged. Whatever was written on this one looked incomplete.

Torres whistled. "Jackpot! A coin, a parchment, and a fragment."

"Sounds like the start of a joke," Gapinski said.

"Alright, love, enough of the theatrics," Celeste said, folding her arms. "What did we find, Silas? And what's that bloomin' addition to the stash?"

Before he could answer, a growling broke through the soundtrack on repeat from above—rising above the waves and seagulls and generator.

Silas's stomach dropped at the sound, nearly dropping the fragment.

"What's that?" He craned toward the opening above.

Torres looked toward the top. "What do you mean?"

"That noise? Rumbling and growly."

"Sounds like the generator to me. And nearing its last leg, by the sound of it."

He walked toward the ladder, spinning back toward the center of the space with furrowed brow.

Not the generator. Engine, one or two of them. Faint but crescendoing into range.

Celeste folded her arms. "No, I hear it as well. A fishing boat perhaps?"

"Or trouble..." he muttered.

Gapinski snorted a laugh. "I think you need a vacation, pal. You hear a rumbly, growly, noisy noise and you automatically think terrorist whack—"

Shouting and a *rat-a-tat-tat* rising above the din cut the man off.

He yelped. "What was that?"

"What do you think, Hoss?" Torres said.

Silas looked at Celeste and frowned. "Company."

The radio silence from the dark web sounded like it had been broken.

He carefully slid the rolled manuscript back into the gold cylinder, then did the same with the other parchment fragment. He retrieved the metal coin and cylinder lid from Torres, then dropped the coin inside and twisted the lid in place.

Retrieving his Beretta, he took off for the ladder. The other three SEPIO agents were close behind, all four reaching the surface as another round of screams and cries and *rat-a-tat-tat* gunfire sounded.

Louder now, more panicked.

They all saw why.

Black raft boats were moored on the rocky beach. Two of them, with high sides and outboard motors that continued rumbling with growly, invasive intent.

And advancing up the coast were two packs of armed men. Four or five to a bunch. Not the black-clad military types they had come to know and loathe. But hostiles in loose tan shirts and brown pants, faces masked with what looked like cloth and arms bearing enough firepower to send the unarmed researchers looking for cover.

It was an invasion. Locals by the look of it.

The warning from the dark web coming at them live.

"*Dios mío...*" Torres said.

"I concur," Gapinski said, whipping out his SIG Sauer.

Celeste did the same. "We need to do something."

"Two to one odds ain't bad."

"We've been dealt worse..." Silas said, mind spinning with indecision.

The Order of Thaddeus was under attack. They had to save their friends. But what about the golden cylinder, and all that it held? Especially the larger scroll bearing the Church's theological code. Were they after it? If so, who were they? Local ISIS sympathizers—the renewed Islamic Caliphate itself? Like other churches in Africa, the Church of Libya itself had endured much violence at their persecuting hands. Or was the threat closer to home—Nous, or the new box-men mystery sect that reared its ugly head last mission?

"*Idiota,*" Torres cursed.

"What is it, mate?" Celeste asked.

"I'm not armed. Left my piece back in the tent."

"Let me give you a bit of friendly advice, sister," Gapinski said. "Never leave home without cold, hard steel. Silas learned that lesson real quick a year ago, didn't ya, pal?"

Wasting no more time, Silas handed the golden cylinder to Torres. "Then it's your job to keep this from our new friends—whoever they are and whatever their intent. Got it? No matter the cost."

"Why? What is this thing?" she asked.

Taking a breath, he said, "The soul of Christianity."

Without waiting for more, he flipped the safety to his weapon off and padded toward the toppled columns where he and Gapinski had come from.

Celeste offered words of safety, as did Gapinski. Soon they were at his side near a group of columns.

Taking aim at a few stragglers from one of the groups bringing up the rear of the hostiles who had stormed the beachhead to the Order's dig site.

"This is definitely outside SEPIO protocol, Master Grey," Celeste mumbled, the group holding their position as the hostiles advanced toward camp.

Silas replied. "I know standard operating procedure requires us to maim, not kill. And only in self-defense. But what other option do we have when our people are being overrun by terrorists?"

"Look, by the shore..." Gapinski pointed toward the rafts. Soon the others saw what he saw.

A woman clutching her arm, propped against a boulder. A man lying prone, face-first in the dirt—probably dead.

No order was necessary after that. As one, they leveraged their triple firepower to defend the defenseless back at camp. And offer a pound of justice for good measure.

Pop, pop, pop, pop, pop the trio responded in sync.

Downing two stragglers in seconds, blood spraying from their gunshot wounds, limbs flailing in muscular spasms from being hit.

And drawing the immediate ire of the other three.

The columns exploded with livid intent, sending the SEPIO agents crouching for cover.

"Seems to be our lot in life of late," Gapinski complained, the gunfire relentless. "Crouched behind ancient Christian ruins while being handed our a—"

"Gapinski..." Celeste warned as the rounds began their retreat.

"What? It's true."

"And what's also true is that complaining isn't a business

model for survival," Silas said, aiming above the parapet of limestone to offer a *pop, pop, pop, pop* reply.

Downing one of three men now advancing toward their position. The others skipped back for their own cover.

Score.

"What, Uncle Sam teach you that little ditty?" Gapinski quipped before reaching around for his own rejoinder and finding the same success. "Money!"

"Not Uncle Sam. Jeff Bezos."

Celeste offered, "How about we save the business fortune-cookie advice for another less dire moment, shall we?"

Silas nodded. "We've got them on their heels. Let's move."

Gapinski scoffed. "Where? We're pinned like The Rock and Hulk Hogan started to tango."

"We're in the middle of it and you're using WWE metaphors?"

"Whatever gets us through the crazy."

More *rat-a-tat-tat* weapon fire ripped through the Order dig site in fits and starts. Yet it was different.

Not so much heading their way as it was heading back—

"Toward camp…"

Silas stood, weapon extended on taut arms and ready for anything, but holding firm until his Army Rangers-honed brain took the lay of the land. Three tours had to count for something.

The last man standing from the group they had been picking off had fled, joining up with the other group who had overrun the encampment now.

Where Victor Zarruq was held, along with the other researchers.

Another smattering of gunfire sounded above the din of waves and the outboard motor and generator, the seagulls having sense enough to flee for safer ground.

Silas sprang from their position. "Come on!" Celeste and Gapinski were close behind.

He took off for the arc of tents now being overturned, falling support poles and tearing canvas punctuated by shouts of protest and followed up with sprays of gunfire. He ran faster at the sound, praying no one had been killed as the terrorists destroyed their camp.

A few of the hostiles were still advancing up the hill, though their clothing blended into the earthy backdrop, making it difficult to take aim. Celeste and Gapinski were following close behind. They opted for a stealth approach, dropping low and using the sparse, aged trees that dotted the hillside and a few mounds of rubble for cover on their approach to a tent at the edge still remaining upright.

Burning wood and sizzling bacon and brewed coffee washed over them on a warm breeze gusting across the encampment. None of it appealed to Silas like it had only a few hours earlier, his stomach having soured from the invasion.

They were almost there, the remaining hostiles having dropped from view in their destruction—though for what reason wasn't clear. He hoped they hadn't made for the researchers, even Zarruq.

God help the Order.

Seriously, Lord. Throw us a bone here!

Coming up to the beige canvas tent starting the camp's faltering procession, Silas held his breath until they were clear from view.

Then he sighed and checked his magazine. Nearly half spent and without a backup.

"On a buck and a prayer, I tell ya," Gapinski mumbled, finding the same damage to his own arsenal.

Celeste went through the same check. "Only spent four, but with six or seven more to go I'm worried."

"I just hope Torres is faring better."

Shouting rose above the destruction, carried on the same wind bearing breakfast. Sounded like a real scuffle, too.

Sounded like Bishop Zarruq!

Silas said, "No time to cry about our rounds, not with all those lives on the line. Besides, by my count we've got thirty between us."

Gapinski chambered one and nodded. "More than enough to take out a coterie of box-men whack jobs."

Celeste did the same. "Or Nous."

"Or whoever they are."

Silas eased his back against the canvas and took a step for a better view to take out the remaining threat.

When a man came unto view. Shirt and pants brown and billowy, a massive gas-powered Avtomat Kalashnikova rifle lowered toward the ground but ready, willing, and able. Better known as the venerable, if not overused, AK-47.

Which was now rising with recognition at the threat.

Now or never.

"Always something," Gapinski complained as he opened up on the guy.

Dropping him without a hitch before Silas could engage. And letting the remaining coterie of whack jobs know where they were.

"Guess that makes twenty-six rounds," Celeste said.

"And a big, fat signal flare fired for all to hear," Gapinski complained.

Silas cursed. Now what.

"Silas Grey!" a voice rang out. Different tone, different timbre than Zarruq's panicked cry they had just heard. "Master of the Order of Thaddeus. Former professor at Princeton University and Sergeant Major with the United States Army Rangers before that."

A cold dread washed over Silas. Didn't recognize the voice

in the slightest, an accented, throaty baritone that apparently knew who he was.

Which also meant there was a better chance than not the hostiles knew what he was doing at the site, along with the Order.

"Come out, come out wherever you are..." the man taunted.

"Do you know this bloomin' bloke?" Celeste whispered.

Silas shook his head. "No clue."

"Sure sounds like he's got the 411 on you," Gapinski said.

"Yeah, I gathered that."

"To the count of ten to show yourself, I will give you," the mystery man continued. "Or the beloved Bishop of Libya gets his head blown off."

The yelling returned. Louder and more menacing.

Sounding familiar. The last person Silas wanted captured.

There was a slap, followed by someone slinging rapid-fire words in some foreign tongue, followed up with a crystal-clear voice that exuded zero fear and made no mistake who was in charge.

"Do not fear those who kill the body but cannot kill the soul; rather fear him who can destroy both soul and body in hell!"

Celeste sucked in a worried breath. "That sounds like Victor..."

"Always something," Gapinski growled.

Silas said nothing. What were they going to do?

There was another slap, followed by a *rat-a-tat-tat* explosion and more screaming.

The SEPIO trio looked at one another, faces drawn with panic and confusion and dread over the meaning of what had happened.

No...

"My final warning shot, that was, Master Grey," the voice rang out.

Silas ran a hand across his unkempt hair growing shaggy.
"One..."
Think Grey!
"Eight..."
"Hey, he's cheating!" Gapinski complained.
"Nine..."
Nothing more to do but the inevitable.
"Alright!" Silas yelled from behind the tent. "I'm coming out and I'm unarmed."

He stuffed his Beretta at his back and walked around the canvas corner, putting his hands out in surrender.

Two of the goons in brown hustled toward them, both bearing AK-47s and looking more than ready to use them.

One of the men grabbed Silas by the wrists and yanked him forward. He stumbled to the ground, just as two other voices sounded from behind.

One very British; one very bald.

"Easy, easy! I'm breakable, bucko!" Gapinski complained.

Two more of the hostiles had rounded from the backside and were leading Celeste and Gapinski toward Silas before joining him on the ground. A short, squat soldier relieved them of their weapons, tossing the Italian- and German-made guns at the feet of someone who looked like the main attraction.

A large man of packed muscle in full military fatigues sauntered over, clearly distinguished from his soldiers' brown makeshift uniforms. His face was masked by a checkered white-and-red scarf that ran up and around his bulbous head, is if it were merely an extension of his neck. He reached behind it and undid a knot, letting it fall to the dusty ground.

Dreadlocks like cords of rope twisted around his head up into a hive that meant business and hung down to his shoulders and beyond the length of his back. The man was African, sub-Saharan, with dark, ebony skin and haunting eyes set behind a flat nose. A jagged scar ran down the side of his face, from his right ear to the corner of his mouth, and his skin was similarly pockmarked with signs of violence.

He flared his nostrils before smiling widely, a gold tooth gleaming from the front. "Pleased to make your acquaintance, Master Grey. I was told I might find you here. And not a moment too soon, considering the hunt that was just announced."

Announcement? And hunt? What the heck was he talking about? And who the heck was this brutish beast?

Arms reached from behind Silas and forcefully brought him to his feet.

The man stepped forward, face falling, eyes narrowing. "Now, I want whatever was beneath the seal of Constantine. I want the emperor code."

Silas didn't flinch, keeping the man squarely in his sights and not giving an inch. Even though inside he was reeling.

The seal of Constantine. Even more worrisome: the emperor code—the very language Markus Braun had used earlier after the Gospel Zero debacle.

That throaty, baritone voice returned, snapping him from his confusion: "I know you were digging for it. So why don't we take a walk, shall we?"

Silas was shoved forward, along with Celeste and Gapinski. He glanced behind to find Victor Zarruq, having been grabbed for leverage by two brawny men, AK-47s slung around their backs. His face was bruised and crusted blood ran down the side of his head. Another two researchers lay prone on the ground, their arms and legs twisted in death.

What were they going to do?

CHAPTER 4

What a nightmare...

Silas had been in tough spots before. Definitely with the Army Rangers and then lately with SEPIO. But this took it to another level with the Order of Thaddeus's muscular arm preserving the faith.

Disarmed and outnumbered, civilian casualties and hostages was not the sort of day he had in mind. And he was the one to solve it. The buck stopped with him as Order Master.

Or the bullet, as the case may be.

Lord Jesus Christ, Son of God, have mercy on us and throw us a life preserver!

The waves continued rolling in from the coast without a care in the world for what was going down a hop, skip, and a jump from their line of entry, the two intruder boats bobbing with every ebb and flow, motors keeping them steady and ready to leave at a moment's notice. The flock of annoying seagulls had even returned, caw-cawing loudly with selfish intent as they jockeyed for space on the rubble poking up from the churning sea.

A warm breeze gusted from the coast, carrying the scent of dead fish and diesel exhaust. And now burning canvas and paper and wood supports, whipped up by wicked winds fanning the emerging flames into a full-on hell, began mixing with it all. Silas nearly lost his bacon and pancakes at the stench, made all the worse by the blow to the head Mr. Gold Tooth gave him five minutes ago.

Adrenaline coursing through his veins and heart pulsing with head-hammering activation, he wanted to take the bastards out—with his bare hands if he had to, given their destruction of life and property. But not with Zarruq marching behind him at the end of a gun, and not with the rest of the Order's researchers at a similar mercy, some wounded, some dead.

A nightmare was right.

Reminded him of the day he and best buddy Colton and a small platoon of Uncle Sam's finest showed up to search a warehouse on the outskirts of some backwoods town he'd forgotten the name of as they continued making their way down the slope back to the dig site. His boys had been sent by the brass knuckleheads to scope out a possible cache of the illusive WMD's that sent him to the blasted country to begin with based on a tip they'd received over night. Not from a local informant, mind you or anything vetted by the Army, but the CIA. And it wasn't clear where they'd gotten their intel. By now, the world pretty well knew the only thing their 'tips' were good for was as a fill-in for depleted Army-issued TP. Even then, answering the call of nature with those tip sheets would leave your backside as burned and bruised as answering the call of duty with them.

Which is what happened that late morning. While their heads were down in the dirt digging holes on a snipe hunt for Saddam's non-existent weapons of mass destruction, what felt like a company of Republican Guard Iraqi military men rode up hard. Only they turned out to be a small, tightly organized squadron of the elite troops sent to hang their asses based on intel from the Iraqi National Intelligence Service. Apparently their tip sheets were more like Charmin Ultra Soft than the RV sandpaper of the CIA.

They'd been beyond screwed, but his boys had held it together. Nearly turned into a Black Hawk Down scenario had it not been for Colton's leadership. Silas made his best friend his right-hand guy once they'd been extracted by a pair of Black Hawks out of Camp Liberty. Never did find the WMDs in that blasted warehouse. And it sure as heck made it difficult to trust another spook. And after that damn roadside IED took out Colton, it made it that much harder to trust another man in uniform, too, after what they'd been put through for those damn WMDs.

After Silas denied they had found anything resembling what Colonel Gold Tooth was after, he'd gotten the blow to the head with the back of the man's pistol. He fell hard, but he didn't change his story.

That's when the camp was set ablaze and the group rounded up like cattle for the whack job's Plan B. Now they were headed down to the dig site. And depending on the math, it could get ugly or be over real quick. Again, depended on the math.

Silas glanced at his new friend, Colonel Gold Tooth, dressed in that military garb. His shoulders were clear of patches or any other official accoutrements, so he probably wasn't really military. Just playacting. He had donned a pair of sunglasses now, his face set as flint toward the site, which they were fast approaching.

He just hoped to the good Lord above that Torres was able to hide the golden cylinder, and they all had the nerve to keep it that way. Otherwise, the Church could be in a world of hurt —considering not only what little he had seen inside, but also what Colonel Gold Tooth had said up at camp.

Announcement. The emperor code.

This had Braun and Rotberg written all over it. And maybe the box-men mystery sect. The new kids on the block that meant as much trouble for the Church as Nous and his brother had meant the past two years.

What a nightmare...

Soon they were back down at the overturned columns. And Torres was coming around to greet the arriving party—out of breath and out of time.

A commotion of rising rifles greeted her, echoing across the site.

Torres threw her hands up in the air. "Whoa, whoa, whoa! Nice to meet you, too, fellas. Sorry, just realized we had company. Was heads-down with a pair of headphones blasting The Boss."

A little over the top, but it would do.

Silas moved in front of Torres, hands out. Five weapons, black and scratched and ready for action, were aimed squarely at his face. He could tell Colonel Gold Tooth was confused.

"I think she means Bruce Springsteen. Gotta love Born in the USA," he explained.

The man furrowed his brow and recoiled slightly. Weapons remained as they were.

Silas laughed nervously and raked a hand over his head. "Anyway, this is our lead researcher, Naomi Torres. She's been down here all morning. Probably didn't hear the commotion down in the hole."

"Ahh, then just the woman I need to acquaint myself with," Colonel Gold Tooth said.

He could hear Torres breathing behind him, heavy and steady, betraying her outward cool-and-collected demeanor. She sure was a good actor under pressure. Had to give her that. He glanced at Celeste and Gapinski, who both seemed equally unsure what came next. Which meant it was on him to get control back.

No, to *take* control back.

It was go time.

Round two.

Silas took a breath, straightened himself, and lowered his hands. "You need to acquaint yourself, you say? I'm not sure we have been properly introduced."

The large man clucked his tongue and threw his head back, that gold tooth glinting in the sun as he grinned and chuckled. Then he bowed and shook his head.

"Forgive me, Master Grey." The man took a step between two of his men, then extended his hand. "Aurelius Chuke, I am."

Silas eyed the hand but took it. They both put an equal amount of masculine fervor into their grips, two bucks squaring off to show who was who without breaking eye contact.

Then they released.

"Aurelius," he said. "Like the Roman philosopher?"

The man grinned. "Like the Christian theologian."

Christian theologian?

Chuke clucked with disapproval. "Aurelius Augustinus Hipponensis. Come now, Master Grey. A man of your stature would have known the venerable early Church father Saint Augustine of Hippo better than that, I should think."

He reddened with embarrassment, but quickly recovered.

"Yes, well, you caught me under the gun. Literally."

"I suppose so." The man clapped his hands and rubbed them together. "Now, where is my treasure? I presume the fair lady with Latin curls behind you would know. Being she is your lead researcher, and all."

Silas stepped aside, praying she was ready for the show of her life.

Torres pushed a lock of curls behind her ear and folded her arms. "What is it you would like to know—Aurelius Chuke?"

"Where it is. The seal of Constantine and the treasure it holds."

"There was no treasure," she said, a bit too eagerly for Silas's liking. He eyed the man, hoping he was convinced.

"Liar," Chuke simply said.

She shook her head and went to respond when the man put up a hushing hand.

"Aware that you have been excavating the East Basilica, I am," he said. "Also aware that early this morning you found a certain symbol belonging to a certain emperor, I am. Two intersecting Greek letters. The Chi-Rho."

Silas sucked in a startled breath. How the heck did he know all that?

As if reading his mind, but probably more a reaction to Silas's own reaction, the man turned to him and grinned. "Eyes and ears across all North Africa. After all, it is my domain, I have."

He silently cursed him for the show of weakness. But then his mind leaped to the only questions that mattered: How could he have known such a thing? And perhaps more importantly, *who* would have told him such a thing? Surely not someone from SEPIO...

Silas banished the thought and stepped forward toward Chuke. "She's telling you the truth. Go on, tell him what you know." He nodded toward Torres.

The man folded his arms and grinned, his gilded tooth glinting in the high-morning sun. "Yes, Naomi Torres. Tell me what you know."

She drilled the man with unflinching eyes. Taking a breath, she explained, "As you apparently know, we spent the better part of four months excavating what turned out to be a baptismal. One of the oldest in the North African Church, by our estimation. And, as you indicated, we did indeed discover this seal of Constantine you referenced. Quite by accident, actually."

The man's face fell. "Accident? What is this *accident* you speak of?"

She sighed and shrugged. "Unfortunately, I dropped a piece of heavy equipment on the tile that hadn't been fully revealed under the remaining sand. It cracked, indicating there was a compartment underneath."

The man leaned forward with eagerness. "And?"

"And, *nada*."

The man scrunched up his brow. "Nada?"

"She means nothing," Silas explained. "There wasn't anything below the tile. Just an empty shaft. Nothing more."

Chuke stepped toward her now, jaw set and eyes hateful. It took everything within Silas not to do anything to stop him. Which would just be rash and accomplish nothing. Trying to pop the guy wouldn't help matters. And he doubted he would get very far anyway.

"You're a liar," he growled.

She swallowed and folded her arms, resting back on one leg and not backing down. "Sorry to disappoint. See for yourself."

The man didn't break his stare, but he did nod toward the excavated hole. One of his men jolted to attention and scampered down the ladder for confirmation. A few minutes later, he returned.

"The woman is telling the truth," the soldier reported. "The center tile is as we were told, but the space underneath is empty." He handed the broken tile pieces to Chuke, who took and eyed them before tossing them to the ground.

Silas held his breath. Every synapse in his brain was firing on all cylinders, and every nerve ending in his muscles was ready to respond to whatever came next.

Chuke spat to the side and grinned, then he laughed before spinning around and grabbing Victor Zarruq by the neck.

The man cried out before a gagging sound was heard. The bishop struggled under Chuke's grip, and the man spun him toward Silas and Torres.

"You and me go way back, don't we, good bishop?" Chuke said through gritted teeth, his neck muscles straining with rage at being denied. "Yes, indeed we do. And I am going to tell this woman, Naomi Torres, one more time to stop playing these games and give me what I came for before I slit your throat! The blood of another worthless Christian spilled on our land won't make a difference to me."

Holding Zarruq's neck by one hand, the poor bishop's eyes bulging under the stress and mouth open searching for air, Chuke extended his other hand in a reach.

A soldier slapped the handle of a long knife into his palm, blade looking sharp and well used. He brought it to Zarruq's neck, pressing against it and drawing a line of blood that ran crimson across his dark skin.

"I am not playing games, Naomi Torres! I am most serious. Tell me now, or Zarruq loses his head."

Panic washed over Torres's face, eyes going wide and mouth going slack and chest rising in fits with clear indecision.

Keep it together...We cannot let the Church's code slip through our fingers.

He transfixed her with telepathic eyes, hoping to convey to her the seriousness of the gun pointed at the Church's head if they lost what they had found. Despite the complementary fact there was a blade pressed against Zarruq's neck!

"Don't you think I know how serious you are?" she yelled, though Silas didn't know if that was the best tactic, given the stakes. "You've got *un maldito cuchillo* at my friend's neck!" Then she took a step forward, eyes watering and face twisting with a plea. "If I had...whatever it is you think I have, don't you think I would hand it over? I would! But I don't have nothing accept that broken tile your man brought up from the empty hole in the ground."

No one moved. No one made a sound.

Not any of the soldiers or any of the SEPIO agents. Not even Aurelius Chuke.

Until he did.

In one motion, he pulled back his arm from around Zarruq's neck—

And he shoved the bishop to the ground.

Silas sucked in a breath.

No...

He watched him stumble, holding his breath and praying like he'd never prayed before.

Then the man rose to his knees, coughing and wheezing and swallowing hard with a hand at his neck.

Staring wide-eyed at the blade still in Chuke's hand, he saw it was clean. Accept for the initial blood drawn at the start, there wasn't a drop more.

"I believe you, Naomi Torres," the man said, stuffing the knife at his hip. "But it doesn't matter anyway. More to find, there are. And find them, my men will. And let me tell you this, Master Grey—"

Chuke stepped toward Silas, neck bulging with indignation and breath smelling of sour milk. "You better pray to whatever god you serve that we don't meet again. Because if we do, Aurelius Chuke will slit your throat and feed your head to the jackals."

With that, the man spun around and motioned for his men to retreat. He strode forth, his men backing up with trained weapons before they reached the columns and quickly followed Chuke back to the moored boats.

Celeste and Gapinski helped Zarruq up from the ground, who insisted he was fine.

"You deserve a medal for what you did," Silas mumbled to

Torres as they watched the hostiles split into two groups down at the shore, climbing back into their boats.

Torres smirked. "Hold off on the ceremony until after we're on the other side of this. Whatever *this* is. Because it ain't over."

No, it wasn't. Not by a long shot.

The two boats sped away as fast as they came ashore, motors throwing up a buzz-saw growl that served as a reminder of their menacing intent.

And leaving SEPIO wondering what the heck had just happened.

Even more: What did Chuke mean there were more to find?

CHAPTER 5

Silas watched his newest enemy fade from view as the others consoled Zarruq, getting an earful from him that he was fine. Had to give the man credit, standing up to Chuke earlier, not backing down or whimpering even while being threatened at gunpoint and then his neck being put under the knife like that—literally. Reminded him of Radcliffe in that way, the same pluck and swagger and obstinance. Maybe it was an old man thing. He wondered if he would get there some day now that he was cresting forty. Probably was already there.

"Slap me some skin, She-Ra Turner!" Gapinski said, holding out his palm and waiting for a slap.

She giggled and grinned, slapping it before Gapinski grabbed it and pulled her into an embrace. "Seriously, sister. Totally amaze-balls on how you nemawashied that guy into giving up his ground. Not gonna lie. Thought you'd get us all killed, but it worked."

"Agree, mate. Absolutely brilliant!" Celeste joined the pair, the three clearly thankful to be alive after what just went down. "Though I agree with Matthew, here. Was mentally walking through my last rites, even though I'm not Catholic."

"While I don't mind being used for bait," Bishop Zarruq said, "trusting full well that I am eternally secure in Christ, I must say—that was a close one."

Torres nodded. "I know, and I'm sorry for that."

"Nothing to be sorry about. You were doing your job. Let's just pray it was worth the risk."

"Speaking of which," Silas said. "The golden cylinder. Where is it?"

She nodded up the hill past the group. "Back at camp."

"What?!" He spun around toward the smoldering remains of their encampment, his legs nearly springing forward with a panic to retrieve the relic.

Celeste joined him. "Back there, in the rubbish pile of soot and ash? How did you manage it?"

Catching a whiff of burned wood and cloth on an updraft of salted fish coming in again from the shore, he turned back to Torres. "Better question is *why* did you manage it?"

Torres pushed a stray lock of curls behind her ear. "Figured once they were through tearing up the joint searching for the goods, they wouldn't return. And if they came looking at the dig site, they'd surely do the same. Then when they set the whole thing ablaze, the plan pretty well took care of itself."

"Let's pray the scrolls we discovered aren't scorched to death," Celeste said.

"*No te preocupes amiga.* Gold is pretty indestructible in fire. Especially the blaze that consumed our camp. Trust me, it's safe."

"How did you manage it, then?"

"Snuck up behind you all when you were, shall we say, distracted with the big guy. Dipped back into my tent and found a place under my cot. No way they would find it again even if they did go back. Then ran back to the rendezvous after they set the joint on fire just in time for you all to come sauntering down the hillside to the site."

Gapinski whistled. "Now that there is legit She-Ra Turner superpower madness."

Silas took a breath, not sure what he thought about it all. Although, he wasn't sure he would have thought of anything better, given the circumstances. But Celeste was right: If the scrolls and fragment did get scorched, then it was all for nothing.

But instead of laying into her with a coulda, shoulda, woulda that didn't matter at that point, he smiled and nodded. "Like I said before Colonel Gold Tooth left, you deserve a medal for what you did. Good work." Celeste and Gapinski agreed.

"Enough dilly dallying around," Zarruq said. "How about we go fetch what it is that nearly got my head lopped off?"

Silas agreed and led the way hustling back to camp. As they neared, he wasn't prepared for what awaited them.

It looked like a war zone. The tents were completely collapsed in on themselves, with blackened wood poles jutting up this way and that and the beige canvas burned to a crisp. Fires still smoldered in places, but mostly the place was mired in black smoke spewing from where they had laid their heads to rest for the night and were just enjoying those pancakes and bacon. A few of the researchers that had been hurt in the tussle were huddled around a man who was lying prone in one of their laps. Dead, by the looks of it.

He sent the other researchers to do what they could with the others. Zarruq joined them, drawing out a string of prayer beads and a small New Testament from an inside pocket in the folds of his cloak to bring them comfort. Silas and his SEPIO agents went in search of the golden cylinder.

"*Dios mío...*" Torres muttered, wandering toward where her tent had stood with hands on her head. Like the rest of the encampment, it was completely gone. A pile of smoldering canvas and wood was all that remained.

And hopefully along with what they had discovered hidden under the seal of Constantine.

Gapinski came up with two large jugs of water. He handed one to Silas, and the two men began dousing the area. The ground hissed with disapproval, white smoke and steam rising. Thankfully, the fire hadn't raged white hot or the gold might have melted, the flames dying quickly to warm embers without anything more to burn.

Torres came up with a long stick and began spreading the debris aside in search of their prize and poking the ground to uncover it. *"Dónde está* you little—

"There!" Silas exclaimed, catching the glint of something buried in the dirt and ash.

He knelt and began digging, grinning widely when he uncovered the blessed sight of gold. He grabbed what he had exposed.

Then recoiled with a shout of pain when he touched the hot metal.

"Yeah, didn't they teach you about energy transference in that high school of yours?" Gapinski said.

"You alright, love?" Celeste said, bending down to take a look.

Silas winced and shook his hand. Hurt like a mother, and it was definitely red and radiating pain, but he'd live.

"I'm fine. Give me some more of that water, would you?"

Gapinski handed him a jug, and Silas poured what remained over the area, the dirt turning muddy and the golden cylinder coming more fully into view, offering a few hisses of protest.

"That should do..." he dropped the jug and gently tapped the cylinder surface with his fingers.

Warm, not hot. Perfect.

He cleared away the grime and withdrew the relic. Which was definitely what it was, given what it held. His inner relicologist began dancing inside. He couldn't wait to pop the top again and verify what he had seen.

Because if they had found what he thought they had found...then this could be the break the Order had been waiting for. Not to mention the break the Church had been waiting for.

Silas walked over to what had been the center of camp where Gapinski had been making breakfast a few hours ago. The others trailed him as he grabbed the gold knob between his thumb and index finger and twisted. The top came off easily, and he handed it to Torres.

He tilted the cylinder, and out tumbled the coin-like object, along with the other smaller fragment. He handed both to Torres.

"What do you suppose this thingy is?" Gapinski asked, eyeing the jagged piece in her hand.

"Don't know," Silas mumbled as he carefully slid the other parchment out from the tube, eager to reconfirm what he had read earlier.

"And then there's the issue of the other fragment," Celeste said, grabbing the thicker parchment for a look. "Did you get a chance to evaluate this one?"

He unrolled his real object of affection. "No, I didn't..."

Then he scanned the first several lines of neatly scrawled Greek letters again. And his breath was taken away as before. He couldn't help but grin at what he was reading.

"But I did get a chance to evaluate this one."

Several seconds passed as Silas continued reading and translating the document that had sat at the heart of the Church for nearly seventeen hundred years.

Celeste, Gapinski, and Torres exchanged looks—all at once intrigued and confused and slightly irritated at Silas's frozen tongue, his head buried in the parchment.

Celeste finally, gently started taking the mystery scroll from his hands.

"Hey..." he protested, eyes going wide and not sure whether to hold on tight or let it go for fear it might rip.

"So how about you let us in on the secret, love," she said, letting him take it back.

Silas cleared his throat and smiled. "Sorry. It's just...I mean, my goodness...It's amazing, isn't it?"

"OMG it's SOOOO amaze-balls!" Gapinski said with dramatic flair. "Are you high?"

Torres said, "I mean, I've gotten used to your ways and all, but even I'm getting annoyed at the theatrics."

Celeste nodded. "Agree. Seriously, what are you playing at, Silas?"

Silas frowned, but took a breath and cleared his throat again. "Alright, try this on for size."

A tremor suddenly seized his hand, perhaps brought on by what felt like an almost holy moment repeating the theological code that sat at the heart of the Christian faith.

He didn't even need to write down the translation. He recited from memory the original that later became the creed billions of people have recited across the generations and centuries, the peoples and nations:

> We believe in one God, the Father Almighty, maker of all things visible and invisible; and in one Lord Jesus Christ, the Son of God, Light of Light, very God of very God, begotten, not made, being of one substance with the Father; by whom all things were made; Who for us men and for our salvation came down and was incarnate and was made man; He suffered and the third day he rose again, and ascended into heaven; from thence he shall

come again to judge the quick and the dead. And in the Holy Ghost.

And whosoever shall say that there was a time when the Son of God was not, or that before he was begotten he was not, or that he was made of things that were not, or that he is of a different substance or essence from the Father or that he is a creature, or subject to change or conversion all that so say, the Catholic and Apostolic Church anathematizes them.

The group sat in stunned silence at the reading of the Church's theological code.

"Is that what I think it is?" Celeste whispered.

"I'm no Catholic, but I'm pretty sure that's the Nicene Creed," Gapinski said. "Or some version of it. Sounded a little funny."

Torres frowned. "You don't have to be Catholic to be familiar with the Nicene Creed, numbskull."

"Christian is the only requirement of familiarity with this creed," Celeste affirmed.

"Not in my neck of the Protestant woods," Gapinski said. "Smacked of incense and liturgical prayers and Papal bulls."

"Which is unfortunate," Silas said. "Because in many ways the Nicene Creed is the bedrock of our faith. Right alongside Scripture, frankly."

"Alongside Scripture?" Torres said.

"Grandpappy is turning over in his grave at such talk," Gapinski muttered. "But if it's the Nicene Creed, then why does it sound so different?"

Silas took a breath and smiled, reveling in the Order's discovery. "Because I'm ninety-eight percent sure it's an original."

"Original?!" the others exclaimed, then promptly huddled around Silas for a closer look.

He chuckled and nodded. "That's right. It's why it sounded funny to you, Gapinski. The original Creed was later amended to become what we now recite. And this here strikes me as one of the original drafts, signed by the original men who gave life and limb to define and defend the faith through the superheated fires of persecution. Look there..." He pointed at the top. "Hosius of Cordoba."

"Who was he?" Gapinski asked.

"The first one to sign the document attesting to the truth conveyed in the Creed. Then there are the ones below him, two presbyters sent by the bishop of Rome. And then the others, tens of hundreds of bishops affirming what the Creed affirms."

"Which is what?" Torres asked.

"The divinity of Jesus the Son and his coequality with God the Father," a voice called out from behind.

The four turned to find Victor Zarruq shuffling toward them, head downcast and looking spent.

Silas glanced over his shoulder to find the group of researchers still huddled together, sobbing and shivering from the weight of the attack.

"How are the others doing?" he asked.

"As well as anyone could expect," Zarruq answered. "One dead and three more suffering injury."

"Life threatening?" Celeste asked.

He shook his head. "Shouldn't be, thank the Lord. One of the researchers had medical triage training, and so was able to staunch the bleeding from one who suffered a gunshot wound and two more with broken arms. The psychological harm is another story..."

Silas understood that, especially given his experience on the field of battle. Civilians often suffered far more harm from the trauma of the experience than actual wounds from battle.

But he couldn't worry about them right now. They had to figure out what the heck was going on with what they discovered. And why that Aurelius Chuke character tried to steal it.

He managed a smile and nodded toward the open scroll. "Come have a look at this..."

Zarruq ambled over to his side, face sagging and eyes tired from the weight of the hour. "What's this you have here?"

"Go ahead. Read it. I assume you've kept up on your Greek?"

"Indeed, I have..." The man took a breath and sighed, then began scanning the parchment. The further he read, his tired eyes began to brighten behind a furrowed brow. Until he gasped and his mouth dropped with recognition.

"Is this...Are you telling me?"

Silas chuckled. "I believe so, yes."

"The Nicene Creed?" Zarruq exclaimed. He returned to the parchment, running a finger carefully up to the top, then pausing at Hosius' name before tracing the others listed with an almost reverent affection. "And signed, no less..."

He nodded. "That's right. The Order may have just uncovered a sealed original copy of the Nicene Creed. The Church's foundational theological code."

Zarruq gasped again and threw a hand against his forehead, mumbling something in his native tongue but conveying what Silas himself felt.

The bishop bear-hugged Silas and started dancing around with the man, clearly excited by what they had found.

"Would love to share in the lovefest," Gapinski said, "but what does it matter? We found an original copy of the Nicene Creed, so what? What does that change?"

Zarruq withdrew from the embrace, catching his breath and grinning widely. "Such a finding, Matthew, is an utterly remarkable and absolutely profound discovery. On par with discovering a hidden original Declaration of Independence or Magna Carta."

"Granted, Victor," Celeste said. "But I do wonder why it matters. Our faith doesn't rise or fall on whether we have an original copy of our faith's central creed. Perhaps an original Gospel maybe."

"Let's not go there, given what we've just been through," Gapinski complained.

"I'll answer that," Silas said. "As a relicologist—or perhaps former relicologist, given my recent career change. Anyway, my whole life work had been reclaiming and rediscovering and retrieving the central elements of the vintage Christian faith in order to offer tangible experiences for people to encounter it."

"And worthy work it was," Zarruq said. "Your reputation on exposing the Shroud of Turin as proof of the resurrection of Christ precedes you, Master Grey."

Reddening, Silas replied, "Yes, well, that line of work nearly got me killed."

Gapinski snorted. "You and us all."

"Back to my point. Gone are the days when the Church can justify our beliefs purely on tradition alone. Personal experience, not dogmatic belief, rules the day. And relics seem to offer people the chance to explore their spiritual questions through objects rooted in historical experience. A copy of the Nicene Creed could remind people what's at the heart of Christian belief—not to mention what's at stake, given the countless stories of the men who came to the Council of Nicaea bearing witness to the truth of Jesus Christ missing eyeballs and limbs and pieces of their body."

"As well as all the martyrs before them who died for those same beliefs," Zarruq added.

"Exactly. Apart from the Bible, the Nicene Creed is as basic as it gets when it comes to Christian belief."

"Alright, fine," Torres said. "So a copy of the Creed could

remind the Church of its theological heritage. But why would Mr. Gold Tooth, some backwoods terrorist, want to steal it? Seems pretty useless to that sort of *hombre*, don't you think?"

Zarruq answered, "I would imagine he would have wanted to destroy it. Like a Russian secret agent during the Cold War days seeking to steal and then shred a copy of the Declaration of Independence out of rage at the democracy rivaling communism."

Gapinski leaned over to Torres. "You know there's a treasure map on the back of the thing, right?"

"Naomi does make a good point," Celeste said. "I can't imagine why the bloke would have wanted such an ecclesiastical document. There must be more here."

The ladies were right. No reason in the slightest Chuke would go to all that trouble to swipe a Christian scroll, no matter how ancient and central.

Silas glanced at the second parchment Torres was still holding, a thought beginning to needle him.

"Unless..."

"What's that, love?" Celeste asked.

He looked up and cleared his throat. "What if they weren't coming for the Creed, but for the other document along with it?"

"Which other document?" Zarruq asked.

Torres held it up with care. "This one."

"What is it?"

"Good question," Silas said. "It was wrapped around the inside of the cylinder along with the copy of the Nicene Creed. May I?" he asked her.

She nodded and handed it over.

He eyed it, along with Torres who came up to his side. She said, "The script and paper are certainly different."

"I see that. Not at all the same scribal hand as the purported Nicene Creed copy. Paper seems of a much higher quality of stock, too. Even the language is different. Latin instead of Greek."

"It's all Greek to me..." Gapinski mumbled.

"And look there..." Torres said, ignoring the man and pointing at the top and then the bottom. "Is it incomplete? The paper seems torn, rather than cut to form. And while I don't know Latin, it seems like there was something written before and after."

"So it's a fragment then?" Celeste asked.

"Looks that way..." Silas muttered before adding, "Do any of you have a scrap of paper and a pen—something I can use to take down the translation?"

Torres handed him a pencil and a dusty notebook she had used for her excavation work.

He thanked her and knelt to the ground, straining to read the Latin characters that had faded with time.

But then it started to come together. And he realized Torres was indeed correct. It was a fragment. Torn at the front and back end.

What it said was confusing.

The implication for the Church was frightening.

CHAPTER 6

Silas re-read what he had translated, double-checking his words against those preserved on the parchment.
Did I read that right?
Then he re-re-read what he had translated, triple-checking his words against those preserved on the parchment, black smoke from the dying flames whirling around him as he sat on the ground checking his work.

Yes, he did get it right. And the translation was positively chilling.

Someone cleared their throat.

Silas looked up.

"Care to enlighten the unenlightened?" Gapinski asked.

Celeste came to his side, staring over his shoulder down at the paper. "What is it?"

He stood. "It's..." He trailed off, head still buried in his translation.

She took it from him and smiled wryly.

"Sorry. Frankly, it's all at once confusing and intriguing and worrying."

"Worrying?" Torres said.

"In what way, love?" Celeste asked, eyeing what he wrote.

Silas took the paper back, returning the wry grin. "It's a partial fragment, as Torres suggested. The top and lower portions having become lost. Or rather, having become torn before becoming lost."

"But why?" Torres asked.

"Why what?" Gapinski asked.

"Why torn? And I would say the jury's out on the lost part."

Celeste folded her arms. "What are you driving at, mate? What do you mean the jury's out?"

Torres held up the golden cylinder. "It's clear whatever was sealed inside here was not lost. Far from it. The cylinder was sealed inside a compartment carefully crafted to hold it, then a tile bearing the seal of Constantine was placed on top—and in a basilica baptismal, of all places."

She tossed it to Gapinski. He startled but caught it with one hand.

"Nice catch, Hoss."

"Gee, thanks."

"So you're saying it was deliberate?" Silas said.

"I'm not sure we can say it was anything but deliberate, given the *loco* lengths whoever put this whole thing together went to hide the dang thing."

He glanced at the fragment, then his translation, the confusion and intrigue and worry beginning to sour into dread.

"Are you thinking what I'm thinking?" Torres asked.

Silas frowned. "That if the cylinder was deliberately sealed with the tile bearing the Chi-Rho, then everything inside was deliberately placed inside?"

She nodded.

"Which would mean the fragment," Celeste added, "the torn parts at both the top and bottom was also deliberate."

Now Silas nodded.

Zarruq asked, "But why do you suppose someone would go to such lengths?"

"To hide the contents from harm," Celeste said.

"Or preserve it for some future purpose," Torres added.

"Not it," Gapinski corrected. "*Them.*"

"Them?" Silas asked.

He pointed at the fragment. "The torn parts at both the top and bottom also means there are at least two more parts. And we could also assume two more Nicene Creed thingies along with two more puzzle piece coin thingies."

"Good thinking, Hoss," Torres said. "Which means we've got three golden cylinders, with three copies of the Nicene Creed stuffed inside, wrapped with three fragments of some other longer parchment, and another three pieces of some coin or medallion or something."

"At least three."

The group fell silent, seeming to consider the revelation.

"Would you mind reading for us what you translated, Master Grey?" Bishop Zarruq asked, breaking the silence. "And what has you so clearly troubled..."

Silas nodded and cleared his throat. He took a breath and read:

And so I asked Alexander to show Arius a degree of consideration and to receive the advice which I gave, insisting that the cause of their differences had not been any of the leading doctrines or precepts of the Divine law of the Christian faith until that time of controversy, nor had any new heresy respecting the worship of God arisen among them in light of Arius' challenge to the manner in which Jesus was considered the Son of God. I insisted they were really of one and the same judgment, and so it was fitting for Alexander and Arius and the entirety of the holy people across the Church's spectrum to join in communion and fellowship at Nicaea. From my perspective, these controversies were small and very insignificant questions, the ones concerning the divinity of Jesus. Instead, what mattered was the profundity of the man's mission of love, teaching a profound depth to human dignity that had not existed before, and modeling the greatest extent of that love on the Roman cross through self-sacrifice. Thus, these divisions over doctrine, which had seemed needless, were in my opinion not merely unbecoming, but positively evil, that such should be the case.

There is only one faith, and one opinion about our religion, and the Divine commandment in all its parts imposes upon us all the duty of maintaining a spirit of peace and grace, in addition to truth and doctrine. I insisted they should not let the circumstance which had led to a slight difference between the two cause any division or schism amongst them and the larger Church, since I believe it did not affect the validity of the whole. We are not all like-minded on every subject, nor is there such a thing as one universal disposition and judgment.

The group stood in silence, the words reflecting the truth of Silas's own reaction: confusing, intriguing, worrying.

"Who's Arius?" Gapinski finally asked.

"One of the greatest heretics to have plagued the ancient Church," Bishop Zarruq answered. "And, shamefully, a bishop birthed from the cradle of my people's country."

"Arius was a Libyan?" Silas asked.

Zarruq nodded. "He was indeed a Libyan presbyter, serving the Church of these ancient lands decades before taking up residence in Alexandria where he breathed the toxic fumes of his heretical, unorthodox teachings, exchanging the truth of

Jesus Christ for a lie built on philosophical speculation and humanistic dogma."

"Tell us what you really think..." Gapinski said.

Silas added, "He was one of the chief architects of the teachings that led to the Council of Nicaea."

Torres hummed. "The very council that produced the Nicene Creed you just read, isn't that right?"

"That's right."

"And what, pray tell, did he teach?" Gapinski asked.

"That there was a time when Jesus, God the Son, was not," Celeste answered.

"Meaning?"

"Meaning, that Jesus was not in the same sense eternally God as God the Father is."

The man crossed his arms and furrowed his brow.

"Arianism is a non-Trinitarian Christological doctrine," Bishop Zarruq added, "which asserts the belief that Jesus Christ as the Son of God was created by God the Father at a certain point in time, so that the Son of God became a creature distinct from the Father and is therefore subordinate to him and of a different substance, while also being God as Son."

Gapinski stared dumbly. "Yeah, you're gonna have to ease the cookies down to the lower shelf on this one. Because that was crazier than a one-legged mule."

Silas explained, "What they mean is, Arius challenged the prevailing orthodox view of Christian beliefs that taught Jesus Christ, the Son of God come in the flesh, was himself God in the same way the Father was—existing from eternity past without having been created."

"As Silas read from the presumed original parchment documenting the agreement at the Nicene Council," Celeste said, "*We believe in one God, the Father Almighty, maker of all things visible and invisible; and in one Lord Jesus Christ, the Son of God, Light of Light, very God of very God, begotten, not made, being of one substance with the Father.'* As the Council concluded, begotten, not made, and being of the same essential being as the Father were crucial to the Church's understanding of right beliefs when it came to Jesus' personhood."

"And crucial to the gospel, I might add," said Bishop Zarruq. "God's revolutionary story of rescue in Jesus Christ is entirely dependent upon whether Jesus Christ really is God, or merely a man, a wise prophet."

"Yeah, I'm with Hoss here," Torres said. "Maybe you could break it down for us more. My training in the Christian faith is a little rusty."

"Mine too, and I was raised Southern Baptist!" Gapinski leaned over to her. "Thanks for having my back with Christian Doctrine Jeopardy."

She winked. "Always."

Silas chuckled. He felt back in his Princeton lecture hall—or better, sitting in his office with a pair of students answering their questions about the Christian faith. Part of the job, he guessed, helping his own SEPIO crew navigate the trickier aspects of Christian belief for the sake of preserving them.

"How about we sit first," he said, gesturing to a set of benches that had toppled in the melee.

Gapinski uprighted one of them and muttered, "We're in for one of those, I see..."

"I heard that."

The man stood wide-eyed before promptly taking a seat.

Silas threw him a wry grin before sitting with a sigh himself. Felt like he could fall asleep then and there after what had happened. But it was still go time. And he sensed bringing everyone up to speed on one of the key doctrines of the Church would be crucial for the road ahead.

Wherever it led.

"Let me say, I do understand the confusion," Silas started. "There's been confusion about who Jesus is and what he came to do from the beginning. Both outside and *inside* the Church."

"How so?" Torres asked.

"Think about it. Outside the Church, Jesus is viewed as one religious teacher among many. There's Buddha, Muhammed, Krishna. And then Jesus of Nazareth—a sort of Gandhi on steroids, right?"

Gapinski snorted a laugh. "Gandhi on steroids. Nice."

"But it's true, isn't it? Which of course makes sense in our modern polytheistic world. It's always been this way, really. The one true God and Lord standing among the other so-called gods and lords, as the Apostle Paul says. So this confusion about the person of Jesus outside the Church is understandable. And to some extent it makes some sense that people inside the Church would be confused as well, because throughout Church history there's been confusion."

"But what's so confusing about Jesus, about who he is?" Torres asked.

"More or less, the confusion has boiled down to his nature," Celeste offered. "Who he is as God, which also has implications for the nature of his work as well—his death on the cross, paying the price for our rebellion in our place, and whatnot."

Silas nodded. "Impressive, darling." Then he caught himself and blushed. She smiled and did the same. "Anyway, early on some people couldn't wrap their minds around the idea that the Creator would stoop so low as to become a creature—bearing all the trappings of creatureliness. Like hunger and sleep and—"

"Constipation and smelly armpits?" Gapinski added.

"Gapinski..." Celeste said, smacking his knee.

"What?" he said, itching his ear.

Silas frowned. "Something like that. Remember what the Book of Hebrews makes clear: God did in fact take upon himself flesh and blood. John wrote in his Gospel that *'God became flesh and moved into the neighborhood,*' as one translation puts it."

"In other words, God became a real live human being," Gapinski said. "That God, well, Jesus *was* really human."

"Bingo. Gold star for Gapinski."

He folded his arms and grinned.

"Alright, so Jesus was a real live human," Torres said. "But what does this have to do with Arius? I thought what he taught was something about his divinity."

"That's right. I was getting there. Because as with the confusion over Jesus' humanity, early in the Church's history there was confusion over Jesus' *deity*. Some believed Jesus the man was adopted by the Father to become the Son of God—that there was a time when Jesus was not God, and only later *became* God."

"And this is precisely the heresy we call Arianism," Zarruq explained, "named after the Alexandrian priest. To clarify what I said earlier, putting the cookies on the lower shelf as you requested, Matthew..." the bishop threw Gapinski a wink; the man smiled and nodded. "What I meant to say was that the false teacher Arius maintained that the Son of God was *created* by the Father and was therefore neither coeternal with him, nor consubstantial. Meaning, Jesus neither existed from the beginning of time nor was he of one substance with God the Father."

"Sort of makes more sense, Victor," Gapinski said. "But why does it matter what he taught?"

"Because in essence what he was saying is, Jesus wasn't *really* God! If he was created and later adopted, then he was a creature and not co-equal with the Father. And frankly, it matters because there is a sort of new kind of Arianism today, perpetuated by progressive Christians who would seek to reimagine a new kind of Christianity for our multi-faith world. This Jesus is said to be *divine*, not God. A sort of Gandhi by nature of his moral example and life illustrating the universal human ideal of love—only on steroids, as you put it, Master Grey," he said with a chuckle. "Like Arius' Jesus, this one isn't the real Jesus either. It is fake."

Gapinski nodded, then frowned and itched his ear. "Yeah, I don't follow."

Zarruq offered a huff, as if exasperated. Before he could respond, Silas intervened. "Maybe this would help."

The bishop nodded and offered a hand. "By all means, Master Grey."

"Central to the Christian faith are the three words *Jesus is God*."

"Yeah, sure. I get that," Gapinski said. "That's basic."

"Basic, yes. But you won't find certain progressive Christians voicing those three important words, much less non-Christians. Instead, they'll say things like Jesus is *'the very movement of God in flesh and blood'* or Jesus is *'the divine in flesh and blood.'*"

"But he is, isn't he?" Torres said. "You said it yourself, or the Book of Hebrews does. Jesus shared in our flesh and blood."

Silas nodded. "True, but notice that, like Arius, these kinds of Christians insist that Jesus is *divine*. While this language seems right, it isn't. It's code language for Jesus being this really good guy who lived the best possible life—who lived *divinely*."

"A Gandhi on steroids," Gapinski said.

"Exactly. The Jesus you find in progressive Christian theology is described as a *teacher* and a *liver* of divine goodness, peace, and love. For them, Jesus the *man* simply showed the world what it means to be human, what it means to live a meaningful existence on this earth that's heavenly, rather than hellish."

"But, again, isn't this all true to some extent?" Torres asked.

"To some extent," Celeste added. "However, to speak of Jesus' *divinity* is not the same as speaking of his *deity*."

Bishop Zarruq hummed with approval. "A very apropos and

crucial distinction, Celeste. You will hardly find progressive Christians giving a positive statement of Jesus' deity. Saying *Jesus is God* would mean all other so-called gods are not. Instead, as Silas said, they will insist that Jesus gives us *'the highest, deepest, and most mature view of the character of the living God.'* Yet again, their Jesus isn't God but merely a person who shows us the divine. The result is that Jesus is left merely as a person who exhibits the divine. He is the *image* of God; he *resembles* and is *like* God. This kind of Jesus embodied and modeled God through his ethics, not his nature."

"My head is hurting..." Gapinski said, itching his ear and glancing around.

"I'm with Hoss, again," Torres said. "And I'm confused what any of this has to do with the note fragment we found, and why we should be so worried about it in the first place."

Silas held up his translation of the fragment. "Because that note fragment seems to suggest that Constantine agreed with Arius, a man who taught things about Jesus that are being parroted to this day!"

"Again, so what? Who cares?"

"Why it matters, is that Arius was the reason for the Council of Nicaea, and the reason why hundreds of bishops throughout the Church put pen to paper to craft the copy of the Creed we found in that golden cylinder that would remind Christians what they believe about Jesus' nature for nearly two millennia. That he was very God as much as very human. And if some new terrorist whack job was searching for it, a fragment we all seem to agree has at least two more brothers—"

"Or sisters, as the case may be," Gapinski added. "Might as well be egalitarian about it..."

Silas frowned. Celeste intervened. "I think what Silas and Victor are saying," she said, "is that the teachings of this bloke Arius aren't anything new. And now we have ourselves a mysterious fragment of unknown origin claiming to support the man condemned by the Church as a heretic, a fragment wrapped around a copy of the Nicene Creed and stuffed in a reliquary underneath a sign and seal that appears to belong to Emperor Constantine. The very emperor who launched the ecumenical council addressing the heretic's teachings in the first place, forming the very creed the fragment was wrapped around."

"And, might I add," Zarruq said, "a *Christian* emperor who launched the council that addressed Arius' heretical teachings. We cannot forget the religious persuasion of the Emperor."

"A persuasion that now seems in doubt," Torres added, "given the fact the fragment offers a glowing endorsement of the heretic."

The bishop held up a finger and shook it. "*Appears* to endorse. Although I can hardly believe my ears, given the man's baptism."

Silas nodded. "You're right. At this point the glowing endorsement is only a conjecture, given we know next to nothing about any of this."

"And yet it doesn't look good," Torres said.

"Now can you see why it's such a big deal?" Silas said. "Especially, since for decades pop culture has claimed Constantine created the Christian religion to serve his powerful ends."

Gapinski smirked. "Yeah, thank Dan Brown for that one."

"And every other half-rate thriller writer," Celeste added, "not to mention the entirety of the New Atheists commune who've spiraled into drunken orgies imbibing on such religious conspiracy theorist pablum."

"Quite the visual you got there, Celeste."

"Which is the farthest thing from the truth of the matter!" Zarruq exclaimed.

Silas nodded. "True, the Church has claimed the Emperor was a baptized Christian who was used by God to protect and prosper Christianity."

"And now some fragment of some letter surfaces that throws shade on that theory..." Torres said.

"Indeed."

"Doesn't smell right."

"Not in the slightest."

Celeste added, "Especially coming hot off the heels of yet another conspiracy seeking to throw shade on the Holy Scriptures."

Silas replied, "This one is almost as bad, because the Church's central creed is center stage."

"With another goon after it," Torres said. "Or set of goons, from a set of competing factions."

Silas took a breath, the weight of the reality settling in.

"So what do we do about it?" she asked.

"Does anyone else hear that buzzing sound?" Gapinski said, itching his ear and shaking his head. "Driving me nutso to the maxo!"

Silas furrowed his brow at the man and glanced around, not noticing anything.

"Must have taken one to the head, mate," Celeste said. "I don't—"

"I hear it now, actually," Torres interrupted.

Gapinski exclaimed, "Thank you! Thought I was losing my marbles."

"Well..."

He stood and started pacing, glancing around before darting toward one of the smoldering tents.

"Hey, that's my—"

"Buzzing satcom unit?" He was holding a device that looked like an old-school handheld television, a thick antenna jutting out and the body looking warped from heat.

"Surprised the thing didn't burn up in the fire."

Gapinski held it out to Torres. "Zoe's on the line."

She took it and answered the call.

"Finally!" Zoe said. "Where have you been? I've been trying to reach you all morning?"

"Sorry, mate," Celeste said, leaning over Torres's shoulder. "We've been having it out over here."

"Hope it wasn't too serious."

"Well..."

Silas came up around for a viewing. "We were attacked by a platoon of whack job terrorists."

"Uh, oh..." Zoe moaned, putting a hand to her mouth.

"Not the words we need to hear right now, Zoe," Gapinski complained.

"What is it?" Silas said.

"I think I know why those whack job terrorists showed up."

CHAPTER 7

'Now what,' were the first words to spring to Silas's mind at Zoe's hint of something bigger going on.

Nearly voiced them, too, his annoyance growing at the things-get-worse cycle that seemed to be having a field day with the Order and SEPIO the past few months—stretching from the moment that box-man tattoo guy showed up at his brother Sebastian's house, nearly sending him to early retirement on God's celestial shores, on through the bombshell announcement of another Gospel to the multiple attacks from two enemies of the Church and ending with Zoe's army of bots fighting that blasted Markus Braun social media titan across his WeNet juggernaut.

But he didn't; Silas held his tongue. He was Master of the Order of Thaddeus, after all. Which demanded that he put on the same big-boy pants he wore in the Middle East leading squads of Uncle Sam's finest to bring home the bacon for the Rangers and end the war that threatened to quickly devolve into a nation-building quagmire.

Except this time he was leading the muscular arm of the Church's finest to suss out what the heck was going down involving a buried baptismal adjoined to an ancient basilica lost to time housing a secret chamber hiding a golden cylinder with what appeared to be an original signed copy of the Nicene Creed, a cryptic fragment of a note seemingly written by Emperor Constantine seemingly championing Arianism, and some puzzle fragment that meant Lord only knew what—and sought after by some local terrorist whack job outfit who knew what ax they were grinding against the Church.

None of it was adding up. And Silas hated math. Always had, always would.

And he feared the equation was about to get real complicated real quick.

Silas sighed and raked a hand through hair growing thicker from need of a good haircut. He also needed a good shave, the five-o'clock shadow turning toward midnight. And a tumbler full of barrel-aged scotch, three-fingers full and neat. He could almost taste the astringent, smoky amber liquid on his tongue. But that would have to wait.

He took the handset from Torres, taking firm command of the moment that he sensed was quickly turning into a SEPIO mission for the Order.

"Alright, Zoe. Give it to us."

She took a breath and pushed those baby blue glasses up the bridge of her nose. "A video surfaced."

"Video?"

"What video?" Celeste asked.

Zoe nodded. "That's right. With a challenge to find a so-called emperor code."

"Emperor code? Isn't that the language Markus Braun used during his maddening soliloquy just two months ago?"

"Always something..." Gapinski growled.

Silas agreed. Always something when SEPIO was involved.

And with Zoe claiming a video had surfaced using the language Markus Braun had used just months before...He had a bad feeling about this.

Silas said to Zoe, "Where did this video surface? On WeShare?"

Zoe shook her head. "No, a different part of WeNet. Some experimental interface similar to the dark web. Apparently, an invitation-only VIP hangout called WeSolve."

"Like Davos or Aspen for the internet?" Gapinski asked.

"That's one way of putting it."

Silas sighed. "Not to channel Radcliffe or anything, but can you get to it, Zoe? What's the deal? What are we looking at and why do you think you know why the goons showed up here—what's the connection to the video?"

"I think they're connected," Zoe explained, "because one of our agents sent along a link on the secure SEPIO comm channel to a video posted on that Davos for WeNet. The one from Rome tracking activity on the actual dark web that led to the chatter about Western activity in Libya."

"Blimey..." Celeste said.

"Looks like after Braun's attempted takedown of the Bible he finally made good on his promise of more things to come by posting an invitation to what you could call a treasure hunt."

"Treasure hunt?" Torres said.

"What does the video say?" Silas asked.

"Here, let me..." Zoe turned toward a laptop and clacked away at her keyboard. Then she turned it around for the group to view on the tiny satcom unit. "The agent flagged the start of the relevant section for you."

She began playing the video:

"...EXACTLY RIGHT, MARKUS. AN INCREDIBLY JUICY FACT ABOUT the history of Christianity is that the religion as we know it was the creation of a pagan Roman emperor—Constantine the Great, who only became a Christian on his deathbed!"

A familiar man with a handlebar mustache and a checkered shirt was sitting on a stool across from another man, who was well-manicured with black hair and high cheekbones wearing an annoyingly SoCal-chic charcoal T-shirt.

"Are you kidding me?" Silas exclaimed. "Markus Braun and Noland Rotberg, having a fireside chit-chat on WeNet?"

Rotberg grabbed one of the handlebars and started twirling it as he continued droning on, Silas's skin crawling at the memory of the Harvard professor from a few months ago who nearly undermined the authenticity of the Bible. The man seriously plucked his nerves.

"It's more of a waterfall-side chat, actually," Gapinski said, "Very Fen Shui."

He was right. The two men sat before a gently cascading sheet of water, black rock glistening from behind, surrounding greenery punctuated by bright red flowers waving with the vibe.

"Quiet down," Celeste said, putting out a hand. "And turn up the volume, would you, dear?"

Silas obliged, cranking it as Rotberg continued.

The Harvard professor leaned back, continuing to play with that one handlebar end. Continuing: "During the reign of Constantine, Rome's official religion was the cult of *Sol Invictus*, sun worship. And the emperor was its high priest. However, the Empire was facing a growing threat of being torn apart from religious turmoil. A conflict between the Church and the Roman cult, between pagans and Christians, the latter of whom had grown with dramatic, exponential explosion. So he decided to do something about it, calling a gathering together of ecclesiastical leaders in AD 325 in order to unify the Empire around a single belief system. The dogmatic tradition of the Church, the religion of Christianity."

Silas clenched his jaw and shook his head. "I don't believe this…"

"Stuff and nonsense propaganda, is what it is," Zarruq said from behind.

"Can't you send one of your bot thingies out onto the interwebs like you did on the last mission, Zoe?" Gapinski said. "Counteract Dear Leader Braun and shut down his feed?"

Zoe looked at them from the screen and snorted a laugh. "Good one."

The four looked back at her across the satcom device as if they were serious about the proposition.

"Oh, you're serious?"

"Well, can you?" Silas asked.

She smirked. "Doesn't work that way." Then she mumbled some frustration.

"What's Rotberg going on about now?" Gapinski asked, pointing at the screen.

"Refocus the viewer on the laptop again, would you, Zoe?" Celeste said. She did.

"Sounds like the oldest canard in early Christian studies," Silas complained. "Constantine and Christianity."

"You have to understand," Rotberg went on, tipping his head back and playing with that annoying mustache tip again. "Constantine was a shrewd, formidable political entrepreneur who understood that Christianity was a rising religion. So he jumped on the bandwagon to bring political stability to the Empire. Figured backing the champion fighter in the arena of religious ideas was the way to go. Which consequently also meant backing the factions that held the power within the Church against the minority voices of the upstart religion. Voices that put pen to paper in order to express their own truth regarding the things of God and teachings of Jesus."

"The Gospels, as Christianity is calling them," Braun said, gesturing with a hand.

"This is a complete rehashing of Braun's last propaganda campaign a few months ago," Celeste said.

Silas nodded but said nothing, wondering where this was going.

"*Gospel* literally means *good news*," Rotberg went on. "And anyone who sided with those other voices, those other forbidden Gospels in the Bible over Constantine's version, was tabled a heretic. That word is a relic of that period of history during Constantine's reign, which is literally Latin for 'choice.' *Haereticus*. Those who *chose* their own truth regarding the Christ of history wore the scarlet letter first."

"Get to it or get new material, buddy," Silas complained.

"I thought Constantine himself was being a Christian," Braun said.

Rotberg scoffed. "Surely you jest! He was a lifelong pagan who had some sort of ecstatic vision of a cross, yes, but was only baptized into the religion through a deathbed conversion. A man who was staring down the darkening barrel of death and too weak to resist the overtures of the powerful bishops who wanted to secure their interests in solidifying Christianity's status and stature as the official religion of the most powerful Empire in the world."

"Don't know about you, but I'd call that new material," Gapinski said.

"What's he playing at?" Celeste asked.

Silas shook his head, again saying nothing.

What indeed...

"And so he converted the sun-worshipping Roman pagans to the Christian faith," Rotberg went on. "He fused symbols, dates, and rituals from the pagan Roman religion to ascendant Christianity—creating a hybrid faith that both parties could live with."

"That's a load of crap and you know it!" Silas cursed the satcom unit.

"Simmer, tiger," Celeste said with a wry grin.

Braun shifted on his stool, crossing a leg over the other and bringing a contemplative hand to his chin. "You are saying the remnant of pagan Roman religion and the symbolism of Christianity was being fused together—the institution of the Church itself and the Roman religious system?"

"Absolutely!" Rotberg said, "For instance, the Catholic saints wore Egyptian sun disks. Isis became the Virgin Mary nursing the Christ Child, a pagan god who had a similarly conceived child who became a blueprint for baby Jesus. All the aspects of Christian ritual—from the miter and altar to the doxology and communion, the act of consuming God in the flesh—all of it was co-opted from pagan religious traditions in an attempt to subvert them and convert them to the Church's cause. That's not even touching on Jesus' birth date, his burial in a hill-side tomb, and resurrection from the dead—all mirroring the pre-Christian god Mithras."

Braun chuckled and glared at the camera streaming the nonsense. "Don't be getting a religious symbologist started on Christian rituals and symbols!"

Rotberg echoed the chuckle. "Oh, you jest, Markus!"

Silas rolled his eyes. He wanted to puke.

"Don't forget that the Church's holy day was stolen from other religious traditions as well," the man continued. "Early Christians honored the Jewish Sabbath, which is celebrated on Saturday. But the good Emperor Constantine changed the day to Sunday, in concert with the pagan's day of sun-worship. Think about that! Most Christians dutifully show up on a day of worship once reserved for paying tribute to the pagan sun god—on *Sun*-day. It's simply madness!"

"Is that true?" Torres asked Silas.

Now Silas scoffed. "Hardly! I mean, yes the Sabbath is honored only because the Church and Israel are inextricably linked by God's original covenant promises and Jesus' fulfillment of them. But to say Constantine *created* Sunday is such historic nonsense it makes me want to spit! The early Church worshiped on the first day of the week because that's the day when Jesus rose from the dead. Not because some Roman Emperor coerced them into it."

He gripped the satcom unit until he thought it would break under his anger.

It wasn't so much that the two blowhards were twisting the truth of his religion and painting it with such ludicrous brushstrokes. That he could take. Had been doing so for some time, ever since back when he was at grad school and then became a professor. Academia wasn't exactly known for being a bastion of Christian tolerance. Religious, yes, but not when the Christian faith and Church was concerned. So he'd been putting up with their kind and their hot-take nonsense for a decade.

No, it was more than that, for he saw how such historical revisionism and blatant lies about the faith had impacted real people—particularly back in the day with his students. Such twisting of the Church's history and beliefs of the Christian faith had planted doubts in their minds thanks to the Rotbergs and Brauns of the world, the religious "experts" and thriller writers alike all making hay with mistruths and mischaracterizations.

The end result was people wondering whether all they'd ever known about Christianity was a lie. Countless people across the WeNet social media platform doubted their faith in Jesus Christ—what the Church taught about the truth of his teachings, and the payment he paid in their place for their sins in death, and his resurrection for opening the way to new re-created life—wondering if it all was a lie. And that wasn't even counting all the others who might doubt whether Christianity offered them anything, whether Jesus himself offered them the hope of rescue and re-creation they'd been waiting for their whole lives.

All of it made his blood boil, which manifested in a tremor seizing the satcom device through his irritated hands.

Silas startled at a hand gently resting on his arm, staying the tremor and checking his anger.

It was Celeste, she was smiling at him with questioning eyes. She didn't say anything, but he understood her perfectly.

You OK?

He took a breath and nodded, then returned to the device. Because the two blowhards were still going at it.

"So where did all of this begin?" Braun asked.

Rotberg sat up with eager interest and took a sip of sparkling water from a green bottle. Perrier, if Silas had it right.

Of course he would.

"Now that is a religious story!" the man said. "We can trace all of it to one moment in time, nearly seventeen hundred years ago. To an ecclesiastical gathering in a backwater, seaside town outside of Constantinople, arranged by Constantine himself. The Council of Nicaea. In attempting to integrate the religions, he needed to bolster the hand of Christianity itself, strong-arming the Church into adopting practices and beliefs through a series of debates and votes—when Easter was celebrated, how bishops would function in the Church, the sacraments and their practice. And the biggest doctrine of them all."

He paused, grinning from ear to ear and clearly relishing the drama of it all.

Braun seemed to take his cue, leaning forward slightly and smiling with interest. "And?"

Rotberg joined him, leaning forward himself and adding lowly, "The belief that Jesus was divine."

"The belief that Jesus was divine?"

"Yes!"

"Explain that, Noland. You are saying the divinity of Jesus, the teaching that he was the Son of God, it was voted upon?"

"Heretical stuff and nonsense, that is!" Zarruq exclaimed.

Silas glanced over at the bishop who looked a shade redder. Seemed the bishop was sharing in his holy rage.

"Agree," he said.

"Absolutely!" Rotberg went on. "Until that singular moment in the history of Christianity, the Council of Nicaea, Jesus' followers viewed him as a prophet, a great teacher and compelling human who offered humanity the best instantiation of the character of the divine. But a *man*, nothing more."

"Are you suggesting he was not viewed as the Son of God?" Braun furrowed his brow, as if he wasn't in on the whole dastardly affair.

Silas clenched his jaw, the anger returning at what was being broadcast from one of the primary information outlets in the world. No way in the slightest Braun wasn't in on the script. Probably wrote it himself after what he pulled months ago.

"Exactly right, Markus," Rotberg said. "The deific designation 'Son of God' was only officially offered as a title and voted upon at the Council of Nicaea. And even then, the result of the vote wasn't a slam dunk, with several bishops siding with a more minority of voices who had a more moderating view of the moral prophet, viewing him as a man who offers humanity a picture of divinity. Rather than *being* divine himself."

"Fascinating."

Rotberg was getting animated now, clearly relishing the spotlight. Truth be told, a twinge of envy was worming its way through Silas. His fatal flaw, coming at the least helpful time. No way in the slightest he should envy the man. Jesus was right: *'For what will it profit them to gain the whole world and forfeit their life?'* No way was he coming out of this waterfall-side chit-chat eternally unscathed.

"Either way," the man went on, "constituting Jesus' divinity was a crucial step in Constantine's masterful plans to bring order and unity to the Empire, as well as establishing the Church's power. The Emperor's maneuver by stamping his imperial imprimatur on Jesus' *divinity* had the effect of transforming Jesus into a *deity*."

Braun hummed contemplatively, putting a hand to his chin. "So in other words, Constantine *made* Jesus God. Not the Church. In essence, he was becoming God through the machinations of the Roman Emperor."

"Exactly! It also had the ancillary effect of transforming the moral prophet into someone and something that existed beyond the human realm. Someone whose power no one or institution or world view could challenge—with the inevitable result that the stewards of that name, the Church, would become an entity whose power and dogma was likewise irrefutable. Which meant both the pagan world and those on the inside of Christianity could no longer challenge the Church. Could no longer question the doctrines and rituals, the beliefs and practices of those in power. Redemption could come only by following the prescribed, sacred path of the Church."

"So it was all about power then?"

Rotberg nodded. "Jesus becoming God was essential for the Empire and the Church to exercise its dual roles. Some even go so far as to insist that the early Church kidnapped Jesus from his disciples. That Christianity coopted the message of the moral prophet, cloaking his humanity inside an unchallenged, irrefutable dogma of divinity that left the Church's expanded power unchecked."

"Which means that almost everything we've been taught about Christianity has been a lie. Not to mention Jesus..."

"The bloke is bloomin' mad!" Celeste exclaimed, crossing her arms and narrowing her gaze.

Silas agreed. And he liked to see her getting worked up about it. Felt solidarity with the love of his life in fighting for the vintage Christian faith.

Rotberg frowned and bowed his head. "I'm afraid that is the truth of it, Markus. Almost everything we've been taught about Christianity has been a lie. Although, there are those in the

Church who know better. That, although Jesus was very human, he was a great and powerful moral prophet who taught and showed humanity the highest, most sincere ideal of divinity. It was Constantine, through his dastardly political entrepreneurship, who reduced the man to a god, and reduced Jesus' life work."

"Two fries short of a Happy Meal, that's for sure," Gapinski grunted.

"That's one way of putting it," Silas said.

"Another is *heretic*," Zarruq said, voice straining under the weight of the social media onslaught.

"Now, this isn't to say that Jesus himself was a sham imposter," Rotberg said, shifting on his stool. "Or that he didn't live in Judea and inspire billions to better themselves and their world. What I am saying is that Constantine leveraged the man's popularity and standing, shaping his religion and giving rise to the Church's power. It was Constantine who strong-armed the Church into transforming Jesus of Nazareth into Jesus the Christ—and three hundred years after his death, no less! Everything before that moment portrayed him and his life and his teachings as a moral prophet. Some of those documents have even been dismissed as merely Gnostic—minority voices within the Christian faith, to be sure, but legitimate ones that were suppressed in the interest of transforming Jesus from merely a man into a deity. And he accomplished it all through the Council of Nicaea, which produced a Creed recited by Christians still to this day. A *code*, if you will."

The SEPIO agents all leaned toward the satcom device at the drop of that line.

"And yet…there is being another code that exists as well, isn't there Rotberg?" Braun said, one end of his mouth curling upward. "Written by Constantine that has been lost to history."

There was that wry smirk again. Silas wanted to smack it off Braun's face.

The smirk turned into a wide grin. He turned toward the camera and leaned in close, as if disclosing a secret.

"Until now."

Then he leaned out of frame, retrieving something that made everyone gasp who was viewing the charade from North Africa.

CHAPTER 8

The air hissed out of Silas like a deflated balloon. Beyond gobsmacked, as Celeste would say, at what the man revealed.

"Are you kidding me..." was all he could manage.

"Holybamoly Batman," Gapinski offered.

"*Dios mío...*" Torres echoed.

"Is that what I think it is?" Celeste said.

Zarruq answered. "I dare say it is exactly what all of us know it is, my dear."

There it was. A golden cylinder. *Another* golden cylinder.

And resting in Markus Braun's hand of all places.

"Several weeks ago," the social media giant began, "some... friends of mine happened upon this relic."

He ran his fingers across its smooth, gilded surface, a flash of white teeth peeking through parted lips hiding his intent.

"But as fanciful as this golden cylinder is, and unbelievably valuable, weighing in at solid fourteen-karat gold, what's inside is what matters most."

The group fell silent as the man twisted open the top. He set it on his lap and withdrew the familiar larger parchment that bore the words of the original Nicene Creed, the Church's original theological code.

Braun unrolled it and took a breath. "*'Pisteuommen eis hena theov patera pantokrotora poieten ouranou kai ges horaton te panton kai aoraton kai eis hena kurion Iesoun Christon ton huion tou theou.'* Or, if you prefer, in Latin: *'Credimus in unum Deum, Patrem omnipotentem, factorem coeli et terrae, visibilium omnium et invisibilium, et in unum Dominum Jesum Christum, Filium Dei unicum.'*"

The man rolled the scroll back into form and handed it to Rotberg. He cleared his throat and recited from memory, "*'We believe in one God, the Father Almighty, maker of all things visible and invisible; and in one Lord Jesus Christ, the Son of God, Light of Light, very God of very God, begotten…'*"

Silas grimaced, the words sounding sour, spoken by a man with an unholy agenda that surely threatened all that Christianity stood for.

"For those not being in the know," Braun went on, "These are the opening words to the Church's code, if you will. What is being known as the Nicene Creed. My brother Hartwin and I recited it as wee lads, and I gather many of you around the world have been reciting it as well. From what I am being told, it is an original copy cobbled together by Constantine and signed by the bishops assembled at his behest. But that isn't the only thing the golden cylinder is being…"

Braun tipped the cylinder onto its side, the familiar puzzle piece metal object falling into his palm and the other parchment. He held up the jagged metal fragment to the camera before setting it down and smoothing flat the parchment fragment. Clearing his throat, he read:

The confession of Emperor Caesar Flavius Constantinus, the Greatest, Pius, Felix, Augustus. Dictated by Titus, my imperial scribe, to be received as my last declaration on the threshold of death.

The Empire knows of my fondness for the Christian religion, how I liberated those who worship the man Jesus and sought the unity of the Church. But that is not the entire truth of the matter, for in him and through this ascendant religion was a new consciousness of human existence, instantiated in his life and emerging through his people across the Empire.

From all walks of life, people are encountering the infinite value bequeathed upon each person by nature of them bearing the image of their Creator. From plebeian to patrician, slave to free, male to female, the entirety of the Empire has encountered a strange new thing in the life of this man Jesus and his followers, the Christians, in Christ's Church. They are encountering a religious community unlike anything seen before, nay, even what the Empire itself has offered heretofore. Something personal and intimate, a connection to the divine apart from personal works and wholly through God becoming man.

I myself encountered this revelation on the battlefield, being wholly struck by the revelation of God's nearness and providential intervention in my schemes. This appearance of our Savior Jesus Christ to me personally and on the field of history more broadly has become known to all men.

Unlike other so-called revelations, this did not immediately make its appearance as a new religion, per se. Rather, and not in no small order, and not dwelling in some corner of the earth but across the entirety of the Empire, the Spirit of God himself helped birth it. For as Jesus himself instructed his disciples, *"you receive power when the Holy Spirit has come upon you; and you will be my witnesses in Jerusalem, in all Judea and Samaria, and to the ends of the earth.*" And unto the ends of the earth it seems God is moving to reveal his heart of love and acceptance before all mankind, through His Spirit and through His Church, as well as through my own hand.

He set down the fragment and fixed the camera with a sturdy gaze. "And there it ends. The start of the confession given by the founder of the Christian religion."

"Founder my ass!" Silas grumbled, a nervous energy winding through him as he waited for the man to get to it.

"Master Grey..." Zarruq said lowly. "I do understand emotions are running ragged, but let's stay the tongue, shall we?"

"Yes, sir." He chuckled to himself, the man sounding all the more like Radcliffe. He was more than thankful the man was along for the ride, wherever it led.

"As you can see, or hear rather, the confession is being cut short." Braun held up the piece of faded brown parchment, the top portion cut square and the bottom looking like the fragment SEPIO found hours earlier, torn and jagged at the bottom with black Latin letters scrawled crisply across its face. "The bottom half was torn away. Which is begging the question: What is being missing? What did the man confess? What did he admit to regarding his faith, regarding *the* faith—the Christian faith and all the beliefs that sit at the heart of the Church's code that Constantine helped construct?"

Braun suddenly stood, the camera adjusting to his change of posture and retreating as he took a step forward. "I am aiming to find out. I and my good friend Noland Rotberg here, the imminently qualified New Testament scholar—"

Silas scoffed again. "Imminently qualified New Testament scholar my—"

A hand clenched his shoulder, and Zarruq cleared his throat.

"Sorry..."

"Today, we are announcing a little treasure hunt," Braun revealed.

"Treasure hunt?" Celeste exclaimed. "What's he playing at?"

Silas shook his head, clenching the satcom device tighter.

"The contest is open only to this private group of distinguished invitees on WeSolve—the Davos of the internet, as I like to call you dear souls. With your help, we will be getting to the bottom of the questions this fragment begs and the ones the religion itself begs. Obviously, there is being at least one more fragment, but we are guessing there are several more that are telling the complete story of Christianity."

Braun paused, dipping his head slightly. "The *real* story, the one the Church has been suppressing for generations, with the help of the pagan Emperor. So we need your help collecting them, ideally by June 19."

He kept his head low, so that the overhead lighting cast dark shadows under the man's eyes, a menacing evil sparking at the center of the cyan ringing his pupils.

A shudder ratcheted up Silas's spine at the sight, sensing a presence, something deeper behind the hunt.

Braun took another step, Silas's heart hammering in his head now and chest feeling as if it would constrict in on itself at the turn.

"To make it worth your while," the man went on, one end of his mouth curling upward again, "I am being prepared to pay the man or woman or even team who locates the other fragments one billion euros—per recovered fragment."

SEPIO gasped as one.

"Did that *loco hombre* just offer a billion *dineros* with a '*b*'?" Torres exclaimed.

"Sounded that way," Celeste said. "And actually it was

euros, but still. A nice chunk of change for a piece of torn parchment."

"I got into the wrong line of work," Gapinski muttered. "Maybe you could teach me a thing or two about the profession, Torres. We could find the others and split the profits."

Celeste smacked his shoulder.

"Ouch!"

"Quiet down!" Silas hissed as the man continued.

Braun said, "Of course, payment will be determined on the basis of verifying the authenticity of each recovered fragment. We are having an entire team dedicated to running whatever may come of the treasure hunt through the gauntlet of tests to determine what, if anything, the good Emperor Constantine wanted to confess about the good religion."

The man flashed a grin and added, "Good luck, WeSolvers, and work quickly. I believe in you. So does the Universe. *Namaste*."

With that, the video faded to black.

And the group faded to stunned silence, the crashing waves and those wretched seagulls the only soundtrack for the moment that seemed too out-of-orbit crazy to be true.

"Can I just say," Gapinski said, "what the hey-ho day was that?"

"Sounded like a right nutter, if you ask me," Celeste said.

"*Si*, but you heard the man," Torres added. "One of the richest men in the world blew a big, fat dog whistle to every treasure hunter in the world, issuing a dog-eat-dog treasure hunting challenge with a billion bucks on the line, the finish line in just a few days."

Gapinski smirked. "Yeah, *Survivor* on steroids."

She turned to him and raised a brow. "You a fan, Hoss?"

He blushed and mumbled, "Maybe…"

"Can we focus please," Silas said, feeling heat rising up the back of his neck at the turn, his nerves fraying from the past day. "Zoe, when did this drop?"

"About an hour before I rang you. Tried calling the minute we got word it was broadcasting on WeNet."

"That explains why the goons from earlier came a callin'," Gapinski said.

"That is a good point," Celeste said. "Must have been part of the super-secret invite-only WeSolve sector of Braun's network."

"Ready to put all his fire tokens on the table for a chance at the billion bucks."

"Fire tokens?"

"It's a *Survivor* reference," Torres explained.

Gapinski grinned and snapped his fingers. "I knew you were a fan!"

"That doesn't make sense," Silas muttered.

"What do you mean?" Celeste asked.

"If it was broadcast on the WeNet dark web an hour ago like we think, how did the hostiles know to come searching for the golden cylinder before the treasure-hunting challenge was officially launched?"

"Good point."

"Perhaps they were tipped off beforehand?" Torres said.

Gapinski nodded. "Came to get a jump on the hunt before every Tom, Dick, and Harry dusts off their fedora and whip, Doc Jones style?"

"Possibly..." Silas said, considering the added element of the hostiles from the morning.

"But are we sure this whole bloody affair is genuine?" Celeste said, ignoring the man. "After all we went through the past few months and uncovered thanks to Torres's ex-fiancé?" She turned to the woman. "No offense, mate."

Torres shook her head. "None taken. And I don't know about the crazy-man Braun's golden cylinder, but the one we uncovered looks pretty authentic to me. No way someone could have buried that thing under all the sand and rubble we excavated the past few months."

Silas asked, "But couldn't some third party have uncovered the whereabouts of the baptismal and dug the necessary chamber inside?"

"Again, no way. The earth we extracted from the site was definitely time-packed, and the objects scattered about inside and around the excavation site perfectly matched the fourth-century dating. Then there's the flooring itself, which was perfectly preserved. No, this was an intact, undisturbed site lost to history."

"But remember, mate," Celeste said, "your ex did manage to fool a Harvard professor trained in this sort of thing, cobbling together the whole bloody package of artifacts and provenance. Perhaps Braun gave the man another few million to orchestrate another conspiracy to bring down the Church."

Torres scoffed. "Even he's not that good."

"She's right. I agree," Silas said. "The gradations of the excavated sediment not to mention the way we found the tile sealing the chamber and the cylinder inside…" He paused considering what he was about to admit. "No, this is legit. I feel it deep down on top of what the evidence suggests on its face."

"Obviously, we'll have to run all the necessary tests to verify the authenticity of the Nicene Creed parchment and the fragment, but—"

A crack, followed by a quick shuffling caused the group to turn toward their smoldering tents.

"Why don't you leave that to me."

Silas's veins flooded with fight-or-flight adrenaline, a large man in military fatigues, hair twisted in dreadlock chords into a hive with half a dozen men brandishing assault rifles, emerging into view.

Aurelius Chuke.

His hand instinctively went for his back.

When the six goons raised their weapons with a rattle.

Silas mumbled a silent curse but obliged the threatening instruction, leaving his weapon be and putting his hands up.

The other SEPIO agents did the same, as did Zarruq. Even the researchers down toward the beach startled at their return. He prayed the Lord would keep them safe and get SEPIO out of the mess.

Again.

Chuke walked toward them grinning, that gold tooth glinting in the high-noon sun. He seized the golden cylinder from Torres and handed it to one of his men, his gaze fixed on Silas with that same golden-tooth smile.

"Master Grey, what am I going to do with you?" That deep, buttery, accented voice was back. Nails on a chalkboard lathered in honey. "A feeling you were holding out on me, I had. A crafty one, I was told."

By whom? Part of the mystery of this whole blasted affair that kept deepening...

Silas took a step, jumping into the fray. Maybe not with both feet, but showing he wasn't backing down was a start.

"We meet again, I see," he said, throwing the same fixed gaze right back at him.

Chuke came in close, so that Silas could smell the man's breath, hot and sour and briny.

He narrowed his eyes. "That we are. Reclaiming what is mine, I am here." Then he called out to his man, "Is it there?"

"It's there," Chuke's man confirmed.

"Both of them? The fragment and the Creed?"

"Aye."

The smile widened back into the grin Silas wanted to slap to kingdom come. "Excellent."

The man turned and began sauntering back to his crew when Silas called out, "Who sent you? Or did you get an inside scoop on Braun's little treasure hunt, figured you'd show up to claim the billion bucks for yourself before anyone else could?"

Chuke turned back again, that golden tooth returning. "What I've recovered is worth more than a billion of Markus Braun's euros. The bloody deed to the Republic of Heaven, it is!"

Silas sucked in a startled breath.

Republic of Heaven...

"But you already know that, don't you, Master Grey?"

Chuke's mouth faded to a scowl. He grabbed the golden cylinder from his man and spun around to leave. But not before leaving one final command for his men.

"Shoot them."

The men bearing the menacing rifles took a thunderous step forward, readying to shoot on command.

Startling the SEPIO agents and sending their hands back up in protest.

"No, wait!"

Bishop Zarruq had stepped out in front, hands outstretched and high and waving a plea.

"Take me instead. As a hostage!"

The hostiles seemed startled at the turn, easing their weapons back until Chuke turned back around.

He threw his head back and laughed, full-belly style. "Now why would I want to do that, you old coot?"

"Because you need me."

Silas went to start forward when Celeste grabbed his arm. She shook her head and gave him a look.

Best to let it play out.

He took a breath and sighed with a nod.

Hoping she was right...

Chuke chuckled again and held up the cylinder. "But I already have what I came looking for. What more do I need?"

Zarruq swallowed and gestured toward the SEPIO agents.

"For one thing, if you kill them and me, you'll stir a hornets' nest. A legion of agents will take their place and hunt you down. After all—"

The man half-turned toward Silas, eyeing him before turning back to Chuke and saying, "—they contend for the once-for-all faith delivered, committed, entrusted to the saints. All of it thanks to Master Thaddeus."

The man waved a dismissive hand. "Idle threats. No match for my battle-hardened men, they are."

"Perhaps..." the bishop went on, "but there's another thing. Something I can give you."

"And what is that?"

"The other golden cylinders."

Silas startled. Did he hear him right? The location of the others? He would give that up to save their lives—even knowing the danger the fragments posed for the Church?

What was he doing?

Chuke stilled, narrowing his eyes. "Negotiating, I do not like."

Zarruq folded his arms and leaned back. "Too bad. You appear to not be having a choice, given the siren call from Markus Braun, broadcasted across the dark sector of WeNet. Every two-bit treasure hunter from sea to shining sea will have been summoned to search after identical copies of that very same golden cylinder you now possess."

The man eyed the object clenched under his arm, his face registering a mixture of apprehension and acquiescence.

Then he stiffened, raising an arm as if he were going to shoot Zarruq himself.

But he didn't.

Instead, he pointed at one of his men and gestured toward the bishop.

"Very well. You will become mine. And if any of your

crusaders come for you and meddle in our affairs, your throat I will not hesitate to slit."

Chuke nodded for his men to apprehend the bishop.

Two did, rushing to grab hold of his arms.

As the hostiles dragged him away, Zarruq twisted toward the SEPIO agents, shouting: "Follow the Emperor, seek the Master, remember—!"

The butt of a rifle slammed into his back, sending him stumbling to the ground and coughing for breath.

Silas went to intervene when Celeste and Gapinski grabbed his arms.

"Let go of me," he growled as two of Chuke's men grabbed Zarruq from behind and lifted him to his feet.

"Not worth it, love," Celeste said. "Not after what Victor offered us."

The hostiles kept going, passing the remains of their encampment and disappearing behind thick foliage.

Taking his new friend and confidant hostage.

Along with the Church's code and the latest threat to the Christian faith.

Constantine's confession.

CHAPTER 9

Silas took off toward the edge of the cliff butting the Mediterranean, cursing himself for how he could let that blasted hostile run off with not only the golden cylinder and all the trouble it held for the Christian faith. But how he could let the man cart Zarruq away as a hostage.

Things had just gotten blown to hades.

Again.

The remaining SEPIO crew called after him, but he didn't care. Wanted to see it for himself, see through the kidnapping of a trustee for the Order of Thaddeus by unknown hostiles.

On his watch!

And yet, they weren't so unknown...

The Republic of Heaven...

Silas had heard that line before. And he knew which horse's mouth the bastard was parroting it from, too. No surprise there. But it made this thing a whole other thing.

He scrambled toward the edge but lost his footing on a pair of rocks, sending him stumbling to his knees.

Just as several buzz-saw growls revved above the din of crashing waves down below over the rocky lip ahead.

He let slip a curse, wincing at the pain shooting up his shins. But he recovered, racing to the edge for a final viewing.

Just in time to find Zarruq being ushered toward a black military-grade inflatable boat, one of two. Looked like the same make and model that had landed upon their shore earlier that morning. Must have returned to confirm whether Torres was telling the truth, but all stealth like and planned out. Not your average hostiles, that's for sure. Far cry from his boys back in Iraq, but definitely not your Rent-a-Whack-Job variety, either.

The bishop was suddenly shoved into the side by the barrel of an AK. He flopped against it before scrambling over the lip inside. At least they hadn't killed him. Held up that end of the bargain. Which really wasn't any bargain as far as the hostiles were concerned, given SEPIO was playing a hand full of blanks.

Then the man himself showed up, Chuke boarding behind Zarruq. The man hoisted himself inside, then stood straight and turned toward the cliff, as if sensing Silas staring down from above.

Silas held his ground, feet firmly planted.

Let the bastard see me. Let him know who his new enemy is.

The man who was going to track him down and exact the vengeful justice of the Lord himself, eye for eye and tooth for tooth.

Within half a minute, the two black boats were shoving off from shore and out to sea. His teammates joined him as the two fish faded into black dots and then from view.

"We'll get him back, chief," Gapinski said, clamping a hand on Silas's shoulder. "No question about that. And then we'll pound 'em into the ground, Hulk-smash style."

Silas took a breath and nodded, throwing his hands up to his head and walking a crunching circle across the rocky bluff in livid frustration. His tenure as Order Master was not going well so far.

"Oh, yeah?" Torres said. "How do you plan on doing that,

Hoss? You heard the guy. He so much as feels the shadow of our mugs on the back of his neck and he'll slit Zarruq's throat."

Gapinski shrugged. "I don't know. Wrangle up SEPIO agents in the field and form a posse—"

"John Wayne style, huh? Maybe rustle up a band of cowpokes while we're at it?"

"Wouldn't hurt. But we just can't leave the guy high and dry on the open seas! I mean, the Rangers practically invented the leave-no-man-behind mantra."

Silas spun toward the man. "I know what the damn motto says!"

He took a breath and closed his eyes, the creed of his former brotherhood flashing from memory: *'I will never leave a fallen comrade to fall into the hands of the enemy.'* He sighed. "Sorry. Didn't mean to bite your head off."

"No prob, Bob."

"And we're not going to leave him high and dry. We'll get the bastards. Believe you me. But we've also got a duty to the Order—to the *Church*, given what we found in that golden cylinder, and then lost. Given what those blathering idiots broadcasted across WeSolve. If I know Zarruq like I think after the past few months, he'd want us to stop whatever the hell is threatening the Christian faith."

"Again…" Gapinski muttered in a huff.

Silas let it go. But he was right. Back in the saddle fighting for and protecting the Church.

"So where do you reckon this leaves us?" Celeste said, planting her hands on her hips and continuing to stare out to sea.

"Bupkis is where it leaves us," Gapinski said.

"Nothing at all, is right," Silas muttered, continuing to pace out his frustrations.

"I wouldn't say nothing…"

Silas stopped, throwing Torres a confused look. "What do

you mean?"

She dug into her pocket and retrieved the jagged piece of metal that had also been part of the golden cylinder package. She held it up with two fingers and smiled.

"That's right!" He hustled up to her and took the mystery from her, eyeing the curious piece of metal and wondering what it meant.

"Slipped it into my pocket earlier. Sort of providential, I guess."

"I'd say!" Celeste said. "Good work, Naomi."

"Slap me some more skin, sister," Gapinski said, opening his palm and holding it up. Torres giggled and slapped his high five. "We needed a win, and you sure delivered."

"What do you reckon it is?" Celeste asked.

"Not sure..." Silas continued eyeing the only piece of evidence remaining from their find. With zero clue what it was. He flipped it over then back again and brought it closer to his face for inspection, brow furrowed and face pinched with concentration. Hadn't paid much attention to it before, but now...

It was clearly old, a layer of grayish-blue-green patina covering parts of it, though most of it perfectly preserved. Probably made from copper or some other metal alloy. One edge was slightly curved with a thickness to it and smooth, but for tiny indentations every quarter inch. The other edges were jagged like a puzzle piece, as if it had been split off from something larger, maybe the size of a baseball. One side was flat and blank, but the other...Looked like raised etchings on its face along the rim. Latin or Greek characters, perhaps, even Coptic. Hard to tell with the degradation of time.

Celeste sidled up to him. "Saw Victor eyeing it earlier. A spark of recognition seemed to flash across his face at one point, which was curious."

"Did he mention anything to you about it?" Torres asked.

She shook her head. "Unfortunately, no."

Silas scratched the object's face with his finger, rubbing off some dirt caked onto the surface.

When he caught his breath in surprise.

"What the heck?"

"What is it, love?" Celeste asked.

He squinted at the object's face and gently pressed his finger against a thin line etched into the metal, tracing a thin V-like shape on its surface that went near one of the jagged edges to the center and down toward another edge.

Looking vaguely like the calling card of a very old enemy of the Order of Thaddeus.

And the Church of Jesus Christ.

No, it couldn't be...

The trio of SEPIO agents crowded around and stared at it in silence while a cold dread washed over Silas, the metal object feeling hot and heavy against his palm now and freighted with significance and meaning.

"Is that what I think it is?" Gapinski asked. "Our resident anti-Christian whack jobs we've come to know and love flashing stick-figure swastika-like ink at every turn?"

"Nous, you mean?" Celeste said.

"Any other resident anti-Christian whack jobs we've come to know and love flashing stick-figure swastika-like ink at every turn?"

Silas raised his head and shrugged. "Too early to tell, but..."

He took in a measured breath and shook his head in disbelief. It wasn't looking good.

"Oh, come on." Torres took the object from Silas's hand and held it up for a viewing. Her brow furrowed and face pinched with the same concentration as Silas, the high-noon sun glinting off spots on the faded metal. "Could be anything..."

"Oh, come on yourself!" Gapinski said. "You've got some fragment of a letter championing some Christian heretic, presumably by the Emperor who has a sketchy relationship with the Christian faith—so says our social media overlord conspiracy thriller writer wannabe. Then some sort of puzzle piece, a medallion maybe, broken up and stuffed down the barrel of some golden doohickey buried in the desert with part of a symbol that looks darn near a match for Nous's bird thingamabob tattoo." He took a breath and shook his head. "Naw, case closed, sister. This has the Church's archenemy written all over it."

Silas considered this. Again, not looking good.

"The Republic of Heaven..."

"What was that, chief?"

He cleared his throat in embarrassment, absentmindedly voicing what he had been mulling over. "I said, the Republic of Heaven."

"The Republic of Heaven?" Celeste said.

"Echo...echo...echo," Gapinski replied. Then put up his hands in surrender as Celeste threw him a look.

Silas nodded. "It's something Chuke mentioned before he left."

"Where have I heard that before?" Torres asked.

He took a breath and sighed. "Rudolf Borg. And my brother."

"That's right!"

Celeste hummed with recognition. "Now that you mention it, I do recall the blokes droning on about the pseudo-spiritual replacement for Jesus' teaching a time or two."

Torres eyed the medallion piece again. "Which means this may very well be Nous."

Gapinski grunted a laugh. "Told you so."

"Alright, alright," Silas said. "We can grandstand when this is over with, when we've solved this blasted caper and Zarruq is safe. But for now, we should assume Nous has both feet planted firmly in...whatever the heck this is. Given Chuke's tongue slip and the fact anything that threatens the faith seems to have Nous firmly planted in it."

Celeste took the medallion fragment from Torres and had a glance herself. "But if this truly is some sort of Nous medallion, its calling-card symbol etched onto its surface, then this pretty much guarantees that what we found secreted away amongst the ruins of a Libyan basilica is the dastardly, devilish deal we thought it was."

"I don't follow," Torres said.

"Nice alteration," Gapinski whispered to Celeste.

"I think what she's saying," Silas explained, moving on, "is that if Nous hid fragments of some confession from Constantine, to be unearthed at some later time in the future, then...well, the Church is in a world of hurt because there's more to unearth that could very well give critics of the Church all the ammo they need to bring their case that Constantine created Christianity to a unanimous jury verdict in their favor —just like Braun and Rotberg insisted on WeNet."

Celeste nodded, folding her arms and saying nothing more.

Because nothing more needed to be said. Such a confession that shed less-than-favorable light on the early days of Christianity's formation and ascension could spell disaster for the faith. At least in the eyes of the watching world...

The four SEPIO agents stood on the cliff in silence, those annoying gulls cawing at each other down below as the waves crashed with greater intensity, the wind wiping up now as it rode a storm front signaled by dark, menacing clouds moving in from the horizon on their already bleak day.

"So what do we do about it?" Gapinski asked.

Silas smiled to himself. Always ready to get down to business, he was—to jump into the fray to save the Christian day and each other's lives. They all were, Celeste and Torres turning toward him, eyes brimming with as much activation and waiting for a plan to knock some heads together.

They were right. It was go time. Twice over.

He began, "First things first, rescuing Zarruq."

"But Victor said a firm no to that one," Celeste protested.

"And Bishop Zarruq isn't Order Master, now is he?" Silas said with a wink. "Not going to do anything stupid, and I have a hunch that the second leg of our new SEPIO operation will take care of the first."

"What do you mean?"

"Something he said before he left. Follow the Emperor, seek the Master, remember…something or other. He was cut off by one of Chuke's goons before he could finish."

"You're right. I recall the cryptic command as well," Celeste said. "You think it's a clue, then, something we should use as a guide?"

"I don't know what else it could be. Especially after he gave himself up on our behalf with the promise to give Chuke the other golden cylinders. He must know something specific. Why else would he offer this last declaration before being dragged away? And what if Nous was next up on the list?"

"Now that you mention it," Torres said, "I do remember the guy spouting off some gibberish like that. But it's not exactly an X-marks-the-spot road map."

"And Emperor I get," Gapinski agreed, "but what about the other dude. Who's this Master dude?"

"Arius?" Silas said.

"But was he considered a master?" Torres asked. "And of what?"

He took a breath to answer, but huffed it out with confusion.

Torres gasped and put a hand to her mouth. "Did I just stump Master Silas Grey, professor extraordinaire?"

He frowned. "Funny. But, yeah, you do have a point."

"I do have to agree," Celeste said. "Arius and Constantine seem like candidates for the first cryptic clues."

Gapinski hummed with contemplation. "A heretic, an emperor, and an anti-Christian sect walk into a SEPIO operation..."

Silas chuckled. "Something like that."

"You think it's a code, don't you?" Celeste said. "Like he was warning us or something?"

"Or steering us into some kind of direction," Silas said.

"Where?"

Torres pointed toward the excavation site. "To the next golden cylinder!"

"Bingo. Has to be." Silas went on, "Something to do with Arius and Constantine, given what we found in the golden cylinder and where it was hiding, under a seal of the emperor. Not to mention Braun's little treasure hunt."

"Brilliant, that Victor is. To steer us in the right direction like that."

"But again, where?" Gapinski asked. "And how the heck are we going to get Zarruq back?"

There was a mixture of fear and anger in his voice and in his eyes. Same for the other two. Silas averted them, not knowing what to say. He looked out across the sea, the water churning now and a rumble of thunder in the distance beneath the darkening sky portending bad things to come. There he was again, standing at the front of the line, men and women looking at him for guidance and direction. Looking at him for answers to questions he wasn't even sure were the right ones to ask yet.

One man might as well be considered down for the count, given the maniacs who took Zarruq. And if he wasn't, he would be if they didn't act fast, though he wouldn't voice his suspicions to the group. Celeste maybe, but later. Then a monumental discovery had just slipped through the Order's fingers, one that could be death for the faith.

Lord Jesus Christ, Son of God, what am I to do?

His people stirred, refocusing his attention to the friends standing next to him who had become much more than that. They were comrades in battle, partners in crime. They were family.

Then a verse from the Bible sprang from memory. The Book of Ecclesiastes, chapter four: *'Two are better than one, because they have a good reward for their toil. For if they fall, one will lift up the other; but woe to one who is alone and falls and does not have another to help.'*

He smiled at the wisdom of the writer, and then promptly said a quick prayer of thanks for the reminder.

He wasn't alone. It wasn't all up to him. SEPIO's strength was in their combined passion for protecting the Christian faith and varied expertise in leaning on each other for success.

So was his as Order Master.

"To answer your question, Matt," Silas said, "I'm not sure. Because this day sure as heck turned sour real quick. But I will —*we* will get Zarruq back. And protect the Church. Agreed?"

"Agreed" the other three said in unison.

"Then let's get the show on the road. Starting with a trip across the pond."

"Which pond?" Torres asked.

Silas pointed out at the Mediterranean, rain sheeting now in the distance. Because what they needed most was lying across the sea.

CHAPTER 10
SOMEWHERE IN LIBYA.

Sebastian Grey didn't know which was worse: the insufferable heat suffocating him like a wet blanket compounded by the deluge thunderstorming through his encampment, or the godawful stench of ripe bodies and some vinegary, cabbagey local slop posing as cuisine wafting through the open tent flap he was trying to wrangle to the ground.

A clap of thunder shuddered from above, his arm jerking with a startle, the rope slipping from his grip to a wicked wind whipping up now from the storm's changing course.

"Sodding piece of—"

He grasped for the damn thing flapping in the wind now like a bucking bronco, the rain sheeting across the encampment as his hired hands rushed for cover and drenching his long blond hair come loose in the effort.

The day had started magnificently, a bright sunny day all happy and warm, their encampment perched on the Mediterranean readying to retrieve a rumor from the bowels of a land long since forgotten. Except there was a problem. A problem with a name tasting of spoiled milk, curdled and chewy.

Silas Grey. His dear older brother playacting some sort of

horrid skit as a cross between the Lone Ranger and Pope John Paul!

But it was more than that. Because the Order of Thaddeus was the larger threat, the band of merry miscreants clutching with pitiful desperation to the superstitions of an irrelevant religion long past its shelf life. Had to give them credit, though. They had stepped up their game the past few months to retrieve relics of its past. Little did they know that one relic above all had laid hidden, one relic to rule them all that would actually pulverize the rest beyond useful succor.

Yet his brother and his religious order wasn't the entirety of what threatened his plans to bring down the Christian faith.

As the newly installed Grand Master of the Church's arch-enemy after Rudolf Borg's death late last year, he had been closely monitoring developments of new pseudo-spiritual sect. An order bearing tattoos of box-shaped men. The annals of Nous history made mention of such men from ages past. *Ecclesia Theotites*, they called themselves.

Church of the Deities. Or simply the Theotites.

It was all very confusing and fluid, and Nous agents were still getting to the bottom of it. But the fog of it all was most disheartening, especially knowing they had infiltrated his own home. He knew he better have answers soon. Or else François Lefevre would and the rest of the Thirteen and Council of Five.

Then he would be done for.

Pain lanced across Sebastian's hand.

He cursed loudly and withdrew it as a thunder clapped closer.

Something attached to the rope must have sliced through his soft skin, drawing a line of blood down his hand in watery rivulets.

His belly quickened at the sight, his mouth watering for the coppery tang of his life force.

"Let it flap..." he cursed, standing and sending his hand to his mouth for the comfort of his blood.

He licked his skin as he sauntered inside his spacious accommodations, head swimming with delight from imbibing his crimson nectar. He padded across an adequate Persian-style rug, evergreen and indigo whorls faded from use, aiming for a modest wooden desk resting near the back next to a queen bed made to his dead military father's exacting standards. Still couldn't shake them after all these years, which was a blessing in disguise. *A clean, comfy camp is a healthy, tolerable one*, Dad had always said.

Reaching the desk, he glanced back at the tent opening as lightning flickered against the sheeting rain, wondering when his sodding hired hands would arrive with the relic, representing the kind of opportunity to vanquish the faith he'd been lusting for since adolescence.

This particular relic wasn't a bone or a lock of hair from some long-dead saint. It wasn't one of the thousands of wood shards claimed as the True Cross or centuries-old nails posing as the spikes that killed that sodding god-man from Nazareth. No, no, no! This one was a confession. A confession to end all confessions, if the rumor held true, the one that had fallen into his lap that nearly prematurely ended his career a few months ago.

Letting go of his hand, having satisfied his desire, he picked up the hefty clay bowl with the markings of an ancient tongue ringing the inside. A Manda magic bowl, it was called, discovered months ago on a fact-finding trip. He had thought it bore a revelation of a secret book discarded from the Christian scriptures, which turned out false. But it made mention of a confession from the *'Emperor of the Way'* that promised a revelation to set straight the *'Code of the Way.'* And when that dreadful Markus Braun made mention of an emperor code, he thought he hit pay dirt!

Sebastian immediately activated Nous's operatives to suss out prospective candidates for the location of this code and this confession. Leading to the encampment of Nous's forward operation in Libya along the Mediterranean to recover the so-called emperor code sending the dark web into a tizzy—especially given Braun's billion-dollar price tag. A well-placed source at WeNet, of all places, had discovered an impending announcement from the social media mogul. Something about a golden cylinder and religious code that bore a striking resemblance to the revelation imprinted on his magic bowl. Just the break he needed to right Nous's ship.

And then it all turned sour.

Mid-morning, Chuke reported that Silas was indeed commanding an outfit of researchers excavating the basilica, but the prize was nowhere to be found. After storming the beachhead where the cylinder was rumored to be buried, an empty hole was all that sat in the ground, void of any sign of the Creed and fragment bearing the supposed confession.

Dimwit gave up after one try. Sebastian scoffed and shook his head at the thought. Chuke was supposed to be the best there was in North Africa, a former warlord won to Nous's cause last year. Which meant nothing to Sebastian. He ripped the man a new one and commanded him to try again. This time without mercy. Even for his brother.

The storm began rolling in from the horizon an hour ago and he had yet to hear from the man. He frowned, considering the omen.

A commotion outside drew his attention to a crowd gathering beyond his tent. Probably some local being shooed away from snooping too close.

He set the bowl down on the desk and reached for a crystal jar filled with amber liquid. A gift from his brother, actually, years ago. One of the few things he had kept from Silas, given its usefulness holding cognac. He poured himself a glass full and took a drink, the spicy yet fruity brandy a balm for his troubles.

But then his mind turned brighter, considering another angle at the day's turn.

Storms shattering the day's peace; darkness overcoming light.

Perhaps it was a prophetic utterance from the Universe itself, reassuring him all was unfolding according to plan.

The line from the Hindu scripture, the Bhagavad Gita, came to mind: *'I am become Death, the destroyer of worlds.'*

Sebastian's mouth curled upward at the line.

Exactly…

Suddenly, the flap to Sebastian's tent fluttered with disturbance. He let slip a curse and readied to finish what he had started when a large man ensconced in fatigues, cords of that dreadful hair sodden from the storm, came barging in. Aurelius Chuke, with that pretentious name that reminded him of that sodding saint he'd learned about in Catholic grade school.

"You've returned."

The man nodded, stepping farther inside.

And bearing a gift.

"Returned, I have. And a gift, I bear."

Sebastian rolled his eyes with irritation at the man's grating Yoda-speak. He threw back a mouthful of cognac and swallowed, his belly warming and head swimming from not just the nectar but the object the man was holding.

A golden cylinder.

Sebastian grinned. "Is this what I think it is?"

"That, it is." Chuke matched his approval, that annoying golden tooth glinting in the dim lamplight.

Coming around the desk, he walked to the man and took it. Removing one end, he peered inside to find a rolled-up scroll and a fragment. His heart skipped a beat at the sight, a thousand hopes and dreams finding their realization in this pretentious imperial cylinder.

Chuke went on, "But that wasn't all we recovered."

He offered a curious whistle and his associate appeared at the tent opening. He grunted something in Arabic, to which the summoned man promptly left and returned.

Bearing a curious fellow the size of a grizzly bear! Beard black and bushy and salted, wearing an off-white sheet embroidered with a putrid pattern with blues and greens and blacks, clutching a hat ringed by the same. He looked like a drenched version of his wretched brother's cat, dripping water across his nice Persian-style rug.

Sebastian turned his nose up at the mawkish man, bronze skin dirty and bearing an ugly gash across his head, blood staining the shoulder of his garments below a watercolor crimson. He didn't have time for a prisoner! Not with the fate of the Church on the line, and with him at the helm of her destruction.

"Who is this?" he sneered.

That annoying golden tooth returned, Chuke grinning like a cat bearing a mouse for his master. "The key."

"The key? To what?"

He spread his arms out. "Everything!"

He set the cylinder down on the desk with a huff. "This isn't a game, Chuke. Tell me what the—"

"He means," the mystery man said, voice gravelly and face drawn, "that I bear the truth of what you are seeking in my lands."

Ballsy, had to give the man that much, speaking up like that, a clear prisoner of the warlord. He stared him down, too, not flinching from Sebastian's irritated gaze. Which sent his pulse throbbing with hate.

"Victor Zarruq, this is," Chuke said. "Former Bishop of

Libya and something of a commanding general with the Order of Thaddeus."

Sebastian's scowl instantly slackened, realization dawning.

He eyed the man. "The Order, you say?"

"Right, you are. Traded his life for his mates, he did. Promised to show us the way, he did."

"As long as the Order remains unharmed," the man called Zarruq said.

This was good. Very good. Should make the next few days easy peasy. And just in time, too, given the free-for-all Braun unleashed with his treasure hunt challenge.

Sebastian grinned. "Excellent. Let's get to work, shall we? No time to waste."

He came out from around the desk and stepped up to the man, who stiffened with a show of confidence yet betrayed it by shifting on bare feet.

"You and I are going to make magic, Bishop Zarruq. And if you don't cooperate, not only will I oversee the destruction of the Church, dancing upon its ashes at the end. I will slit the throats of every last one of your precious SEPIO agents myself. Beginning with my brother and ending with you."

The man swallowed, his breath escaping with a betraying whimper.

Excellent. With a whimper, is right.

His breath and the Church's last.

MEANWHILE, ON ANOTHER SHORELINE NOT FAR AWAY, MARKUS Braun didn't know which was worse: the fact that one of the clues to the emperor code had been discovered outside the boundaries of his little WeSolve treasure hunt, or that a competitor had bested him by snatching it—*the* competitor at that, stretching back centuries deep.

Braun slapped the silver mouthpiece of the nozzle against his palm, the one attached to the multi-colored, finely blown glass hookah sitting on the ground in front of his perch mounted on a stack of gold-tasseled crimson pillows—contemplating all that should be done about it all.

All that *he* should do about it all.

Reports of an ambush by a well-financed local Libyan warlord turned militia-for-hire had reached him moments ago. One of the men gifted him by the spiritual sect that had radically redefined his life bore the news—the sect giving him purpose and an aim for not only his money, but his humanitarian vision for the global community.

A vision where the Human Will—capital 'H', capital 'W'— in all of its universal-conscious glory could spread like a well-crafted meme across the expanse of his interconnected humans. Promoting peace and prosperity and progress, for humanity—with him firmly at the helm of making that utopian dream come true.

Because that was the thing about utopia, that mid-16th century word first used by Sir Thomas More. Based on the Greek *ou* and *topos*, a utopia was literally *not place*. It existed nowhere on the planet. An imaginary plot of *not-place* land in the middle of nowhere, enjoying the utmost perfection in legal, social, and political systemic progress.

And it was Markus Braun who would dream it, will it, forge it into existence. By force if necessary, but preferably by persuasive means. Which is where the emperor code came in.

The last such place was arguably the Roman Empire. Surely not the sort of *place* of perfection Thomas More had written about, given the ongoing threats and diseases and rudimentary technology. But it was close, having reorganized much of the world, known at least, under Pax Romana. The peace of Rome. Where rule of law ruled and the average citizen could make something of themselves. Even slaves were treated far better with very strict legal rights than anything dreamt under previous Western regimes. Combined with government-instituted infrastructure projects, from roads to baths, one could consider the Roman way quite the way.

But something had begun to threaten the stability of it all. Not so much a force as an idea.

Christianity.

It wasn't so much that the upstart religion from the backwards Judean province itself threatened the Roman status quo. After all, even the upstart prophet did *'render unto Caesar the things that are Caesar's.'* The two had co-existed for centuries, mostly because of the mighty thumb under which the State held the Church. Something the Western world could surely learn a thing or two. But with its unforeseen explosive growth, from all corners of the Empire and from each social strata—whether slave or free, plebeian or patrician—inevitably there would be a clash of kingdoms.

That was the genius of one Emperor Caesar Flavius Constantinus, the Greatest, Pius, Felix, Augustus.

Constantine the Great.

Not only did he wisely lift the persecuting sanctions that would have torn the Empire asunder. He leveraged the religion for his own political ends, creating and coaxing and crafting the faith in his own image. One he had never truly embraced until his deathbed. And even that was suspect.

Especially given what Braun had discovered to exist that would completely upend the Church's narrative surrounding the faith, particularly the singular dogma that it seemed to hinge upon.

The deity of Jesus.

Braun held the mouthpiece in his hand and smirked at the thought before shoving it into his mouth and drawing in a contemplative inhalation of the heavenly hashish that was burning at his breath above a coal at the center of the Persian device.

How Jesus became God had been something of a fascination of his when he tossed aside his childhood faith. How embittered factions had formed on either side of the ballsy claim that the man from Nazareth had been more than human.

With Constantine the Great squarely at the center of the controversy.

He puffed on the hookah, smoke pluming from his mouth out into the cavernous tent anchored near the Mediterranean, the rain pattering on the canvas reminding him of home. Then he wrapped his mouth around the nozzle again and drew lungfuls of the tetrahydrocannabinol-laced smoke.

The emperor code was the first clue needed to uncover the Church's dirty little secret. Or rather, what was rumored to have accompanied copies of the code Emperor Constantine had strong-armed into existence, giving sure footing to the fledgling faith he himself had cast off like a soiled sock. And according to that rumor, the emperor had shared his opinion of that sock. Which diverged radically from the Church's record.

But the plan to collect the pieces had already begun to unravel, a spy having infiltrated his network like a virus and managed to secure one of the fragments of the Emperor's confession.

Braun withdrew the nozzle slowly, exhaling a final mouthful of smoke. Then he slammed it against his palm with exacting self-flagellation, then harder and again with even more force—bursting the capillaries underneath his smooth skin.

He inhaled sharply, the sensation filling his head with a mixture of pain and pleasure. It was a modicum of recompense for his transgression, perhaps a hold-over impulse from his childhood faith that exacted vengeance for fleshly transgressions, eye for eye and tooth for tooth.

It was also a ritual of self-denial he had learned from an obscure sect of Gnostics in southern Iraq, having embedded himself with them for a season to fully learn their ways of plumbing the Universe's depths of knowledge and insight and revelation after he was contacted by—

A car door slammed shut just beyond his tent, startling him from his trip down memory lane.

He straightened on the stack of pillows, his heart leaping at the sound of a voice and then the slosh of boots through wet ground before another door clicked open and slammed shut a moment later.

He saw the sandals before he saw the man. *The* man, as the case was. Face marked by that intriguing tattoo he himself had etched on his back months before.

The cubist box man, echoing a distant memory of secret knowledge preserved through the centuries for such a time as this.

As much cash and cultural cache he had amassed the past few years, the truth of the matter is everybody's gonna have to serve somebody, as Bob Dylan so eloquently put it.

Fell in love with the singer-songwriter during university. Felt a kindred spirit with the man. Until he discovered his conversion to Christianity, that is. Which apparently the song originated from. What a zero, he was, giving up his power to some dead god long since butchered. Both literally and metaphorically, as Nietzsche put it best.

That soured their relationship real quick. Which turned him onto one of the man's musical interlocutors, as one-sided as it was, much more preferring John Lennon's "Serve Yourself" rejoinder anyway.

Serve yourself, indeed...

Head shaved with wide shoulders and hairless olive skin, tastefully dressed in a plain, well-tailored *thawb* soaked from the afternoon rainstorm, the man who entered had come to him at his headquarters in Palo Alto, California, a year ago without announcement and without a retinue of handlers. A good-looking fellow who called himself Sha. That was it.

Braun fancied the name, but thought it was a joke. Given the name matched an acronym that had brought him billions. Secure Hash Algorithm was a family of popular one-way hash algorithms used to create digital signatures that formed the backbone of WeNet security, allowing a billion people around the globe to interface securely with one another, without fear of government recriminations or phishing schemes from rich Nigerian princes seeking to park their treasures abroad.

A deeper dive behind the name after the man left brought up all sorts of interesting things.

In Japanese, *sha* means *'person.'* In Chinese, *'to kill.'* Which sort of fit the bill, given the man's offer. Then there was *'darling'* in French and *'to turn'* in Hebrew. But it was the Arabic that sounded closer to what the man intended. *'To will,'* which was a typical Muslim refrain combined with Allah: *'InshAllah'* or *'In sha Allah.'*

If God wills or *God willing.*

Given the man's origin, it sounded right on the money.

His money, actually, which the man was seeking in exchange for the keys to a kingdom that would give him far more power than a simple social media platform.

What the man named Sha was offering was nothing short of divinity itself. Which made sense, considering the spiritual sect he had been stewarding for decades.

Ecclesia Theotites.

The Church of the Deities, with mankind assuming what was rightfully theirs.

The right to be a god unto themselves. Deciding what was good and evil.

And yet there were barriers. One had almost bested him on his very own network. The other pretty much did. And it seemed both had just stolen his thunder. Again. Something he would have to change, and probably atone for.

"*As-salam alaykom*," Sha said, bringing his hands together and bowing slightly.

"*Wa Alykom As-salam*," Braun said, hoping he didn't mangle the Arabic reply.

The man chuckled. "I see you have been practicing your Arabic." Sha stretched out an arm and motioned with his hand for him to come down.

Braun took a breath, unsure what he would tell the man—how much he should tell him until he had a firmer grasp on the situation. After all, what good were his billions if he couldn't buy his way to victory.

He stood and climbed down, bracing himself for the tongue lashing.

Instead, the man opened his arms up with a smile.

Hesitant, he stepped forward then obliged, the two embracing in an unexpected greeting.

Sha let go and clasped his shoulders, eyes fixing him with probing orbs of darkness. "I am understanding that you have lost the first lead on the emperor code."

Braun swallowed, his billions in that moment about as good as toilet paper. "That is being correct."

"Lost first to the Order of Thaddeus and then to Nous."

He flashed surprised eyes at the man before blinking away the tell, wondering how he had known of the development so quickly.

Sha chuckled again. "I see surprise written across your face. Remember, Braun: I have ever-seeing eyes that are always perceiving, and ever-hearing ears that are always understanding."

That's a Persian mystic for you.

"But none of that matters. What does, is that we appear to have our next lead. And it is not far from here."

Relief flooded his face.

"Don't look so relieved, Braun." Those haunting, dark eyes returned. "For surely our enemy is close at the heel. And without the code, our arrangement will be for naught."

Dylan was right. Everybody's gotta serve somebody. But in serving Sha, he would be serving himself. For what he offered was the font of life.

Braun nodded. "Tell me what you are wanting me to do."

CHAPTER 11
ROME, ITALY. JUNE 16, LATE EVENING.

The Gulfstream hit the tarmac during the early night with a bounce before the engines grew to a wicked *whoosh*, bringing the jet to a halt—sending Silas reaching for his armrest.

"No worries, love," Celeste said, resting a reassuring hand on his tensing one. "Matthew's a clever one. I'm sure he has things under control up front."

He took a breath and relaxed it, throwing her an embarrassed smile. "Why do you think I'm tensing up so? If I remember correctly, last time Gapinski flew a chartered jet he nearly landed it in the Caribbean."

"Because some crazy psychopath from some super-secret Mormon special-ops crew sabotaged it!" Gapinski bellowed from the front.

"So you say…" he mumbled as the jet slowed and began easing toward a private hangar.

Celeste playfully smacked his arm. "Remember, never insult the pilot until we've come to a complete stop at the gate. No telling what he might—"

The plane suddenly jerked, the brakes being suddenly applied.

Silas gave a cry and gripped his armrest with white knuckles again before the plane started moving.

"Psych!" came Gapinski over the loudspeaker, the man's bald, round head peeking over the captain's chair with a Cheshire grin. "You forget who's still flying the plane, chief."

Silas huffed and relaxed, Celeste stifling a giggle at his side. He yelled, "And you forget who's still signing your paychecks, pal. A spigot that can be turned off at will."

The grin faded and Gapinski returned to the controls, mumbling an announcement about their arrival at the hangar in just a few minutes.

And not a moment too soon.

Once Victor Zarruq was carted away by Chuke and his goons, Silas and Celeste activated reserve SEPIO agents out of Rome to mobilize, flying to Libya to secure the archaeological dig site, clean up what remained of the encampment, and protect it if need be. Meanwhile, Torres and Gapinski contacted the local law enforcement they had worked with to establish the dig site to begin with, coordinating triage support for the researchers and their extraction. Hours later, the day quickly fading to night, the four SEPIO agents chartered a separate jet out of Benghazi to Rome in order to continue the hunt for anything that might help them bring clarity to the mess that began that morning using the best research tools in the ecclesiastical business.

Archivum Apostolicum Vaticanum.

Better known as the Vatican Archives.

Normally not accessible to the public but only to scholars once they are seventy-five years old, the Order of Thaddeus had a special arrangement with the vault of Church creeds and confessions and papal papers stretching back centuries. Given their entire encampment had been roasted by Chuke and his henchmen, it only made sense to leverage the Order's access to the troves of research. Especially given the specific nature of the threat—the Church's code encapsulated in the Nicene Creed and a supposed confession of Constantine that threw shade on the veracity of its compilation. Soon the SEPIO agents were piling into a Black G-Class Mercedes, Gapinski's car of choice it seemed, and heading toward the Vatican.

Housed in a fortress-like part of the Holy See, the secretive nature of the Vatican along with the hidden trove of ecclesiastical documents within have fanned the flames of speculative fiction and conspiracy theories for decades. The central repository in the Vatican City for all the acts put into effect by the Holy See also contained precious documents stemming from the Church broadly for centuries. Particularly germane to the Catholic branch, the state papers, correspondence, papal account books, are archived within, as well as many other documents which the Church has accumulated over the centuries.

Silas was hoping those "other documents" would point them in the direction that would shed light on this so-called emperor code and even the confession of Constantine that had drawn Braun and Rotberg and whoever else onto the hunt.

Because so far, things were not looking good. And it was up to SEPIO to stem whatever tide might be ready to engulf the Christian faith. With Silas ultimately in charge of it all.

After shoving off from the airport, they made a quick stop at the Order's Rome operation, understandably the largest of their outposts outside their DC headquarters. Last time they were there, a resurgent Knights Templar had tried to take out Islamic terrorists bent on leveling Saint Peter's Basilica. What a trip that was! Grabbing new mobile phones and weapons and a change of clothes, they headed out into the cramped, winding Italian streets to the crown jewel of the Eternal City. The Vatican. More specifically, the vault holding precious resources that would blow the conspiracy wide open. That was the hope, anyway.

Silas had visited the city a few times before, both sweet and sour. First on leave from the Rangers during the hell of war in the Middle East. Had to re-center his soul, and Saint Pete's Square seemed as good a place as any. Had done him a world of good to reconnect to the Catholic side of his faith he had left behind during college. And while he had gravitated toward a more Protestant Evangelical flavor of Christianity after his on-base recommitment to Christ, he had still reveled in the ritual and rhythm and rootedness the visit brought him. That was the sweet part.

Then there was the sour part, when he was dragged by his former war buddy Eli Denton on some crazy, hoaxy mission to authenticate the Gospel of Judas that nearly cost the Church its reputation. With his brother Sebastian squarely at the center, of course—the beginning of the end for him. Nearly cost Silas his own reputation, too, had he not put two and two together. The mission had been one of his first official ones working for the Order. Now look at him—Master of the Order of Thaddeus.

A full moon shone brightly in the sky, a sea of diamond sparkles strewn across the obsidian sky mostly obscured by the city lights. But the clearness was a welcomed relief after the rainy onslaught they had left in North Africa. Again, with his brother no doubt firmly at the center of it all. Probably squeezing Bishop Zarruq now for all the intel he held. Torturing him even.

He winced at the idea. At what his brother had become. Hadn't always been that way. Of the two, Sebastian had been the one destined for a life in the Church while Silas was far more interested in worldly pursuits. All before that damn priest ravaged his brother's soul, using and abusing him for his own selfish ends.

Gapinski drove out of the congested city and along the Tiber, the dome of Saint Peter's Basilica peeking just above a line of buildings. One end of Silas's mouth turned upward at the sight, a beacon of faith for millions of believers. He himself still appreciated the level of beauty and pageantry the Catholic Church brought to the faith, unlike his Protestant brothers and sisters who seemed more interested in fancy lights and fog machines.

Though he agreed that through the blood of Christ we have direct access to the throne of God, as the book of Hebrews teaches, the veil being torn and the gift of grace and mercy dispensed directly to believers by the Spirit—still there was something about the high-church churchiness of what he had experienced as a boy that did something for his faith that more low-church varieties couldn't. Perhaps that's why he enjoyed the Order of Thaddeus's headquarters located in the Episcopal Church building of the Washington National Cathedral, and the Anglican faith itself—Protestant doctrine and Catholic ceremony, the best of both worlds. Though he wasn't all that interested in parsing out folks who embraced Jesus as Lord and Savior. If it was good enough for the Apostle Paul, it was good enough for him—whether high-church or low-church.

Soon they were idling at a military police checkpoint at the *Via della Conciliazione* with Saint Peter's Square dead ahead, the dome gleaming a brilliant white underneath the glowing moon and a canister of lighting strategically aimed to draw the eye toward the holy place. Sitting in the passenger's seat, Celeste explained their appointment at the Apostolic Archives. After a radio check and confirmation, the MP let them through, but they were led by an escort of Vatican gendarmerie in a small white car.

The black cobblestone road, normally bustling with tourists, was completely barren, the variously shaded brown five-story buildings almost pressing in against them as they made their way down the long corridor of businesses and apartments guided by the orange glow of lamps mounted high on stone pillars. The escort sped toward the square before veering right and then left.

And just like that, they were within the boundary of Vatican City, slowing at another military checkpoint guarded by two more Vatican gendarmerie in fatigues at an idling humvee before turning into a small side street guarded by a wrought-iron gate. Reminded Silas of the sorts of posts he would man back in Iraq, sending a flash-back chill up his spine.

Gapinski snorted and pointed out the windshield at a pair of men dressed in colorful Renaissance-era uniforms striped in red and blue, orange and yellow, necks ringed by white collars and heads fitted with black berets.

The Pontifical Swiss Guard.

"Definitely not in Kansas anymore, Totos..." Gapinski said.

"Which means we should be mindful to be on our best behavior," Celeste advised.

He scoffed. "When am I not on my best behavior?"

She raised a brow and cocked her head, and the rest of the car fell silent with the same inquisition.

"Whatever. Won't catch me dead wearin' one of those getups."

"Thank the Lord for that..." Silas muttered as he leaned forward for a better view.

The drive in was even quieter than the main roads in Rome outside the Vatican, as if they had entered into a completely other dimension. Looked about like he expected an ecclesial compound to look, with manicured bushes and lawns, buildings styled in Roman and Baroque and Gothic architecture. They bypassed a small parking lot adjacent to a six-story building, dipping inside a small arched entryway that led inside to a vast courtyard that served as a parking lot for the Archives and other ecclesiastical departments for the Holy See.

Gapinski parked, and so did the escort. The Vatican officer, dressed in a crisp, black uniform with slick, styled hair, stood at attention as the four piled out of the SUV. Then he motioned toward a set of glass doors leading into the stately building.

Silas nodded and followed the man who led the way, breath feeling shallow at the excitement of entering into one of the most hallowed spaces in Christendom, if not fraught with secrecy and conspiracy. Walking a short set of stone stairs and entering inside, his senses were instantly flooded with the smell of aged paper and old furniture and vintage artwork—everything you'd expect in a museum or an archive of the Church's affairs.

"Blimey..." Celeste said, craning her neck around in wonder.

"I hear ya, sister," Gapinski said.

"Me, too," Torres agreed.

So did Silas, his breath now fully taken away by the vast, sparsely lit space, a faint white glow filtering down through large windows above anchored in the finely gilded ceiling. He'd been in some pretty impressive ecclesial buildings before, and this ranked high on the list for capital-I impressive.

Stone angels peered down from above anchored to several archways supported by thirty-foot chocolate marble columns with similar marble tiling the floor in a cream and brown pattern with more of the chocolate marble decorating the walls stretching in all four directions. The gilding continued in abundance around the inner arches and ringed the perimeter of the ceiling, Latin phrases too dark to read etched inside. Stone angels peered down from on high. Biblical figures and other Christians saints made of similar stone rested in alcoves stretching the length of the space in between a series of arches that seemed to stretch on forever.

The group stepped farther inside, their footfalls echoing in the silence of their awe. They reached a small section and stared agape toward the ceiling, an alighted dome painted sky blue with floating angelic beings amidst a cloudy swirl of pinks and yellows and whites mesmerizing them.

Another set of rushing steps soon jolted them from their

trance. Coming toward them from the other side of the building was a tall, trim man in a black cassock, a bright purple sash wrapping his waist and the same color edging the sleeves and neck and buttons in bright piping, the uniform marked him as an upper-level ecclesiastical official of some sort. He looked younger than Silas expected, with a clean face, bright blue eyes, and a chock of dirty-blond hair.

Reaching them, he smiled and bowed. "Greetings, in the name of the Father, Son, and Holy Ghost."

The SEPIO agents returned the same greeting.

"I'll leave you to it, then," said the Vatican security official who had escorted them, leaving the way they had come.

Silas extended his hand to the man. "Silas Grey. Thanks for the help."

"My name's Bartholomew Braley," the man said, looking American and sounding Southern. "I gather you're with the Order of Thaddeus, am I right?"

"That's right. We're hoping to crash your library for the night. In a bit of a bind and praying we find something here, a book or letter or tract from the Church's past, that will give us some clarity."

"Ahh, something of import and intrigue, I gather?"

"Something like that."

"Well, you've come to the right place if you're looking for something from the Church's past. May I ask what this is about?"

He hesitated, glancing at Celeste for guidance. Surprised the man was in the dark, but he guessed the rest of the world was as well, along with the Church, given Braun's dark-web invitation.

"Celeste Bourne," she said, extending her hand. Bartholomew shook it. "Forgive us, and forgive the late hour, but we're not at liberty to divulge our specific interests. I assure you, any help you can offer us tonight will be of vital interest to preserving and protecting the interests of the faith."

She penetrated him with unyielding eyes, and the man seemed to blush under their weight. Silas stifled a grin, knowing how persuasive those eyes could be. Even for men sworn to celibacy.

Bartholomew smiled and bowed again. "I understand. I also understand that if the Order is calling upon the Holy See for help, I can trust its urgency. No reason to tarry, how about we get to it?"

Silas said, "Appreciate the help. Lead the way."

And lead he did, walking to an ornately decorated bronze door and removing a large ring of bronze keys. Finding one in the mess, he stuck it in the lock and turned. It unlocked with a *click*, and he swung the door open on well-oiled hinges, giving not a squeak or sigh.

Bartholomew motioned for the agents to enter. "In we go…"

"Just like that?" Gapinski said, stepping toward the opening. "The door to the Church's secret archives is chillin' right off the main entrance?"

He shrugged. "What did you expect? A series of keypads followed by complicated puzzles and booby-trapped corridors?"

"Uh, yeah…"

Bartholomew slapped him on the back with a chuckle. "Sounds like you've been reading a few too many conspiracy thrillers for your line of work's good."

"Actually, it's the best preparation for my line of work."

"How about we get to it, fellas," Silas said. "Braun and my brother ain't going to wait another second to bring down the Church, and neither should we trying to save it."

The man nodded and continued onward, leading them down a corridor with walls decorated by the same chocolate marble and the same cream-and-brown tiles stretching its length, joined by saintly statues in memoriam. Same for the ceiling, paved in gilt, with carved angels watching their movements from above.

"Say, you wouldn't happen to be *the* Silas Grey, would you?" Bartholomew asked. "Princeton professor and relicologist?"

"*The* Princeton professor?" Celeste whispered to Silas with a giggle.

"What are we, chopped liver?" Gapinski muttered.

Reddening, Silas cleared his throat. "*Former* professor, but yes, that's right."

"Thought so," Bartholomew said proudly. "Your work is the reason I donned the white collar."

Silas was shocked. He didn't think anyone had paid attention to his obscure academic work. "Really, which part?"

"The Shroud of Turin, what else? Had zippo interest in religion, much less Christianity. But I caught some special of yours airing on some news network around Easter jabbering on about Jesus' resurrection. About how central it is to the Christian faith, the *why* to our faith, the reason we believe. About how we can trust that the Father brought the Son back to life again, not only because of the testimony of the Holy Scriptures, as historical and factual as they are, but also because of the testimony of science with the burial cloth."

He chuckled to himself at the revelation, remembering the interview clearly. It had been early in his tenure at the university and several years into his pet project proving the Shroud an authentic relic proving Christ had indeed been raised from the dead. He remembered how proud he felt being on national television. And prideful, his head blowing up like a balloon at being tapped for the limelight. What the Book of Proverbs says is right: '*Pride goes before destruction, and a haughty spirit before a fall.*' For a few years later, he was sacked.

They came to another set of bronze doors at the end of the long hallway, this time with a keypad entry. Bartholomew withdrew a key fob separate from the ring he had used earlier, waving it at the security device.

With a *click*, the doors unlocked, withdrawing to reveal an elevator.

"Yes, siree," the man went on, leading the group inside. "Fascinating stuff, that was. Eventually brought me to the faith, and all of this," he said with a flourish.

"Really?" Silas said with surprise, that pride returning.

"Sure thing." He swiped the fob at another keypad, bringing the carriage to life, the doors closing and elevator descending with a shudder. "Made me pick up and read the story of Jesus for myself, it did. Long story short, I eventually confessed Christ as Lord and Savior, was confirmed in the Church, then studied to be a priest and eventually ended up at the Vatican."

"Quite the journey," Silas said, amazed at how the Lord had used him, if unwittingly. Apparently he did at least one thing right while at Princeton.

His ears popped the farther they descended. Had to be four or five stories by now. Then the carriage slowed and eased up with a lurch, and the doors opened to reveal a well-lit hallway of white-washed stone walls, a red runner with golden tassels across a polished walnut floor leading the way through. Modest, unassuming, and entirely discrete. Could have been any number of offices or university corridors strewn across the globe.

The air was sweet and sanitized, temperate and climate-controlled. Which made sense, given the kinds of documents and relics preserved beneath the Vatican Archives.

He just hoped there was something in them that would blow open the conspiracy. Because they were running out of time. And with Zarruq's life on the line on top of the faith's credibility threatened—it all was turning out to be a disaster for the Order.

"Just down the hall is a room you can use," Bartholomew

said. "And this floor contains all the relevant documents you may need."

"Relevant?" Celeste said, giving Silas a sideways glance.

Silas gently grabbed the man's arm. "Why do you say relevant, Bartholomew? You asked earlier why we were at the Vatican...playing as if you didn't know."

The man stopped and offered a knowing grin. He said lowly, "Come now, Master Grey. We're the Vatican, and the fate of the faith is hanging in the balance. I assure you, we know. Now come along, just a few more doors. I've pulled a few things that may be of use."

Silas didn't know whether to pull back or lean into the man's offer for help. He looked at Celeste, then at Gapinski and Torres, all shrugging as the priest reached a nondescript door.

"Can we trust him?" Celeste said.

"Can we trust the Vatican, our patrons?" Gapinski asked. "Is the Pope Catholic?"

"Seems eager to help," Silas said. "Normally, I like to keep things close to the chest. But I suppose we need all the help we can get."

"I'm sure. Certainly was a bit star-struck back there," Celeste added with a wink.

Blushing, Silas followed after the man, who entered through the door, then stopped short when he felt a buzz at his leg.

He retrieved his phone. A text from Zoe. He read it, his face falling at the message.

Not good.

CHAPTER 12

Silas followed Bartholomew inside, his head swimming with the possibilities of what was happening. He went to show Celeste the message when he gasped at what he saw inside. The other three SEPIO agents followed close behind, their gasps and hushed amazement echoing his own.

The workroom looked more like a CIA black-site warehouse, stretching the length of a modest basketball court and nearly another story in height. And all the chocolate marble walls and creamy brown tiles from the main level were replaced by the utilitarian white walls and charcoal carpet he'd grown to loathe from his Ranger days. A black cage stood in one corner, wires coming out the top with tiny blinking red and blue and white lights behind a mesh fence. Looked like a sophisticated server, powering several workstations silently arranged in a neat row on one wall. The far end was anchored by a set of four flat-panel displays arranged as a massive display, like the situation room in the belly of the White House.

The whole environment also reminded Silas of SEPIO headquarters back in DC and their outposts strewn across the globe. Which was impressive, considering the sclerotic nature of the Church that was often a century behind the times. Pretty advanced for the Vatican as well, that's for sure. And here he thought the Order was ahead of the technological curve when it came to bringing the Church into the twenty-first century.

But that wasn't all of it. And not at all what delighted and surprised him.

Along the opposite wall and running down the middle were tables piled with ancient manuscripts. Very ancient, by the look of it. And smelling all metalicy and pulpy and musty from age.

"*Dios mío...*" Torres marveled. "I could get used to these accommodations for my work."

"Why can't we spring for a joint like this to conduct our research, chief?" Gapinski said. "Looks more like Jack Bauer's pad than anything the Vatican could cook up. No offense, or anything."

Bartholomew chuckled. "None taken. And the entire room is something the Order of Thaddeus cooked up, actually."

"Really?"

"Sure is."

"How is that?" Silas asked.

"A one Rowen Radcliffe helped modernize much of the technology you see here, from the server to the workstations. Even the catalogue of Vatican records that furnished what I was able to pull from the actual archives of the Archives was brought into the twenty-first century thanks to him."

His face fell at the mention of the former Order Master's name. He glanced at Celeste, whose head was bowed with the same quiet memorializing of their fallen friend.

"Sent over a crew of very professional and proficient techies," the man went on, "led by one Zoe Corbino a few years ago. A godsend, to say the least. How is Rowen doing these days?"

The four fell silent, the man's memory falling hard in the center of the room.

Silas cleared his throat and said, "He passed, late last year."

"Oh, sorry to hear." Bartholomew added softly, "Come, let me show you what I've pulled so far."

The man brought them to the tables stacked with the Church's cache of documents stretching back centuries. Reinforced steel cases of thick glass that meant protective business housed fragile-looking parchments browned with age and scrawled with neat Greek and Latin characters, their pages well preserved. Not surprising, considering the Church had perfected the art of climate control. A few codices bound by stiff leather and smelling of the heavenly hides sat together on one table. One was open, and beautiful hand-drawn marginals ran up and down the page next to the text, bright and colorful flowers and vines and cherubs blowing golden trumpets.

Silas was salivating at the sight, both ends of his mouth curling with wonder at what the texts held. He reached for one when his hand vibrated. He looked at the mobile device still clenched in his fist.

'Well?'

His face fell. That's right! Zoe's news had slipped his mind with the sight of all the parchments and codices.

"What is it?" Celeste asked, leaning in next to him.

"Zoe. Something's happened. Or happening, as she texted. In her words, *'Braun's released Pandora's box.'*"

"What does that mean?" Gapinski asked, reading the text over his shoulder.

"Maybe we should find out," Torres said.

"Bartholomew," Silas said, "What're the chances we can connect those displays at the end of the room to SEPIO headquarters back in DC? Something's come up and I need to check in with my people."

"Absolutely. Just give me a minute." The man hustled to a desk anchored in front of the massive display wall and started typing. Within a minute, Zoe's face was the size of a small swimming pool. She pushed her baby blue glasses up the bridge of her nose as she clacked away at her keyboard.

"About time!" she said. "I'm guessing you got my message?"

"Something about Pandora's box?" Gapinski said.

"Which means what exactly?" Silas asked.

She scoffed and rolled her eyes. "Hello, Greek mythology. Like when Prometheus stole fire from heaven and Zeus got his revenge by presenting Pandora to Prometheus' brother Epimetheus. Who then opened a box of sickness and death and—"

"Jar," Gapinski interrupted. "Not a box, a jar."

She leaned back with a wry grin. "Touché. Impressed a fella from Georgia is so well read in the Greek classics."

"Hey, some of us buck-toothed yokels got game."

"Zoe, can we get on with it, please?" Celeste said. "What's the point?"

She huffed. "The *point* is that's exactly what Markus Braun and his lackey have done with their treasure hunt!"

"What are you playing at? What's happened?"

"See for yourself." The display faded to black. A beat later, a grainy video clearly shot with a phone inside a dimly lit chapel somewhere started playing.

Silas folded his arms as shouting was heard from speakers in the ceiling before a group of men were seen storming around inside. Each of them were brandishing something long that was obscured by the pixilation of the video, but it was clear they were weapons of some sort. As the men overturned a Eucharist table, they started yelling something in a foreign tongue.

Zoe explained, "Abraham analyzed the demands and concluded they were looking for a golden cylinder hidden in the chapel."

He reached a hand for the bridge of his nose, closed his eyes, and sighed. Every Tom, Dick, and Harry logged onto WeSolve were probably searching for Braun's billion-dollar golden eggs strewn across the Mediterranean. And doing whatever it took to lay their hands on them and the billion-euro prize.

Pandora's Box is right.

"SEPIO has received reports from the field of other churches like this one as well as other Christian landmarks having been raided by parties searching for the same object Braun described."

"Always something," Gapinski huffed.

Silas ran a hand through his hair. Not good. "Where was this shot?"

"At a Coptic church in Egy—" she was cut off by the sound of gunfire.

Silas and Celeste both spun around toward the door and withdrew their weapons—before realizing it was coming from the video. Bartholomew startled and crouched at the sight.

Several people flopped dead from the on-screen blasts before the camera fell with a jerky dip behind a bench and the video cut to black.

"Sorry about that," Silas said, stuffing his Beretta at his back. "You've got some nice surround sound in here. Thought we were being invaded. Zoe, how many more like this?"

She came back on the screen and replied, "At least eight that we can confirm. Everything from small chapels like this one in Syria and Turkey to sites of veneration in Israel."

Which meant they needed to kick it into high gear. On the double.

Celeste said, "Any reports on WeSolve describing anyone actually discovering any more golden cylinders?"

"Not yet. Just these chickens running around with their heads cut off, drunk on Braun's golden-goose carrot sticks."

"Mixing metaphors there, Zoe," Gapinski said.

"Like three," Torres added.

"Thanks for the 411," Silas said. "Monitor WeSolve and the

broader WeNet platform for anything from Braun. And make sure SEPIO agents are giving you updates every hour on what's going on around the Mediterranean with these churches and Christian sites. Let me know the minute anything more changes. We're going to be up to our eyeballs in research here at the Vatican, but I'll keep an eye on my phone."

Zoe said she understood and signed off.

Silas turned to Bartholomew. "How about we get to it."

The man nodded. "Certainly. Anything to help."

"What you got for us?"

The man grinned. "This way." He led them to a series of large glass cases. Inside were manuscripts that looked like coffee-stained paper towel, all wrinkled and brown. He slipped on a pair of white cotton gloves and opened a case, gently pulling one out. Surprisingly, it held up well as he handled it.

He instructed Silas to don a pair of the same gloves and then handed him the manuscript about the size of a half-sheet of paper.

"Are you sure?" Silas said, a flutter running through his belly at the prospect of handling the ancient Church document.

"Absolutely. I think you will find it quite enlightening."

He took a breath and nodded, then received the parchment that looked like a letter. He gasped at what he saw.

"What is it, love?" Celeste asked, hovering over his shoulder now. Then she gasped, as did Torres when she leaned in for a look.

Gapinski said, "Guessing if I lean in for a closer look-see I'll gasp like the rest of—" And he did. "Hey, is that what I think it is?"

There it was. An *X* imposed over a *P*. The Chi-Rho.

The sign of Constantine.

"Go on, read it." Bartholomew added with a wink, "Unless your Latin isn't up to standard after retiring from Princeton."

Silas smirked. "I think I'll manage." Then he started translating in his head while reading it aloud:

Constantine the Great Augustus, to Arius.

It was made known to you in your stubbornness some time ago, that you might want to come to our headquarters, so that perhaps you could enjoy the privilege of seeing us. We are quite amazed that you did not do so immediately. Therefore, hasten to come to our court. This way, once you have been in our company and obtained favor from us, you may be able to return to your own country. May God protect you, beloved.

Gapinski exclaimed, "Arius? Ain't that the guy mentioned in the first fragment we found?"

"That's right," Silas said, considering the letter.

"It sounds like the Emperor ain't too happy with the man."

"You're right," Bartholomew explained. "He wasn't. But if you think that was bad, check out this other letter sent by the Emperor to the heretic. Gives a whole new level to the phrase 'tried by fire.'"

He retrieved another aged parchment from the case and handed it to Silas, returning the first one back to its resting place, safe and sound.

Again, Silas translated the words in his head and offered a translation for the others:

The great and victorious Constantine Augustus to the bishops and laity: Since Arius is an imitator of the wicked and the ungodly, it is only right that he should suffer the same dishonor as they.

> If any writing composed by Arius should be found, it should be handed over to the flames, so that not only will the wickedness of his teaching be obliterated, but nothing will be left even to remind anyone of him. And I hereby make a public order, that if someone should be discovered to have hidden a writing composed by Arius, and not to have immediately brought it forward and destroyed it by fire, his penalty shall be death. God will watch over you, beloved.

"I don't get it," Torres said after he finished. "Clearly Constantine was ticked at the dude."

Gapinski snorted an agreement. "Yeah, can't get clearer than suggesting the man's writings be used as kindling."

"Even going so far as suggesting that harboring them was a pretext for a death sentence," Celeste added.

"So what gives?" Torres said.

"This is what gives..." Bartholomew handed Silas yet another parchment. Same color, same black script, bearing the same sign of Constantine. He returned the other back to its rightful spot.

"You'll note this one carries a remarkably different tone than the previous two."

The parchment was longer, the letter itself double-sided. And the script was smaller, allowing for more content to fill the crinkled, pale paper. Silas's head was hurting from the mental workout, but he carried on, consuming the Latin script and translating it for the rest:

> The victorious great Constantine Augustus to father Alexander, the bishop:
> I understand that you are engaged in an epoch

struggle for the holy Church, the man from Libya having stirred the pot of belief. But you should know that Arius came to me at the encouragement of most everyone. He promised that he now holds to our catholic faith as laid down and confirmed through us at the Council of Nicaea.

So you see, I have written this letter, not simply to inform you, but I expect you to receive these men, Arius and his fellow workmen, who are approaching you for forgiveness. And so if you find that they are now laying claim to the apostolic, orthodox faith, which was set forth at Nicaea and gives eternal life—and in fact we have confirmed that they do — then I encourage you to provide what they seek. For if you should show care for these things, then the grudges will be conquered by unity. So come to the aid of unity. Share the goodness of friendship with those who are not separated from the faith. Make sure that I hear a report of peace and unity between all of you, for which I hope and even long.

God will watch over you, our most honored Father.

"Well that was unexpected," Celeste said. "One minute the Emperor is condemning Arius' writings to the flames and those that shelter them to death. The next he's suggesting Arius was an orthodox believer and should be embraced as a brother in Christ!"

"Always something," Gapinski complained.

Silas agreed. He hadn't paid much attention to Arius during his graduate work, nor the controversies surrounding his teachings on Jesus' person and the nature of his divinity for that matter. Now he wished he had, and he felt foolish for his ignorance for a part of Church history that now seemed far more significant than ever.

He handed the letter back to Bartholomew. "Does add a level of confusion into the mix, that's for sure."

"That's putting it mildly," Celeste replied. "From the sound of it, Constantine seemed to have warmed up to the fellow."

Bartholomew nodded. "It is true that there was a hot-cold dynamic to their relationship. And that's probably because of this final letter."

The man handed Silas one more from the case. "I won't say anything about this one. Just...well, you'll see."

A slight tremor took hold of Silas as he retrieved the final parchment, his gut telling him this might open up the conspiracy in a direction he would rather let stay hidden away in the Vatican Secret Archives.

He was right.

Again, reading the Latin and translating it for the SEPIO agents, he said aloud:

Arius and Euzoius, presbyters, to Constantine, our most pious emperor and most beloved of God.

O sovereign emperor, we offer a written statement of our own faith, and we protest before God that we, and all who are with us, believe what is here set forth.

We believe in one God, the Father Almighty, and in His Son the Lord Jesus Christ, who was begotten from Him before all ages, God the Word, by whom all things were made, whether things in heaven or on earth; He came and took upon Him flesh, suffered and rose again, and ascended into heaven, whence He will again come to judge the quick and the dead. We believe in the Holy Ghost, in the resurrection of the body, in the life to come, in the kingdom of heaven, and in one Catholic Church of God, established throughout the earth. We have received this faith from the Holy Gospels.

> If we do not so believe this, and if we do not truly receive the doctrines concerning the Father, the Son, and the Holy Ghost, as they are taught by the whole Catholic Church and by the sacred Scriptures, as we believe in every point, let God be our judge, both now and in the day which is to come.

It went on, but Silas trailed off, confused by the confession—and dreading its implication.

"Wait a hot minute," Gapinski said. "Did the so-called heretic just confess to believing what we found buried in the Libyan sands that was hijacked by Muammar Gaddafi—to believing in the Nicene Creed?"

His gut went watery with recognition, seeing how the man at the center of one of the Church's greatest earliest controversies and conspiracies seemed to be voicing approval of historic Christian orthodoxy. That he believed in one God and in Jesus, who was begotten from him, eternally existing.

Or was he truly confessing this? Plenty of wiggle room in there and shades of meaning that were far more gray than black-and-white belief.

He handed it back to Bartholomew and ran a hand across his head. "I don't buy it."

"I don't know, Silas," Torres said. "Seems pretty clear to me. Or at least his heresy is less obvious."

"Which is the problem. For Arius, Jesus was the *moral* Son of God, not the *metaphysical* Son of God. Rather than God himself becoming a human being, Jesus was viewed as a man who merely embodied the deepest meaning of life, as even some contemporary teachers would say."

"Cue Oprah's Super Soul Sunday theme music," Gapinski said.

"She's not the only one, pal. Remember Trevor Bohls?"

"The megapastor-turned-WeTuber from last mission?"

"That's right. He'd join Arius in the same sentiment, that as the moral Son of God Jesus' life embodied the universal human ideal of love. That's what makes him divine, not that he is actually God. Which is diametrically opposed to the vintage Christian faith. For them, our human problem hinges on the view that bad habits are formed by bad examples and ignorance influences us to sin. That's what makes us sinners. Thus, we need a better example to form better habits in order to form better patterns and systems of living."

"A classic heretical view of human nature," Bartholomew added.

"That's right. And that's why they think Jesus is important. To *show* us our best version of ourselves."

"Gandhi on steroids," Torres said.

"Exactly."

Gapinski moaned, "My head is hurting, chief..."

Silas chuckled. "Sorry, but stay with me a minute. Because all of this matters to whatever the heck is going on here with the Nicene Creed and Constantine. When some people talk about Jesus and his importance in the world, what they mean is that he gives us a better, truer example for living. Jesus was the vehicle of the Divine because of the way he lived and taught."

"Uh, isn't that what he did?" Torres asked. "Give us a good model to live by. The whole love your neighbor as yourself thing, love your enemies and the rest?"

"That's true, yes. To an extent. But what happens when we take an Arian view or something close to it is that Jesus' divinity is downplayed. In fact, as a human, Jesus isn't even all that unique. He is merely one spiritual teacher among many—although perhaps a tad more special than the rest."

"This picture of Jesus," Bartholomew said, "couldn't be further from the image painted by the Holy Scriptures and the historic faith. The Church has always believed God is Jesus

Christ and Jesus Christ is God. Jesus is not simply the most mature view of the character of God or the divine in skin and bones. Jesus is God himself. Listen to how Cyril of Jerusalem preached Jesus' deity."

The man reached into his cassock and retrieved a phone, then typed before clearing his throat and quoting: "'One who has seen the Son has seen the Father, for the Son is in all things like him who begot him. He is begotten Life of Life, and Light of Light, Power of Power, God of God; and the characteristics of the Godhead are unchangeable in the Son.'"

"Hey," Gapinski said, "that's like what you read from the super-ancient Nicene Creed stuffed in that cylinder we found!"

Silas nodded, bringing out his own phone. "You're right. Cyril's teachings on Jesus' person reflected the consensus in the early Church that was codified in the Creed. The great Reformer John Calvin continued the early Church consensus. Listen to this: 'All the offices which properly pertain to divinity, Scripture ascribes to the Spirit as to the Son. It ascribes to Him the faculties of wisdom and eloquence, which our Lord told Moses are proper to His majesty alone. Likewise, by means of Him we come to participation in God, and thus we feel that His power gives us life.'"

Bartholomew cleared his throat and folded his arms. "Excuse me, but did you just quote one of the leaders of the Protestant Reformation in the Vatican Archives?" A scowl slowly faded to a wry grin. "I thought you were batting for the same Catholic team."

Silas chuckled. "We're batting for the *Church's* team, including the Catholic end of the bench. But my favorite is Karl Barth's summary of the historic Christian view of Jesus, saying God is wholly and utterly in his revelation in Jesus Christ."

"So Jesus is God," Torres said. "Got it. But what does it matter? I mean, I get it's important, but why?"

"It's important because if Jesus isn't God, but rather simply a divine-acting human, no way do we have forgiveness and salvation, or rescue from evil, sin, and death! This is why the early Church fathers went to the mat for decades in their battle with Arius and his followers. No mere mortal could defeat evil, sin, and death, because all humans are born sinful and incapable of saving themselves. A sinless sacrifice was needed. Humanity needed someone who had the power to defeat sin and conquer death. Only God could do that. Only he could provide the needed, perfect, sinless sacrifice to pay our price in our place. All of which people like Markus Braun and Noland Rotberg deny in their reimagining of Jesus as merely a divine example and model of love."

He fell silent then chuckled and shook his head. "Sorry for the impromptu sermon. Not meaning to get preachy but this is why what's been going down is so important. This is what's at stake here. Jesus made himself nothing by taking on the nature of our humanity in order to live the life we could not live and die on the cross, being resurrected three days later by the Father—bringing forgiveness and salvation and rescue to all the world. Jesus isn't just this really nice guy who did and said really nice things. He is the Son of God, the firstborn over all creation, in whom and for whom all things were created!"

Then he clenched his jaw and made a fist, anger rising at what Braun and Rotberg were doing with their conspiracy to bring down the Church. Again. This time bringing down the Church's central Creed concerning Jesus Christ himself.

"Mess with how we were created, mess with human nature," he went on. "But don't mess with Jesus! God's crazy love through his life, death, and resurrection are at stake—which impacts the real lives of real people and their eternity."

A chime interrupted him, coming from the ceiling speakers.

He caught his breath from the impromptu homily and realized it was an incoming call, Zoe reappearing on the screen.

Face fallen.

What now...

CHAPTER 13

Silas ran a hand through his hair growing shaggier than the close-cropped Army-issued cut he was used to maintaining. His tongue tingled for a shot of nicotine, his fingers itched to hold a cigarette between his lips to take the edge off a situation that was becoming increasingly fraught as the hours ticked by.

A tumbler of scotch would do, too. Its smoky, spicy amber liquid numbing his head that was beginning to run wild after a jolt of anxiety pinged his brain, chased by a worry he would be overcome with shortness of breath and a rapid heart rate, the vestiges of a plague left over from a case of PTSD he'd suffered after his tours in the Middle East a decade ago.

Get it together, Grey...

He said to Zoe on the display, "Please don't tell me another church or Christian site was attacked by treasure hunters."

Zoe shook her head. "Worse. Or better, depending on your perspective I guess."

"What are you playing at, mate?" Celeste asked. "What's gone on?"

"They've found another one."

Silas sucked in a breath. "Another golden cylinder?"

"Righto."

"Who?"

"By the look of it, some African dude and…" She trailed off, glancing down at her keyboard.

Silas didn't even have to guess. Her face said it all.

"Sebastian," he said flatly.

"A live-stream video was posted to the WeSolve newsfeed dedicated to Braun's gimmick."

"Live? Are they still at it?"

"Just launched five minutes ago. Called the minute I knew things were up."

"Let's get on with it then," Celeste said. "I assume you have the video at the ready?"

Zoe nodded, then the screen faded to black before another image appeared.

The African man they had met earlier, Aurelius Chuke, was standing dutifully next to a table inside what looked like a large tent, the canvas sides glowing from yellow lanterns hung off camera. Next to him was another man mirroring Silas's own features, high cheekbones and broad shoulders, but with blue eyes and blond hair.

Holding a golden cylinder in one hand and a fragment in the other.

Silas swallowed hard, his mouth longing for both that cigarette and tumbler of scotch. Both would have to wait.

He said, "Bartholomew, could you turn it up?"

The man did as Sebastian continued his introduction.

"…group of intrepid humanitarians seeking to enlighten the world with the best knowledge and insight the Universe offers."

"Intrepid explorers my ass…" Silas grumbled, folding his arms. Now he really did want the shot of nicotine and scotch. Pronto.

"We believe in a coming Republic of Heaven, in which the world benefits from the best spiritual teachings history has to offer. Admittedly, from the man from Nazareth known as...Jesus," Sebastian said, twisting his face slightly and puckering his lips as if the name was sour on his tongue. "But what we must realize is that Jesus didn't come to start a new religion but to announce a new way of life. He was the founder of a new countermovement to all other human regimes. You see, the human problem is dysfunctional systems and destructive stories. Thus, we need a new system and a new story to repair and heal us. The upstart Jewish prophet provided humanity the solution through his teachings on the Republic of Heaven and example of higher living that transcends this chaotic one."

"What a load of bull," Silas muttered. Celeste shushed him, nodding toward the television as the man continued.

"This is precisely where the Church has gotten it wrong all these ages. Jesus invited the world into a new way of living, into something that was emerging into our day and age as the Republic of Heaven, which is an invitation into the Übermensch—humanity emerging beyond itself as envisioned by the German prophet Friedrich Nietzsche. The entire human experience has been one of constantly emerging from what we were and are into what we can *become*. Jesus understood this better than anyone during his day, and anyone since—except, perhaps, Master Nietzsche himself. Recall the words of the man who laid bare the reality of our religious world."

Sebastian cleared his throat and stiffened, almost reverently, then began reciting a parable Silas had heard before.

"Have you not heard of that madman," he said, voice almost wistful as he stared into the camera, "who lit a lantern in the bright morning hours, ran to the marketplace, and cried incessantly: *'I seek God! I seek God!*—As many of those who did not believe in God were standing around just then, he provoked much laughter. Has he got lost? asked one. Did he lose his way like a child? asked another. Or is he hiding? Is he afraid of us? Has he gone on a voyage? Thus they yelled and laughed."

Then one end of Sebastian's mouth curled upward, and he took a step closer to the camera, fixing it with a mad obsession. "The madman jumped into their midst and pierced them with his eyes. 'Whither is God?' he cried; *'I will tell you. We have killed him—you and I. All of us are his murderers.'*"

Silas rolled his eyes and huffed. He'd heard the tale told by the German idiot and plenty of freshman ones back at Princeton trying to impress him with their rote memory and indifference toward religion. But he knew the truth of the matter. It wasn't that God was dead; the matter was that belief in him was dead. There was a mile-wide difference.

"*'We have killed him—you and I. All of us are his murderers.'*" Sebastian went on. "Oh, that Spaghetti Monster in the sky still pops his head up from time to time on those crazy religious cable television shows. But through science and brute force, humanity has finally begun to transcend its baser religious selves, rising to become like the gods—not merely knowing good and evil, but deciding what is good and what is evil. God is dead. God remains dead. And we have killed him."

He paused, raising the golden cylinder still clenched in his hand. "And we have discovered the truth of the matter. That not only have we killed God, we invented him in the first place! Particularly the one that has reigned supreme the past two millennia, ruining the world with its Crusades and Inquisition and witch trials, with its horrid apocalyptic literature and contemporary music."

"Hey, don't dog on my DC Talk," Gapinski complained.

Still clutching the cylinder, Sebastian set down the fragment and picked up a larger parchment from the table, rolled like a scroll. He unfurled it and flashed a wicked grin from the other side of the camera. He leaned in and whispered, "Now we know the whole Christian edifice was a construct. In fact, a political one, cobbled together by the Roman Emperor Constantine in order to maintain order throughout the Roman

Empire, vaulting the Church to a position of power along the way. This is a copy of the venerated Nicene Creed, signed, sealed and delivered to Emperor Constantine with a rather juicy bit of correspondence. Alas, it is just a fragment. However, we have also found another. And I must say they are rather enlightening. Just listen for yourself."

Silas flashed Celeste a worried look. She nodded the same.

He set down the purported Nicene Creed original and retrieved the fragment he set down earlier, then Chuke handed him another.

"You don't suppose," Gapinski said, "that jackass has the fragment that we found, do you?"

"That's exactly what it is," Torres replied. "And by we, you mean *I* found, right?"

He bowed. "But of course, Madam."

She giggled and tapped his shoulder.

Silas interrupted their banter: "Hold up. Listen..."

Sebastian began reading the first fragment. Which confirmed what they all knew. It was the one they had discovered across the pond in Libya.

The back of Silas's neck was inflamed now, and anger churned in his belly. Because not only did that mean they had part of the mystery surrounding the emperor code. It meant they also had Victor Zarruq.

"Always something..." Silas mumbled, echoing Gapinski. The man glanced his way with a raised brow.

He was interrupted by Sebastian switching fragments. "Now take a listen to this second parchment piece, which picks up the plot perfectly from the previous one." He read aloud:

But there have been obstacles to this movement, primarily from a certain controversy surrounding a certain bishop from Africana. A scourge to some and brother to others, Bishop Arius has been a blessed comfort to me, instructing me in the ways of Christ at various times and confirming the essential tenets of the Christian faith, confessing what I myself came to confess, believing what I myself came to believe. Mainly, in one God, the Father Almighty, and in His Son the Lord Jesus Christ, who was begotten from Him before all ages, God the Word, by whom all things were made, whether things in heaven or on earth; that He came and took upon Him flesh, suffered and rose again, and ascended into heaven, whence He will again come to judge the quick and the dead; and also in the Holy Ghost, in the resurrection of the body, in the life to come, in the kingdom of heaven, and in one Catholic Church of God, established throughout the earth. This is my confession, and it is that which Arius had thus plainly spoken to me, and which I took at face value.

However, I understood that the origin of the controversy that emerged from the north of Africana, and what Alexander demanded of the priests, that they each testify to the opinion they maintained respecting a certain passage in Scripture concerning the divinity of the man Jesus, known as the Christ. Arius, for whom I shall have greater words below, inconsiderately insisted on what ought never to have been speculated about at all, or if pondered, should have been buried in profound silence. Hence, a dissension arose between two factions —Alexander and Arius—and fellowship was withdrawn. Consequently, the holy people of the Church itself were rent into diverse factions, no longer preserving the unity of the one body, of which I have felt a certain responsibility, having taken God's people under the shadow of my wings, like a nursing mother. Which is

> why I have intervened in the Church, seeking to build up the body of faith as if it were my own, responsible for its making.

Sebastian set the fragment down on the table. "Now as you can see, this is also a fragment, picking up where the other left off, but missing its ending. The previous one was missing its beginning—which we believe was read by Markus Braun on this platform when he launched his challenge to recover the pieces to expose the Christian faith for what it is."

He shifted, leaning back against the table and folding his arms and widening his mouth into a satisfied grin. "What it makes plain is that there was a conflict between two early Christian leaders. One man didn't like what the other was teaching, and so sought to excommunicate him. Which would have been bad politics for the good Emperor Constantine. So what did he do?"

Sebastian's voice rose to a fevered pitch, and he grabbed the parchment again, saying: "He, and I quote, *'intervened in the Church, seeking to build up the body of the faith as if it were my own, responsible for its making.'* The man took the bull by the horns and made the religion into his own image!"

Silas's head was swirling with the possibilities of what the man was suggesting. It wasn't at all a foregone conclusion that's what Constantine was doing, making the Christian faith in his image, as Sebastian's rhetoric suggested. There were any number of reasons why Constantine would want to *'build up the body of faith'* as he said—which oddly echoed what the Apostle Paul had written about the Church.

But still...there was an air about it that seemed heavy-handed, especially him feeling responsible for the Church's making. Which could deliver both Sebastian and Braun the victory they wanted: exposing the Church as some imperially manufactured religion.

Not good.

Sebastian had stood again and was stepping toward the camera. "I promise not to rest until the final pieces of this puzzle about Constantine's role in formulating the Nicene Creed and constructing the Church into his own image and any other conspiratorial nonsense is revealed—for humanity! The Republic of Heaven depends on it."

With that, the feed faded to black.

Silence again enveloped the space.

And again, Gapinski was the first to eventually break it. He whistled, then said, "Well that takes the cake, doesn't it?"

"Stuff and nonsense, it is," Celeste said. "A right nutter, that one is."

"Are we even sure the thing is genuine?" Torres asked. "I mean, we all know any two-bit hustler can cobble together parchment and provenance, given our last mission."

"Given what Grant cobbled together, you mean?" Silas said.

"Like I said. Two-bit hustler."

He threw her a grin and took a step toward the display, arms folded as he considered something he had seen.

Celeste said, "I don't know, he sounded pretty convincing to me."

"You saw it with your own eyes," Gapinski said. "The golden thingamabob. A spittin' image of the one we had and the one Braun displayed."

"Right. And the fact he has in his possession the one previously uncovered by yours truly—" she motioned toward Torres, who took a slight bow.

"And stolen by that Chuke whack job," Gapinski added.

"And that, which sounded exactly like the missing fragment previous to the one that Sebastian just read us, the two fitting together quite nicely."

"True," Torres said. "And I guess what he read seemed to confirm what we had just been talking about, with Arius and the central Christian belief about Jesus' identity and all."

"Zoe, play it back, would you?" Silas said, interrupting the conversation.

"The whole thing?" she asked.

"Just the last ten seconds. I'll tell you when to stop."

She jumped the video back several frames and started it again.

"There!"

"What is it, love?" Celeste asked.

He pointed to the desk. "See that object lying on the table?"

"Next to the parchment, right after Sebastian set it down?" Torres asked.

"That's right. Zoe, can you capture that and zoom in on it a bit?"

"Sure thing. But I'll do you one better than that. Hold tight."

After a few minutes ticked by, she displayed a captured selection from the frame Silas wanted and enlarged it on the screen. But it looked far better than what had caught his eye.

She said, "I cross-referenced the object you noted with all the other frames from the video to create a composite from all angles. Hope it suits your fancy."

"Holybamoly," Gapinski said, "we've got the computing power for that sort of CIA maneuver?"

"*Psht*. You kidding me? The CIA ain't got nothing on SEPIO."

"Perfect, Zoe. Nice work." Silas took a step toward the display, mind spinning with possibilities.

"Is that what I think it is?" Torres said, joining Silas at his side.

A jagged piece of metal or ceramic was displayed, a bit pixelated but clear enough that Silas knew in his gut it matched the one they had recovered from their own golden cylinder.

"The metal puzzle-piece thingy!" Gapinski exclaimed.

Silas turned to Torres. "Do you still have the one we recovered?"

She fished for it in a pocket and handed it over.

He held it up to the massive display. Similar, but different. Not only in shape and form, but in content. The V-like shape didn't match. Close, but flipped around, so that it was on the opposite side and upside down.

He frowned, confused by it all.

Until it hit him.

"Wait a minute..."

He stepped closer, his breath growing shallow at the possibility that was quickly becoming a probability.

Silas held the piece they had recovered up in front of him. Looked similar, that's for sure. He lined it up to the one on the display. Then he turned it, matching one end to the other.

"Zoe, please shrink the image by like ninety-five percent."

"OK..." She did as she was asked, the image shrinking down to size, framed by a black background. And Silas held the recovered piece closer to the display.

"*Dios mío...*" Torres exclaimed. "Looks like a match to me!"

"Always something..." Gapinski growled.

"Not perfect," Celeste said, tilting her head.

"And not really a medallion."

"Maybe we were wrong on that front. Can't know for certain without the other pieces."

"Does sorta look oddly like the newfangled swastika hands to that pagan bird symbol of Nous, I'll give you that."

"Would you send a copy of that image to my phone, Zoe?" Silas said, disbelieving the truth of it.

"On it," she replied.

Celeste folded her arms and huffed. "I just knew they had their prints all over this conspiracy."

Silas clenched the metal fragment before stuffing it back in his pocket, then sighed. Seemed that way. And yet...

He turned to face the room. "Except we all agreed there's no way Nous could have gotten what we recovered down into the chamber under the buried basilica baptismal. Isn't that right, Torres?"

She nodded. "Not the one we recovered at least."

"Which doesn't rule out the possibility," Celeste added, "that the blokes could have orchestrated this whole bloody affair from centuries past. Stuffing the nonsense down inside those golden tubes and then burying them in the sand, biding their time for the day they unearthed their conspiracy to undermine the Church."

"I don't know..." Gapinski said. "That's quite the long con. Even for our resident pseudo-spiritual whack job terrorists."

Silas nodded. "I agree. And why would Chuke, who is clearly with Nous, and—well, Sebastian...why would they be hunting these pieces down as much as Braun if Nous was responsible?"

Celeste shrugged. "A sort of amnesia, perhaps? Nous conspired way back when to manufacture false evidence to suggest Constantine created Christianity, then forgot where it hid their manufactured pieces. But they somehow held on to the memory of their conspiracy until unearthing it one day for all the world to see on WeNet."

There was silence from the group as they considered the narrative.

"Sorry, darlin'," Silas finally said, "that doesn't make any sense."

She playfully smacked his shoulder, then frowned. "You're right. It's bullocks."

He turned to her and grinned. "Oh, really. I'm right, so that would make you..."

"Don't press your luck, hot stuff."

Gapinski and Torres both cleared their throats.

Silas chuckled. "Sorry. Where were we?"

"Trying to save the Church," Gapinski said, "from no uncertain doom and destruction at the hand of pseudo-spiritual terrorists?"

"Oh, yeah. That."

"So what are we gonna do about it? I'm about tired of holing up in the belly of the Vatican, no offense," Gapinski said, turning to the priest.

Bartholomew held up a hand. "None taken."

"I'm rearin' for a fight, if you know what I mean. I think we've done enough damage from our heads down in the books. Time to come up with guns blazing."

"I agree," Torres said.

"I as well," Celeste added, "So how about we start with recapping where we're at with this whole bloody affair."

Gapinski shrugged. "No different from all of SEPIO's other bloody affairs. An anti-Christian social-media mogul with a chip the size of the Vatican on his shoulder launched an *Apprentice*-style treasure hunt to find evidence the Church covered up the true origins of its central belief, Jesus' divinity. But not before we found evidence first, right before it was stolen from us and ended up on WeNet next to its sibling. That about the long and short of it?"

"Yikes! *The Apprentice* and *Survivor* analogies in twenty-four hours?" Torres said. "You got a man-crush on Mark Burnette or something, Hoss?"

He frowned and dipped his head. "Maybe…"

"Alright, folks, let's focus," Silas said, walking back over to the manuscripts and codices on display. "We're now short another golden cylinder thanks to my brother, on top of the one his henchman Chuke stole from us." He checked his watch, a cheap Seiko gifted by Dad and pockmarked from two decades of wear. "Now we've got less than seventy-two hours to bag this cat before the rest of WeSolve does."

"Seventy-two hours?" Bartholomew questioned.

"That's right."

He hummed. "Interesting."

"Why is that interesting?" Celeste asked.

"Because it's the anniversary of the adoption of the Nicene Creed by the bishops gathered at the First Council of Nicaea."

Silas sighed with recognition. "That's right! June 19, AD 325."

Gapinski whistled. "Quite the statement-making ticking clock."

Torres folded her arms. "If that doesn't put an exclamation point on the mission, I don't know what does."

Celeste said. "Which means this is clearly about bringing the Nicene Creed to its knees."

"And the Church," Silas said.

"As if there was any doubt."

He nodded toward Bartholomew. "Good catch. Got anything else for us? Not that you haven't done enough for us already," he added, sweeping an arm across the aged ecclesial archive.

The man offered a smile and nodded. "My pleasure. Anything to serve the Order, and the Church. However, there is one other thing."

"And what's that?"

"Seems the best course of action is to follow the two characters at the center of this sordid tale."

"You mean Arius and Constantine?" Celeste said.

"I do."

"Follow the Emperor…" Silas muttered, Bartholomew's advice connecting to the memory of Zarruq's warning from earlier.

"What was that, chief?" Gapinski asked.

"Remember what Zarruq said? Follow the Emperor, seek the Master, remember something or other? What Bishop Zarruq shouted back when he was being dragged away by Chuke and his thugs."

"That's right," Celeste said. "We wondered whether Master was referencing Arius. And Victor was cluing us in, perhaps steering us in a direction to find the remaining fragment."

"Exactly." Silas turned to Bartholomew. "What do you make of that?"

He shrugged. "I suppose the man's honorific title as bishop could consider him a Master of the Church."

"It's about all we have to go on. Emperor and Master."

Celeste nodded. "Constantine and Arius."

"Yeah, but where do those names take us?"

"Constantinople and Ptolemais," Bartholomew announced proudly.

"Consta-Tola-who?" Gapinski said.

"The seat of Constantine, I recognize," Torres said. "Not so much the other."

"Not only the Emperor's seat of power," Silas said, "having moved the Roman capital from Rome to modern Istanbul, but also his final burial."

"And Ptolemais?"

"The home of Arius," Celeste said. "And the bishop of Ptolemais, Secundus, was a patron of Arius and listed among those present at the Council of Nicaea."

Silas smiled. "That's my girl." She smiled back and blushed at the compliment.

"So Istanbul and back to Libya," Torres said.

He nodded. "Back across the pond, we go."

"So how should we split the teams? Boys against the girls again?"

Celeste wrapped her arm in Silas's. "About time we pair up."

"I agree," Silas said.

"Which means I'm stuck with Hoss, here," Torres complained.

Gapinski cleared his throat. "Stuck? What am I, chopped liver?"

Torres giggled. "At least we have ourselves some solid leads this time around."

"Yeah, but I have to imagine Bishop Zarruq had the same 411 on the locations."

"Which means Nous has the same 411 on the locations as well," Celeste said.

Silas nodded. That he did. And that they did.

Which meant they needed to hustle. On the double.

Before his brother and Braun knew what was what.

CHAPTER 14
ISTANBUL. JUNE 17.

It was going to be a hot one.

The feel of the air, humming with stick and suffocation, signaled to Silas they were in store for one of those summer days he remembered growing up as a teenager in Falls Church, Virginia. The kind when his football pads and jersey stuck to his skin like a trash bag during summer practice, and every pore of his body thirsted for Gatorade relief under the high-noon sun and sweltering, swampy Northern Virginia lowlands near the Potomac.

Wasn't in his nature to complain about the weather. Figured there wasn't a point. Like complaining water was wet or the Detroit Lions can't pick up a single yard. It's just the way things are. But he sure preferred his heat dry, especially after suffering for summers on end in the South Pacific with Dad and Sebastian, and then in Northern Virginia when pops was transferred to the Pentagon. Figured he'd done his penance plenty times over.

So he was in a bit of a mood pulling out of Istanbul International Airport in a humid sweat wondering how the day would turn out.

After taking a breather in some Vatican housing unit to rest up and freshen up, the SEPIO pair had left the Vatican in the dead of night to get a jump on the connection between Constantine's confession and the emperor's christened Roman capital city—if any even existed. They wished Gapinski and Torres luck on their own goose chase and asked if Bartholomew would keep looking for any further connections from the Vatican Archives that could help them unravel the mystery. He would, and was eager to offer any help he could.

Their flight over had been uneventful enough, a quick three hours in the wee morning hours using an Order-issued Gulfstream he had gotten to know well the past few years since joining the Order, zipping from mission to mission with SEPIO saving the Church from no uncertain doom. Hated flying, but the creamy leather seats combined with the mahogany wood paneling and trim work, not to mention the well-stocked wet bar at the back and concierge service, made it bearable.

Silas had slept hard the minute he'd strapped in tight for the flight over. He and Celeste had touched down in the early dawn half an hour ago, but finding a rental car had been a real pain, which probably started the mood on top of the humidity. Given their early arrival, they were left with a rattly Peugeot with a wheezy air conditioner that reminded him why he didn't much care for the French. The fan worked well enough but offered up cold air only when it suited its fancy, coughing it out like a pack-a-day smoker.

Like the French.

Soon enough, they were zipping through the D020 with minimal traffic on toward the Church of the Holy Apostles, the original burial site of Constantine the Great. Should make it in a little over half hour. Which suited Silas fine considering the Frenchie he was driving and its unreliable set of lungs.

Had never been to Istanbul himself. Had known some NATO-coalition boys from the Iraq War who had visited on leave, but he hadn't much wanted to after the Turkish parliament killed U.S. plans for a northern front in the war against Iraq, refusing to authorize the deployment of U.S. troops on Turkish soil. Not that he cared much about such realpolitiking maneuvers nor did he care much about mounting his donkey and tilting at such windmills now. But back in the day, in the shadow of 9/11 after Dad had died at the hands of terrorists in the Pentagon, his twentysomething self bled red, white, and blue at any slight toward Uncle Sam. Now, not so much.

As they drove, Silas ran through what he knew of the city from his grad school days, and how it connected to their mission searching for Constantine's confession.

"Led by the hand of God," as one early Church historian suggested, he built a considerable level of Christian accouterments in the city. In his new palace, he anchored an enormous bejeweled cross at the center of his bedroom ceiling. He replaced pagan temples with a massive church-building campaign that would give Church-State separatists a coronary. Even commissioned fifty Bibles to be used in the newly built churches. One of the most famous was *Codex Sinaiticus*, preserved in a monastery in Egypt at the foot of Mount Sinai still containing half of the Old Testament and the entire New Testament. This new abundance of Christian trappings symbolized a decisive victory for the Church over pagan gods.

And they were heading toward one of the most famous of those church buildings, Church of the Holy Apostles. Which really was no longer a church anymore.

Built in AD 330 by Constantine the Great and later enlarged and reconsecrated by Justinian in AD 550, the Church of the Holy Apostles was traditionally the burial place for the imperial family during the early years of the Byzantine Empire, beginning with the remains of Constantine himself. Unfortunately for SEPIO, the tombs were plundered by the Crusaders during the Fourth Crusade. And when Constantinople fell to the Ottomans in 1453, the Church of the Holy Apostles became the seat of the Ecumenical Patriarch of the Greek Orthodox Church for a brief period before being demolished in 1461 by Mehmet the Conqueror to make way for the Fatih Mosque.

What they sought wasn't at the church at all, but just beyond at the Istanbul Archaeological Museum. And on a buck and a prayer, as Gapinski said.

A car drifted into Silas's lane, trying to squeeze between him and a beat-up blue Volkswagen that looked like a holdover from when it joined NATO in '52. Not another car around, yet there it was, elbowing in for Lord only knew what.

Irritated and reaching for the only smidgen of control he could in the past day that had sapped him dry, Silas accelerated to close the gap. The other car had the same idea. Nearly kissed the blockhead's bumper before he braked hard and broadcast his anger for the early morning world with his horn.

Celeste placed a hand on his leg.

"Would you look at that jerk!" he exclaimed, the car exiting and speeding off, leaving Silas to honk again as his only passing recourse.

"Simmer, tiger. Or else you're liable to start a street brawl."

"I'd win, too."

She grinned. "I'm sure you would. But then we might end up in one of Erdogan's prisons, and that'd be the end of it."

Holding the steering wheel with one hand, he wrapped his fingers from the other in hers. "I guess you're right."

"No truer words have ever been spoken. And don't forget it when we tie the knot."

"I wouldn't dare!"

She giggled, and he drove on. How could he have been so lucky? It was just two years ago he was single and consumed with his work at Princeton when she fell into his lap. Or rather, she saved his ass after terrorists nearly blew it to smithereens.

Since rescuing him from that bombed out chapel at Georgetown University and then saving him again in the bowels of the Church of the Holy Sepulchre and countless more times, he couldn't imagine life without her. And then when he nearly lost her last fall to the Devil himself, he did the only thing that made sense—the only sensible thing he had probably done in his life, other than signing up to defend his country after 9/11. He asked her to marry him.

Thankfully, she said yes. He was eager to get to it, quite content to exchange vows at the local courthouse if need be. But she would blow her brunette top if he suggested it. Wanted a princess wedding in a church all the way, which he wouldn't have taken her for. Fine by him. At least they were finally alone and working together side by side to protect and preserve the Christian faith. Probably the next best thing to marriage.

Til death do us part.

Celeste said, "Constantinople was also known as *Christoupolis*, isn't that right?"

Silas nodded. "Christ's city. The Emperor was originally buried here in the Church of the Twelve Apostles. Surrounding his tomb were twelve other tombs, signaling his belief he was a thirteenth apostle of sorts, charged like Peter and Paul as an evangelist to broadcast and extend the gospel across the globe."

"Pax Romana style?"

"Something like that. Some have viewed the arrangement as an *alter Christus*, a sort of altar around which the Christian faith, the *apostolic faith* would be served by his life. Since then, people inside and outside the Church have been arguing about the meaning of that life for Christianity's rise."

"Arguing is right."

"Obsession, more like it. Markus Braun and Noland Rotberg are in good company."

Celeste asked, "So what do you make of this whole obsession with Constantine, anyway?"

Silas shrugged. "Makes perfect sense in our postmodern times, with its obsession over networks of power and power differentials and accusations of minority voices getting the shaft."

"To be fair, there has been plenty of that going on for decades. I think Harvey Weinstein pretty much made the closing argument on that one."

"No, you're right. That's fair. And the Church itself has certainly perpetuated and exploited such power imbalances."

"From across the ecclesial spectrum, too. From Catholic pedophile priests to Evangelical womanizing pastors. Your own brother fell victim to such sinful power plays."

He nodded. "The headlines certainly play into the narrative that it was old white men who pulled the Church's strings to angle it in some massive conspiratorial power play against other voices to arrive at the epicenter of power. Whether it's the priesthood, excluding women from serving, or the traditional view of Jesus' divinity and humanity, or the existence of hell and necessity of exclusive faith in Jesus' death and resurrection for eternal life. So, yeah, Braun's and Rotberg's own power play is entirely convenient given the spirit of the age."

"To be fair again," Celeste added, "Constantine was the most powerful man in the known world at the time who certainly had some sort of conversion experience. What's the arch say that still stands in the Roman forum bearing an inscription to the man? *'To the Emperor Caesar Flavius Constantinus, the Greatest, Pius, Felix, Augustus, inspired by divinity, in the greatness of his mind...'*"

"Impressive, Celeste Bourne. Oxford taught you well."

"I may have had a mild obsession with the man in grad school."

Silas propped an elbow on his window ledge to steer and leaned back, flashing her a wry grin. "You never mentioned another man in your life."

"What's the saying, never study and tell?"

He laughed. "Something like that."

"I do tend to agree with the debate about whether the conspiracy theorists are right in his use of the faith for his own powerful ends."

Silas shook his head. "Such a cynic."

"Such a *realist*."

"Then what do you think? Was he a true believer?"

Celeste took a breath and a beat, then answered, "I believe Constantine believed his mission in life was to preserve and strengthen the Roman Empire by means of Christianity. To reach this goal, the man reshaped the public sphere in profound ways that pushed Christianity into culture in ways previously unheard of. You could say he baptized the public space with it, given all of his reform efforts."

"Which wasn't all bad, was it? Considering the alternative was rampant persecution. It was largely because he normalized the faith, gave it room to breathe and exercise in public, that it flourished and grew, that the gospel went forth and people found Christ."

"Well, there are varying views on that," Celeste responded. "But I do grant you this wasn't all bad, considering the alternative was a state-sponsored, all-out assault on the faith, as you said. But Constantine's alternative was the other extreme, believing a key purpose for marrying the Empire so closely with Christianity was the earthly blessings it afforded the State. Which is why he exempted clergy from being required to perform civic duties and pay taxes."

Silas considered that, and marveled at her depth of intelligence. He was marrying up for sure, whenever that was.

"I don't know," she went on, "it all seems like merely accoutrements of power. Minting coins to depict him praying to God and busts of him with eyes fixed toward heaven. Even the restoration of the Church's civil liberties was a pretty ingenious power play. Backing the winning horse, and all."

"Wow, you sound like Braun, dear."

"Now them are fightin' words, as you Yanks say."

Silas laughed. "Which sounds far better in Queen's English than a John Wayne Western twang. And you've got a point, about backing the winning horse, but there was also a deep concern for the purity of the church and its doctrines, particularly the unity of the Church."

"Perhaps he fell somewhere in the middle, then," Celeste acknowledged, "having a genuine faith-transformation experience while also putting his finger on the scale, so to speak, for his own political purposes."

Silas said, "I would submit our job isn't to judge whether Constantine was a Christian based on particular theological or denominational standards. But rather, what we can see is the totality of the man's life and actions, whether he was concerned merely with building the Kingdom of Constantine or the Kingdom of God."

Celeste leaned against her window toward Silas. "And your conclusion, professor Grey?"

He shrugged. "There is no question in my mind that Constantine was a great blessing to the Church. Within a single generation, Christianity went from suffering its greatest persecution to enjoying its greatest privilege. His pledges through the Edict of Milan restored Christian freedom enjoyed before the Great Persecution, even going so far as to extend and enlarge those freedoms. He also launched a massive campaign to build church buildings across the Empire to give the growing movement tangible places of worship."

Celeste chuckled. "Of course, you have to deal with the optics of him killing his own son from a previous marriage by poison and then boiling his wife in a bath."

"Jesus' teaching about loving your neighbor as yourself went out the window with that one, I grant you that."

"Then there is the issue of his baptism."

"His baptism? What about it?"

Celeste said, "I should think it is worth noting that Emperor Constantine wasn't baptized until he was splayed about on his deathbed. Arguably, he didn't confess Christ until he was one foot in the grave."

Silas scoffed. "I wouldn't go so far as to say he didn't confess Christ. Perhaps we should conclude that Constantine was a Christian man, but one with deep flaws who at times used his faith as a political tool for maneuvering the Empire through tenuous times. Yes, he seemed to take his mission on earth to be more political than spiritual. But he was the Emperor for goodness sakes! Doesn't mean he was not Christ's son or outside the grace of God. And considering all that the Lord used him to accomplish during the great upheaval almost seventeen hundred years ago, it's clear Christ was with him."

"Touché," she said. "But perhaps we're going to just have to agree to disagree on this one, love."

"I don't know if I can handle not being on the same page with something so important."

"Just wait until I school you in the proper way to dispense a roll of toilet paper."

He furrowed his brow. "What do you mean? It's under and out all the way."

"Barbarian!" she exclaimed. "Over and down, or I'm calling off the engagement."

He went to reply when his phone buzzed with an alert. "Here we are...."

Celeste craned around, brow furrowed with confusion. "Here we are? Where are we?"

"The site of the original Church of the Holy Apostles."

She paused a beat, taking in the area. "How depressing..."

She was right. It was.

They were on a boulevard divided by a narrow strip of blooming trees and grass wet with early morning dew. Buildings towered above them four, five stories. Silas pulled over and parked at a corner in front of a beige-trimmed, white building. Looked like some sort of fast-food restaurant, called *Sedef Iskender*, whatever that was. Across a narrow street opening up to the right was a woman's clothing store, an upscale affair with black granite architecture selling high-end dresses.

But no church.

"I don't understand," Celeste said. "Where's this church that's supposed to be housing the remains of our infamous Emperor?"

"It ain't here, sweetheart. Just on the way to our real target."

"What do you mean it isn't here?"

Silas went to answer when one end of his mouth curled upward. "Don't tell me my Harvard-trained brain knows something the great Celeste Bourne doesn't know."

"Ha, ha, very funny. Don't forget my Oxford-educated brain just schooled you in the finer points of Constantine's religious persuasion."

"Apparently Oxford-educated ain't what it used to be."

She frowned. "Cheeky bugger. Just tell me what's what and let's get on with it."

He chuckled and pulled away from the curb. "The place was long gone, since around the fifteenth century."

"Then what's that mean for Constantine's remains? And weren't a number of other Byzantine emperors buried alongside him at the cathedral?"

"That's right. But they all eventually ended up at one place. The Istanbul Archaeological Museum, just down the way."

"Seems fitting. And you believe Constantine is there? Or rather, the next clue is there?"

"There are several theories where Constantine's remains ended up, but they most certainly are not at the museum or any other place in the city."

"Don't tell me we flew across the Mediterranean in the dead of night only to smack into a dead end."

Silas patted her knee. "Have faith, darlin'. I've got it all under control."

"That's what I'm afraid of…"

Soon they were pulling up to the entrance of a park that sat just outside the museum.

And Silas was praying he really did have everything under control.

Otherwise it would be SEPIO's most expensive sightseeing trip to date.

CHAPTER 15

Dawn's first light began making its appearance as Silas pulled the parking brake to their Peugeot rental at a gate guarding a park at the base of their target, the humidity slapping him in the face again as he opened the door.

Yep. A hot one indeed.

But they had bigger things to worry about. Like praying to the good Lord above that some golden cylinder had survived the test of time—Crusades, grave robbers, Muslim hordes—stuffed away in some imperial sarcophagus sitting outside the Istanbul Archaeological Museum.

The Lord works in mysterious ways, they say. Silas had seen him work mighty-miracle wonders the past two years alone while on mission with the Order. He just hoped the Lord was in the mood to serve up another dose of grace and mercy for their time of need. In a big way.

Because SEPIO needed it. And the Church.

A line of purple began splitting night from day across the horizon as the pair hustled through a park darkened by large trees. Sycamores by the looks of them, soaring high with boughs sagging from age and signs of summer. Negotiating his smartphone for direction, he led Celeste to the location he had researched where the targets were held. Hated parking their getaway so far away, but there was no good route up to the museum building's perimeter where the old Byzantine tombs were resting.

Wood and steel park benches rimmed by white paint lined the walkways. A few homeless men were still snoozing away, having made them their abode. The SEPIO pair made it a point to sidestep around them through the grass, giving them a wide berth. The last thing they needed was a civilian spotting them, as confused as they might be.

The sky was growing a more pronounced bruising as Silas and Celeste neared the museum complex, so they picked up the pace, stepping back on a path of mismanaged cobblestones caked with dirt and moss from neglect before padding toward their target. Didn't have much time before the city began emerging from its slumber. So they picked up the pace, eventually spotting a five-story beige building rising in the middle of the park, windows darkened and hiding their historical treasures.

Along with something Silas was not at all expecting.

"Is that a—"

"Wall..." he moaned, panic rising to the surface with each step. He swallowed hard and stuffed it away before it threatened to take over.

Get it together Grey...

"You didn't say anything about a bloomin' wall," Celeste complained as they neared, bright green vegetation spotting the dark bricks and confirming the truth of it.

Probably thirty to forty feet high, the damn thing ran the entire length of the park, shielding the museum with protection from would-be invaders in the early dawn seeking treasure in the shape of a golden cylinder from an early Church sarcophagus connected to the Church of the Holy Apostles.

"Why didn't you say anything about a wall?"

"Because Google maps didn't show me no bloody wall!" he hissed, holding up his phone to consult the app on full display before regretting it.

He glanced around the brightening space before taking a breath and huffing in frustration. Both at his outburst at Celeste and his incompetent planning.

"Sorry. Not called for."

"No worries," she said. "Now let's find a way in."

They ran the length of the wall in both directions, searching for anything that could give them leverage inside. All the gates were closed and barred. It had to be over twenty feet, the whole way around. So it seemed like they were out of luck.

"What are we going to do?" Celeste asked, running a hand through her hair as she stared at the wall.

Indeed. What were they going to—

Then he had it.

"The benches!"

"The wha—Hey, where are you going?" she called after him, but he was already racing down the lawn toward the path.

Reaching a wooden bench, he grabbed hold of it. Then prayed like he'd never prayed before pulling back. Hoping it wasn't bolted to the ground.

It gave.

He closed his eyes and sighed.

Thank you, Lord!

The thing was heavy, but he managed to hoist it on his shoulders and start back up toward the wall.

Celeste met him on the way. "Oy! Where are you taking that bloomin' thing?"

"Where do you think? Care to join in the infiltration fun? Think you can manage?"

"I like the way you think, Silas Grey."

Took some doing, but within several minutes they had each lugged three benches up the incline back to the base of the wall, the sky turning the shade of a bruised strawberry now as morning emerged.

"We don't have much time," Silas said, as he positioned one bench against the wall. He took another and set it on top, angling it so that the feet at one end were resting on the other end of the bench part. He did the same with the third and fourth and fifth, alternating the angles, until they had a makeshift ladder—as sketchy as it was.

"See, that's why Rowen made you Order Master."

"To stack park benches like a boss?"

Celeste giggled. "No, silly. To save the day."

"Are you flirting with me, Celeste Bourne?"

She folded her arms. "Perhaps..." Then she eyed their contraption skeptically. "Although, I don't know...seems pretty dodgy to me. Good effort, but something only a man would build, I reckon."

He snorted a laugh. "Probably why men die before women."

"And Yanks before us Brits."

The sound of traffic faintly picking up pace beyond the trees reminded Silas they didn't have much time before the world was fully awakened, along with the museum.

"You want to do the honors," he said, "or shall I?"

"Ladies first," Celeste said, stepping up to the plate. "Besides, I'm going to need a firm hand at my backside if I'm to hoist myself up to the top."

He smiled. "My pleasure."

"Don't get any funny ideas, mister. We're months away from marriage."

Holding her one hand, Silas helped her step up to the first bench. Then he did as he was told, keeping her steady as she mounted the second. She did the rest, climbing it like a boss herself and reaching the top with ease. She grabbed hold of the top of the wall and hoisted herself up, turning around on her bottom and giving two thumbs up.

Relieved, he climbed onto his contraption and started for the top.

She said, "Long way down to the bottom. Not sure how we'll make it back out once we're inside."

"We'll cross that bridge when we get what we came for."

Reaching the top, he grabbed hold of the wall next to Celeste.

When his foot slipped on the bench, banging into the side and sending one of its legs skipping through the armrest.

Which had the domino effect of jostling the one beneath. And then the other below that one.

Uh-oh...

Jumping and hoisting himself farther onto the wall, he escaped the bench ladder as it collapsed into a heaping, raucous pile below.

He finished pulling himself up and straddled the top, glancing down to the ground with a regretful wince. "So much for the element of surprise."

"If those homeless blokes weren't clued into our incursion, they are now."

"Then let's get to it."

Celeste was right. The jump down was far. But they'd managed, landing on the cobblestone like the pros they were, having been trained well by their respective governments.

"What are we looking for?" she said, taking out her smartphone and shining its light toward the museum.

Light caught a lush garden, punctuated by pedestals mounted by the detritus of history.

He answered, "Four imperial sarcophagi used for past Byzantine emperors and coming from the now-vanished Church of the Holy Apostles. Should be set in red porphyry rock standing in front of the museum."

"Where?"

He shrugged.

"So a needle in a Constantinople haystack?"

"Basically."

"And me without my Turkish delight."

They raced toward the front of the museum beyond the garden, a stately looking thing of Roman and Baroque architecture that seemed misplaced, blackened by weather and pockmarked with age.

He stopped in the middle, shining his own smartphone's light around for a better look. "Let's split up. I'll look around here if you want to search near the museum."

"Cheerio," she said before taking off.

The sky was brightening now, his beat-up old Seiko confirming it was almost six. Not much time left. They had to pick it up.

On the double.

Silas waded through the garden of full-size statues and pedestals crowned with the tops of ancient Corinthian columns and weathered birds and totems—all of it, as interesting as it was, looked like the picked-over bones of a mastodon historic site.

He sighed and planted his hands at his hips, glancing around and coming up dry. A needle was right. The targets could be anywhere.

A sudden call rose above the garden. From the museum.

"Over here!"

Celeste.

That was fast.

He raced onto a path and past a statue missing her head, then padded across a cobblestone courtyard toward three boxes the size of their rental glowing red in the dawning morning sitting just outside the museum.

Bingo...

"Nice work!" he said, coming up to her side as she shined her smartphone light across one of the boxes.

"Don't thank me too soon..."

"Why, what's wrong? What have you found?"

"Nothing, that's the problem," she said, shutting off her light. "I've looked all over these bloomin' boxes and can't find anything that would help. Look—"

She pointed the light at the top, a deep crevice edging the perimeter separating the lid from the boxy part—clearly having been opened. Surely anything that might have been inside would have been picked clean centuries ago.

Desperate, he turned on his own light and started searching the surface of the pockmarked red slabs of stone that had housed the remains of Byzantine emperors from centuries past —for anything at all that might signal some hidden chamber or any other clue to the location of the golden cylinder housing Constantine's confession and emperor code.

"Did you check inside?" he said hunched over as he continued his search.

She frowned. "Are you mad? How do you expect me to get inside? The cover must weigh a few hundred kilos."

He ignored her, continuing his search as dread grew in his belly. He came up with the same answer as Celeste.

A big fat negatory.

"Besides," she went on, "grave robbers would have cleared out the innards centuries ago, anyhow, probably during the Crusades or after Constantinople fell to the Ottomans. And I have to imagine any archeological museum worth its salt would have scoured them years ago looking for—"

"Well then, what the hell are we doing here?"

She huffed. "I don't know, *Master* Grey. You tell me! You dragged our bloomin' bums across the Mediterranean in the dead of night—"

"Alright," he interrupted, throwing up a frustrated hand before raking his other through his hair. Then he stopped and sighed. "Sorry. Not called for. Again."

She folded her arms and nodded.

Didn't make sense in the slightest. Sure, she was probably right. But if something had been found, surely the Order would have known about it, and the Vatican. But there wasn't anything of reference in the Archives. Unless it was still hidden, somewhere, somehow in one of the three—

"Wait a minute…"

He twisted around and counted the red boxes.

One. Two. Three.

"There were supposed to have been four boxes!"

"What are you playing at?" Celeste asked, coming to his side.

"There's another one, somewhere on the perimeter."

She looked around and then glanced at the sky, which was now far bluer than Silas would have wanted.

"Let's go," he said, taking her hand and leading her to the left across the museum's outer edge, racing now as the clock cycled down to zero.

But there was nothing. Just a bunch of scaffolding and plastic sheeting for renovating museum walls. They backtracked toward the other end, stumbling across more of the same as they sprinted now, desperate for something to make the trip worth it.

And help them safeguard the Church.

Lord Jesus Christ, Son of God, throw us a bone here!

They kept at it, padding along the museum and lifting more of the same plastic sheeting draped across blocks and statues and columns, finding plenty of broken pieces of history underneath the protective plastic. But nothing—

Then they saw it, both at once.

A ray of sunshine had splashed down from the rising sun through parted clouds, a slice of gold splitting through a pair of buildings on the eastern side and landing on another box farther down.

Now that's what I'm talking about, Lord!

The ray of light split wider, as if heaven itself had opened up a rift in the fabric of reality and deposited the tomb on their doorstep in answer to his prayer.

"Thank you, Lord..." Silas mumbled before the pair flashed each other a hopeful grin. Then they took off, stopping short a few feet away when they saw the full measure of it.

There it was. Yet this sarcophagus was different from the other three, a gabled tomb in white marble.

And marked by the Chi-Rho cross.

The symbol of Constantine the Great, set inside a laurel wreath.

"If that don't scream X-marks-the-spot," Silas said, "I don't know what does..."

"I bloomin' well think so."

At either end of the *X* openings of the Greek letter Chi were two other Greek letters, an Alpha and Omega, representing the name of Christ offered in the Book of Revelation, chapter 22 verse 13: *'I am the Alpha and the Omega, the first and the last, the beginning and the end.'* Above the Chi-Rho on either side were two eight-petal flowers and the symbol set inside the wreath was tied off by a vine.

Silas took a hesitant step, then moaned. "Look..."

He pointed to an opening tunneled into the top, between the lid and the box. "Could have been used by a child or small person to crawl into it and root around for treasures."

"Which means there is a good chance the tomb is empty."

He sighed and nodded at the truth of it.

"Cheer up, Charlie," she said, stepping up to the massive object and running a hand along Constantine's symbol. "A bit of thirteenth-century grave burgling has never stopped SEPIO. Perhaps they missed something."

Perhaps...but doubtful.

He joined her anyway, searching the other sides while she

continued searching the symbol itself. He inched along the backside, shining his light along the surface as he squeezed through a narrow opening between the sarcophagus and the museum, his own backside getting scraped in the process.

Nothing but pockmarks from centuries of wear.

Reaching the other side, a noise caught his attention.

He stepped toward the sound, holding up his phone's light. "What was that?"

A skittering or scraping.

Or footsteps.

He held his breath, continuing to hold his phone high.

"Probably just a critter," Celeste said, continuing to work.

Unsure whether to hold steady or lend a hand, another rustling from the garden to the right drew his light.

Right before two squirrels came bounding out, one chasing the other.

He let out his breath with a sigh, wiping his brow with the back of his hand.

"Here, help me with this," Celeste said. "Think I found something."

Silas spun around. Celeste was hunched over part of the Chi-Rho, the top portion that looked like a *P*.

"What did you find?"

She flashed him a grin. "I think it's a wax seal, caked over with mortar that's been flaking off for some time. Have a look."

Shining her light, she picked off a grayish-white substance, a large piece flaking to the ground. Underneath was clearly some sort of substance, gray and clouded. Perhaps it was some sort of wax resin, like she said.

"You wouldn't have a knife, would you?" she asked.

Silas reached into his boot and withdrew a long steel blade, handing it to her handle first.

"Army issued," he said smiling.

"Brilliant..." She took it and got to work.

He looked on, doubtful at first. But the more she worked the blade in the eye of the Rho, the more hope rose. Something sure was caked in there pretty good, the mortar she first identified completely scraped away and even more of...something lodged inside.

Celeste gasped. The blade had completely sunk down inside. She turned to him and grinned before pulling it out. "There's a chamber."

Silas aimed his phone's light at the spot. Sure enough, there was a blackened hole where she had removed the knife. He flashed her hopeful eyes.

Then was distracted by another noise, more clangy than rusty this time.

He went to walk toward it when Celeste muttered: "Got you, you little bugger."

He turned around. She had scrapped out the rest of the wax resin and was reaching down inside the void.

There it was again.

Silas spun back toward the garden, taking a step toward what he had sworn he'd heard.

Are my ears playing tricks on me?

"I'd say we won the jackpot, wouldn't you?" she said.

Turning back toward the sarcophagus, he found Celeste holding a golden cylinder.

He grinned. "Golden."

"My sentiments exactly."

Silas glanced at the sky, then at his watch. "Time to jet."

He started toward the other side of the courtyard, "By the way, it's hit the jackpot."

"What are you talking about?"

"You said won the jackpot. What's that, some sort of Britishism?"

She scoffed. "How about you worry about the task at hand

instead of comparing my impeccable linguistic skills to your Yankish idioms—like where's our bloomin' exit."

"Whatever you say, dear. And I think it's this way." He hustled faster past the garden and threshold to the museum. "Saw a section in the wall earlier when we were scoping out the other side. Should be...there!"

He turned into a lot filled with broken columns and large chunks of stone sitting behind a knee-high gated stone wall. He climbed over it, helping Celeste do the same. Dead ahead was the top of the wall and the green fence meant to keep away the riff-raff.

"Going to be dicey, but—"

"We've stormed the ramparts of greater threats with reckless abandon?" Celeste said.

"Something like that."

Silas climbed on the wall and jumped for the top of the fence, grabbing it and pulling himself up with ease. Soon, he was easing over the top and jumping to the ground.

"Toss me the cylinder, through the fence."

Celeste did, then repeated Silas's maneuver, landing next to him. "I reckon we should tarry no longer. Let's pop the top before straying too far. If it's a bust, we may need to make a return trip, even inside the museum once the gates open."

"Agree."

They found a bench next to a massive sycamore a ways down the hill, trunk clinically obese and standing like a crazy old uncle, boughs jutting up this way and that. They slumped down, then got to work.

Silas clenched his jaw and twisted up his face as he tried working the end cap loose, the hold tighter than the last time he remembered. He kept at it, unable to twist the cap loose.

"Here, let me try." She eased it from his reluctant hands, and he gave up. Long ago he learned it was best for Mars to pick battles on Venus wisely.

And that was neither the time nor the place.

"Be my guest. But it's on there pretty—"

It popped loose on her first try.

He frowned. "You do know I loosened it for you, don't you?"

She giggled, shinning her smartphone light inside and flashing him a grin. "Jackpot."

"Don't you mean we've *won* the jackpot."

"Best mind your tongue before you find yourself missing it."

He laughed, reaching inside for what he assumed was tucked within.

Jackpot was right.

He pulled out another copy of the Nicene Creed, as well as the familiar fragment. Glinting down below was another jagged piece of metal.

Keeping the fragment, he rolled the copy of the Creed inside the golden cylinder and handed it to Celeste. He then started scanning the next piece to Constantine's confession.

A few seconds ticking by, Celeste said with impatience, "Well, what does it say?"

Silas smiled. "Sorry." Then he took a breath and cleared his throat. He read the Latin and translated aloud:

> Some would say that no new religion can easily arise within the lands that other religions have long been practiced, such as Roma. To survive, a religion must have a hierarchy, legal decrees, ordered practices, and, most important, consistency of doctrine. Thus, humbly I offer the following dogma as a means to foster and perpetuate that which we have hammered and honed the past two decades—and yet not merely by my own hand, but what the Church itself has established at its birth:
>
> Although an angry God full of vengeance and spite might be preferable to a kind, loving one, that is not the

case. As the Apostle John writes so eloquently: *"For God so loved the world that he gave his only Son, so that everyone who believes in him may not perish but may have eternal life. Indeed, God did not send the Son into the world to condemn the world, but in order that the world might be saved through him."* Thus, although we proclaim obedience to the teachings of Christ, it is not the manner in which we are saved. Salvation is through Christ, not Christianity; through the life, death and resurrection of Jesus, not of works lest anyone should boast. The only way to obtain the resurrection of the dead and life everlasting is through faith in his finished work on the cross.

Although fear of perpetual hellfire suffering could be used to keep people under our control, it is not necessary. For as John continues, *"Those who believe in him are not condemned; but those who do not believe are condemned already, because they have not believed in the name of the only Son of God."* Thus, it is not necessary to craft a list of sins in order to instill fear in people. However, may the Church continue to make clear that rejecting Christ is the surest path to rejecting God's forgiveness of sin and embracing the fires of hell! It is not merely that people cannot dwell with God unless they are absolved of their sin through the Christian faith, as if mere intellectual assent to a set of dogmas was the cure. It's that God himself has extended his hand of friendship, offering the forgiveness of sins to all who seek it, resting in the death of Jesus as a ransom for sacrifice in personal faith.

While other religions offer spiritual immortality and reincarnation, the blessed hope of Christ is the resurrection of the dead, as the Council reiterated and the Creed declares. Not a spiritual resurrection, but a physical one, where the soul is rebound to the body on the new earth, with Christ as King. This isn't something we create or define, but the scheme of Jesus Christ himself, who has been declared to be both Savior and Judge.

We must not tolerate even a whiff of false teaching. Although treason is a capital punishment, and one might be tempted to similarly deem heretics worthy of execution, know that the wrath of God is stored up for them instead! Nothing from their mouths can be tolerated. Let their deeds act as a clarion call to warn others against falling away. Instead, we must pay greater attention to what we have heard from the testimony of the Church, so that we do not drift away from it. It is unchanging, and the survival of the faith is not dependent upon keeping it relevant for the tickling ears of the masses.

Above all, dear brothers and sisters in the faith, remember the essence of Christianity is found in the words of our Lord, who when asked the greatest command he spoke thusly: *"you shall love the Lord your God with all your heart, and with all your soul, and with all your mind, and with all your strength.' The second is this, 'You shall love your neighbor as yourself.' There is no other commandment greater than these."* Let us rejoice with unity in these commands, being mindful to obey all of what Christ taught us and serving our neighbor in humility and love.

The pair stood in stunned silence, the weight of the words and gravity of their revelation setting in.

Did he say what I think he said?

CHAPTER 16
DIRSIYAH, LIBYA.

Gapinski whistled as he slow-walked around the beut resting in the over-sized, darkened, hot-and-humid hangar of corrugated metal smelling of Aunt Betty a hop-skip-and-a-jump from the Gulfstream that had just touched down at Al-Marj Airport. Glad to have his dogs back on the ground after what happened back across the pond.

Especially with the hunk of German metal and rubber and leather staring him down.

Had had some mechanical difficulties coming out of Rome in the wee hours of the night after Silas and Celeste took off. An indicator light flared up something fierce. After what happened in Miami on some wild goose-chase mission to Nicaragua a few years ago, he was more than happy to delay their travels and let the grease monkeys get their hands dirty under the hood.

That is, until they were told there was no going back into the city for more R&R beforehand. Had to wait it out inside the plane sitting on the tarmac until all was well. Which suited Torres just fine, since the plush leather seats seemed suited for her Latin frame. Snored to beat the band the whole time, which wasn't even the worst of it.

Gapinski was usually beholden to the hometown Gulfstream manufacturer from Georgia, but General Dynamics had nothing on Mercedes-Benz, at least for the make and model that was supposed to be carting their butts across North Africa. Seats were definitely not for his Southern-fed, six-foot-four frame.

So while Torres slept the hours away without a care in the world, he tossed his way with mumbled curses through the drilling and jackhammering and fiddling around under the bird's hood. About the only thing that kept him sane was the well-stocked minibar. Even then, the accompanying bag of peanuts and pretzels couldn't fill a thimble!

Three hours later, they finally ditched the plane for another SEPIO bird that had come in from the field for a debrief on the current situation that got the Order's knickers in a twist. An hour after that, the SEPIO pair finally made the hour-plus-change jump across the pond back to the godforsaken sands of Libya.

Gapinski had complained loudly the first time they'd landed a few days ago. Didn't see no point traipsing around the country that threw his own country the middle finger eight years ago when the embassy was attacked by radical Islamic whack jobs. It would be another year before he'd get out of the military, but he was stationed in Germany as a Marine liaison with the Airforce when the whole crapstorm was brewing. Remembered well the bodies showing up at Ramstein Air Base, coffins draped by American flags. He wanted to load up then and there and be the first boots on the ground for Uncle Sam's response. It never happened, except for a fifty-member Marine FAST team being sent to Libya to 'bolster security,' and a posse of feds to 'investigate' the atrocities, and increased surveillance by unmanned drones to 'hunt for the attackers.' All of which was an expensive way of brushing the whole cotton pickin' thing under the rug to appease the watching world.

So when the Order came to root around some basilica stuck in the sand a few days ago, the jarhead alumnus wasn't happy. Didn't open his yapper then nor when Silas sent him back with Torres to follow up on a cryptic word from Bishop Zarruq in search of some imperial seal lost to history. But he was a grumbly, mumbly mess the flight over.

The only silver lining was the gray beast he was climbing into, his head growing dizzy and fingers tingling from massaging the sweet, smooth leather. Like a freshly powdered baby's bottom.

More than made up for the night's hassle.

He flexed his fingers, as if a marathoner readying for a race, then pushed the '*Start*' button. The twin-turbo V8 engine roared to life.

"Now that's what I'm talking about..."

Torres finished loading their gear in the back, the typical SEPIO package of satcom units with direct connects to Zoe back at HQ in Washington for mission support, a couple of high-powered SIG Sauer MCX rifles, a pair of SIG P320 full-size pistols with backup magazines, night vision goggles and binoculars—in other word the usual getup for the Church's band of roving Navy SEALs for Jesus.

She closed the trunk and hopped in the front. "What is it with you and these hunks of Italian-engineered junk, anyway? You're like obsess—"

Gapinski gasped with interruption, grabbing his chest with dramatic flair. "Di—" he swallowed hard and coughed. "Did you say junk?" He scoffed and held up a finger. "Not only that, but *Italian*-engineered?"

He peeled out of the hangar and out onto a service road, the Libyan landscape bleached by the blinding mid-morning sun.

"This Mercedes *German*-engineered G-Class 500," he went on, "pairs upscale refinement with off-road ruggedness. Definitely not a hunk of junk. I'd say the perfect combo for any

SEPIO mission and anything Nous or those crazy box-men whack jobs or Braun or whoever wants to throw whatever at us!"

"Yeah, yeah, yeah. Silas know about your little expenditure? Seem to remember him putting the kibosh on these sorts of things."

"Silas gave me carte blanche—"

"To find the golden cylinder!" Torres said. "Not hot rodding in the Libyan outback in four-figure SUVs."

"Pretty sure the outback's an Austrian thing."

"Au-*stralian*."

"Oh, yeah. Always get them mixed up. Irregardless—"

"Not a word."

Gapinski twisted up his face as he pulled out onto the main drag. "Whatcha talkin' about? Irregardless. As in, without concern as to advice, warning, or hardship."

"Which is simply *re*-gardless."

"Tomato, tomahto. Let's call the whole thing off and get to the task at hand, shall we?"

Torres snickered. "Just bustin' your chops, Hoss."

He threw her a frown. "Ha, ha, ha. Very funny. Sure, mock the fella who had the foresight to get us a sweet ride for our Libyan gig. You'll thank me later, with all this creamy leather and V8 horsepower."

"It's all Greek to me. Mercedes this, BMW that."

"Upscale refinement with off-road ruggedness, Torres. That's where it's at. And Mercedes offers it in spades. Besides, Silas and I came to an understanding after the hostel fiasco last mission in Miami."

"If you say so."

"Anyway...so Ptolemais," Gapinski said, passing a supermarket with the scent of grilled meat and baking bread that made him remember how hungry he was.

Torres nodded. "The port and former archdiocesan city of

the Pentapolis during the early centuries of the Church. And dead ahead in modern Dirsiyah."

Gapinski merged into another artery flowing with steady traffic, bringing the GPS navigation to life and charting a course. "What's the deal with the city, anyway? Why'd Silas send us here?"

"Apparently, it was one of several Libyan cities where the earliest Sabellian teachings flourished."

"Cabelas who?"

"No, not the sporting goods store, dingbat. *Sabellian.*"

"What's that?"

"Not sure exactly, but something that connects to our boy Arius. Something about downplaying the divinity of Jesus."

"Which also connects to our conspiracy du jour about the Nicene Creed."

"That's right," Torres said. "I did a bit of research on the flight over, and apparently the succession of bishops in the city during the years surrounding the council that led to the Church's theological code included Arian bishops. In fact, Secundus, who was bishop of Ptolemais during the day and a patron of Arius, was listed among those present at the Council."

"That's deep."

"I'd say. The dude was a delegate of ancient Libya to the First Ecumenical Council of Nicaea who advocated the Arian view and defended Arius himself."

"So what's here to explore?"

She shifted in her seat toward Gapinski. "A basilica. Built according to the typical threefold leaf floor plan similar to what we were digging at the past several months in Apollonia. With three naves, a chamber off the north side, and thick Byzantine walls that still remain in spots."

"Sounds like our city then."

"For sure. The city has an interesting connection to

Constantine, too."

"Really? Two for the price of one, then."

"Basically. A magnificent archway was built in dedication to his victory in Rome. A large, lively Christian community existed in the city, and for five hundred years they roamed the streets and worshiped in homes—until the Arabs ravaged it like much of North Africa. Decimated the Christian population, along with the Jewish one as well, through forced conversion to Islam, or death. Excavations of the site began in 1935, but have languished."

"Well, aren't you just a regular Wikipedia entry of info..." Gapinski muttered.

Torres turned to him. "Excuse you, but what bee crawled up your rear?"

He glanced her way and frowned. "Sorry. Just starving, is all. Haven't eaten since—"

"The flight over?"

He scoffed. "Like a packet of peanuts the size of my pinky! Anyway, blood sugar's getting low, and if I don't get something in me quick, my stomach's gonna start chewin' at my ribcage."

"I'd prefer turning into a pumpkin to that visual..." She stretched out in her seat and fished something out from her pocket, then tossed it into Gapinski's lap.

He twisted up his face and picked it up by two fingers. "A Clifbar?"

"Always carry a spare with me, just in case."

"What am I supposed to do with this?"

"Uh, eat it?"

He threw it a disdainful look, right before Torres snatched it back.

"Fine, you don't want it—"

"No, no, no! I'll take it. Blood sugar, remember? Blood sugar!"

She threw it back in his lap. "Alright, Mr. Crankypants."

He tore it open and took a bite. "Thanks. And not half bad. Reminds me of Grandpappy's raisin cookies, all chewy and oaty and, well, raisiny."

She laughed. "You're welcome."

"And to answer your earlier question about my obsession with cars, it was Grandpappy who roped me into it all. Brought me to car shows in neighboring Atlanta. Him and me even restored a '57 Monte Carlo. So, yeah, it was all Grandpappy..."

The SUV fell silent, except for the humming V8 engine and outdoors.

Torres put a hand on his knee, sending a welcomed jolt up his thigh.

"How have you been since his death? It's been over a year now, hasn't it?"

He took a breath and nodded. "Yeah. Emotions come and go. Some days worse than others. But mostly try to focus on all the memories, you know? How he literally saved my life..."

"Sounds like he was great."

He smiled. "He was...A gentleman and a scholar, he was, for sure."

They left the hustle and bustle of the town and into the countryside, heading for the basilican ruins.

"So, it's been a while since we've paired up," Gapinski said, tossing the last remains of the Clifbar into his mouth.

Torres said, "Wasn't the last time hunting down Farhad, chasing after the Passion relics?"

"Yeah, I think you're right. God rest his soul."

"Speaking of which, that reminds me..."

"Yeah, what's that?"

She turned toward him. "You never told me how you got roped into this gig."

He laughed. "Now that's a story."

"Looks to me like we've got time. Come on, Hoss. Spill it."

He put the SUV into cruise control and leaned back. "It's

like most things in life, right? A funny combination of luck and God's providential intervention. Though I tend to err on the side of the Almighty poking his finger in our business more than just fate messing with us."

"What do you mean?"

"Well, near the end of my time with the Marines, I wandered into a church in Germany. One of those big, stony monstrosities, with stained glass and a big pipe organ smelling like wet wood and old people. Sat down in front of some dude during one of the mid-afternoon prayer times to contemplate where on earth I was heading and what on earth I was doing with my life."

"I hear that," Torres agreed. "Spent a bunch of days at a cathedral in Miami after I was canned by my uncle."

"So get this," Gapinski went on, "afterward I got to talking to the guy behind me. Could tell I was an American and wondered what I was doing in Kaiserslautern, the nearest city where the air base was located. Told him I was nearing the end with my duties with Uncle Sam, came to pray about next steps and all that jazz. Then the guy offers me a job, right then and there. Turns out the guy was some Master of a super-secret religious order that had been protecting the Church and the faith for centuries."

"Radcliffe?"

"Righto. We got a bite to eat and talked more about it all. I basically went for the free beer and bratwurst, thought he was a bit off his rocker and needed someone to humor him. But the more he went on about Project SEPIO, the Order's Navy SEALs for Jesus outfit, as we've been called, the more this reassuring warmth and this peace began to overtake me. Like it was meant to be, you know?"

"Radcliffe certainly has that effect on people."

Gapinski chuckled at the memory of the man. "Sure does. Or rather, did. Anyway, apparently he was in the area on Order business and stumbled into the church himself. Never did find out what it was all about, but he said the Lord up and told him to do his morning prayers at the joint."

"Weird..."

"Right? I mean, I had heard the whole 'the Lord works in mysterious ways' mantra in my neck of the Bible-belt woods. Never had it happen to me personally, God dropping into my life all cloak-and-dagger like, moving so obviously and weirdly, as you put it. That was six years ago, and haven't looked back since."

"Mysterious ways, indeed," Torres said. "And here you are, barreling down the backroads of Libya, driving a six-figure hunk of *German*-engineered metal toward a stack of ancient Christian ruins."

He laughed. "Don't you know it. Speaking of which..."

He eased the Mercedes SUV to a stop off the road, pointing toward a set of ruins that looked like the ribcage of some picked-over prehistoric dinosaur—with partial walls and columns jutting up from the rocky ground this way and that.

But that wasn't all of it. Not even the best part.

Tents. Six or seven of them. The same canvas monstrosities SEPIO had been using just a few days ago before all hell broke loose.

And there was a good chance the Devil himself was holed up in there somewhere. With not one golden goose, but two, maybe three.

Gapinski shut off the car. "You hear about any other dig going on in these parts the last few months?"

Torres shook her head. "*Nada.* And believe me, had something of this scale been carrying on in our backyard, I would have heard about it."

"Which means this was slapped together the last day or so."

"Right after Braun launched his little treasure hunt competition on WeSolve."

"Which also means these ain't friendlies, ready to invite us over for tea and crumpets."

"No doubt Nous or the other crazy whack jobs with boxmen tattoos. And they beat us to the punch."

"Always something..." Gapinski growled, rolling down his window for fresh air.

It was cool and tinged with salted fish, blowing in off the Mediterranean a few kilometers up the way. Not another soul around, other than the mess of worker bees digging up the ancient Christian site like it was nobody's business.

"What a desecration..." Torres muttered, the pair continuing to take in the view. "All that history, just getting picked over like that. Where's the respect? Vultures, all of them."

"I guess respect for the past ain't worth a whole lot when a billion bucks are on the line."

"We should find a spot to plant ourselves for a while. Take in the lay of the land before we go in and bust open some heads."

Gapinski craned his neck, spotting a cluster of tightly packed trees that butted up against the archaeological site half a klick north. Looked like a decent spot for observing the enemy and planning their infiltration.

He twisted the steering wheel and went off-road, aiming for the perch.

Torres gave a yelp and braced herself against the window as it bounded over the rough terrain.

Gapinski chuckled. "What did I tell ya, Torres? Upscale refinement with off-road ruggedness."

"Yeah, right..."

Soon Gapinski was backing up their ride into the foot of the forest, low branches scraping against the roof and swallowing it whole. Would take a real set of eagle eyes to spot them secreted away. He threw it into *'Park'* and shut off the engine, then the SEPIO pair got to work.

Torres threw open the trunk hatch and opened another of the black cases housing their gear. She grabbed one of the binoculars and handed one off to Gapinski. He threw it around his neck and accepted one of the satcom units as well.

She said, "Probably best to leave the firepower alone once we get the lay of the land."

"No way, sister." He flipped the lid to another case and grinned. "You're forgetting Gapinski's first rule when engaging potential pseudo-spiritual whack job terrorists."

"Oh, yeah? And what's that?"

He held out one of the P320s before shoving another in the front of his pants. "Never leave home without cold, hard steel. And in our case, never leave our Mercedes G-Class without cold, hard steel."

Torres smirked and accepted the gift, as well as a backup magazine. "Whatever you say. You're the boss."

"You'll thank me later." Gapinski grabbed the two MXC rifles, handing one to Torres.

She held up a hand. "Not my kind of firepower, Hoss." Instead, she grabbed a smaller caliber handgun that she stuffed at her boot.

He shrugged. "Suit yourself." Then he closed the rear door and sauntered to the edge of the treeline. Torres followed, the wind whipping the dry Libyan ground spread before them on an updraft of heat that made him want to climb back into the air-conditioned comforts of their ride.

Using the binoculars, they started scanning the remains down below.

There they were. A handful of pseudo-spiritual whack job terrorists running around, draped in taupey garb with black and tan man scarves wrapped around their heads and face. And brandishing black weapons that looked like they'd seen a fight or twelve.

"Sure got the jump on us…" Torres said.

Sure did. Gapinski focused on the tents, a massive one at the center with two smaller ones on each side and a few more, scanning the area from each of the dwellings to count off the visible hostiles. Thirteen, so far. Bad ju-ju number, that's for sure.

"Are we sure this is Nous," she went on, "or that other mystery sect? Granted, not sure I've ever seen this kind of firepower at an archaeological dig before, but—"

"There! Center tent," Gapinski interrupted, pointing out into the desert void. "The Ringling Bros and Barnum & Bailey big-top tent at the center."

Stepping out into the blinding, hateful sun was a familiar face.

"That *idiota* from Apollonia," Torres cursed. "The one who stole my golden cylinder!"

"Don't you mean *our* golden cylinder?"

"Whatever. I found it, fair and square."

"A bit possessive over our desert-junk finds, aren't we?"

She scoffed. "You try sweating it out for months on end, getting eaten alive by bugs and baking in the desert sun, dirty and stinky and sandy and then come—"

Gapinski whistled with interruption, extending a hand again toward the dig site. "Would ya lookie there...."

Torres gasped. "Bishop Zarruq..."

"And the Head Honcho himself, all blond and coifed."

Sebastian Grey.

"You're just jealous he has hair," Torres said. "But, yeah. There they are. Sebastian and that Chuke character. At least Zarruq is looking good."

"Looking alive, maybe. But who knows what those whack jobs did to him."

"Which means we've got two missions now. The next clue and the bishop."

Gapinski went to offer a reply when a rustling and crack cut him off.

"What the..."

He spun around to find one of the hostiles staring them down, an automatic rifle aiming for Gapinski's head. Tall guy about his height who could stand to use a few Big Macs to put some meat on his bones. His taupey getup all billowy and dripping off his sad frame.

Which should make it easy to put the poor guy down, if it came to that.

The man, face shrouded by one of those Persian man scarves, started slinging a bunch of Arabic their way. Voice high and heady, weapon waving around all frantic and frazzled. A Russian made AK assault rifle, by the look of it. Big, black thing, too. Could do a lot of damage if he wasn't careful.

"Hold up, bub," Gapinski said. "We no speak Arab. *Hablo ingles, por favor.*"

Torres scoffed. "Why do *gringos* always default to *español* whenever there's a language barrier? And it's *habla*, not *hablo* knuckle—"

"What are you doing, standing here in trees?" Arab Man shouted with interruption.

Gapinski lifted the binoculars. "Bird watching?"

He rattled the rifle, which made Gapinski chuckle at the dramatic flair.

Then he waved it toward the dig site. "Come with me! Both of you."

"No, no," Gapinski said, stepping forward with hands raised. "We didn't see anything, pal. Just a bunch of desert sparrows. A real let down, actually. Was hoping to catch a glimpse of the Yelkouan shearwater. All we got was bupkis on that one. Although, I guess we're too far inland to—"

"Silence!" Arab Man shouted. Then he grabbed Torres by the arm and shoved her into Gapinski.

Wrong move, pal.

An angry heat ran up his back and blossomed at his neck. He narrowed his eyes and dipped his head. "Now, is that any way to treat a lady, Aladdin?"

With hands still raised, in one motion Gapinski slapped a massive open paw on the side of the carbine barrel, stage left, clenching it like a vice and wrenching it from the man's grip with ease—all of it happening in a flash before he butted the poor bastard square in the face with the stock.

Gapinski almost felt bad for the guy, stealing his manhood like that with one puff of air.

Almost.

He spun the weapon around and took aim as he crumbled down to the ground like a used bathrobe.

"*Dios mío!* Where did you learn to do that, Hoss?" Torres exclaimed.

Gapinski knelt beside the man and checked him over for any other weapons. "Marines, sister. Where else?"

"The few, the proud, right?"

"Damn straight."

Coming up dry, he flipped him over and yanked down the man's collar.

"What are you—"

"Checking for ink. Nothing, which means the dude ain't one of the new kids on the block."

Torres leaned in for a look. "No box-man tat. What about the wrist?"

"Checking now..."

He frowned. But not out of surprise, but irritation at the confirmation.

"There we have it, then," Torres said at the familiar intersecting lines bent at each of the four ends.

Gapinski stood and nodded. "Nous."

"Was there any doubt?"

"Never know. But that means the dude was on some sort of patrol from the main camp."

"Which means he's going to be missed at some point."

Gapinski said nothing, but she was right. Not good prospects for laying low in the near future.

Torres smiled and shuffled around to the guy. "I have an idea. Help me take off his clothes."

"Umm, if you have a thing for the fella, maybe we should wait until he regains consciousness."

Torres slung a string of Spanish under her breath, which he took as cussing. "No, knucklehead. We're going to undress the dude so you can take his clothes, put them on, walk into camp as one of the pseudo-spiritual whack job terrorists, rescue Zarruq, and swipe whatever they've found."

"Oh, is that all…"

"I'm serious! Come on, help me get—"

"Whoa, whoa, whoa," Gapinski said, waving his arms. "You seriously want me to traipse into a camp crawling with hostiles like a fox in a henhouse and steal the goose that laid the golden cylinder?"

"I think you're mixing metaphors there, Hoss. But, when in Rome…"

"In case you haven't noticed, we're not in Rome anymore, sister. We're in Libya!"

"Even better."

"Are you insane!"

"You got any better ideas? Besides, it's the perfect ruse!"

"Except I don't speak Arabic. You heard me! I can barely string two English sentences together let alone the *langue française du territoire libyen*!"

"Did you seriously just speak French?"

"Dated a French lass back in the Marines."

Torres frowned. "I think you'll be fine."

Gapinski sighed, running a hand across his bald head.

"Except the dude I took out looks about a hundred pounds wet. Don't you think his posse will think something's afoot if I come waltzing into town stuffed inside his threads?"

She shrugged. "Maybe. But what else can we do? You saw the place. It's at least seven to one out there. You got a better idea?"

He opened his mouth to answer, then held his breath and held it open.

He didn't. And he instantly knew it was the right play.

Then he closed his mouth and frowned before huffing with resignation.

"Fine. You win. Help me get his pants."

Within minutes, they'd stripped the poor lad down to his skivvies, and Gapinski had managed to stuff himself inside Arab Man's clothes—complete with the dudes Hammer pants, billowy shirt, gloves. Even got the headscarf to cooperate around his head and face. Although, he was already feeling like he was drowning in his own hot and humid breath.

Torres cocked her head with assessment. "You look the part enough to get into camp. After that, who knows…"

He frowned and tossed her the keys. "How reassuring. Keep her safe for me, alright? I wanna be able to get my deposit back."

"Yeah, yeah. And don't sweat the objective, Hoss. You'll be fine. Besides, if you get into trouble, I've got your back. But don't forget—"

She tossed him Arab Man's assault rifle. Gapinski caught it with one hand.

Then he took a breath and nodded. "Alright, sister. Here goes nothing."

He crossed himself, which felt weird because he grew up Southern Baptist, but it felt right. Then he plunged out of the trees into the desert void.

On toward destiny.

CHAPTER 17
ISTANBUL.

Silas's heart was pounding, his head following suit, hammers of confusion rapping against his mind over what he had read and translated aloud for Celeste.

Had he read that right? Had he *translated* that right? He went back over it, reading the original Latin from the top.

"Did he say what I think he said?" Celeste offered as he re-translated his work. "I mean, did he *confirm* what I think he confirmed?"

Silas looked at her, taking in a measured breath. He swallowed and nodded. "That for his last dying breath, Emperor Constantine basically confirmed the essence of the Christian faith—you mean, is that what I think he said, what he confirmed?"

She sucked in a breath of her own and nodded. "Basically."

He went back to the fragment, picking back up where he left off in his confirmation.

"But why would he write this," Celeste asked, "of all things before his death?"

"And apparently, just before his baptism?"

The pair fell silent, Silas continuing to read back over the fragment under the tree as the early dawn began widening into the full morning, a curious ray of hope niggling at the back of his brain.

He muttered, "I'm wondering if this thing is at all what we think it is…"

"What do you mean? What could it be instead?"

He set down the fragment. "Think about it. We've assumed this has been some sort of repudiation or at least some sort of recantation of Emperor Constantine's Christian faith—and then something that confirmed what the religious conspiracy theorists have been peddling for decades, that the Emperor basically created Christianity to serve his powerful, political ends."

"That's because it bloody well sounded like it!"

"Yes, but only from a handful of fragments. Now…" He returned to the part of Constantine's confession that felt far different.

Celeste folded her arms and stared off in contemplation. "Alright, but what about that first paragraph?"

"What of it?"

She took the fragment and pointed at its last sentence, beginning to reread it aloud: *"Thus, I offer the following dogma—"*

"Wait a minute," Silas interrupted. "You can read Latin?"

She scoffed. "Of course, love. I am Oxford educated, after all."

"Then why didn't you tell me?"

"Wanted to let you have all the translating fun," she said with a wink. "Anyway, look here." She pointed again and read, *"'Thus I offer the following dogma as a means to foster and perpetuate that which we have hammered and honed the past two decades.'* That bloody well sounds like what the Markus Brauns and Noland Rotbergs of the world have been crowing about for decades."

"That Constantine created Christianity, that he influenced what the Church believed and practiced."

Celeste nodded. "Right, at the expense of other minority voices. Fostering and perpetuating, hammering and honing what he and his co-conspirators wanted to become the dominant view within the Church for the sake of the Empire, not to mention Constantine's own political ambitions—and the Church's"

Silas folded his arms. "You sound like the Brauns and Rotbergs of the world."

"Only the messenger, love. Neither advocating nor parroting the message itself. So put away the daggers."

He smiled and nodded, then leaned back on the bench, considering it all—what they had witnessed and read and discovered. From the initial find in Libya, with its cryptic references, to the one Braun himself had uncovered, to the man's treasure-hunting contest and the subsequent revelations of his brother's involvement.

Again.

Then there were all the historical and theological dimensions. Constantine's seemingly on-again, off-again relationship with Arius, the heretic who had tried to re-write the Church's understanding of Jesus' identity, overemphasizing his creatureliness and humanity at the expense of his divinity and co-equality with God the Father. The early Church bishop who was at the center of the reason for the Nicene Creed in the first place.

There was something about it all that they were missing. Something—

Silas sat up, remembering the other missing element from the cylinder they had found.

"Pass me the golden goose, would you?"

Celeste handed it to him. She had twisted the end cap back into place, so he twisted it back off and tipped it.

Out tumbled the familiar metal piece, landing in his hand. Same jagged edges, same etched lines on its face.

Except this time...

"Hold on." Silas held up the metal fragment, taking out his smartphone and shining its light onto the metal object's face.

And confused by what he saw.

"Check this—"

The emerging morning was pierced by *rat-a-tat-tat* gunfire, the stout sycamore behind them exploding with menacing violence, splintered wood and shredded leaves falling around them.

The metal fragment tumbled from Silas's hand at the sudden turn. He went to reach for it when Celeste grabbed him by the collar and dragged him to the ground.

The object skipped off the bench and path before landing in the grass.

Just as another round of *rat-a-tat-tats* buzzed them overhead and splintered more of the tree.

Still managing to hold fast to the cylinder, Silas stuffed the parchment inside then slapped the top back in place and twisted it shut.

"Run!" he yelled, leaping to his feet and dashing around the wide berth of the sycamore, Celeste close behind.

They lunged behind the tree for protection, finding it just in time as another set of *rat-a-tat-tats* thudded into the wood.

"Thanks for the save," he grunted, withdrawing his Beretta and twisting toward the onslaught. "I owe you one."

"Believe the debt is mounting with every passing SEPIO mission, love." She threw him a wink before slinging a *pop-pop-pop* leaden rejoinder into the park, all shots going high and wide and meant more as a deterrent than anything. "Where the bloody hell did they come from?"

"And who the bloody hell are they?" Silas replied, offering

his own *pop-pop-pop* reply to hold off the hostiles before stealing a look around the tree trunk.

Six of them, that he could see, coming down the embankment leading to the wall in front of the museum.

"Must have been after the same thing we were after."

"What's the American saying? Finders keepers, losers weepers?"

Silas chuckled. "Something like that."

"So what do we do?" Celeste said, twisting around for a look herself.

"Get the heck out of Dodge?"

"I count six, taking up positions now behind the other trees. Wearing black and bearing long-barreled rifles."

"Sounds like your perfect bargain-bin Kindle thriller, black-clad villains and all."

"Sure, but from SEPIO's experience it's the truth of the matter when it comes to hostiles at the center of a conspiracy to take down the Church. At least it's three to one."

"Vegas odds."

She popped off *one-two-three* shots, grinning afterward and blowing the top of her barrel. "Make that five."

"Show off."

She grinned. "Always."

He smirked. "And now much better SEPIO odds as far we've had recently."

"How about we get ourselves back to the car, shall we?"

"First things first. Give me covering fire."

"What for?"

He leaned out and nodded back toward the bench, another set of *pop-pop-pops* forcing him back behind the tree for cover.

That was a close one.

He swallowed hard and said, "The metal fragment. I dropped it in the grass."

"Who cares! We've got the bloomin' fragment and Creed copy. What more do we need?"

"Caught sight of something on the face of the metal before hostiles showed up. Might be something about it that matters to this whole blasted conspiracy."

She sighed and shook her head. "If you say so, Master Grey." She aimed her SIG Sauer back out into the park. "Ready?"

He nodded, handing Celeste the cylinder for safekeeping. Then he took aim and fired before shuffling out from behind the tree and over beside the bench.

Celeste followed suit, popping off *one-two-three-four* rounds to give him cover.

Which was just enough to get him to kneel at the side of the bench before the hostiles themselves opened up fire.

It was a decent spot, shielding him from a direct hit of the five remaining hostiles, whoever they were. Could be Sebatian's goons, could be the new mystery sect sporting box-men tattoos they hadn't yet pinned down. All they knew was that they were somehow working with Braun and Rotberg on—whatever the heck they were doing!

Either way, he wouldn't last long before he used up his nine lives and was sent packing to Saint Pete's pearly gates.

So he got to work searching for the metal fragment even as more gunfire started coming in hot and heavy, splintering off the obese sycamore behind and skittering along the concrete path at the base of the bench.

Didn't know what exactly, but the set of lines had made a curious bend and point that looked different from Nous's calling card, which they thought had been some sort of signal from the past of the Church's enemy's involvement in the conspiracy. Could have just been a variation or some scratches from the passage of time, but there was something about the new medallion piece that looked different.

And raised questions.

But there was nothing lying on the path, and nothing on the bench itself.

Where the heck is this cotton pickin' thi—

Then he saw it. Glinting in the grass from the morning sun rising higher now. A bit far for comfort, but he would have to go for it.

Go big or go home, as they say.

As well as now or never.

He took a breath and crossed himself on instinct. Old Catholic habit, he guessed. But it was also appropriate, making the sign of the cross and all. Never hurt to invoke Christ's protection when launching oneself headlong into no uncertain doom for the sake of the Church.

Especially for the sake of the Church. Because if the last few years taught him anything, fighting for the Christian faith was the most dangerous of all lines of work.

Before lunging out for the prize, he steadied his aim toward the closest hostile. Might as well make his covering fire count for something.

Man in black, face masked and edging out from behind a skinnier sycamore than they'd been using.

Perfect.

The top of the bench splintered before he could act, sending him crouching for cover.

Silas recovered once a window opened up and retook his aim, searching for the sycamore among a sea of lookalikes and sizing them up for—

There you are...

He popped off *one-two-three-four* rounds before making his move, Celeste joining in as well, opening up a relentless cover as he swiped the metal fragment from the grass—catching a glimpse of the hostile snapping backward before crumpling to the ground.

Rushing back to the tree, Silas rounded it for cover just as the edges splintered with menacing violence, one of the bullets grazing his back before sailing past into the park.

He cried out, more from surprise than pain, twisting an arm around to feel the damage.

"Cutting it a little close there, love," Celeste said, twisting back around herself. "You alright?"

"Just a scratch." More than that, actually. Hurt like crazy. "But yeah, close call."

Celeste lifted his shirt and winced. "A good bloody grazing that will leave a scar, I reckon. But no more damage."

"Like I said, close call. I'll be fine."

She slid out an empty magazine and shoved a fresh one inside. "Got what you were looking for?"

Silas nodded, checking his own magazine for damage. A quarter tank left. He swapped it for his other one, sticking it in his back pocket for back up.

"Safe and sound," he said, "but now what?"

There had been a brief lull in the firefight, but now it was picking back up again. Sounding more like the kind of feigned offering he himself might put up if he were advancing forward.

Which he confirmed when he glanced around the sycamore's girth.

Four left, picking their way toward them from tree to tree.

Silas twisted back in a huff. "This isn't working. We're pinned here. And before long either the police are going to show or the hostiles will overtake us. Which would be bad either way because this—" he retrieved the golden cylinder from Celeste and held it up. "This would fall into hands we don't need right now."

"We should split up then," Celeste said. "Draw their fire in two directions."

"Good idea. Then meet back at the entrance and get the heck out of here."

She popped off a *one-two-three* warning shot, clearly ready to get to it, then nodded. "Right. Meet you back at the car."

"Wait—" Silas reached down at his boot and handed her his Army knife. "Just in case."

She smirked and took it, shoving it at her own boot. "You need this more than I. But thanks for the backup just the same."

"On three?"

"Screw three! No use dilly dallying when hostiles are at the ramparts."

Good point.

Another spatter of gunfire confirmed it, and she gave him a kiss on the cheek before running north, toward the fence perpendicular to the one leading to the exit and their car.

He twisted around and offered some covering fire of his own before taking off stage right back toward the entrance.

Praying to the good Lord above he kept his fiancé safe.

And him.

CHAPTER 18

In short order, Silas saw her plan unfold for the good, peeling off a pair closest to him.

Which meant the other two went tearing after Celeste.

But he knew she could take care of herself. Probably better than he could take care of himself.

So he shoved the golden cylinder at his back and took off down the path they had come down earlier, not giving the hostiles a foothold in their pursuit. Smaller trees lined the path, as well as some lamp posts along with benches, so there was enough intervening barriers to cover his escape.

Glancing back, in the light of the now blazing morning sun filtering into the park through the ancient trees, he could see one of the hostiles raising his weapon to meet the challenge.

Silas spun back and fired off a *one-two-three* punch, bobbing on the pads of his feet like a champion boxer and offering another *pop-pop-pop* before twisting back and continuing his retreat.

Tearing down the walkway, he spotted in the distance the white limestone entrance they had come through hours ago before dawn. Then he spotted a perfect rest stop along the way that would give him a chance to regroup. Another one of those gnarled, well-endowed sycamores.

An angry rejoinder to his covering fire started up from behind, so he sprinted for it.

When a homeless man lying on the bench they passed earlier sat up, stiff as a board.

Startled him crapless, seeing another figure pop up like that! Although, the man himself was probably startled crapless by the weapon fire and Silas running toward him with two black-clad hostiles in hot pursuit.

He yelled, "Get dow—"

The man's head snapped back with interruption, a single bullet hole blooming with blood before the back of the bench shattered. He tumbled overboard, face first onto the cobblestone path.

Silas mumbled a curse under his breath and crossed himself as he zagged past the man onto the grass toward the tree he had spotted earlier, fully knowing that bullet was meant for him.

He ducked behind the wide sycamore, another *one-two* rounds echoing from behind and sinking into its trunk.

Instead of continuing on, he took advantage of the rest stop to regroup, glancing back to find the nameless face bleeding out on the stone walkway and one of the perpetrators padding between the trees. Still a ways off but closing in fast.

He extended his weapon around his tree, most of his body protected by its trunk and took aim.

Take this, you bastard...

With a *one-two* punch he dropped him hard, the man crumpling from a headshot, the back shattering away.

Which seemed like appropriate payback justice for the homeless man.

He pivoted around to the other side, separate weapon fire

echoing toward him from the distance now, Celeste clearly getting into it with the other two hostiles.

Or, more likely, the other two getting into it with her. He felt sorry for them!

Easing around, he eyed the park from where he had come.

Nothing. No one.

The one guy he had dropped—or gal, depending on whether the box-men tat mystery sect was an equal opportunity employer—he was lying still now at the base of a trunk. But there should have been one more left.

Yet no one else was near.

The back of his lizard brain was sending up all kinds of red-flag signals now, screaming the same kind of caution and care and circumspection that kept humanity alive from the Stone Age through the Bronze Age all the way through post-classical history until Adam and Eve's progeny dropped the atomic bomb—which pretty much threw out all the caution and care and circumspection from humanity's built-in playbook, but still.

He wasn't going to make a move until he knew what was what. No need to get gobbled by a mastodon when one could muster up some patience and wait a few beats for the target to make an appearance. Same went for hostiles in Iraq back in the day and the pseudo-spiritual whack jobs roaming out in front of Istanbul's museum of archeology.

He pivoted back around to the other side for a better view.

Same story, same red-flag signals.

Silas gripped his weapon tighter, aiming for the trees beyond the bench where the body of the bastard he'd taken out still lay. Searching, discerning, intuiting any sort of movement or shift in the shadows or—

He heard it before he saw it.

Then he felt it.

A strong arm, thick with cords of muscle from a muscle-head who'd been preparing his whole life for that moment, reached around from behind—cinching with a vice grip that threatened to collapse Silas's neck while pressing a pistol against his temple.

"Where is the golden cylinder?" a gravelly voice growled in his ear.

On instinct, Silas arched his back and reached a hand up to pry away the arm. "I think you've mistaken me for someone else," he said lowly, voice choked by the hostile's grip. "I'm just the gardener."

"Stop the games, Grey. I know you have it. Saw you and that vixen of yours scurry away."

The man kept at it, tightening with bulging arms and threatening to cut off Silas's air. Hurt like a mother, too. And he knew if he didn't do something soon, it would be lights out and he'd be out the golden goose.

Time to roll the dice and put all those basic-training dollars Uncle Sam threw at him to work. Never trained for this specific scenario, but he'd been through enough sticky wickets to know how to handle himself.

He just prayed his head didn't end up blown off like the poor homeless man lying face down a few yards away.

Figuring the best way out was down, he collapsed his legs into a pretzel curled underneath, forcing the goon to support his two-hundred-some-odd pounds of nearly middle-age muscle and bones in a flash.

Almost popped his head off, but it worked.

Hanging for a second as the momentum shifted, the goon began tilting forward at the unexpected shift before letting go.

Giving Silas the window to use every one of those middle-age muscles at his core and back and hips to twist onto his back and sink three into the man's chest, the golden cylinder digging into his spine.

The goon recoiled, popping off a sudden burst himself at the shift.

One round came dangerously close, sinking into the trunk just over Silas's shoulder, but the goon fell hard, the weapon loosening from his grip and falling with him to the ground.

Grasping for desperate breaths, Silas sat up and brought a hand to his neck. Ached something fierce, but he'd live. And he was living, which was more than the goon could say crumpled at his feet.

Another sound caught his attention. A *thump, thump, thump*, like feet padding through uncut grass. From beyond a clump of younger trees obscuring his vision just beyond the well-endowed sycamore he was resting against.

Not again...

He rose to his knees, his neck and throat and Adam's apple barking out a wicked ache that threatened to lay him out. But he swallowed and waited, readying his aim.

When Celeste popped into view, throwing her hands up.

Silas sighed and rose to his feet.

"Heard the shots and thought the worst," she said, shoving her weapon at her back.

"You underestimate me, dear," he croaked, massaging his neck again and shoving his Beretta at his front. "Looks like you managed alright."

She smirked. "The blokes didn't have a fighting chance."

"I bet."

"You still got the goods?"

He brought out the cylinder from behind his back. "Safe and sound. How about we get the heck out of here?"

They returned to the cobblestone path, running for the entrance as dawn turned into morning, the sky a bright blue now with the sun cresting above the trees and the city awakened to life.

Silas could see the car through the gated turnstile. Still

parked where they had left it. Unoccupied and unguarded, from the looks of it.

He motioned toward the car and ran. "Come on!"

They shoved through the park entrance and came up quick to their vehicle.

When he heard the crunch of boots and the cocking of a gun.

"Not so fast, partner…"

Silas skidded on the concrete then spun around.

A man stepped out from behind the waning morning shadows nestled against the entrance, holding a weapon that looked oddly like a Colt Single Action Army Revolver. Hence the cocking sound he'd heard, which many of those bargain-bin Kindle thrillers he referenced earlier got all wrong—pistols like his trusty Beretta or Celeste's adequate SIG didn't cock.

Except for the Colt pointing in their direction.

But the man stepping toward them with hateful eyes and a dead-center aim wasn't one of the men clad in black. They'd taken care of that without mercy.

Instead, it was someone who Silas wasn't at all expecting.

"Noland Rotberg?"

The man with that annoyingly ironic handlebar mustache hustled up to Celeste and threw an arm around her neck and pressed the Colt against her temple.

Which sent all the hairs on the back of Silas's neck standing at angry attention.

"Let her the hell alone," he growled, head dipping and eyes narrowing with rage.

The man grinned, a set of crooked but white teeth gleaming through. "Nice to see you, too, Doc Grey. And fancy seeing you here. Wouldn't have an ancient gilded cylinder about, oh, yea big, stuffed behind your back, would you?"

Celeste struggled under Rotberg's grip, throwing Silas not frightened but determined eyes that said all she needed to say:

Don't you dare give up the bloomin' cylinder we just fought like hell to retrieve.

He didn't want to, but he didn't see any other way. Not with Celeste at Rotberg's mercy.

"Figured you'd be rootin' around here," the man went on, "given the city's significance for Christianity, being the Emperor's capital and all. Just happy to have stumbled upon you before you ran off with the goods."

He took a shuddering step, shoving Celeste forward and jamming the pistol into her temple now, cocking her head at a wicked angle. She gave a muffled squeak, clearly in pain.

Silas clenched his jaw and took a step forward himself. Everything within him wanted to tear the man to pieces. But Celeste shook her head before darting her eyes at the ground, then back to him before glancing down again.

Knew she was signaling something. At first, he thought she was reiterating her opinion of the matter, that SEPIO didn't negotiate with terrorists when the Church was on the line, even for their own.

Then he saw it, the familiar black handle poking up for attention from her boot.

He grinned and nodded his agreement to go along with the plan.

"Fine," Silas said. "But you should know this ain't at all what you think it is."

Rotberg smirked. "And what, pray tell, do you think I think this is?"

Silas took out the golden cylinder from behind his back and set it on the ground, but far enough away that Celeste had to kneel and step forward.

Giving her a window to do her thing.

He said, "You think it's every Da Vinci-code conspiracy wannabe's fantasy, combined with the genius of the New Atheists who'd want nothing more than to take down the Church with some long-lost secret confession from the architect of the Christian faith, verifying his political ambition and heavy-handed stranglehold hold on the Church. You think if Dan Brown and Richard Dawkins had a man-child, this would be it."

Rotberg sneered at the suggestion, those handlebars wiggling with irritation, fingers flexing around the butt of his Colt into a white-knuckle grip that made Silas think he went too far.

"You have no idea, Grey," the man growled. "What we have been able to uncover will prove that all the world has ever known about Christianity is a lie!"

"We'll see about that..."

"Yes, we shall. Let's get to it."

Still holding Celeste, arm firmly wrapped around her neck and Colt pressed against her temple, Rotberg took a shuddering step toward the golden cylinder still glinting in the morning sun.

"Now pick it up!" he said.

Flashing Silas determined eyes, Celeste did as she was told.

"Easy now..." the man said, the Colt pistol trained on the back of her neck as he loosened the grip.

Silas held his breath, praying like he'd never prayed before.

Because one wrong move, and Rotberg wouldn't hesitate to blow her head off.

She knelt, but instead of reaching for the golden goose, she eased out the silver knife from her boot—the one Silas had given her, just in case.

Called that one, didn't I?

In one motion, she yanked it out and thrust it into Rotberg's thigh, the blade sinking fast into his muscle like a knife carving a pumpkin.

He screamed, startling backward.

Silas feared Rotberg would discharge the Colt in their direction—in Celeste's direction.

But she didn't give him the chance.

With a perfectly executed roundhouse kick, Celeste swept the Colt from his hand, the weapon skittering across the concrete. Then she launched a push kick that threw him stumbling against the park's stone wall.

Silas quickly retrieved the cylinder, and the two got into their car. Rotberg struggled to recover, doubling over and heaving for breath. But it didn't matter anyway.

The SEPIO pair sped away, joining the morning traffic and easily escaping.

"Where d'you learn how to kick like that?" Silas asked.

Celeste shrugged. "Her Majesty's service, where else?"

"The Queen of England taught you a roundhouse?"

She frowned. "No, silly. But I wouldn't put it past the seasoned woman to sock it to a would-be assailant if it came to it."

"I suppose she did defend the Falkland Islands in the face of the military junta."

"That was Margaret Thatcher, but good try."

"At any rate, mad I lost my knife though."

"Knives can be replaced, love. Fiancé cannot."

He laughed, putting a hand on her knee and squeezing it with a grin. "Indeed."

"We should check in with Zoe, then try Bartholomew to see if he found anything further to aid us in our endeavor."

"Agree. I just hope Gapinski and Torres are having less drama than we've had."

CHAPTER 19
DIRSIYAH.

A day without SEPIO-level drama sure would be nice...
Gapinski finally neared the encampment after hemming and hawing the last hour since leaving Torres, unsure how to approach the merry band of Nous mercenaries wielding Soviet-made assault rifles like it was nobody's business.

Except it was apparently their business to be wielding them, with SEPIO on the receiving end of their entrepreneurial exploits.

"Just what I needed. To go traipsing across the sands of Tripoli—"

Sands of Tripoli?

He scrunched up his face and slowed his pace, mumbling the song he'd been forced to put to memory back in the day. *From the Halls of Montezuma, to the shores of Tripoli...*

There it was. "Just what I needed. To go traipsing across the *shores* of Tripoli—"

But that didn't work either, because he wasn't anywhere near a shore. Although, he did catch the distinct smell of dead fish and briny seas on an updraft of warm air gusting across the rocky ground. And the Mercedes GPS showed they were close to the Mediterranean, so he figured he was close enough to make it fit.

Either way, he was a grumbly, mumbly mess sauntering across the sands of Tripoli or Al-Marj or Ad Dirsiyah or wherever the hell they were as he closed the distance between him and no uncertain doom.

He went back to the Marines' Hymn that had been drilled into his noggin' back in basic training, singing under his breath: *"'We fight our country's battles in the air, on land, and sea; first to fight for right and freedom and to keep our honor clean; we are proud to claim the title of United States Marine.'"*

Yes, sir, commander sir.

Gapinski adjusted the AK-103 assault rifle slung around his shoulder Torres had swiped from the terrorist whack job he rifle-butted an hour ago. Glad she handed it off to him, too, because he figured he'd raise a brow or two if he waltzed into camp with anything other than the Mikhail Kalashnikov designed weapon that had made the Russian small-arms designer and lieutenant general famous. Or infamous, depending on one's politics. The AK line had pretty much put him on the military map, the 47 version the one that sealed the deal. The 103 was a mainstay of the Libyan army and later confiscated by ISIS, so it made sense the dude had been carrying in. A bit overkill, but Gapinski liked the size of it, and the 600-rounds-a-minute rate of fire was nice. Especially when you're up for whacking a bunch of whack jobs.

Whether on the sands or shores of Tripoli, didn't matter to him. He only hoped he'd have an opportunity to put the thing to good use before the day was through, given what they'd put SEPIO through the past few days.

The high-noon sun had been unrelenting. Gapinski was nearing the encampment now, thank God, but he was boiling like an overdone potato in his getup, the MC Hammer pants sticking to his legs now from sweat. Gloves were nice, though, a good fit that would hide his Georgia-white skin. The headscarf was a special sort of pain in his rump, the thing coming loose and billowing down around his bald head while making him feel like he was suffocating to death when in place. No wonder ISIS was filled with a bunch of cranky-pants terrorists. He would be too if he had to run around in taupe-colored getups, face wrapped in a headscarf that made him feel like he was drowning!

And baking like an Idaho-grown russet, wrapped in aluminum foil and cooked to perfection like Grandpappy used to make 'em. Sliced down the middle with a third cup of sour cream stuffed down the gully, topped with bacon bits and shredded cheddar and a pinch of chives, complementing a big, fat, juicy porterhouse the size of his head grilled to medium-rare perfection and dripping with grease and smothered in A1 sauce, washed down with a brewski that—

Gapinski's food fantasizing was interrupted by a boulder the size of his porterhouse, sending him sprawling in the rocky sand and headscarf unfurling across the ground within sight of the encampment.

"Sonofa—"

Gunfire interrupted his situational cursing.

The familiar *rat-a-tat-tats* of a chorus of assault rifles sent him scrambling from the ground after his headscarf and ducking behind a cluster of barren bushes that hadn't seen sight of a good bottle of Dasani in half a month.

Gapinski crouched low, slinging his rifle over his shoulder and fiddling with the damn headscarf to get it to cooperate. He wrapped it up and around and over his face as best he could. Apparently one needed a degree in headscarf wrapping to get the thing to cooperate, but he got the job done. Although the crazies on the other side of the line of tents might have a thing to say otherwise.

More gunfire erupted, followed by hootin' and hollerin'.

Which made him think something had happened, something they were celebrating. Sounded mighty familiar, like the ISIS dudes he'd seen on TV prancing around the streets of Iraq and Syria after a successful battle.

Might as well join in the fun.

He was within reach now, anyway, the nearest tent only twenty or thirty feet away. Time to bite the bullet, put on the big-boy pants, and get the job done.

Here goes nothin'...

He stood and went to step out from his hiding spot.

When another guy stepped out from around the tent.

Gapinski quickly crouched again. Probably not the best thing to do. Made him look more guilty than he already was.

He sat still, hoping against hope and praying to the Lord Almighty the guy had missed him.

A string of foreign words that were all Greek to him were slung his way.

Or Arabic, considering.

"Always something..." he muttered, continuing to crouch while the dude approached. He chanced glancing over his shoulder, catching sight of a battered AK-47 aimed in his direction.

Not good.

But what could he do? He didn't know a lick of Arabic, and knew the guy would be interrogating him like a crazed CIA black-site operator.

Then he had it. About the only thing he thought to do in the moment.

He hiked up his taupey Hammer pants gifted to him by the terrorist he'd taken out. Then he pretended to be taking care of business, right there in the open desert behind the bush. Because where else would a terrorist whack job take care of business than behind a bush? Didn't suppose they brought in Porta-Johns while on the warpath. Although these dudes seemed a horse of a different color, with their fancy canvas tents and military-grade inflatable boats and AK-103s and—

Another string of Arabic interrupted his thoughts, so that he nearly let his bladder loose then and there.

The man came closer, speaking lowly with his weapon raised. Only a few feet away now, Gapinski twisted toward the man, shaking his head and pointing underneath before waving a hand in front of his nose and twisting up his face.

Telling his new Arab friend all he needed to know.

The man groaned and backed away, speaking something more before turning back and disappearing behind the tent.

Relieved—figuratively, not literally—he waited a minute to make sure the coast was clear, then quickly stood and put his getup in place. He hustled along the encampment's outer rim away from the tent his new friend disappeared into. Coming up to another, the larger big-top spectacle he had glimpsed from the treeline, he adjusted his headscarf and walked into the camp.

Show time...

The thirteen or so men he had glimpsed earlier were gathered at the center of a dusty courtyard the size of a suburban cul-de-sac, the sun-bleached beige tents arrayed in a horseshoe around the center where a set of ruins stood. Another chorus of *rat-a-tat-tats* rattled off into the air, the way he knew peeps in them parts celebrated pretty much anything.

Gapinski padded closer to the group but held back, not wanting to draw attention to himself but also not wanting to look conspicuous.

Beyond the already crazy level of conspicuousness he was putting out.

A set of columns on the far side of the dig site stood the test of time, some intact, some cracked in half, like a row of teeth mounted on mortar gums. Some sort of palace or provincial building, he imagined. The surrounding soil was nothing but packed, sunbaked dirt and rocks, but he imagined much of it was rubble strewn about what had been a significant town back in its heyday. Another larger, more intact building stood farther beyond camp, archways and carefully cut bricks piled expertly on top of one another still standing in defiance.

Couldn't make heads or tails of any of it. All that mattered was what the raucous was all about. And what stood at the center of it.

As he neared, Gapinski stood on his toes to see above the men crowded around. Several broken walls stood at the center, chest high, with narrow walkways between them, as if they had served as entrances inside the crumbled edifice. The rest of the structure had broken down years ago, but beyond the broken wall was a crescent-shaped bowl, some sort of leftover basin stuck right there in the ground. A pair of stairs descended below on either side of the crater, where tiny tiles sat at the bottom, white and brown. Along with a very familiar symbol.

The Chi-Rho.

The middle of the symbol had been smashed to pieces, but he could still make out the curvature of the Rho's *P* and the arms of the Chi's *X* arranged by the tiny tiles. A hole was all that was left of the tiles. Strike that: more like a shaft, leading down into the ground. Gapinski didn't even have to guess what had been inside.

He didn't have to wait long to find out, either.

Out from the middle of the pack strode a familiar face, framed by blond locks and wearing all the cockiness of a man who's always gotten his way in life.

Sebastian Grey.

He was grinning and cradling a familiar object. The golden cylinder. Must have just pulled the thing from the ground, the goons throwing up their *rat-a-tat-tats* and hoots and hollers again, clearly celebrating mission success.

Another man joined him, quieting the others. Again, familiar. A big, bulky, brawny meathead wearing military fatigues—though Gapinski didn't know how the heck he managed in the heat—his head spun up with a hive of dark dreadlocks that fell beyond his shoulders. And that ridiculous name that sounded like a comic book villain—although maybe that was the point.

Aurelius Chuke.

On instinct, Gapinski eased the rifle around to his front, gripping it tight at seeing the man a third time in nearly two days. He wondered where he had stashed Zarruq, whether the bishop was even still alive.

Glancing around the encampment, Gapinski spotted a small tent with sagging sides planted next to the big-top bonanza. Like the main attraction, where he presumed Sebastian lived in luxury, the thing was guarded by two men, one on either side. No other tent had a posted guard. He looked to Chuke, who was now hunched over in consultation with Sebastian about something, then glanced back.

Dollars to doughnuts Zarruq was stashed away in there. Why else guard it with two of Sebastian's goons?

Speaking of which…

"Gentlemen," the man said, voice rising above the crew of Nous hostiles. "Meet your next billion-dollar prize!" He thrust the golden cylinder into the air, the men erupting in *rat-a-tat-tat* celebration, with more hoots and hollers hot on its heels before Chuke silenced his men again with a growly string of Arabic.

Gapinski stepped around a trio of men, inching a few feet closer to the pair he wanted in order to get a closer look at target Numero Uno.

Except his forehead itched like a mother under the headscarf, a line of sweat beading something fierce and throwing up the itches. And with the rest of the getup sticking to his oversized body now from the heat of the day, he thought he'd lose his stuff.

Keep your head on, ya big lug...

He left the headscarf alone, fearing the thing would come unwrapped if he touched it, then positioned himself close enough to listen to the pair now, focusing on them and their conversation to ward away the crazy itch nibbling against his head like rabid mice while keeping another ear at the crazy down at the center.

Sebastian had handed the cylinder over to Chuke, affirming him for taking Zarruq hostage as the man had apparently been a cash cow of information—leading to the billion-dollar prize the man was opening with a twist. Popping the top, Chuke dumped out the contents.

Gapinski strained forward to see the familiar jagged metal thingamabob thumping into Sebastian's hand. The man eyed it with confusion, turning it over this way and that before handing it to Chuke and dismissing it with a mumble, as if he had never seen the thing before. Which seemed odd if the whole conspiracy was a Nous hatchet job from another life. But what did he know?

Chuke shook the cylinder now, and an equally familiar copy of the Nicene Creed slipped out. Sebastian showed little interest in it, unfurling and giving it a once-over before handing it back to his second-in-command. Then he grabbed the cylinder from the man and shook it for the apparent main prize.

Another fragment fell out. What Gapinski suspected was part of the so-called Constantine confession or emperor code or whatever the heck it was.

Sebastian handed the cylinder back to Chuke and spread the fragment open. He held it between his hands and read in silence, his eyes darting this way and that before the ends of his mouth began rising with delight—clearly pleased with what he was reading.

But then they fell, wilting like a daffodil in a Georgian heat coming in hot and heavy from the gulf. His face went slack, his mouth fell open slightly, his manicured brow furrowed with deep lines of confusion, indignation even.

Gapinski threw up his own furrowed brow underneath his headscarf, gripping his weapon tighter and unsure what the clear shift in the dude's vibes meant.

What had he found? What had Constantine written?

Snatching the golden cylinder back from Chuke and stuffing the fragment down inside, Sebastian rushed off in a huff, the man brushing dangerously close past Gapinski before pushing past his guards and disappearing beyond a flap of canvas into the big-top tent.

Chuke followed, not paying Gapinski any mind, believing he was one of the fellas. The others began dispersing, sauntering to a few parked pickups caked with desert grime or back to their own meager accommodations arrayed around the ancient ruins.

Now what?

Wanting to look neither conspicuous for standing around with his finger up his nose nor get into a convo with one of the whack jobs that required a crash course from Rosetta Stone, he sauntered to the perimeter, looking this way and that, as if he were on patrol. Which would buy him enough time to figure out Plan B, but just barely. Because sooner or later, one of the ISIS wannabes was gonna figure out the big beluga with a misshapen headscarf and a taupey Hammer pants riding his ass was not who he should be.

Now what, was right.

Wandering to the edge of camp, he leaned against one of the limestone columns to figure out what the hell he should do next.

It gave, a chunk crumbling from the side of the ancient edifice and the thing shifting off its base.

"Always something..." he muttered, his bowels flopping to

the dirt even as he spun around to catch the damn thing before it crashed to the ground.

Thankfully, he did, setting it back in place and glancing around to make sure the coast was clear. It was, and he set back toward the tents.

Alright, don't feed the animals or lean against the architecture. Got it.

Gapinski knew time was not on his side. Sebastian found what he was looking for, so he would be on to the next golden goose—and stat. But what he found seemed to cook his gander, to carry on the metaphor, which was odd.

He passed one of the pickup trucks, the three occupants lying lazily inside. One of them was drinking from a canteen, the water dribbling down his chin and reminding Gapinski how thirsty he was. The man had also removed his headdress and was splashing water down his head and face, reminding him how friggin' hot he was.

The dude glanced his way, and he quickly looked at the ground, continuing his walk. He shook his head and kicked the ground, thinking about the mess SEPIO was in. Clear as day, Sebastian found what he came looking for, which meant at least four of the fragments that threatened to rewrite the Christian faith had been found. Five, if Silas and Celeste had any luck on their end. How many more were out there? One, maybe two?

And yet...

He couldn't shake the look on his face. What was it? Surprise, astonishment? That wasn't exactly it. Disappointment, that was it. Like something in the fragment didn't match what he expected to find.

Which meant he needed to infiltrate that tent and get hold of the fragment. Could be an important clue to blowing up the whole dang conspiracy threatening the Church. The second one in as many months.

But how?

Sighing with frustration at his options that looked about as appealing as a bad Vegas hand, he saw another truck a few feet ahead, its lone occupant taking a snooze in the back propped up against the cab. He crunched across the gravel slowly, so as not to awaken the dude, then stopped at what he saw farther up ahead.

One of the men guarding Bishop Zarruq was motioning with his hands to the other guard before scurrying away. He watched the dude as he slipped around the corner of the tent and out of sight. Probably finding a spot to take care of business out back.

Which left only one terrorist whack job guarding Zarruq.

He had to act. And fast. But how? What?

He went to run a frustrated hand across his bald head when he remembered himself, and what he was wearing, nearly unfurling the dang headscarf before the watching world.

Cursing himself for the slip, he adjusted the thing back into place when he noticed something lying on the truck's tailgate.

A canteen, made of tin and marked with dings and scratches from use. The top was secure, and it gave him an idea.

A stupid one at that.

But as they say: Go big or go home.

Time to roll the dice.

Now or never...

He looked around, feeling like he was going to pass out from heat stroke now and recycling his own carbon dioxide. But he pressed forward, padding toward the truck on careful feet that probably made him look like a hippo doing a pirouette out in the blazin' sun on the sands of Tripoli. Or shores, whatever it was.

Coming up quick, he kept an eye trained on the sleeping man and another on the others around him. No one watched, no one cared. That he could tell, anyway.

Reaching for the canteen, the back of his lizard brain screamed for him to stop and run away, trained on too many hoary Kindle thriller novels and television shows that had the baddie waking up just as his beat-up tin canteen was being swiped from a tailgate of a beat-up pickup truck in the middle of an archaeological dig sit in Libya. But training told him such things rarely happened.

At least he hoped they didn't that day.

He shook away the worry and snatched it, then kept on walking, the whack job none the wiser.

Thank you, Lord Almighty...

One down, one to go.

Which was the real test.

Making sure his AK-103 was firmly in place around his soaked midsection, he strode toward what he presumed to be Zarruq's tent, Full Bladder Dude still MIA. He prayed to the Lord Almighty he had a bad case of the runs, because he needed him to stay away just a few minutes longer.

Plan was to stride right past the guard left standing and right on in under the cover of caretaking the prisoner's hydration needs. Fake it 'til you make it had been sound wisdom pretty much his whole life. And he was hoping the wisdom carried him through to the other side of the flap of canvas waving lazily in the breeze.

Just a few more steps. The guard's head was down, and he was resting against a wood pole at the opening.

He stiffened when Gapinski approached, and he raised his slackened rifle on instinct.

Jesus, take the canteen...

Gapinski held up the tin object and nodded toward the opening, not breaking his pace for nothing and not giving the dude a moment to break his advance. Probably helped he looked to have two hundred pounds on the guy. What was with the genes out in those parts? Or was it the food, eating lentils and goats instead of corn and beef?

Either way, he held his breath as he reached the tent threshold, giving the man his best don't-even-think-about-it look while leading with the canteen.

The man didn't say a word. Took a step back even as Gapinski entered before slumping back against the post, the entrance flap falling back into place for privacy.

It was dark. And hot and humid. And smelly, like something had died and gone to the outhouse and back. He thought he would hurl what little water and that raisin Clifbar was left in his belly. But he held it together, waiting for his eyes to adjust and praying to the Lord Almighty he'd chosen the right door.

"*Psst,*" he whispered. "Bishop Zarruq? You in here, chief?"

Something rustled against the back, startling him and catching his breath in his chest. Something big and bulky. Wearing a cream-colored cassock with wicked-cool black and blue and green embroidery that fit in with the land to a T.

The bishop. It had to be!

Gapinski rushed over. The man scurried against the canvas, raising a fearful hand.

He stopped short and knelt, holding out the canteen. "Bishop, it's me. Matt Gapinski."

There was a moment of disbelief, before quickly turning into full-on relief. Zarruq threw his arms around his neck, offering a word of praise to the Lord before pulling back and throwing both hands on his hips.

"What the blazes are you doing here?" he asked, accent thick with fatherly irritation.

"I'm here to rescue you. Well, that and retrieve the new fragment. Here, have this." He passed the canteen to the bishop, who took it with thanksgiving and began chugging it.

Finishing, he sat back and sighed. "So they found it then, the next fragment?"

"Apparently. And I'm guessing with a bit of insight from their resident Order of Thaddeus trustee?"

His face fell, and he nodded. "I promised, for your sakes, that I would point them in the right direction. Given the Arian entanglements in the most recent ecclesial brouhaha, I figured Ptolemais was as good as any place to look. Apparently, I was correct."

"That you were. One of the ancient ruins hatched another golden goose. Or laid another golden egg. Still confused on that one. Either way, yeah, Sebastian's got another golden cylinder, complete with Nicene Creed and fragment and weird Nous coin."

"That's not what it is?"

"It's not? Then what is it?"

A whistle outside the tent cut off the bishop's answer. From over his shoulder and coming 'round the bend.

Full Bladder Dude's bladder was full no more.

Crapola.

CHAPTER 20

Where's an SUV with upscale refinement and off-road ruggedness when you need it. Maybe Torres would catch some sort of telepathic plea and come riding in on a gray Mercedes to haul his and Zarruq's butts out of there.

Come on, Lord. Toss me an SUV here!

Gapinski stood and took back the canteen. "I gotta go."

"Wait!" Zarruq said, grabbing his sleeve. "What is your plan?"

"What do you think? I'm gonna bounce you and the Constantine code or imperial confession or whatever the hell it is on out of here. Although, where's a good Mercedes G-Class when you need one..."

"Get the fragment, fine. But leave me."

"No way, chief."

"That's an order!" he exclaimed with a barely contained whisper.

Gapinski went to reply but thought against it. Instead, he went to the door and whispered: "Sit tight. I'll be in touch."

Then he left, holding up the canteen and nodding to the dude wilting against the post in the mid-afternoon sun. And hoping to the Lord Almighty that Full-No-Longer Bladder Dude didn't get suspicious.

He kept walking, the back of his head feeling four eyes glaring at him as he strode toward the center of the encampment, weapon clanging against his back and hammer pants sticking against his legs now from the day's sweat.

Fake it 'til you make it, right? He hoped his confident performance called off the dogs. Otherwise things could get real interesting, real quick.

A truck full of the pseudo-spiritual Nous whack jobs were pulling out, a trail of dust kicking up as they wound past the set of ruins with cracked teeth, columns jutting up this way and that. Didn't know what it meant, but probably a sign they were getting ready to pull out. Made sense now that they had the golden goose. Or golden egg, or whatever metaphor was apropos for the occasion.

Gapinski stopped at the threshold of what he assumed was another baptismal where the third golden cylinder had been found, taking stock in the remaining men—seven by his count, not counting Sebastian and Chuke and Zarruq.

When a hand grabbed his shoulder and twisted him around.

Full-No-Longer Bladder Dude, with his wilting sidekick hanging back but looking like he was ready for backup if need be.

The man spit a bunch of Arabic gibberish his way from behind one of those brown-checkered headscarves. Didn't understand a word of it. A beat-up AK-47 caked with gunk and grime hung from his shoulders, at his back, which meant he wasn't alarmed, only suspicious. But it was still in reach if he went to DEFCON 1, with nukes on the launchpad and ready for action.

Always something...

He looked away from the cacophony of Arabic, noting a few

men from one of the remaining pickups he'd passed earlier starting to take an interest as the man shouted now, gesturing toward Gapinski's hand. It was still holding the empty canteen, but he forgot about it as he gawped for words. Only limited Spanish rose to the surface. Torres was sure right about—

The man suddenly grabbed the hand still holding the canteen and yanked at it, drawing back a pasty-white wrist that caused the dude to startle.

Their eyes met. Cold, dark eyes with the dawn of revelation that Gapinski wasn't one of his own.

Party's over. A good 'ol boy from Georgia in a camp of bronze-skin Libyans pretty much sealed the deal on that one.

But not *game* over. Not by the grace of the Lord Almighty, anyway.

Guess Zarruq's rescue was getting cashed in early.

If he got that far.

Full-No-Longer Bladder Dude backed up and reached around for his 47, another cry of gibberish seeming to activate the others around. Even Backup Boy started raising his weapon to engage the man who had been fingered a hostile.

Sorry, pal. Not today.

Gapinski was quicker on the draw, spinning his own Mikhail-Kalashnikov designed Muscovite specialty weapon around and letting her rip.

Rat-a-tat-tat. Rat-a-tat-tat.

And just like that, Full-No-Longer Bladder Dude flailed his arms around something wild before landing on his back, crimson blooming from his chest in arching spouts as it shredded under the weight of lead.

Even Backup Boy got in on the fun, Gapinski's aim better than he expected. Though the truth of the matter was more that the heft and power of the AK-103 was enough to blow right through Nousati Numero Uno and check Numero Dos's queen before he was able to take out King Gapinski.

He shuddered with the same recoil but with far less flair, crumpling to the ground like a used bathrobe.

But not before getting off a *rat-a-tat-tat* punch-back of his own, a spray of bullets slung his way.

One of them grazed past in a wicked burn, slicing through the ridge of Gapinski's upper arm and out the other side leaving behind a nasty rut of torn skin and muscle that hurt something fierce, bleeding more than he'd expect.

Pain bloomed at the point of impact, and Gapinski faltered his weapon for a moment as it lanced down his arm. But that wasn't even the worst of it.

That pickup he'd passed earlier, full of the becoming-interested Nousati hired guns were now fully engaged, jumping out and armed to the teeth. And Chuke had stormed out of the big-top bonanza, followed by Sebastian hot on his heels and their two guards.

Putting it somewhere around seven to one. Not even Vegas odds, and definitely more than he'd faced before.

Worst. Odds. Ever.

Come on, Lord. Toss me a bone here!

Instead of a heavenly helping hand, a volley of *rat-a-tat-tats* were thrown his way.

Gapinski threw himself over the chest-high wall leading to the baptismal, landing on the ancient stone with a bruising crunch but thankful to have a sturdy barrier between him and the Worst Odds Ever.

He tore his headscarf off from his head—no need for that now that the cat was out of the bag—and wrapped it tight around his arm, blood winding down his massive biceps in multiple rivulets. He pulled hard, one end firmly between his teeth, grunting from effort and feeling like he would pass out. Hurt like a mother, but he'd live.

That is, if he narrowed the odds and made it out of the hornets' nest he'd just stirred up!

The bullets were unrelenting, smashing into the broken wall with wicked abandon and chewing the ancient stone with a ravenous appetite Gapinski hoped wouldn't be sated by his hide. It went on like this, bullet after bullet, his back to the stone wall without a window in the action for a look-see, until the rhythm behind the assault started shifting.

He figured it was from reloads, a whack job can only whack so long until his weapon runs dry. But the farther apart they came, the more he feared it was to reposition and open up a new front on their assault.

Then he saw it. Out of the corner of his eye.

A pair of them. All taupey and billowy, faces wrapped in the headscarves he'd be sure as hell fine with never again seeing in his lifetime.

And taking aim.

Whack job flank!

Throwing himself down, he took aim and let loose, throwing them off their game. But just barely.

They slid behind a group of toppled columns and answered round for round, two other hostiles joined them now and amplifying the firepower.

Four to one. Them SEPIO odds. Which had rarely turned out to be good odds. But something he might be able to work with.

Mumbling a curse, Gapinski rolled along the dirty floor and into the baptismal, narrowly missing a FastPass to Saint Pete's pearly gates as bullets skittered across the blackened stone floor where he'd been lying.

He landed hard on his knees but recovered in time to slam against the wall on the other side facing the assault and take aim, sending a *rat-a-tat-tat* reply that gave the bastards pause.

He held it until a pair of the bullets sailed straight into a face that peekabooed with ill-timed intent. The dude's head snapped back, but Gapinski didn't catch the highlights because he was taking aim for round two, his bullets chewing through another's chest.

Both flopped hard to the ground like fish.

Gapinski chuckled. Like shooting fish in a—

An eruption of gunfire on his right sent him pancaking to the tiny-tiled floor, the smashed Chi-Rho resting a few feet away.

Bullets skipped across the ancient stonework overhead, sending puffs of mortar and brick splintering with menacing violence. The gunfire was coming from where he had tumbled into the drained well, behind the broken wall.

He sent up his own burst of gunfire, then another, more a cover than anything else. Did enough of a job to let him scurry back to where he had come to close the angle of assault, quickly coming to the retaining wall flanked by the pair of narrow stairs.

Just as the two other Nousati hostiles from the earlier quartet came barreling from his flank.

The dudes managed to pop off several rounds that fell too close for comfort before Gapinski caught their incoming assault. But he spun around just as they threw up a crazed war cry he cut short by a *rat-a-tat-tat* spray. Sent both whack jobs slumping fast, their heads cracking against the first set of broken walls in harmony.

That puts a nail in my left flank's coffin. Literally.

But it was far from over.

He sprang to his knees and took aim over the baptismal lip as another pair of remaining hostiles paused their gunfire to snake closer.

Gotcha...

He squeezed but clicked empty.

"Sonofa—"

Another round of *rat-a-tat-tats* cut him off.

Not from ahead over the baptismal lip at the broken wall, but now from his right flank.

They were hesitant and sporadic, keeping their distance and trying their hand, like they were poking a fish to see if it was still alive.

And now he was trapped.

Fish is right.

Now *he* was the fish—in a stone baptismal, no less!

Come on, Lord. Toss me a bone here!

The answer came sooner than he expected.

The whine of an engine was suddenly heard from overhead. Big engine, heaving horsepower, lots of oomph and plenty of cylinders to get the job done.

And upscale refinement with off-road ruggedness.

A Mercedes G-Class barreled between two of the tents at the far end of stage right, crash landing just inside the encampment.

It braked hard and spun sideways like a pro—throwing up all kinds of dust and rubble and pots and pans. Just like in the movies, the tail leveling one of the tents and creating enough chaos and confusion to throw off the whole equilibrium of the hostiles' charge.

Gapinski grinned. The cavalry had arrived.

The Naomi Torres Division.

An eruption of *pop-pop-pops* answered the call of duty from just over the front end. Small arms, not the hulking Avtomat Kalashnikovas. Not what he would have led with, but it wasn't his call to make. Nor was it his complaint to make.

As his late grandpappy might say: Beggars can't be choosers when a bunch of pseudo-spiritual terrorist whack jobs are riding your ass!

He was just glad she opened up a front that would sure give the Nousati bastards a run for their euros.

As they decided what course of action to take, Gapinski wasted no time.

He threw aside the AK-103 and slid out one of his trusty SIG Sauer P320s. Sending *one-two-three* rounds into one of the right-flank hostiles with his finger up his nose, and another pair toward his partner.

Nousati Numero One fell, Numero Dos skipped back behind a massive tree, its trunk all gnarly and leafy branches sticking up into the sky all catawampus. Reminded him of the Ents from Lord of the Rings.

Irregardless—or *regardless*, as Torres would have surely corrected—he skittered out from his spot and scampered up the far side set of stairs, getting the jump on the last of his right flank and the others ahead who had shifted their firepower on the Mercedes.

His heart sank at the sound of bullet after bullet pinging off metal. Although, better that then sinking into flesh. His or Torres's.

Speaking of which...Time to join his partner.

With the firepower now focused on the Mercedes, he dashed from the edge of the broken baptismal walls, hooking around past the toppled columns. He gave the fallen Nousati bleeding out on the parched beige ground a wide berth and aimed for the last of the tents now toppled from the force of Torres's grand entrance.

Bullets whizzed by, kicking up the packed soil and thudding into the fallen tent. He offered a *pop-pop-pop* reply for cover then dove behind the torn canvas draped across the back end of the SUV.

"Torres! You read my mind. Or heard my prayer, one of the two..."

"Figured you could use a helping hand." She popped of a *one-two* punch then cheered. "Got another. Three by my count."

"Which means there can't be many left. Saw a pickup truck full of Nousati leave an hour—"

Livid gunfire cut him off. From the far side of camp, at the dirt road winding inside from the main. A bed full of Nousati hostiles *rat-a-tat-tating* and aiming for the Mercedes dead-center mass.

"Always something..." Gapinski growled, backing up against the rear driver's side door and aiming through the shattered windows for the newcomers.

Who were really just oldcomers coming to reinforce their dwindling comrades.

"Who are they?" Torres asked, crouching low.

"A pickup full of Sebastian's buddies, that's who. Look out—"

Gapinski pulled Torres to the ground as an unrelenting surge of lead smacked into the Mercedes, shredding the driver's seat and blowing out more windows.

"Thanks," Torres panted, swallowing hard and wiping her brow glistening in the mid-afternoon sun. "Owe ya one, Hoss."

"This ain't working..." he grumbled. "And we're not even close to retrieving our two objectives."

"Maybe this could help." She slid out one of the high-powered SIG rifles from the back seat and handed it to Gapinski.

"You've been holding out on me?" he complained.

"Just holding it in reserve until the right time."

More lead thudded into the Mercedes, threatening to blow the thing to kingdom come.

"I'd say now is as good a time as any." He knelt and peeked over, the firefight dying down as the goons repositioned. He caught sight of Sebastian directing Chuke to do...something.

Which meant they didn't have much time.

"I've got an idea," he said.

"Oh, yeah? What's that?"

"Cover me while I go retrieve the golden goose. Or egg, or whatever the hell it is."

"On your own?"

He shrugged. "Someone needs to lay down covering fire like it's nobody's business."

As if agreeing, Torres slid out another rifle and angled it around toward the front end and propped its barrel up top. Then let out a *rat-a-tat-tat* burst, and another.

"You best get to it. I don't know how much more this hunk of Italian-engineered junk can take."

"German!"

"Yeah, yeah, yeah. Get to it, Hoss." She turned to him, adding: "And be careful."

He nodded, dropping the rifle and shoving his SIG Sauer at the front of his pants. Then he crouched and padded behind the overturned tent she had taken out earlier.

Wasting no time, he padded along the perimeter to the Big-Top Bonanza, coming up to it quick and sliding to its base. Withdrawing a knife from his boot, he took a breath and sent up a message to the Lord Almighty, praying it was empty and the golden goose was where he thought it should be—hopefully along with the others.

He knelt and thrust the blade into the beige canvas, its taut fibers giving quickly against the sharpened Swiss surgical steel.

Then he paused, waiting for a reply.

None came, except for the back-and-forth volley beyond.

Satisfied, he took a breath and swallowed, then put his hands inside and readied to part the curtain and step on through.

Here goes nothin'...

In one motion, he spread the canvas and hiked one leg through, pushing inside the darkened space toward destiny.

Empty.

Except for a mound of cushions at the center that looked

like a bad remake of Alibaba and the Forty Thieves and a hazy cloud that hung in the still air, smelling of a bad high school memory when he'd tried cheap street ganja the first time.

Mercifully, the entrance flap stood close, the *rat-a-tat-tats* picking up pace again and snapping him back to the task at hand.

He twisted his face up at the smelly fog, then smiled.

A wood table with spindly legs stood a few feet away.

And sitting at the center was a leather satchel. Shiny, shimmering tubes poking out.

The golden gooses! Or eggs, or whatever the hell they were. The original SEPIO found in Apollonia and the goon Chuke swiped, the new one Sebastian read off on WeSolve TV, and then the one he just uncovered at the dig site.

"Come to papa..." he muttered, leaning toward the satchel with one leg left outside and reaching a long arm across the table toward the target, a massive paw ready to grab and go.

Just as a tall, slender man with moppy blond hair threw open the entrance flap and popped inside.

Their eyes locked. Sebastian stood, arms at his side, mouth agape. Gapinski's bulk hung between the slash in the tent's side and the wooden table, palm open and hovering an inch above the sack of cylinders.

Time hung.

And then it didn't.

Gapinski snatched the leather strap.

Just as Sebastian pulled out a mean-looking piece of hardware and took aim.

But so did the SEPIO agent. Who was a former Marine. And much quicker on the draw. Even half-suspended between the two worlds inside and outside the tent.

Using his one leg caught outside and his well-muscled core, Gapinski pulled himself back outside, dragging the bag with him, even as he whipped out his SIG. It was perfectly executed, if not a bit odd, given his size and pose. But it did the trick.

He sent *one-two-three-four* bullets sailing toward Sebastian. At least one caught him in the shoulder and jolted it back with a violent jerk.

But not before Sebastian let loose himself, popping off a *one-two-three* reply.

All high and wide but completely disrupting Gapinski's carefully executed maneuver, sending him alley-ooping backward and crashing hard against the packed ground and the cylinders tumbling out of the satchel along with him.

He winced, his spine and back and muscles crying out in pain from the force of the fall.

He lay still, breathing and checking himself over.

None of them hit; he was fine.

But he had to move. On the double.

Scrambling from the ground, he gathered the golden eggs and stuffed them in the satchel, securing the flap shut. Then he raced to Zarruq's tent and repeated what he'd just executed.

But not before offering a *pop-pop-pop* warning back into Door Number Two from Sebastian's tent to ward off the crazy.

He jabbed the knife into the canvas and tore a new opening, top to bottom, and this time all the way to the ground to accommodate his bulk.

Consequences be damned, he pushed through with his weapon raised and ready to put to good use.

But it was empty.

No Zarruq.

"Sonofa—"

An explosion cut him off, a flash of crimson and black blooming beyond the tent.

Dear God, please—

And then the sudden whine of an engine. Different tone,

different timbre than the bucket of bolts that had ridden in moments ago.

Slinging the satchel around his shoulders, Gapinski pushed through outside.

Fearing what he'd find.

CHAPTER 21

Thick black smoke billowed high into the sky from beyond the line of tents, the acrid smell of burning rubber and fuel and paint washing Gapinski's way on a gusting wind and sending him into a coughing fit.

"*Torres!*" he yelled between coughs, his throat dry as sandpaper and feet stumbling across the uneven ground as the desert raged with fire.

Oddly, the gunfire seemed to have—

Another explosion sent him stumbling forward, his knee jamming into the damn rubble. He went to brace himself and bent his hand, landing on the shoulder still screaming from earlier.

He cried out, but he pushed off the ground and pushed forward, racing back toward the Mercedes.

"*Torres!*" he yelled again, breathless and panting and stumbling toward the Mercedes, praying like he'd never prayed before that Torres was still in one piece.

There she was, sitting on the ground back against the SUV's rear wheel, head tilted back, blood caked to the side of her face, a wound still gushing blood above the ear.

"Oh, dear Lord Almighty!" Gapinski rushed to her side, completely ignoring the threat that raged just across the hood.

"I'm fine!" She shoved him and reached out to stand.

Seemed her cranky self, so that was probably good.

He helped her up to her knees. "Are you sure? Did you get clipped by a round?"

"Smacked my head trying to avoid one."

"Speaking of which…"

He popped his head above the hood for a look-see.

Not at all expecting what he saw.

Which was no one. At least no one alive.

Several bodies were strewn across the ground, the pickup the hostiles had ridden in on smoldering now.

"Looks like you cleaned up pretty good, Torres." He raised a hand to high five her.

She grinned and slapped it. "Thanks."

The pair ventured out into the no-man's land, weapons ready but realizing the truth of the matter.

Nous had fled, or what remained of them. Sebastian, probably Chuke with a few more.

And Zarruq…

"The bishop?" Torres said, shoving her weapon at her back and nodding toward the tent.

Gapinski frowned and shook his head. "At least I managed to grab these before they left." He slung the satchel from around his back and reached inside, pulling out a golden cylinder and tossing it to her.

She caught it and grinned. "Nice. I suppose the gash to the head was worth it covering your ass."

"Unless they're empty…"

Torres fixed him with wide eyes. "You didn't check them before you left?"

"Sorta didn't have time. Sebastian came in just as I grabbed the thing. But he took one to the shoulder, so I made up for it."

"Moment of truth then..." She twisted up her face as she strained against the top. Eventually she loosened it and tossed the cap to the ground. Reaching inside, her frown turned upside down.

She tipped the cylinder and out came the familiar metal fragment. She tossed it to Gapinski; he caught it. "The rest is inside, safe and sound. Check the others."

Gapinski stuffed the metal thingamabob in his pocket and checked the other two. He took a deep breath and sighed with a grin, confirming all was safe and sound.

Until he turned around to assess the damage to their Mercedes.

Not good.

Half of the front windshield was riddled with bullets and splintering like a spider web, the other half had fallen out altogether. The front tires were flat and the engine was hissing, a plum of white steam still rising.

He shook his head and sighed. "Yeah, we ain't getting our deposit back on that one."

"Our deposit is the least of our worries. What about the big, fat bill Silas is gonna get for the thing?"

"Yeah, my ride allowance is toast."

"That, and the fact we don't have a ride to begin with."

Gapinski glanced up the main road back into town, a dirt thing with deep ruts humming with heat and humidity now.

"A couple miles, tops. We'll find a ride back to the airport."

Torres mumbled something in Spanish, then walked to their slain beast. "Best get to it, then."

The pair gathered up their weapons and the satcom unit, then set off back toward the coast. Gapinski figured it was time to check in with the chief. He punched in the direct-line auto dial to Zoe back at SEPIO command, who then patched them through to Silas and Celeste.

"Where the heck have you been?" Silas said, voice raised

with an equal amount of worry and exasperation. "We've been trying to reach you all day."

"Sorta been tied up, chief."

He and Torres gave a rundown of that day's events, infiltrating Nous's camp and retrieving the golden gooses, but ending with Bishop Zarruq's fumbled rescue attempt. Then Sebastian and Chuke getting away.

"Sounds like quite the ordeal," Celeste said.

"A shame about Zarruq," Silas said. "Don't beat yourselves up, but...a damn shame."

Gapinski glanced at Torres and sighed. "Don't we know it."

"But bravo for securing the fragments," Celeste said.

"Yeah, bravo on that front," Silas affirmed. "We'll get Zarruq back. Mark my words. And we understand being tied up. We've been having it out over here ourselves." He filled them in on their own details, ending on their own fragment recovery.

"So now we've got three of the four known cylinders," Torres said. "Maybe more if Silas and Celeste lucked out. That should count for something."

"We're getting close, that's for sure. What can you tell us about the new one you recovered?"

Gapinski answered, "It's all papery...and stuff?"

"Sort of goes without saying."

Celeste said, "Well, did you read it? What's it say?"

"Did I read the fragment written in Latin?" Gapinski asked.

Torres snorted a laugh. "Yeah, he can barely read English."

He frowned. "I just saved your ass and that's the thanks I get?"

"You saved my ass? You seem to be forgetting I rolled up in your Mercedes G-Class not too long ago."

"Upscale refinement and off-road ruggedness."

"Exactly!"

"Kids!" Silas shouted from the satcom unit. "Hash out who

saved who later. Now's the time to put this whole blasted conspiracy to rest."

"Sorry, chief," Gapinski said, shaking a finger at Torres. She just smiled and giggled. "What's the plan?"

"The plan," Celeste answered, "is to rendezvous back at the Church's Archives."

"Vatican again?"

"Know any other Archives of the Church?" Torres muttered.

Ignoring her, Gapinski added: "Seems like a wasted trip, going backward to Rome when we should be going forward to…who knows where!"

"I would agree," Silas said, "except Bartholomew found something that could help us."

"Oh, yeah? What's that?" Torres asked.

"He didn't say. But apparently something that should shed some more light on the whole thing."

Gapinski looked at Torres and shrugged. "I guess it's back to the Eternal City we go."

"See you in a few hours," Silas said before ending the call.

He stuffed the unit in his back pocket, his dogs barking now from the walk and clothes drenched with sweat.

"How much longer?" he panted.

"At this rate, another hour."

"Shoot me now."

SEVEN HOURS LATER, GAPINSKI AND TORRES WERE PASSING through the now-familiar gates leading to the Vatican Archives, the Pontifical Swiss Guard still standing guard and at attention in their blue, red, yellow, and orange getup—complete with MC Hammer pants and black beret.

All Gapinski had was the tight-fitting getup of the Nousati whack job he'd taken out in the desert, having abandoned his original clothes after all the drama at the archaeological dig site with the authorities coming in hot and heavy. Smelled of sweat and BO and burning car. The flight over didn't help matters either, since they had to fly commercial out of Benghazi. Something about a mechanical issue with one of the indicator lights on their Order-issued Gulfstream stuck back at Al-Marj Airport. Plucked his ever-living nerves after the fight they'd had, having to drive another hour to the city that had taken out those Americans almost a decade ago. Wanted to take a crowbar to the flight dashboard, too, but he relented. The SEPIO pair found a ride to the city located on the Gulf of Sidra and a Tunisair flight two hours later that eventually made it to Rome.

So now he was a grumbly, mumbly mess needing a hot shower and soft bed and stiff drink. A cigar wouldn't hurt either, one of those newfangled Nicaraguan Joyas he'd heard good things about, hints of roasted coffee, nuts, and leather on the tongue and the nose, perfectly humidified with the slightest of crinkle that—

"We're here," their escort grunted, parking with a squeal that made Gapinski wonder whether the brakes would have held when it mattered.

Gapinski grunted an acknowledgment himself, tweaked his cigar-and-scotch fantasy was so rudely interrupted when he couldn't imbibe.

He opened the door and stepped out. "Thanks, bub."

Torres followed, and the driver left the way they'd come.

The soaring pontifical edifice was just as they had left it: shrouded in darkness and secrecy. "Here's hoping our ass-kicking was worth it," he moaned as they climbed the stairs, every bone and muscle and ligament and toenail screaming for that Joya and a tumbler full of three-fingers worth of Macallan, the oaky, amber liquid taking him away to a land far, far—

"There you are!" another voice called from inside.

He huffed with irritation at the interruption. The daydream about his twin loves was about all he had to go on, given the ongoing mission.

It was Silas, waiting for him and Torres along with Celeste just inside the entrance.

"Please tell me you've got a Joya and a growler of Macallan waiting for me down in the bowels of the Archives."

Silas raised a brow. "I'm not sure the Vatican is the cigar-smoking and whisky-drinking kind of place. But I'm sure we can rustle up a bottle of Chianti somewhere."

"Always something…"

"And what the heck are you wearing? You look like a cross between Aladdin and Rambo."

Gapinski glared, saying nothing yet saying all he needed to say: Back off, dude.

"Don't poke the bear," Torres whispered, getting her own glare in return.

Celeste giggled and reached in for an embrace. "I'm sure Matthew could do without the ribbing, considering what you two have been through."

He winced, pulling away and moving his arm to ward off the pain in his shoulder.

"Ooh, sorry. Forgot about your battle scars."

"Just a flesh wound. But, yeah, leave the threads alone. Not what I would have chosen by a mile. You can thank the Nous dude I put down for those."

Silas laughed. "Point taken. So do you have them, then? The golden cylinders?"

Gapinski pulled the satchel around from his back and handed it over. "Happy to get rid of these things. A real pain in the ass going through security, I'll tell you that."

"Nice work. Now let's rustle up that bottle of Chianti. I'd say you earned it!"

"Damn straight."

Silas led them down the corridor leading to the doorway that led down to the room they had been at before. Apparently, he and Celeste had arrived a few hours ago and discovered newfound privileges of being Order Master, which gave him certain keys to the Vatican Archives kingdom. He was a bit showy about it, which normally wouldn't have bothered Gapinski, but he was in a mood. And he really wanted that bottle of Chianti!

"Ahh! You made it safe and sound," Bartholomew said, greeting them from inside the tricked-out Archives research room.

"I don't know if I'd describe it as safe…" Gapinski grumbled, slumping in one of the couches.

"Don't mind him," Silas said. "He's just in desperate need of some libation."

"Ahh! I've got just the thing," Bartholomew said, scurrying away to the exit.

"A bottle of Chianti?" Gapinski asked from across the room.

He gasped and spun around, twisting up his face with revulsion. "Heaven's no! A Bruno Giacosa Barolo Falletto, from 2015, I believe."

Gapinski twisted around on the couch. "*Excusez-moi?*"

"It's a Barolo, Hoss," Torres said. "You'll be pleased. Full of body and ripe fruit, great depth and density."

"Well, aren't you a regular Italian sommelier?"

She smiled and shrugged. "A side hobby."

"If it's red and will dull the pain, I'm in. But you wouldn't happen to have a thick, juicy porterhouse steak to go along with it, would you?"

Bartholomew shook his head. "Sorry, but I think the Barolo will do the trick anyhow." Then he left.

"Alright," Silas said, sitting across from Gapinski on another couch with the satchel. "Let's see what you've brought us…"

Gapinski pointed out which one was the new one. Silas

twisted off the end of the cylinder and emptied it of its contents, the Nicene Creed copy and the other parchment fragment. A musty smell floated his way, like Grandpappy's basement. Had probably been sitting down in that hole in the ground for over a thousand years! Crazy to think about.

After sizing up the Creed, Silas handed it to Torres who did her own sizing. Then the chief took the fragment in hand, carefully spreading in flat and taking a breath, as if he were about to run a marathon. He licked his lips and glanced around at the rest of them before diving into the parchment.

Gapinski glanced back toward the door, looking for Bartholomew and his Barolo, or whatever the heck it was. His stomach did a massive growly flip, reminding him he hadn't eaten in like a day, and regretting that he mentioned the porterhouse.

"Here we go," Silas said. Then he began to translate the thing, reading it aloud:

I could not have been more wrong.

Having come to my senses, by the power and conviction of the Holy Ghost, I exhort all to withdraw with a good will from these temptations of the devil to neglect the good news that has been proclaimed to the world since the dawn of the Church, that which was handed on to all Christians from its dawn as of first importance: that Christ died for our sins in accordance with the scriptures, and that he was buried, and that he was raised on the third day in accordance with the scriptures, and that he appeared to Cephas, then to the twelve, and then to more than five hundred brothers and sisters at one time. And to this the necessity that Jesus is the reflection of God's glory and the exact imprint of God's very being, that he sustains all things by his powerful word, and that when he had made purification for sins, he sat down at the right hand of the Majesty on high.

Our great God and our common Savior has granted us all the same light of revelation. And as a steward of this faith, I sought to successfully bring my task to conclusion, under the direction of the Lord's providence, to be enabled, through my exhortations, diligence, and earnest warning, to recall his people to communion and fellowship around the unity of the faith.

It is true that religions and empires often rise together. Such was the case with the former ways of Roma. But it is equally true that religious creeds and practices can often be co-opted by civilization. That is the situation we find ourselves in the not too distant future, I'm afraid, a Church that is accommodating civilization and a faith this is being eaten alive by it! The same is true for the factions vying for control within itself, so many varying perspectives on what should or should not be held to be Christian belief, neglecting the once-for-all faith entrusted by Christ himself to God's holy people. So many different truths of the person and work of God and our Savior. Our religion must not merely align with the ideals of the society in which it finds itself. Its practices and beliefs cannot simply accommodate the general worldly sentiment or merely accommodate every whim and wind that blows.

Silas's heart was thrumming in his chest at what he had just read.

There he was, Emperor Constantine, quoting the Apostle Paul! And claiming to be a steward of the faith, not its architect as the Markus Brauns and Noland Rotbergs of the world had contended. And boy did his warning ring true, that the Christian faith was in danger of being co-opted by culture, accommodating it according to whichever way the wind blows.

The door opened at the back, and Bartholomew entered. Gapinski clapped his hands together and stood. "Just in time! Because I don't know what the hey-ho day we just heard."

"His confession," Silas said with marvel reading back over what he had just translated.

"I'm not sure about that, love," said Celeste, standing and moving to one of the tables.

"How can you say that? You heard it yourself."

Gapinski returned with the bottle of Barolo red uncorked and a wine glass filled to the brim. "This should be good…" he said, taking a sip and sitting with a pleasurable sigh.

"Heard what ourselves?" Torres asked. "Can I get some of that?"

Bartholomew handed her a glass, and Gapinski poured. "Bottoms up…"

"First Corinthians 15, that's what." Silas retrieved his phone from his pocket, opening it to a Bible app and scrolling to the passage. "Take a listen: *'For I handed on to you as of first importance what I in turn had received: that Christ died for our sins in accordance with the scriptures, and that he was buried, and that he was raised on the third day in accordance with the scriptures, and that he appeared to Cephas, then to the twelve. Then he appeared to more than five hundred brothers and sisters at one time, most of whom are still alive, though some have died.'*"

Gapinski swallowed back another swig of wine. "Hey, that's what our buddy Constantine said!"

"Most of it, nearly word for word!" Silas said. "Which amounted to a sort of early creedal confession of the Church, declaring that Christ died for our sins and then was resurrected, physically appearing to the Twelve Apostles and then to hundreds more. Which Constantine then combines with another crucial passage about Christ's identity."

Silas inputted another search into his Bible smartphone app, then read: "*Long ago God spoke to our ancestors in many and various ways by the prophets, but in these last days he has spoken to us by a Son, whom he appointed heir of all things, through whom he also created the worlds. He is the reflection of God's glory and the exact imprint of God's very being, and he sustains all things by his powerful word. When he had made purification for sins, he sat down at the right hand of the Majesty on high, having become as much superior to angels as the name he has inherited is more excellent than theirs.'"

"Nice catch, Silas," Celeste said, walking over bearing another parchment. "Hebrews chapter one."

"Exactly! Which gets to the very heart of the early Church controversy that led to the Nicene Creed."

"What do you have there?" Torres asked Celeste.

She replied, "One of the other fragments. I wanted to check something at the front end of our new one. May I?" she asked, gesturing to the one Silas was holding.

He handed it over. "What do you have?"

She matched the bottom end of the one to the top of the new fragment.

Silas smiled. "Perfect match!"

"I was wondering about Constantine's remarks at the start."

"About being wrong? I wondered that as well."

Celeste nodded. "Right."

"And what was he wrong about?" Gapinski asked, throwing back another mouthful and refilling his glass.

Eyeing the parchment fragment she brought together with the new one, Celeste cleared her throat. "Here it is, and I quote: '*There is only one faith, and one opinion about our religion, and the Divine commandment in all its parts imposes upon us all the duty of maintaining a spirit of peace and grace, in addition to truth and* doctrine. *I insisted they should not let the circumstance which had led to a slight difference between the two cause any division or schism amongst them and the larger Church, since I believe it did not affect the validity of the whole. We are not all like-minded on every subject, nor is there such a thing as one universal disposition and judgment.'* Then he says in the one you and Torres just discovered, *'I could not have been more wrong.'"*

"About the Christian faith?" Torres asked.

Silas took the other fragment from Celeste, hope rising within. "I don't think so. I think he meant the controversy between Arius and Athanasius. Suggesting he was wrong to say the divisions and schisms were only slight and not affecting the whole of the faith. Perhaps even suggesting he was wrong to say there isn't a universal, once-for-all faith that was threatened by Arius."

Celeste added, "That's what I wondered as well. Which would seem to throw this whole conspiracy stuff and nonsense into another orbit, wouldn't it?"

He stared off, considering what they had read. Was Constantine really disavowing Arius and his heresy that sought to disrupt the unity of the faith? Was he confessing what the Church had always confessed about Christianity, about Christ?

Then he shook his head. "There's still something more to this, something missing."

Celeste held up the parchment piece Gapinski and Torres had just recovered. "Another fragment, you mean? The end of this one is torn, leading me to believe there is still at least one more out there."

He shook his head. "No, something more. Another clue to bring clarity to this whole blasted conspiracy."

"Oh yeah, I almost forgot." Gapinski reached in his pocket and tossed the familiar metal fragment on the table. It landed on the side with the etchings. Throwing back the rest of his wine, He said, "Sorry, pal. Looks like another part of the Nous symbol."

Silas picked it up and eyed it. Then they went wide with surprise.

"I'm not so sure about that..."

CHAPTER 22

What could this mean?

Silas leaped from his seat and hustled over to a worktable he and Celeste had been working at earlier before Gapinski and Torres arrived. He was looking for the other two matching medallion pieces they had been carting around the past few days.

"Where's the fire, chief?" Gapinski said, leaning back and taking another sip of wine as Torres and Celeste stood.

"Matthew's right. What are you playing at, Silas?" asked Celeste.

He ignored them as he turned over papers scattered about the table and set aside books looking for the other medallion fragments, his mind reeling at what he held, the familiar lines etched into the aged metal looking not at all what he expected.

Gapinski is right: A missing piece to this whole blasted conspiracy puzzle...

Or was it?

Best not to get your hopes up, Grey. Not until—

There they were, the other metal fragments they figured formed some sort of medallion. One from Apollonia. The other from Istanbul, the one he and Celeste had just recovered. And then this one from Gapinski, which seemed like a mirror image of the one buried in the Libyan sands

He cleared a space on the dark wood of papers and books, then laid out the first two medallion pieces, Gapinski's new one and the original, fitting them together with care. They slipped easily into one another with memory, like a hand sliding into a well-used leather glove.

"What do you mean?" Celeste said, coming up to his side. "That you're not sure it's another piece to the Nous symbol?"

"I'll let you know in a minute. Give me the other two golden cylinders, would you?"

Torres handed him the satchel. He fished out the only other medallion piece, the one Sebastian had found and announced on WeSolve. He set the one he and Celeste had found earlier at the top, then held his breath as he positioned the new missing fragment, sliding it between two others like a piece of pie.

A perfect match...

Two gaps at the nine to twelve o'clock positions indicated two more missing pieces—one they knew of from the earlier WeSolve broadcast that Braun had revealed—but the fitted fragments indeed revealed more of the puzzle.

He opened his phone and pulled up an image of that one piece, zooming in and angling the image before positioning his phone to fill part of the gap. Then he grinned with satisfaction.

"Look." Silas pointed, his heart hammering in his head and chest heavy with the significance of what they'd discovered.

"Holybamoly, Batman. What is that?" Gapinski said, coming up from behind.

"That ain't Nous, whatever it is," Torres offered.

No. It ain't...

Instead of the one end at the top bent left to form the head of Nous's phoenix bird symbol, both sides were bent forming an upside down 'V'. And where they had thought the two other portions of the symbol were the wings, angled inward toward the body at the center, Silas had turned the pair around so that they formed an actual 'V', with a stem rising to meet the larger medallion fragment.

"Blimey..." Celeste said, folding her arms. "Is that an anchor?"

"Looks that way..."

The four stood at the table, staring at the shattered, incomplete medallion that seemed to depict the nautical device.

Gapinski was the first to speak, asking what everyone else was thinking. "So...just gonna go ahead and ask: What the hey-ho day is an anchor etched on the face of a medallion doing shattered into pieces doing stuffed down golden cylinders with copies of the Nicene Creed and torn fragments of some confession or recantation or whatever the heck we think it is this side of Sunday—and then all of it scattered around the world?"

"I'm with Hoss," Torres said. "What gives?"

Silas took a breath and rubbed his face now prickled with several days of stubble. Good question.

Early Christians had adopted the anchor as a symbol of hope for the future, given it was regarded in ancient times as a symbol of safety. For the Church, Christ is considered to be a believer's unfailing hope. Saint Peter, Saint Paul, and several early Church Fathers spoke of this sense. But like Gapinski asked, what does it all mean?

"'We have this hope, a sure and steadfast anchor of the soul,'" Bartholomew intoned behind them, continuing: "'a hope that enters the inner shrine behind the curtain, where Jesus, a forerunner on our behalf, has entered, having become a high priest forever according to the order of Melchizedek.'"

"The Book of Hebrews, chapter six," Celeste said. "I was thinking the same thing, where the ancient symbol of the anchor is explicitly connected with Christ."

"But that begs Matt's question," Torres said. "Why was this symbol shattered and placed inside these cylinders, then scattered around the Mediterranean?"

"Because that definitely ain't Nous," said Gapinski, finishing another glass of wine with a belch. "Which, at this point, means the idea this is a conspiracy brought on by the Church's archenemy is sketchy at best."

Silas ran a worried hand through his hair as he studied the broken symbol. Because what the man said was right. This was starting to look like a whole other thing. But *what* exactly...that's what worried him.

"Perhaps the symbol of the anchor is meant to act as we had assumed it was all along," Celeste said.

He turned to her. "And what's that?"

"As a calling card."

"But in this case," Torres said, voice brightening, "definitely not the card we thought was being played."

"Not from Nous's deck, you mean?" Gapinski asked.

Celeste nodded. "Right, that was what I was thinking. A different symbol from some other source entirely. Perhaps connected to Nous, but probably not."

"What about the new kids on the block, the box-men tattoo guys that reared their ugly heads the past few months?"

She folded her arms and shook her head. "Perhaps, but I don't believe so."

Silas returned to the arranged puzzle pieces, the ends of his mouth curling upward with hope now. "I agree. This definitely seems connected to the Church somehow."

"But how?" Torres said.

"And not just how, *who*?" Gapinski asked, folding his arms.

The group fell silent for a moment in the face of all the questions.

Yet for Silas, for the first time since this whole blasted mission began hope was emerging. Just like the anchor symbolized. Hope they were on to something that could save the Church and protect the faith.

"I wonder..." Bartholomew said, turning away and shuffling over to a workstation.

Silas turned his way, curious what he was thinking about all of this. Celeste interrupted him.

"Oy, what's this?" she exclaimed, bending toward the reconstituted medallion, eyeing the pieces Gapinski and Torres had recovered.

"What's what?" he asked, turning back around and joining her.

She pointed along the edge. "This. Are those letters? Some sort of characters etched there along the edge of these pieces?"

He squinted, searching along the edge in the dim light. His eyes widened with a mixture of disbelief and curiosity.

Looked exactly like she said!

"I didn't notice those before," Torres said, joining the pair.

"I remembered some scratches caked with grime from the one in Apollonia," Silas said, taking apart the medallion puzzle and eyeing the two new pieces closer. "But didn't think anything of them until now."

Celeste did the same with the first piece they had discovered in Apollonia, and Torres joined her by examining the new one she and Gapinski had recovered.

"This one's pretty beat up," Torres said, squinting one eye and picking at parts of the edge with her fingernail. "And dirt and other gunk is caked in the crevices pretty well. Probably why we didn't notice it before."

"Same with this one," Celeste said, wetting a finger and rubbing it against the edge.

"Eww, gross," Gapinski muttered under his breath.

She hit him; he yelped. "Instead of sideline commentary, how about you go do something useful. Find us some water and a hand cloth to help scrub away the grime."

"Yes, ma'am..."

"This doesn't make any sense," Silas mumbled.

"What doesn't?" Celeste asked.

He pointed. "These characters look like a jumbled mess of Greek characters, see the Chi there." He pointed to the now familiar *X*. "But if it was stuffed down a Roman cylinder, I would have expected them to be Latin characters along the side. Especially post-Nicene Creed, around Constantine's death."

"It's all Greek to me," Gapinski said, walking up with a pitcher of water and cloth towel.

Torres shook her head. "Never gets old, does it?"

"Good boy," Celeste said, taking the towel and getting to

work. "I agree, that does strike me as odd, even more so given the presence of the Nicene Creed. If this were now some Christian sect, one would also expect Latin since one can argue it became the Church's official language in the 4th century."

"And with the characters all running together," Silas went on, turning the fragment for a better view, "I can't make sense of it, since my piece clearly starts in the middle of the string of Greek letters. Or the beginning or end, depending."

Then he had an idea.

Taking a scrap of paper nearby while Celeste continued her work, Silas scribbled down the characters in their English equivalent at the top, the ones visible from Braun's piece on his phone and the one he and Celeste had recovered in Istanbul:

EPAGONIZESTHAITN

He folded his arms and stared at the characters, trying to make sense of them.

"Yeah, I got nothin'," Gapinski said over his shoulder.

Me either...

"I'm finished with my fragment," Celeste said, handing the cloth over to Torres, who got to work on her own piece, and then handing the piece to Silas.

"Thanks. Let me just..." He squinted again holding it up to the light for a better look.

"I managed to rub away much of the dirt that had been encrusted to the edge, but it still isn't in the best shape."

No, it wasn't. But Silas could make out most of the characters, again in their English equivalent, which he wrote down underneath his own, skipping a space for the missing piece:

EPAGONIZESTHAITN

NTOISAGIOIS

He checked over his work but was satisfied he had rendered the characters correctly. He folded his arms and stared at the new set, clenching his jaw and huffing a frustrated breath. This was going nowhere. They had nothing more than a handful of crudely cut, badly damaged maybe-Greek characters.

Although...

He caught his breath with recognition.

"This here, *TOIS*," Silas said, pointing at the end of the new string, "is probably an article, plural."

"Probably?" Gapinski asked, brow raised.

"I'm finished now as well," Torres said, intercepting any bite-back from Silas.

She handed over her piece, cleaner than Celeste's had been. He got to work copying down the characters:

PARADOTHEIS

Now they were getting somewhere! He combined these new ones with Celeste's, fitting the pieces next to each other:

PARADOTHEISETOISAGIOIS

"If this is an article..." Silas said, marking a dark hash mark between the *S* and *A*, the Sigma and Alpha. "Then this next word should be..." He counted off the characters with his pen, considering the words they could form—

Then made a mark and dropped the pen in shock, bringing a hand to his face and rubbing his stubbled chin.

PARADOTHEISE/TOIS/AGIOIS

"Come on," Gapinski moaned. "Don't leave us hanging!"

He looked back at the characters, agreeing with his assessment. But what did it mean?

Celeste leaned in, translating: "'To the holy ones.' Or 'to the saints,' whichever you prefer."

"As in, Christians?" Torres said.

"Wait a second," Gapinski said. "I thought this was some conspiracy by pseudo-spiritual terrorist whack jobs!"

Silas returned to the set of characters he had first written down, heart thumping now and head swimming with possibility—catching another article, at the end of what he had written down from his medallion.

Heart pounding and breath shallow on an adrenaline high, he separated it off from the other characters with another dark hash mark:

EPAGONIZESTHAI/TN

And Silas knew exactly what that first word was. He offered a drunken giggle, delighted at what it said.

"Contend..." he muttered.

"Content? What content?" Gapinski asked. "Or perhaps *content*. Lord knows we could all use a bit of peaceful happiness and bliss..."

Silas shook his head. "No, not *content* or *content*. *Contend*. Struggle for, protect."

Torres twisted up her face in confusion. "Struggle? Protect? Contend? And for what?"

Celeste folded her arms and grinned. "For something that was important to the holy ones, the saints."

"You thinking what I'm thinking?" Silas said, turning to Celeste, mouth running dry now at what he knew deep down had been stuffed in those cylinders.

She nodded, brows raising with excitement. "I would wager that we are indeed on the same wavelength with this one."

The two fell silent, both staring at the medallion pieces with bemused smiles.

"Hello..." Gapinski finally said, tapping the top of his closed fist with two fingers. "Is this thing on? Care to fill us in? We're dying over here!"

"Yeah, what gives? What's this about?" Torres asked.

"You both should know as much as we do," Celeste said.

"We should?"

"Contend...for something for the saints? Ring a bell?"

The two went silent, staring at the medallion pieces as Silas and Celeste waited for it to dawn.

"Yeah, I got nothing?" Gapinski said.

"Me either," Torres muttered.

Celeste explained, "It is only the motto of the very organization that cuts your paychecks each week."

"*'Contend for the faith that was once for all entrusted to the saints,'*" Bartholomew said from behind again. "Verse three, from The Letter of Jude Thaddeus."

Torres smirked. "Our founding father, of course!"

"Oops..." Gapinski said, rubbing the back of his neck with embarrassment.

Silas fitted all the pieces back into place, then folded his arms and marveled at the medallion, characters fully restored:

"Exactly. Jude 3." Silas pointed at the last untranslated word, *APAX,* and said, "That word means *once* or *once-for-all.* Guarantee you the missing Greek word is *PISTEI.*"

"*Faith...*" Celeste said.

He threw her a knowing grin. "The *once-for-all faith,* or *faith once for all entrusted,* as *PARADOTHEISE* means here." He pointed at the word from Torres's medallion then folded his arms in contemplation.

Torres said, "But why on earth was this rather obscure verse—"

"Obscure verse?" Celeste said with raised brow.

"Watch who you're talking about there, Torres," Silas said. "That verse is *our* verse."

Gapinski snorted. "Yeah, don't bite the hand that feeds ya, Torres!"

She rolled her eyes. "I only mean that Jude 3 is not John 3:16. I mean, how many Christians even know about the Book of Jude let alone can quote this verse."

Silas smiled. "I hear you. Just giving you a hard time."

"But she has a point, chief," Gapinski said.

"And what's that?"

He picked up one of the metal fragments. "We've got this obscure verse—" he stopped short before quickly adding: "Torres's words, not mine! And here it is, just ringing some medallion broken into probably six pieces, stuffed down the necks of these golden thingamabobs. Like she said, what gives?"

"So that's the question *then,* isn't it," Celeste said. "Why this verse on this medallion?"

"It makes perfect sense," Bartholomew said from behind again.

Silas turned around. The man was arms crossed, wearing a wry grin. "It does?"

"But of course! And you yourself should know, *Master* Grey. Especially after giving your comrades such a hard time."

He glanced at his fellow SEPIO agents and furrowed his brow, confused at the man's show. "Why's that?"

Bartholomew stepped forward and snatched the piece from Gapinski, cassock whispering across the floor in the silent room. He placed it back on the table and fitted it with the others.

Then he said, "Because that symbol is your own symbol."

CHAPTER 23

Could it really be true?

    A weak tremble seized Silas's hand at the possibility. He clenched it shut, embarrassed at the show of weakness which was really a show of embarrassment at his ignorance being exposed. He was the Order Master for crying out loud! And he didn't even recognize what was flat staring him in the face the past few days?

That the clarity they had been seeking about the conspiracy had been with them the whole time? That what they had been chasing wasn't at all the ruin of the Christian faith but a potential boon for its authenticity? And the Order of Thaddeus itself had been responsible for secreting it away for such a time as this?

He swallowed and took a breath, stuffing down his pride and turning back to the massive clue resting on the table in front of them, the HVAC hum from the carefully climate-controlled facilities the only soundtrack as they took in the gravity of the revelation.

Lord Jesus Christ, Son of God, is this clue the hope we've been looking for?

"What on earth are you playing at, Bartholomew?" Celeste

asked, turning back herself and running a finger across the thin lines that formed an anchor, the hope of Christ.

"What I'm playing at, Ms. Bourne, is that medallion, resting on that table is the Order of Thaddeus's. Because that symbol is the Order's symbol."

Silas and Celeste looked at one another, faces registering the same dumbfounded disbelief and confusion.

"It's no secret," the man went on, "in the Roman Catholic Church at least, Jude Thaddeus is the patron saint of desperate cases and lost causes."

"The saint of hope..." Silas marveled.

Bartholomew nodded. "That's right. And apparently, during the early days the apostle's religious order took for itself the anchor as a symbol of all that they sought to accomplish in preserving and protecting the faith, the hope of Christ. After all, what better hope can the Church's saints offer the world than the once-for-all faith entrusted to them? A hope anchored in the finished work of Jesus on the cross through his shed blood for the forgiveness of sins, hope in the resurrection of the dead and the life to come."

The man was right about that anchoring hope, which the Church had found in Jesus. But that it was a symbol of the Order was news to Silas. And apparently the rest of the gang.

Gapinski crossed his arms. "This is nutso to the maxo, as Zoe would say."

"I agree," Torres said.

"Why haven't we heard of this until now?" Celeste asked, clearly taken aback as much as Silas—which gave him a bit of comfort. "I know you chided Silas in jest a moment ago for not recognizing the symbol, but I've been with the Order for years and have heard neither hide nor tail of it! Even Rowen Radcliffe never brought it to our attention."

The man shrugged. "That's not surprising, since it has been lost to history."

"What do you mean, lost to history?" Silas asked, confused more than ever.

Bartholomew took a breath and waved them over. "Look here."

He led them to a workstation with a large monitor displaying an aged manuscript in familiar tea-stained brown, what looked like faded black Greek scrawled across.

"When I heard you were coming a few days ago, being tapped on the shoulder to greet your arrival and shepherd you through our collection, I did a bit of digging."

"Snooping you mean?" Gapinski asked with a chuckle.

The priest shrugged and smiled. "What can I say? I'm an archivist. Curiosity gets the best of me."

"And kills the cat..."

"So what did you find," Silas said, moving the conversation along.

Bartholomew put up an apologetic hand. "I was...snooping, as you said, through the historical archives of the Order going back centuries, far back through Vatican II, the Reformation—which was quite a doozie of a snoopfest! All the way through the Renaissance and so-called Dark Ages of civilization, which was really one of the heights of the Church's intellectual endeavors thanks to the Order, actually, in partnership with the Benedictine and Franciscan monks, all the way through the early Councils of Chalcedon and Nicaea to its founding. It was all quite fascinating and quite revealing. You should have a look sometime!"

"Perhaps when this is over, Bartholomew," Celeste said, "and we've solved the caper. But you indicated you found something of interest to us."

"That's right. References to the symbol that had faded from use during the Enlightenment as the Order struggled to hold fast to its mission, rooting the Church in the historic faith and anchoring the believing community in the essentials of Christianity. So when you fit the pieces together and revealed the anchor symbol, something clicked in my head and I found this in our extensive database of digitized archives, part of the Digital Vatican Library, a vast digitization project that aims to digitize the entire Archive's collection of manuscripts, tens of thousands of codices and papal bulls and encyclicals and charters from the earliest Christian orders." He smiled and pointed to the screen, adding: "Including the Order of Thaddeus."

A holy hush fell across the room. Silas and the others leaned closer toward the monitor at the revelation that the founding document of the organization they worked for was staring them in the face.

"Blimey..." Celeste whispered.

"Holybamoly..." Gapinski added.

"*Dios mío...*" Torres said.

"All of the above," Silas said in agreement, the sketch of the rest of the medallion in faded ink on parchment confirming the truth of the matter.

And also confirming something in his head.

He turned toward his SEPIO agents. "That means this isn't at all some sort of Nous conspiracy to bring down the Church."

"I'd wager not," Celeste said. "But what do you make of it then? A splinter group within the Order?"

"No, don't you see? What if it was the Order of Thaddeus who took Constantine's confession and tore it into several pieces, splintering a medallion with their symbol, a sort of official seal of the Order and stuffing it down inside golden cylinders, along with copies of the Nicene Creed?"

Celeste narrowed her eyes in thought. "Perhaps, but for what purpose?"

"Obviously not for some conspiracy to undermine Christianity," Torres offered.

Silas nodded. "Exactly. Not at all, but instead to support its authenticity. Maybe even bolster its credibility by having the

Emperor himself give his own confession of faith. Possibly a sort of imperial imprimatur."

"That's a big possibility," Celeste cautioned.

"True, but also a big *probability*."

She went to respond but closed her mouth instead.

Gapinski laughed. "Did Silas just render Celeste speechless?"

She gave him a look, which forced him behind Silas for cover.

Silas stifled a laugh and returned to the seal affixed to the screen, then brightened. "Looks like I was right."

"About what?" Celeste said leaning over.

"About the remaining medallion piece. Look there," he said, pointing to a Greek word arrayed around the seal. "*PISTE*. The word missing from the Jude 3 inscription etched around the medallion pieces we retrieved."

"Which means there is a remaining medallion piece," Torres said. "Another missing link."

"And another missing parchment piece," Gapinski added.

Silas nodded. "We know of at least one other one we don't have."

"Markus Braun's fragment."

"Exactly, which means there's one remaining torn piece to Constantine's confession. It's the missing link that will blow this whole thing wide open. I just know it will confirm what we're already confirming."

"And what's that?" Torres asked.

He turned to her. "That Constantine disavowed Arius, affirmed Nicene Christianity, which is to say historical, biblical Christianity, and confessed his belief in Jesus Christ as Lord and Savior."

"I realize your hopes are high on this, love," Celeste said, voice laced with skepticism, "but we have little proof with any of this. Only conjecture at this point. And besides, based upon everything we have seen so far from what we do have, both from the retrieved manuscript fragments as well as the historical record, the jury seems out on that accord, regarding both Constantine's relationship to Arius as well as his relationship to the Church and confession of faith in Christ."

"Maybe not entirely," Bartholomew said.

Silas turned to him. "What do you mean?"

His brow flickered with a mischievous glint, and one end of his mouth curled upward. "Because there was something else I discovered while you were away."

He turned toward the door to leave, then motioned for the group to follow. "Come along. Some supplemental findings I should think will bring more clarity. And ammunition."

Silas eyed his SEPIO agents and shrugged, then followed after the man.

Bartholomew led them back toward the elevator. Once inside, he punched in a code at a keypad. Gears snapped into motion, taking them farther below.

He winked. "Down we go...."

"Again," Gapinski complained, looking up and around and swallowing hard.

"You afraid of elevators, Hoss?" Torres asked.

He frowned. "Maybe..."

She smirked as they continued descending, several floors by the feel of it.

"I'm taking you to my personal office," Bartholomew said. "Well, office might be a bit generous. Closet more like it."

"To do what, exactly?" Silas asked.

"To show you something I found while you were away. I put it in my office for safekeeping."

"Safekeeping?" Gapinski said, twisting up his face with confusion. "From Vatican peeps?"

He flashed him a knowing look. "One can never be too sure who is lurking about..."

The elevator pulled up before coming to a stop.

"Here we go. Heads down, by the way."

Heads down was right. They were met by a low-slung ceiling of brown cut stone, with the same architecture leading the way on the floor. The walls were of the same variety, large blocks fitted together. A strong smell of must and dampness, decay even followed them as they made their way forward. LED lights ran the length of the floor and other lights glowed orange from recessed canisters above. Reminded him of SEPIO HQ back in DC, but smelling like an over-ripened basement.

"What is this place?" Silas asked.

"The bowels of the Vatican," Bartholomew answered. "And actually, it had once been part of the network of catacombs running throughout Rome from the earliest of centuries."

"Catacombs?" Gapinski said with a start, flashing the walls a freaked-out eye.

Bartholomew chuckled. "No need to worry. The bones have since been cleared out. Offices and closets are all that remain. Speaking of which…"

He pulled up to a nondescript steel door, a keycard pad mounted at the right with a red light. He flashed it a gray card held in his palm before stowing it back inside his cassock. The light changed to green, and the door unlocked with a *click*.

Bartholomew pushed through. Silas followed. A closet of an office was right.

A small desk was set in the corner of the room about the size of his childhood bedroom, lights dimmed yellow and smelling far more like his Falls Church childhood basement. A heavy safe sat next to it on the ground and a worktable stood behind it, piled high with books, some looking very old, their browned pages peeking through under stiff, warped leather bindings.

Bartholomew crouched next to the safe and punched in a code. It unlocked, and he swung open the door on tired hinges.

He removed a stack of parchments in plastic sleeves and brought them to the worktable. He turned on a lamp; its fluorescent bulb flickered to life.

Silas joined his side, marveling at the Latin script looking surprisingly crisp against the beige parchment. Then he startled at something he saw. Something small, imprinted faintly in the upper right corner.

The Chi-Rho.

Reaching for the top parchment sheathed in plastic, he hesitated. "Sorry. May I?"

Bartholomew gestured toward the document. "By all means. But do take care. It is very old."

"How old?" Celeste asked.

He looked at her and winked. "You'll see. Go on, read it."

Silas swallowed hard and took it, then obliged his request:

The effects of that envious spirit which so troubled the peace of the churches of God in Alexandria continued to cause Constantine no little disturbance of mind. For in fact, in every city bishops were engaged in obstinate conflict with bishops, and people rising against people, causing in him sorrow of spirit; for he deeply deplored the folly that had been exhibited by the deranged Arians.

Turning to Bartholomew with furrowed brow, he asked, "Is this what I think it is?"

He nodded, grinning widely. "It is."

"Is what what you think it is?" Gapinski asked.

"A copy of Eusebius's *Life of Constantine*," Silas answered.

Bartholomew shook his head. "No, the *original* copy of his *Life of Constantine*."

"What?" Celeste exclaimed, grabbing for the parchment.

Which Silas held back with a grin.

"Not to worry," Bartholomew said, reaching toward the pile. "There are more to go around." He handed one to Celeste, a longer piece but in the same condition with the same imprimatur.

She took it and scrunched up her face into a victorious grin, then started translating the Latin, eyes wide and hungry.

"What's this here?" Torres said, pointing to the Chi-Rho at the corner. "We've seen it elsewhere. The official symbol of Constantine, right?"

Bartholomew nodded. "The Emperor had this account by Eusebius the Historian specially commissioned and drafted for his personal affects. I pulled a few pages that seemed particularly relevant."

"And what does the good historian have to say," she said, clearing her throat and glaring at Celeste when she raised her head.

Celeste pushed a stray lock of hair behind an ear. "Here, let me..." She cleared her throat and read aloud:

As if to bring a divine array against this enemy, he assembled a general council and invited bishops from all quarters, expressing his honorable estimation. When they were assembled, it appeared evident that the proceeding was the work of God. For those who had been most widely separated, not only in sentiment but also personally, as well as by country, place, and nation, were brought together, forming as it were a vast garland of priests, composed of a variety of the choicest flowers.

She handed back the parchment to Bartholomew. "So it

appears that Constantine was acting in good faith when he assembled the council after all to combat the Arians."

He retrieved it and set it back on the table. "That he was. However, consider this other parchment." Bartholomew reached for another sleeved manuscript page and handed it to Celeste.

Silas leaned over for his own viewing. Looked like a list of locations at first glance.

"What's this?" she asked.

"A listing of the Church's representation at the Council. You'll see it's quite diverse."

Again, she translated the Latin, which noted ministers from all the churches across the spectrum of the Church—from Europe, Libya, and Asia to Phoenicians and Arabians; delegates from Palestine and Egypt and from the region of Mesopotamia; a Persian bishop and even a Scythian; those from Pontus, Galatia, and Pamphylia to Cappadocia, Asia, and Phrygia; even from the remotest districts like Spain.

Torres folded her arms and sighed. "So much for the argument that white Europeans created Christianity. Just look at that representation from the Church!"

"I'd say," Silas said, retrieving the parchment from Celeste. "Note what else Eusebius says of the Emperor: *'Constantine is the first prince of any age who bound together such a garland as this with the bond of peace, and presented it to his Savior as a thank-offering for the victories he had obtained over every foe, thus exhibiting in our own times a similitude of the apostolic company.'*"

"A bit high on the man, if you ask me," Celeste muttered.

Silas leaned over and whispered, "You're just mad you were wrong about the bloke."

She gave him a look that told him to back off, yet a wry grin struggled to push through.

"That's what I thought," he said with satisfaction.

"So from across North Africa," Bartholomew said, playing

interference, "and the Middle East and Asia Minor, and then into Europe—the whole representation of the universal Church was present at the Council of Nicaea to make one of the most decisive decisions about what was central to the Christian faith: the nature of Jesus Christ, his equality with God the Father."

"Fascinating, Bartholomew," Celeste said, "but what does this have to do with finding Arius?"

He put up an apologetic hand. "Sorry. I'm digressing a bit."

"I don't know," Silas said, "I think it shows the Council was truly an ecumenical and international affair. Not something cobbled together by the Emperor for political gain."

"Precisely! But the most fascinating part is his speech to the council."

Silas took in a startled breath. "The speech?"

The man grinned, reaching for a folio of bound pages, perfectly preserved and similarly sleeved but presented as a sort of tract.

He handed it to Silas. "Go on. Read it."

CHAPTER 24

Silas's heart was thrumming a mean beat, his hands growing moist and head swimming with possibility at what he was holding.

The very words of Constantine given to the Council of Nicaea. Both parties at the center of this blasted conspiracy.

It was a small folio of pages, preserved through the centuries given its significance, the Church keen to safeguard and showcase the imperial words offered to Christianity's first great ecumenical council. The binding was stiff and solid in his hand. He pressed against the cover, the leather surprisingly soft and flaring up a heady sweetness. He cracked it open, a flutter hitting his stomach at seeing the script running across the aged parchment and Chi-Rho insignia at the top. He gently fanned them, the pages whispering the possibility of secrets and flaring up another heady scent, pulpy and musky.

What would they reveal, what truths of Constantine's feelings about the Arian controversy and Christian claims to Jesus' deity did they hold?

Celeste rested a hand on his shoulder. "Go on, love."

"Yeah, time is a little of the essence here, chief," Gapinski complained.

Silas frowned, then swallowed and turned to page one. An elaborate drop cap opened the first sentence, gilt ink wrapped in green vines and what looked like blue and red birds resting on their leaves. Marginals ran up and down the sides as well, of cherubs and saints and a long cross stretching top to bottom.

He cleared his throat and began translating, reading aloud:

I pray that no malignant adversary may interfere to mar our happy state, and that it has been forever removed by the power of God our Savior. For strife within the Church is far more evil and dangerous than any kind of war or conflict. As soon as I heard the news of your dissension, I judged it to be crucially important, desiring that I might aid in finding a remedy for this evil.

And now I rejoice in seeing you assembled. However, I feel that my desires will be most completely fulfilled when I can see you all united in one judgment, and that the common spirit of peace and concord prevails among you all. Delay not dear friends, you ministers of God, and faithful servants of him who is our common Lord and Savior. Lay aside whatever has caused such disunion among you. Remove such controversies by embracing the principles of peace.

"An interesting revelation into the mind of the good Emperor," Celeste said, "with his talk about unity of the faith and sharing in the common Lord and Savior, Jesus Christ."

"Agree..." Silas said, marveling at the words, though not as much a slam dunk as he had hoped. "There's more."

The words continued, a whorl ornamental break separating the next paragraph from Constantine's speech. Translating, he read aloud:

> Speaking these words, the Emperor gave permission to those who presided over the Council to deliver their opinions. Several assertions were put forth by each party, and despite early accusations and controversy, the Emperor gave patient audience to all, receiving every proposition with steadfast attention. By occasionally assisting each party, he gradually disposed even the most vehement disputes and brought about a reconciliation.

Gapinski said, "Doesn't sound like someone with his thumb on the scale, that's for sure."

"Not at all," Bartholomew agreed.

Torres added, "More like a judge playing referee between two parties pleading their case."

"And it goes on—" The priest pointed at another paragraph over Silas's shoulder and took the lead translating aloud:

> By the affability of his address, he persuaded some and convinced others by his reasonings, praising those who spoke well and urging all to unity until he succeeded in bringing them to one mind and judgment, respecting every disputed question.

"He persuaded?" Celeste said, sounding equally stunned and skeptical.

"And convinced by his reasoning," Torres said.

Bartholomew nodded. "That he did. As we saw earlier, he had fiery words for the Arian dissenters that would seek to undermine the historic Christian belief in Jesus' identity as the

Son of God. And Constantine himself took point in making the case for the historic belief in Christ's identity."

"Well, now we're back to the dude having his thumb on the scale," Gapinski said. "Isn't that what Braun and Rotberg have argued?"

"And those bargain-bin Kindle thrillers?" Torres added.

Bartholomew smirked. "Not entirely. This was not a political power play but rather a personal conviction of faith shared by the rest of the Church. He also instructed the churches to respect this very verdict from the Council of Nicaea."

The man reached for another of the parchments resting on the dark wood desk. "Upon completion of the Council of Nicaea, after the verdict basically anathematized the Arians, by a wide margin mind you, and reaffirmed the Christian conviction in Jesus Christ the Son's co-equality with God the Father in power, essence, and glory, Constantine sent a letter to the churches throughout the empire urging them to respect what had been rendered."

This time Celeste took it from him, looking it over. "Says here the good Emperor had wanted to ensure *'that unity of faith, sincerity of love, and community of feeling in regard to the worship of Almighty God, might be preserved'* amongst the Church.'"

"Which absolutely would have included the belief in Jesus' divinity," Silas said.

"He goes on: *'Every question received due and full examination, until that judgment which God, who sees all things, could approve, and which tended to unity was brought to light, so that no room was left for further discussion or controversy in relation to the faith.'*"

Gapinski shifted and put a hand to his chin. "So the dude says there was a full hearing of all sides arguing the matter."

"Indeed," Celeste said. "And he ordered the churches to *'Receive with all willingness this truly Divine verdict'* and *'as the gift of God.'* The bloke binds them *'from that time forward to adopt for yourselves, and to require others to adopt the Council's code.* He even suggests 'the cruel power of Satan was removed by God's aid through the agency of our endeavors in Nicaea.'"

"Clearly the Emperor appealed to the bishops' ruling," Torres said, "for the obedience of the churches to believe in Christ's deity."

"And basically fingered the dudes," Gapinski added, "who sought to undermine that belief as agents of the Devil!"

Celeste said, "And did you notice how he rooted the decisions coming out of the Nicene Council as being divinely directed, a gift of God even?"

Silas smiled and nodded. "I did. Which again adds weight to this controversy surrounding this central belief of Jesus' divine nature being far more personal to his faith."

A measure of hope was surging now, these revelations Bartholomew had found buried in the Church's archives plus the picture emerging from the assembled parchment fragments combining to paint a very different picture than the conspiracy he had feared just days ago.

Bartholomew set the parchment on the growing stack of read manuscripts. "As you can see, the Emperor transmitted a faithful copy of this letter to every province, wherein they who read it might discern as in a mirror the pure sincerity of his thoughts, and of his piety toward God, along with copies of the Nicene Creed."

He reached for one final folio, a handful of tea-stained pages peeking up under another stiff, solid leather binding. Opening the tract before them, the heady scent of ink and pulp and musk escaped into the air, making Silas long for a library to escape to from the madness of the past few days. A nice terry-cotton robe and sherpa-lined slippers and king-size bed would be nice, too.

"Here is the final document from the Archives I wanted you to read. I think it puts to rest any doubt about the Emperor's allegiance."

Silas took the tract of pages, anticipation welling in his belly. Scrawled across the pages was familiar black ink, along with the gilded drop cap at the start with red-and-blue detailing, along with some marginal illustrations and familiar Chi-Rho insignia affixed to the corner. Again, he wondered what revelations it held, and whether it would be the final key that clicked it all into place.

He glanced at the other SEPIO agents and cleared his throat, then got to work translating and reading aloud one final account from Eusebius, the Emperor's farewell speech:

> O Christ, Savior of mankind, be present to aid us in our hallowed task! Direct the words which celebrate your virtues, and instruct us worthily to sound your praises. We give thanks to you, our God and Savior, according to our feeble power.
>
> Unto you, O Christ, supreme Providence of the mighty Father, who both saves us from evil and gives us your most blessed doctrine. Who is worthy to declare your praise, of whom we learn that from nothing you called creation into being and illumined it with your light—that you brought harmony and order from chaos?
>
> Chiefly we mark your loving-kindness. For you have caused those who have given their hearts to you to earnestly desire a divine and blessed life. The Son of God invites all men to practice virtue, and offers himself to all who open their hearts up to him for salvation. Unless, that is, we will deceive ourselves and remain in wretched ignorance of the fact that he has secured the blessing of the human race by coming to earth.
>
> How can anyone doubt God's presence and help? He has easily delivered us from many dangers and terrors at his simple nod. I believe this is the sure basis of faith, the

true foundation of confidence, that we find such miracles performed and perfected at God's command. Even in the midst of trial, we find no cause to deny our faith, but retain an unshaken hope in God. When this habit of confidence is established in the soul, God himself dwells in the inmost thoughts. The soul is invincible; it will not be overcome by the perils which may surround it. We learn this truth from the victory of God himself. Though grievously insulted by the malice of the ungodly, God is intent on blessing mankind.

Constantine went on, but Silas handed the folio back to Bartholomew, who then set it back on the dark wood table along with the others he had chosen for SEPIO.

"That pretty well settles it then, doesn't it?" Torres said.

"You mean that Celeste was wrong and Silas was right?" Gapinski asked with a wry grin, nudging Celeste with an elbow.

She glared at him and frowned before one end of her mouth curled upward. "Under normal circumstances, I would have given you a right good slap for that."

"Oh, buddy..." he said, backing away.

"But, as much as it pains me to say it, you're right. Seems to be a right heartfelt confession by Emperor Constantine. As surprising as it sounds."

Silas rubbed his chin, considering what he had read—and all that they had seen. Glancing at Celeste, he said, "While I agree, that it appears I was right and you were wrong—"

"Watch it," she interrupted, holding out a finger.

"Yes, dear," he quickly said. "While it appears Constantine was indeed an orthodox believer, I still don't know..."

"What's not to know?" Torres said. "Even I was skeptical, yet he said so himself: Jesus Christ was the Son of God, the Savior who saves us from evil."

"I'd still like to get ahold of that final piece, the last missing parchment fragment would seal the deal."

"Yeah, but where?" Gapinski asked. "Seems like the proverbial needle in the haystack."

Silas shook his head, hopeful at what had been unearthed from the Vatican Archives but discouraged the trail had gone cold. After all they had recovered—all they had gone through.

"Perhaps I could shed some light on that one," Bartholomew said. "While I was rooting around our database for anything that could aid your endeavor, I also did a bit of digging into more of the history of the Order."

"Don't forget what happened to the curious cat..." Gapinski said.

"I know, but curiosity is why they pay me the big bucks. At any rate, in another section of the Order charter I showed you, the one that showcased the insignia, I found a curious reference to a place of refuge for the brotherhood, the *koinonia*."

"Koino-whatchamacallit?"

"Greek for *community*," Silas explained. "Or brotherhood."

Bartholomew nodded. "That's right. And among the bits speaking of wonderful men committed to contending for and preserving the deposit of faith given to the Church by the Holy Spirit and committed by Christ himself through the apostles of our Lord—the brotherhood continuing what Jude Thaddeus himself started—the charter promised that the Order would always have a place of refuge, a source of encouragement and safety when the world goes dark."

Silas's eyes went wide with hope. He glanced at Celeste who matched his surprise.

He said, "What place of refuge? Where?"

"A place known as Edessa, in modern Syria."

He smiled, which turned into a toothy grin before he laughed with recognition. Of course! The place where it all began for Jude and his efforts at contending for and preserving the memory markers of the faith.

"Edessa?" Gapinski said, face scrunched up in confusion.

Silas turned to him and the others. "As the story goes, it's where the disciples had sent the apostle as an answer to King Abgar's request to Jesus for healing. Our Savior wrote that he couldn't go, however Jude did after Christ's ascension into heaven and was able to offer healing to many while in Edessa, including the king himself. It's also believed he bore with him, either then or at some other point, the Holy Shroud."

"Yeah, I still don't get it."

"Don't you see? It's the tributary to the Order of Thaddeus, where the apostle first bore evidence that would help contend for the faith." He turned to Bartholomew. "You said it yourself. The refuge for the Order, a place of last resort for all it needs to find safety."

Torres added, "And you think that's where the final resting place is for the final parchment fragment?

Silas smiled and nodded.

Only one way to find out.

CHAPTER 25
URFA, TURKEY. JUNE 17, LATE EVENING.

Silas snapped his seatbelt into position with a *click* as the Gulfstream readied to land back into Turkey, this time at a regional airstrip just outside the modern equivalent of Edessa, the city of Urfa.

The gray tarmac was coming into view now outside the window in the fading daylight. It was nestled in a curious plane of green resting inside a bowl of jutting hills painted various shades of brown, the lowering sun casting wicked shadows between the giants hunched over with ill intent. By the time they left Rome late morning, it was nearly noon in Urfa. Between the nearly 1500 miles and rough turbulence through a storm crossing the Aegean Sea, they were pushing dinner time and Silas was more than ready to get boots on the ground.

He breathed deeply and closed his eyes, leaning back to ready for impact on the approaching airstrip. He hated flying as a rule, but he was especially queasy about landing in some backwater airport.

Another flight, another landing, another date with destiny.

Such was the life of a SEPIO agent heading off a conspiracy that could bring down the Church. Or in this case, expose a lie that thousands, millions even, had believed about the Christian faith. That Christianity had been cobbled together by competing beliefs and dogmas offered by competing centers of power within the Church. To double the conspiratorial impact, Emperor Constantine was styled as a powerbroker, a kingmaker of sorts who picked the winning horse in order to keep the Roman Empire from collapsing under the infighting weight of a religion that had risen to enormous heights of popularity and acceptance by broad swaths and sectors of the Empire by the fourth century.

From rich to poor, slave to free, peasant to politico, it was nothing short of a miraculous moving of the Holy Spirit that the Church had not only survived the furnace fires of persecution—in some cases literally, where believers had been burned at the stake, or worse. Instead, the Christian faith had flourished under such superheated threats and grew to overcome the imperial religious cult of the Roman Empire as well as other pagan superstitions of the Roman citizens. Becoming not only an officially recognized faith in the Empire, but a sanctioned one as well. Though it wasn't accurate to say Christianity became the official religion of the Roman Empire, it was certainly its de facto faith. Especially given Constantine's conversion with putting his faith in Jesus Christ.

And yet, to think some would seek to dismiss this movement that should have died with the death of its prophet at the hands of the Empire in AD 33, nailed to a cross on a hill just outside the walls of Jerusalem, yet didn't—to dismiss it as the invention of white Roman Europeans, and one white Roman European in particular—Emperor Caesar Flavius Constantinus, the Greatest, Pius, Felix, Augustus—was sheer madness. Conspiracy theorizing run amok that was intellectual nonsense and delusion, making no sense of history whatsoever. Given Silas's previous life as a relicologist, and the reason he was dragged into SEPIO in the first place, he knew why.

The Shroud of Turin. Or more accurately, and dogmatically:

the resurrection of Jesus, the memory of which the Shroud bore witness.

No way a bunch of freaked-out twentysomethings hunted by the ruling religious and political class and factions of their day would go to their deaths for a hoax—willingly enduring lion maulings and upside-down crucifixions and boiling vats of oil. They would have endured none of it if belief in Jesus' resurrection was not a fact of history.

For the simple reason: Why die for a lie?

Because if Jesus lives, defeating death itself after being raised from the dead on the third day, as the Nicene Creed codifies, then everything else about Christianity must also be taken seriously. Including Jesus' ransom payment for the sins of the world, paying the price for our rebellion against God in our place; the hope of the resurrection of the dead for those who put their faith in Jesus; the reality of judgment at the last day, and a separation of those who are in Christ from those who are not.

This also included Jesus' divinity as the Son of God—co-equal in power, glory, and honor with the Father and the Spirit. A central Christian belief which the Church's code, made possible by Emperor Constantine—so in many ways, as Markus Braun suggested, the *Emperor* code—instituted in the first place, which was reasoned and written by dedicated men to defend, protect, and preserve what Christians had believed from the start.

And which SEPIO was now going to the mat to defend, protect, and preserve. Not only for the sake of the Church, but for the sake of Christians.

A sudden dip and hard series of bumps jolted Silas from his thoughts on the matter, his breath catching in his chest as the buzz-saw growl of jet engines aided the brakes in bringing the Gulfstream to a halt a few yards from the end of the tarmac.

He eased in a stabilizing breath, glancing outside at the

green landscape now dominated by the parched beige of the surrounding hills. Which told him it was go time.

He just hoped they were right about Edessa holding the final clue to busting open the conspiracy threatening the faith, and that the final fragment confirmed what he had suspected.

Otherwise things could get real interesting for the Church real quick.

"Good news, love," Celeste said across the aisle, making him jump with a start. "Sorry! Flying still give your nerves the jiggles?"

He sat straight and nodded. "Something like that. What do you got?"

"Well, good and bad, I suppose. Zoe sent through a message during the flight that chatter on the dark web and some intel gathered from SEPIO agents tracing movement with Nous operatives suggest we're on the right course of action."

Now he leaned forward with interest. "What do you mean by right course of action? Flying to Edessa?"

"Right. Looks like Nous also got wind of it being a possible location for the final resting place of the final fragment."

Silas frowned and leaned back. "No doubt extracted from Bishop Zarruq."

"No doubt. And extracted is the truth of it," she said quietly. "At any rate, I suppose that means we chose wisely."

"It also means we're going to have company."

"No doubt."

The jet finished taxiing to a private hangar. Awaiting them was what looked like a BMW SUV. Gapinski was going to be disappointed. Which was an understatement.

"What the heck is this hunk of junk?" he complained at the bottom of the airstairs, hands on his hips and face twisted up with revulsion.

"Move it, would ya?" Torres equally complained as she pushed past.

"Come on, mate," Celeste said from behind. "We haven't got all day." He took a step forward, making room for her. "Not a Mercedes, but it should do the trick."

"You're kidding, right?" he said, still planted at the end of the airstairs.

"We don't have time for games," Silas said, brushing past him from behind. "Are you driving or am I?"

The man huffed and frowned. "I'll drive."

"Then saddle up. It's go time."

"Yes, sir...Just tell me the thing is packing heat."

Silas opened the trunk, revealing a SEPIO infiltration package, complete with enough SIG Sauer pistols and assault rifles and backup ammunition for the crew. Including his trusty Beretta.

"At least we've got that going for us," Gapinski muttered over his shoulder before turning toward the driver's side door.

The crew loaded into the car that felt surprisingly smaller than the more spacious G-Class they were used to riding. Eliciting not a small amount of complaining from Gapinski. But they buckled up and shoved out into the unknown Turkish world.

"So where are we heading?" Celeste asked.

"About that..." Silas said from the front, pulling out his phone. He connected it to the SUV with its Bluetooth connection, then dialed Zoe back at HQ. While in flight, he had asked her to coordinate with Bartholomew at the Vatican Archives on a possible location for their infiltration plan.

He hoped the pair had found something useful, or else the trip would be a complete waste of time.

Time they didn't have to waste, given the stakes.

"About time," the petite Italian answered. Silas imagined her pushing those oversized blue glasses up the bridge of her nose.

"Hello to you, too," Silas said. "We're making our way down

to Edessa—or Urfa, rather, and we're hoping you've put together a plan for us."

"It's been like three hours!"

"You've worked with less."

"But not coordinating with a third party with a countdown on our hands."

"So you're saying you've got bupkis?" Gapinski asked.

"Now, I didn't say that. Here, let me—"

The connection went silent for several seconds. Silas wondered if they lost her, but his phone continued ticking by the call's seconds. Soon a familiar voice was heard.

"Howdy, agents," Bartholomew said. "Ready to put this conspiracy to rest?"

"Ready when you are," Silas said. "Have you found something we can use?"

"Perhaps…"

He glanced back at Celeste, brow creased with worry and growing frustration. They didn't have much time left. They needed answers, and those two were their lifelines at this point.

"At first glance," Bartholomew went on, "Urfa appears to offer nothing of Christian interest for the Church, even when you get there. From what I understand and according to my research, there is not a single Christian church in the vicinity, and certainly not an ancient one still standing. Instead, the Muslim minarets are all-pervading."

"Then what in the world are we doing here?" Torres complained.

Silas answered, "Because if we could turn back the clock a little over a thousand years, say to the mid-900s, we would find an entirely different place."

"That's right, Master Grey. The city had been one of the centers of Christianity for centuries, rivaling Jerusalem and Ephesus early on, and then Antioch and Alexandria and Rome in later centuries. Despite the city having finally fallen under

Muslim control through Arab conquest a millennium ago, we would have found a full-blooded Christian city, literally brimming with Christian churches and monasteries, numbering more than three hundred, according to one Arab geographer of the time."

"Wasn't there something like three different rival Christian sects represented as well?"

"That's right. And the Christian pilgrim and tourist trade was already at least six centuries old and flourishing during Edessa's high point."

Torres smirked. "Proving the Church has always been divided and all too eager to make a buck off the faithful."

Silas frowned. "At any rate, we need a possible location for where the final fragment of Constantine's confession might rest. Please tell us you found something."

"Like we said," Zoe answered, "possibly."

"What do you mean by that?"

Bartholomew cleared his throat. "Apparently, the Great Mosque of Urfa, Urfa Ulu Camii, built in 1170, sits on the site of a former Christian church the Arabs called the *Red Church*, due to its crimson hue. It even apparently incorporates some of the remains of the church on the northern wall."

"I'd wager that seems right promising," Celeste said, flashing a hopeful grin at Silas.

"That's not all. As tradition holds, a well has been identified somewhere inside the compound as that into which the burial cloth of Jesus was thrown. Something about keeping it safe during early conquests of the city, but it's not clear."

"Are you kidding me?" Silas exclaimed, making Gapinski veer sharply before steering back on course.

"That's right."

"Where is this well?"

"Not exactly clear on that front," Zoe added, "given mosques aren't exactly our forte, and Urfa isn't exactly a roaring tourist destination. It's never even been on our radar until now."

Silas ran a frustrated hand through his thickening hair. Super odd that SEPIO wasn't aware of all that the city held, given how important it was to the early days of the Order, but whatever. First the medallion depicting the Order's apparent early insignia and then this? He wondered what else from its history they had been missing all these years.

"There seems to be some sort of large fountain in the courtyard," Bartholomew explained. "But then another SEPIO agent sent along an image he found during an intel sweep on the internet of a stone-like structure built into the inside of the mosque itself that seems more on point. Perhaps part of the early church structure that had been demolished by the Arab invaders."

"I vote for diving into the courtyard fountain," Gapinski said.

Ignoring him, Silas asked, "And there's nothing else you can tell us about the place?"

"Sorry, chief," said Zoe.

"Then we go in blind."

"Wait a second," Torres said. "Are you serious?"

Silas turned around toward her in the back. "Serious about what?"

"You're telling us we need to bust inside a Muslim mosque in order to find some long lost piece of a confession that may or may not help the Church?"

"Exactly."

"Always something…" Gapinski growled.

"Look, I know it's not much to go on, but what choice do we have?"

Torres went silent, slumping back and staring out the window.

Silas rested his scruffy chin against a hand and stared out

the window as well, the sun sinking lower toward the horizon with a line of blazing orange. "It's about all we've got until the clock runs down—"

"And *BOOM!*" Gapinski interrupted.

The car loudly complained.

"Alright, alright! Jeez, tough crowd."

Silas sighed. "Anyway, soon the sun will set and it will be go time."

"Again..." he muttered, the headlights coming on as if to emphasize Gapinski's complaint. "Can we at least grab a falafel or something? My stomach's been doing gymnastics something fierce since we strapped in for dear life during that stretch of rough air."

"Not a bad idea, actually," Celeste said. "We're going to have to wait for *salat al-'isha* anyway before commencing our mission."

"Salad? I ain't fueling up on leaves for a SEPIO gig facing no uncertain doom!"

"No, moron," Torres moaned. "*Salat al-'isha* is the final obligatory prayer by practicing Muslims, between sunset and midnight."

Celeste nodded. "Right. Which means we have a few hours to kill beforehand. Wouldn't want to have a sneak up on the praying faithful, now would we?"

"I suppose that would end things real quick," Silas said.

Gapinski snorted a laugh. "Yeah, straight into President Erdogan's little shop of penitential horrors."

The drive was a quick hour south to the target drop zone, which lasted half an hour longer because of the dinner pit stop. After finding Gapinski some food—ironically, a falafel stand at a rest area along the highway—and the rest of the SEPIO agents fueled up as well, they reached the former epicenter of the fight to preserve and protect the Christian faith.

The sun was dipping low now, a blazing mixture of reds and

oranges that bruised the sky purple as it sank beneath the horizon. The city itself was surprisingly hopping, the evening giving way to a nightlife full of clubs blasting Eurodance tunes a few decades too late and restaurants servicing patrons outside under a canopy of emerging stars and a full moon drowned out by bright white lights overhanging crowded streets. Shops along the main thoroughfare selling dresses and handbags and electronics reminded Silas that the rest of the world was much like his own: men and women and children and families living life, making sense of the world, and trying to better themselves and the ones they loved with a new pair of shoes or middle-class service job.

Gapinski muscled the car through town, the buildings white and tall and surprisingly well-ordered. Reminded Silas of Russia, in all of their utilitarian exactness and blandness, but with a Turkish flair of ornamentation. Even Eastern European nations he had visited, like Romania and Ukraine, with small towns that felt like time capsules of Soviet occupation from the 40s and 50s. Which made sense, given Turkey's early relationship with the U.S.S.R. before Stalin's death.

Soon the crew was parking in front of a shopping mall, the thumping bass of that Eurodance music intruding even inside the BMW.

"You sure about this, chief?" Gapinski said, eyeing the street and the passersby. "Us lily-white folk are gonna be pretty tough to blend in with this crowd."

Torres smacked his shoulder. "Speak for yourself, *gringo*."

Looking at his phone, Silas said, "It's about the best we can do. Zoe sent over a map of the neighborhood and there's no way to get closer. Need to hoof it from here. So let's arm up inside, then head on out."

Celeste and Torres grabbed the pistols and assault rifles from the back and handed them out as couples and groups of rowdy nighttime revelers laughed and stumbled past outside.

Silas slid out his magazine and checked it before shoving it back inside with purpose. "You got the goods, Torres?"

He turned toward her as she slid out a manila envelope from the inside of her jacket. "Safe and sound, chief. All fragments present and accounted for."

He nodded. "Alright, let's do this. And keep your eyes open for Nous and our other mystery sect. As Zoe confirmed, there was chatter about this location on the dark web, and it looks like at least one of them is on the way. Let's just hope we make it before they do."

"And can get out before they can give us a hidey-ho at the end of an AK-47," Gapinski said, shoving a SIG Sauer P320 pistol in the front of his pants and slinging a SIGM400 assault rifle around his back, throwing on a coat over the gear for safekeeping.

Soon they were armed up and heading out into the night, Silas taking point with Celeste following at his side and the other two bringing up the rear a few paces back. He led them between a high-rise mall that quickly faded into two-story, drab buildings from eras gone by. Those Soviet-era buildings, in all of their utilitarian, bland glory, contrasted sharply from their upscale cousins out front. Apparently, the Turks were no different than the rest of civilization in shoving aside the ramshackle for the glitz.

Head down and following the map Zoe sent along, Silas led them down a twisty-turny, dimly lit alley that wasn't even a side street. Low-level, beige buildings of cut stone stained by weather and time pressed in against them, lead pipes and air conditioning units attached to the walls added to the obstacle course, and open windows smelling of curry and roasting meat hovering above made them all long for comfort. A dog barked in the distance, too close for Silas's comfort. Sagging dark wires hung between the roofs, and more snaked along the roofline and around corners, darting down a maze of confusion. He ran his hand along the rough walls to keep his bearings, and thanked the good Lord above for Zoe's intel, which said they should be arriving, just about...

"There!" Celeste shouted, pointing to a barred gate down at the end, arched stonework above the bars looking even older than the surrounding buildings.

The four agents padded toward the end, the dog continuing its rant along with the bassy thumping of that blasted Eurodance music.

Silas took a knee on a patchwork of gray cobblestone running from the alley and beyond into a courtyard, eyeing the mechanism still stuck in the Cold War. Satisfied, he took out a lock pick from his back pocket and got to work.

"Looks simple enough..."

"That's what they all say just before getting cold-cocked by a pseudo-spiritual terrorist whack job," Gapinski muttered from behind.

"Charming," Celeste muttered herself, shining a penlight over Silas's shoulder at the simple mechanism.

"Why is it," Torres added, "that we're always breaking into religious buildings under the cover of darkness?"

"It's the gig you signed up for, sister," Gapinski said.

Silas inserted the narrow metal pick into the open lock mouth and started working it back and forth. Tall trees stood guard beyond, stretching higher than the modest city dwellings. The scent of juniper and pine gusted on a hot breeze blowing lazily from the courtyard through the alleyway, followed closely by the smell of earth and stone. Gray bricks led into a quiet, empty place that was void of any overhead lighting. Not a soul was around, neither coming nor going.

Making it the perfect target for their incursion.

He just hoped what they sought was where they hoped it was.

In a few twists and turns, the gate unlocked with a *click* and

Silas was shoving through, the hinges giving an irritated, squealing reply before going silent. The others followed closely—

When a light from behind, white and blinding, flared up without warning.

CHAPTER 26

Silas spun around to find a security lamp perched high above on the stone arch. Must have been motion activated.

A wire snaked down before disappearing around the corner of a massive brick tower that soared eight or nine stories high. He followed the power source into the shadows, padding onto dirt ground and staying clear of the light before he could reach for it and yank it low.

"Always something," Gapinski grumbled before leaping over a knee-high wall at the right. Celeste and Torres followed him to escape being seen.

Withdrawing a blade from his boot, Silas slit the wire, dowsing the light and bringing the world back into darkness.

That was close. He just hoped it wasn't an omen of more to come.

He shoved the knife back in his boot, stepped back to the path, and frowned, disappointed that the church-turned-mosque, once dominating the region with Assyrian Christians living and worshiping in the ancient city formerly known as Edessa, looked more like a sad loaf of bread with a knife thrust down inside with that tower. Black mold streaked down the sides of the surrounding buildings' stone walls, their facades pockmarked by age but well-kept otherwise. Small windows were arrayed along the perimeter structures, darkened inside by paneling or curtains.

A far cry from the gleaming beacon of hope that bore the torch of historic orthodoxy centuries ago.

"We best be getting to it, I reckon," Celeste said, joining him back on the path, Gapinski and Torres close behind.

"Agree, come on," Silas said, leading them past more towering trees before padding down a short set of stairs into a main courtyard bearing stone benches with a cemetery off to the side, gates bared and tall headstones jutting up this way and that like dragon teeth.

It was far quieter than the alleyway, and much more so than the street before that, the sounds of the city nightlife fading into a sacred peace thanks to the surrounding buildings.

"Now what?" Torres asked, the other agents eyeing the area with her.

"There," Silas said, padding over to a pavilion-like structure, eight columns holding steady a circular stone roof above a white limestone fountain.

"There's Door Numero Uno that Bartholomew mentioned," Gapinski said. "Any sign of Constantine's, well, sign?"

Silas ran around the perimeter, searching for the now-familiar Chi-Rho. Celeste joined him, searching inside and out along the basin, but both came up empty.

"Must be inside."

"That's what I was afraid of," Gapinski muttered.

He nodded toward the main building that anchored the southside of the courtyard, fronted by an arched colonnade. He ran toward a door at the center, a large pinewood plank bound by iron ribbings, fully expecting another blinding white light to activate as he padded across the expansive courtyard, like a prison-yard jailbreak foiled by the state penitentiary security.

Other than the full moon shining down from above, darkness still shrouded them in secrecy.

Silas came up to the door and pulled at the latch. Bolted tight, which he expected.

He knelt on the cool, gray brick, withdrawing his pick again and getting to work a second time.

"Not much for security, are they," Torres said.

"I cannot imagine they have much need for it," Celeste said. "Who in their right mind would steal into a mosque in the dead of night?"

Gapinski smirked. "Thank you for making the exact point I was making earlier."

A gentle clicking was heard. Silas stood and pulled on the door latch, the wooden door hefting open on cranky hinges.

They piled inside and quickly shut the door, then waited. Waiting for any security apparatus or light or siren that might announce their arrival.

None came.

Suffocating darkness and the even more suffocating smell of musty, old carpet and plaster walls was all that greeted them.

Celeste clicked on her penlight, casting white light and wicked shadows across the cavernous space of pale limestone. Crimson carpet interweaved with cream dots and parallel, interspaced cream lines ran across the length of the vast space. Other than stout columns holding the ceiling above, and a dome of steel and glass the size of a swimming pool hovering above, the large hall was empty.

"Nice weave," Gapinski commented, bouncing his knees with each step. "I could get used to bowing down on this."

"Let's spread out," Silas said, holding up his phone for more light. "Search for anything that might look like an old well, with stone or perhaps brick."

They split into pairs, the guys going one way, the gals going the other. Quickly working the length of the vast hall and searching for the Chi-Rho that would give them the final clue to unraveling the conspiracy threatening the faith.

And coming up with nothing.

Just white walls, along with tacky bronze sconces and circle chandeliers adorned with nothing more than glass bulbs.

Silas ran a frustrated hand through his hair. Where could it—

"Over here!" Torres shouted.

He pounded toward the voice, followed closely by Gapinski. "Did you find it?"

The two women were standing in front of a glass door edged by more bronze, Celeste's penlight held aloft.

He went to it, cupping his hands against the glass to look inside. Beyond looked like another large hall. And who knew how the door was wired.

But they didn't have time to second guess. It was go time, on the double.

"Through the looking glass we go..." he muttered before tugging at the door. It gave without issue.

They came into another vast space, not as large as the first but still sizable. It was carpeted in a basil green and long lines of interspaced sections of crimson red, all running the length of the hall. They were greeted by the same basement scent and stale carpet that reminded Silas of his childhood parish.

Leaving the others behind, he raced forward, holding his phone high even as Celeste shone her penlight from behind.

And praying the white light couldn't be seen from outside, or else their misadventure would be cut short real quick.

That's when he saw it. Anchored to one wall near the middle of the room across from a door he assumed led back outside. Nearly missed it buried in an alcove in the white limestone wall were it not for light glinting off a silver metal bucket setting on top a wooden box wedged over the target. Yet there it was.

Looked like a large boulder, about the size of a manhole cover, jutting up a foot or two from the floor.

The well...

Silas reached it and tossed the bucket to the floor, a long rope snaking from its handle, along with a blue cup that must have been used to quench the faithful's thirst—physical and spiritual. He threw open a pair of warped wood doors that covered the well and shoved his phone inside for a look.

His white light glistened back from down below. Quite a ways down, actually. Looked like a good twelve to thirteen feet, maybe fifteen. Hence the rope.

But he noticed something else, too. Something that gave him hope.

"Help me with this..." he said, motioning to Gapinski as he began wrenching the wooden box free from the alcove. Took some doing, but the two managed to break it loose, tossing it to the carpet and revealing a large hole, enough for a single person to climb down inside.

Which gave him an idea.

Gripping his phone and shoving it down into the hole, he took a breath and eased inside. It was tight, but he managed to stretch down, the rock rubbing against his shirt and frustrating the heck out of him.

But he managed to press himself inside a shaft that led down to the water below, the air warm and humid and smelling of algae and stale water.

And yet...

It was moving!

Which meant it was coming from somewhere and was being taken away somewhere else, down below the mosque, which had been a church where the Image of Christ had once been secreted away for a time.

Not only that, it seemed to open up to some sort of cavern.

Silas eased himself out, hope rising at what might be down below.

When he saw it. Faint but there.

An anchor, etched into the well's side. An insignia, signifying a definite connection with the Order of Thaddeus. What, he could only guess, but it was something. He had to believe it was something...

He grinned widely, his belly fluttering now with possibility.

"Look!" He scrambled back and pointed.

The others crowded around, bending over for a viewing.

"Blimey..." Celeste whispered.

"*Dios mío...*" Torres added.

"A and B for me, too," Gapinski agreed.

"Grab that rope and help me down," Silas said.

"What?" Celeste exclaimed, looking at the bucket lying on the floor. "Are you mad?"

"Have to agree with your lady friend, chief," Gapinski said, reaching for the rope. He stretched it out and eyed it. "Doesn't look like it can barely lower the bucket down below let alone two hundred pounds of muscle."

Silas set his Beretta on the floor and removed his jacket, stuffing the bottom of his shirt in his pants. "There's water down below, and it looks like it opens up into some sort of cavern."

"And you think our golden goose is hiding down below?"

He shoved his phone inside his pocket and put a leg inside the well, then the other, sitting at its lip. "I don't know. But I've got a feeling about this."

Celeste scoffed, folding her arms. "A feeling? You're bloomin' mad! What if you get stuck and we can't retrieve you?"

He turned toward her. "Yeah, a feeling. I know it's crazy, but something is here. It's gotta be if this was once a key location for the Order of Thaddeus. And you saw the anchor, the Order's insignia. Call it the movement of the Spirit or whatever, but something inside is telling me this is it. The end of the road leads down below."

The others went quiet, eyeing one another before eyeing the well.

Then Celeste let her arms drop with a sigh. "If you get bloomin' stuck down there or the rope breaks or—"

"I'll be fine," Silas said, grabbing her hand. Then he let it go and got back into position, sitting on the lip of the well and letting his legs flop inside.

Gapinski got into position himself, bracing a leg against the well's rocky wall, and handed Silas the rope, the bucket clanging behind as if in protest. "Ready, chief?"

Silas nodded. He tied the rope around his waist good and tight, then eased himself down inside until his bottom was clear off the lip. He grabbed hold of the rope and began the descent, Gapinski grunting behind as he slowly lowered him down below.

Thankfully, the rope held steady. But the space was tighter than he expected, the rough rock wall making it difficult to get down inside. He let gravity do the work, his body just small enough to slowly descend. That smell of algae and earth and basement mildew grew strong now the closer he reached the bottom, five or six feet now from the surface.

Then he broke through with a sudden pop, falling straight down the shaft and into the water with a splash.

Plunging down several feet until his feet hit the water, cold and moving swifter than he expected.

Only reason why he wasn't dragged clear down the underground river was because of the rope still tied to his waist. But he felt the current tugging against him. He didn't wait for it to work its magic.

Grabbing hold of the rope above, he heaved himself up while kicking with his legs, reaching the surface with a gasp.

"*Silas!*" he heard above, distant and echoey. "*Silas!*"

Silas gasped for air again, water running down his face and in his mouth, then heaved another pull.

"I'm alright!" he managed to shout back, his voice echoing back to him off the cavernous rock walls.

A shaft of light fell down the hole from above and spread across the water, filling his world with the faint glow of white.

Illuminating something entirely unexpected.

A small platform the size of a kitchen table, made of brick and carved into the side of the wall, sitting seven or eight feet away.

Celeste was shouting something from above, but he didn't hear her.

For the light was glinting faintly off from something etched on the wall.

Am I crazy? Is this a mirage?

He blinked, his eyes adjusting now to the darkness and the faint white light he assumed was from Celeste's penlight making it clear what he saw was not his mind playing tricks on him.

"Gapinski!" Silas shouted.

"*You're alive!*" he shouted back.

"You could say that! Let up the rope, I've found something!"

"*Found something?*" Celeste shouted. "*What are you playing at?*"

"Just give me some slack and I'll see!"

The rope suddenly loosened. He splashed back into the water, but he was ready. He swam the few yards to the brick platform, hoisting himself up on top.

A drunken giggle escaped his lips as he pressed his palms into the cold hard stone, slippery from algae and the humidity of the subterranean chamber.

Thank you, Spirit of the Lord, for your confirmation...

It was indeed real. A patchwork of gold tiles arrayed in the familiar symbol of Constantine.

Which meant he had work to do.

He stood, the wall now facing him, the Chi-Rho clearly visible.

Silas took a step forward when the rope cinched against his waist.

A curse slipped, and he shouted, "Give me some more slack!"

"*Can't! That's all I have left.*"

"Always something..." he grumbled before catching himself. "And now I'm apparently channeling Gapinski."

He stepped back and grabbed the rope then pushed it down, wiggling it down his waist. He stepped out and let it fall back into the water.

"*Silas? Did we lose you, my man?*"

"No, I'm still here!" he shouted back. "Just give me a minute. And keep the light going, would you?"

"*Will do!*" Celeste shouted back.

Taking a step toward the wall, he pressed a hand against the Emperor's insignia. It was slick with condensation and felt cool to the touch.

Then something crawled over it, its many legs sending up a pitter-patter across his skin.

He pulled it back with a start, his hand coming away from it feeling clammy and creepy. He furiously brushed the creepy-crawly something away, then stomped the ground for good measure.

A shiver ran up his spine and he darted his eyes around, the walls glistening with the white glow of Celeste's penlight now pressing in against him.

Time to get to it.

Whipping out his phone and praying to the good Lord above that it still worked, he pressed the '*On*' button.

It worked. It's why SEPIO shelled out the big bucks for equipment that could survive a deep plunge.

Activating its light, he shined it at the Chi-Rho. It was ringed by tiles, the center round one looking like a similar covering tile as before. He pulled his knife from his boot then shoved it into a crack, grinding it this way and that.

The mortar chipped with ease, having suffered under the molestation of humidity and time. Slowly but surely, he worked the knife around the entire round Chi-Rho tile. Then he thrust the blade back into one side of the groove and pressed toward the wall.

Until the tile popped loose and shattered on the stone platform floor.

His breath caught in his chest at what he saw.

A round chamber and an object stuffed down its gullet glinting in the light of his phone.

Shoving his hand inside, he withdrew the object. Confirming what he had known to be true in his gut up top.

Another golden cylinder. Perhaps the *final* golden cylinder.

"*Silas? Please tell me you haven't been eaten by the Loch Ness Monster?*"

He smiled at Celeste's voice shouting from above. "I'm fine! And I've found it!"

"*The golden goose?*" Gapinski shouted back.

"Oh, yeah! And I'd wager—"

His foot caught on a spread of sludge, sliding forward and wrenching his other leg all catawampus. He lost his balance in the sudden turn, throwing his arm out to stay himself.

And lost the cylinder in the process.

It fell to the stone platform with a clang before bouncing and spinning toward the edge.

He reached toward it, grabbing the end with two fingers.

But it slipped, toppling down into the water rushing past.

"NO!!"

"*Silas? Everything alright?*"

Panic seized him like a rabid dog as he saw the gilded object sink through the water. But he didn't let it take hold.

Please, dear Lord. Please, dear Lord...

He shoved his phone in a pocket and plunged back inside, the frigid waters shocking the breath out of him, the current tugging against his chest and legs and arms.

But he didn't let it take hold.

Diving underneath, he began a frantic search without the benefit of his phone's light. Thankfully Celeste still sent down a beacon from above, its light doing some good in the crystal-clear water flowing from some artisan spring.

Silas spun around under the water's surface, trying to catch a glimpse of anything that looked like the ancient relic.

Rocks and detritus from the city and dead things littered the ground, but no cylinder.

He reached for the surface again, heaving a desperate breath, his mind running wild now from his carelessness.

How could he be so stupid! Slipping on damn sludge without the sense to hold on for dear life.

Please, dear Lord. Please, dear Lord...

Betting the current may have taken the object farther down, he bobbed along the surface, his toes touching the floor in spots. Couldn't have gone far because of the cylinder's weight. But under water and with this current it could have—

His foot hit something, sending it skittering across the channel's floor.

He sucked in a hopeful breath, praying again like he'd never prayed before.

Please, dear Lord. Please, dear Lord...

He dove underneath after it, pushing his arms in front and grasping at anything his hands found.

Another rock.

Then something round! With a long neck.

Just a bottle.

Then he found it, nestled against the chamber wall.

Curling both hands around the cylinder, he seized it and pushed back for the surface, heaving a thankful breath and confirming the truth of it.

"*Silas!*" he heard in the distance.

He heaved another breath then swam for the sound and light, glimpsing the rope still swinging from the well's hole up top.

"I'm here! Had a momentary setback, but I'm coming in!"

Easing back into the loop he had pushed off earlier, he brought it to his waist and tugged twice. Then braced for Gapinski to bring him to the surface.

It was tight, tighter than last time with the cylinder, but soon he reached the top.

Celeste was the first to greet him.

"I thought I lost you!" She threw her arms around his neck and squeezed. Then she let go and smacked him on the shoulder. "I have half a mind to throw you back down into that bloomin' hole! Don't you do anything like that again, alright?"

He smiled. "Alright. But look—"

He handed her the golden cylinder, retrieving his Beretta with a shivering hand and putting his jacket back on to get some heat into his soaked bones.

Her frown turned into a grin. "The final fragment, then?"

"That remains to be seen, but I'd wager it is."

Celeste began spinning off the top sealing one end shut, soon removing it and handing it to Torres. She tipped it, the familiar metal fragment thudding in her hand. Then a scroll came loose and another fragment.

"Look!" Silas said, pointing to its bottom edge.

Rather than the expected ragged edges on both the top and bottom, the end was flat. As one would expect from the end of a normal piece of paper.

"The final fragment," Torres marveled.

He nodded at her. "Indeed."

Celeste grinned, handing the fragment to Silas. "I would wager you definitely deserve the honors."

He smiled and took a breath, then began translating and reading it aloud:

As I lay gasping for life, I am reminded of my greatest contribution to the world: putting to rest the dog Arius and unifying the true believers around the essence of Christianity. And so, with my last dying breath, I confess now before my baptism that which the Church itself confesses to be true:

We believe in one God, the Father Almighty, maker of all things visible and invisible; and in one Lord Jesus Christ, the Son of God, Light of Light, very God of very God, begotten, not made, being of one substance with the Father; by whom all things were made; Who for us men and for our salvation came down and was incarnate and was made man; He suffered and the third day he rose again, and ascended into heaven; from thence he shall come again to judge the quick and the dead. And in the Holy Ghost.

And whosoever shall say that there was a time when the Son of God was not, or that before he was begotten he was not, or that he was made of things that were not, or that he is of a different substance or essence from the Father or that he is a creature, or subject to change or conversion—all that so say, the Catholic and Apostolic Church anathematizes them!

This is what I believe, and I believe it is what makes me what I am: a child and friend of God in Christ. I did not create it, but rather it is what has created me anew. It is not the invention of any man, whether bishop or emperor; instead it is the very truth of God, gifted to the world through his Spirit and the Apostles.

In nomine patris et filii et spiritus sancti,

It was signed in the now familiar symbol of Constantine:

Celeste grabbed Silas's arm. "That settles it then," she said in a whisper.

He wet his lips, agreeing but wanting final confirmation.

"Torres! The fragments."

She handed him the manila envelope and he withdrew four plastic sleeves, parchment fragments browned by age stuffed inside. He slid each of them out and arranged them on the floor, one on top of the other until the torn edges aligned.

Silas grinned. Perfect matches.

Sliding out his phone, he opened the camera app and snapped a picture, then another. He stuffed it back inside his pocket and took a breath, pressing his palms against the green carpet and leaning over the completed puzzle, readying himself for the task at hand.

One final translation to verify the Emperor's confession one final time.

He cleared his throat to get to work.

When a clang sent him bolting to his feet.

CHAPTER 27

Silas whipped out his Beretta and spun around on the floor to aim toward the doorway at the end of the hall, the distant clang returning to confirm the first time wasn't a mirage.

Someone was there.

Or someones...

"Don't suppose that was a mosque mouse, do you?" Gapinski asked, standing next to Celeste and aiming the barrel of his M400 dead ahead as well.

No. I suppose not...

Gathering up the parchment fragments, Silas shoved them inside the manila envelope then stuffed it inside his jacket for safekeeping. Their time was up.

"Cut the light," he instructed Celeste.

The room plunged into darkness, and the four stood still—waiting, intuiting, discerning what might be approaching.

Could be nothing. Could be something.

Odds were it was more than a mosque mouse. Perhaps the imam, coming to ready the space for pre-dawn prayers.

Or worse.

Time seemed to slow, the seconds ticking by through Silas's hot open-mouth breaths and his heart hammering in his head.

His eyes adjusting now with the help of the full moonlight filtering down through windows above, he chanced a step forward. Toward the glass door and back to the vast hall with red carpet where they had originally started.

Thankfully, the well-padded carpet Gapinski had quipped about before offered blessed cover for his steps, so he quickened his pace. The others joined him, Torres and Celeste having withdrawn their own weapons and taken aim along with the fellas.

The door was dead ahead now, the clear glass offering no reflection and one of the double doors standing ajar as they had left it.

Coming up to it fast, Silas eased against the wall nearest the open door, aiming through the opening into the space beyond. Celeste joined him at his back, and Gapinski and Torres took the other side.

He glanced behind at his partner, who nodded him forward, weapon ready to offer whatever backup he needed.

Silas nodded back and widened the opening with his extended arm, taking a step forward, then another.

When a beam of light sliced across the crimson carpet.

Then another.

Until there were four or five bands of white sweeping the room, bobbing this way and that on headlamps strafing side to side and coming in fast.

Before he could respond, a single bullet shattered the glass door, sending Silas stumbling back behind the wall before a *pop-pop-pop* finished the other one off.

Then all hell broke loose.

Gunfire erupted in *rat-a-tat-tat* waves, finishing off the glass and vandalizing the rest of the structure.

"Guess that confirms it ain't no mosque mouse!" Gapinski

quipped, twisting back himself before nosing the end of his M400 through the void and offering his own *rat-a-tat-tat* reply.

"Who do you suppose it is?" Celeste asked, sheltering behind him as Silas followed through with his own rejoinder. "Security or city police?"

"I'll give you two more guesses."

A black figure came into view, white light at his head nearly blinding him as it turned to face their position.

But he had something else in mind.

With a *pop-pop-pop*, Silas leveled the guy before the hostile could do any damage.

But that didn't really matter because—

"We're sitting ducks here!" Gapinski grumbled as relentless gunfire forced them back.

"Yeah, about to get our gooses cooked real bad!" Torres added from behind.

"Mixing metaphors a bit there, aren't we?"

As if chiding his sarcasm, another menacing *rat-a-tat-tat, rat-a-tat-tat* ripped through the doorway, chewing at the ancient stone masonry and shredding what was left of the bronze door jamb that had been deglassed.

Silas looked for a window to reply, but none came. Just an unrelenting advance of lead.

Not good...

But then it all at once ceased, falling chunks of stone and a large section of the jamb clanging to the floor the only sound left in its retreating wake.

Or was it...

White light sliced through the open doorway now. Three or four beams joining to direct their collective light their way from a cadre of unknown hostiles.

And then an all too familiar voice echoed from beyond the threshold.

Which sent Silas's stomach crashing to the carpet.

"Come out, come out wherever you are, big brother."

Gapinski threw him a surprising glance across the threshold, eyes wide and mouth dropping. Celeste grabbed his shoulder from behind and squeezed with empathetic solidarity.

Sebastian...

"I know it's you, Silas, and your merry band of Navy SEALs for Jesus. That you're here rooting around for the final fragment to Constantine's letter. Remember, I still have an insider speaking sweet nothings into my ear about your SEPIO outfit."

Celeste sucked in a startled breath. "Victor..."

"Now what..." Gapinski said.

Silas looked at him, mind spinning from the turn. He had no idea. Especially if Zarruq was being dangled at them as bait.

A cold dread seized him, and his mind filled with a foggy, confused panic that hadn't gripped him in a while. The same dread and foggy panic that started in Iraq and had been kept at bay with pills and therapy, popping up here and there with situational stress but not having been an issue for months.

Yet there he was, his chest now tightening and heart barreling through him like a freight train, his ears ringing with a tuning-fork ting that told him everything he needed to know.

Panic attack.

Lord Jesus Christ, Son of God, not now...

He closed his eyes and heaved a breath, starting to count backward from a thousand to force himself back to the moment.

999, 998, 997, 996...

Another breath, still more coldness and fogginess and heart-thumping panic.

982, 981, 980, 979, 97—

"Give up, Silas!" Sebastian called out again, interrupting his countdown. "You're surrounded, and there's no way in hell you're getting out of here alive with the final parchment fragment. You or your friends."

"What do you propose we do, Master Grey," Celeste said lowly from behind, that hand returning to rest on his shoulder.

Her touch snapped him back to the moment and a surprising peace that surpasses understanding descended on him—whether from her reassuring presence or the presence of the Holy Spirit, he wasn't sure. Probably both.

And a good question. What was his proposal?

"I say we go out in style," Gapinski said. "Guns blazing in a cloud of firepower glory."

"*Idiota...*" Torres mumbled. She did have a point.

And yet, what other choice did they have, other than handing themselves over to Nous—to Sebastian.

Over my dead body...

Then he had it.

"The door," he said, just loud enough for the other SEPIO agents to hear. "The one back near the well."

"You think we can use it to escape?" Celeste whispered. "Don't you think Nous has that one covered as well?"

"Doubt it. Look at them. I see four beams of light. Maybe they have four more."

"Two to one odds. I like the sound of that," Gapinski said. "Them Vegas odds."

"Better than Vegas odds!" Torres said. "Best damn odds SEPIO's had in a long while."

"I'm waiting..." Sebastian crowed from beyond the blown-out door.

Silas huffed. "Anyway, that's near well the most Nous has brought to a showdown. Doubt they've got more."

"Well, do you have any clue where the door leads?" Celeste asked. "That it can carry us out under the cover of darkness?"

Nope. Not a clue. And it frustrated the heck out of him they were left flatfooted and caught by surprise.

He turned back toward her and said, "If you've got any better ideas, I'm wide open. Otherwise, that door is about the only bet we can place. And we best get to placing it."

She nodded. "No, you're right."

Silas nodded toward Gapinski. "I'll lay down covering fire. You and Torres dart across the threshold."

"Roger that."

"Hate to be so pedestrian, so cliché about it all," Sebastian shouted again, sounding irritated as heck, "but I'll give you to the count of three to show yourselves. One..."

Again, baby brother: Over my dead body.

Silas clenched his jaw with resolve and gripped his Beretta tight, getting into position and readying himself for the diversion.

When a fiery, furious explosion rocked the hall.

From behind and back toward the well.

The other door. Their plan of escape!

An updraft of fire bloomed briefly into the vast space behind, followed quickly by acrid smoke and splintered wood, white lights bobbing through the smoke attached to six or seven black-clad hostiles, armed to the teeth with jutting black barrels that quickly coagulated around their position.

Apparently, I was wrong about the manpower...

And Sebastian was creating a diversion, holding their attention away from the secondary point of takeover. Mildly impressive. And irritating as spit.

"Yeah, about those odds, Silas..." Gapinski complained.

Silas mumbled a curse under his breath and threw Celeste a worried look.

"No use putting up a fight outnumbered and outflanked," Celeste said.

"Sensible woman, I'd reckon," a voice said from behind.

It was Sebastian, appearing silhouetted in the headlamps of

his men positioned just beyond the chewed-up doorway even as more padded toward them with menacing purpose.

Instinctively, Silas whipped his Beretta toward his brother.

Gunfire ricocheted off the ceiling from behind, mortar and stonework raining down and reminding him who was really in control.

"I would think very hard about your next move, professor," a bassy, buttery voice echoed at his back. One he recalled very well.

Chuke...

The hostiles surrounded the SEPIO quartet, brandishing shiny Heckler & Kochs, Nous's weapon of choice. They quickly unarmed Silas's teammates even as he continued training his pistol at Sebastian's smirking face shrouded in the blinding light, arms folded and eyes dark with ill intent.

"Time to lay it down, love," Celeste said, even as she was jerked violently to the ground and hands wrenched behind her head.

"Get your hands off her, you bastard!" Silas growled, spinning with his weapon toward the man in billowing beige and brown, face masked with those damn ISIS-like headscarves.

Which had the immediate effect of attracting four barrels directed at his head.

A hand came from behind and rested on his shoulder.

"Checkmate, big brother," Sebastian said. "Best listen to the missus. Lay down your weapon and I assure you all will be well."

Silas closed his eyes and sighed. Hated to admit it, but he was right. Checkmate, indeed. Then he put his hands up, Beretta dangling from a finger.

One of the Nous hired guns promptly relieved him of the weapon, and the others lowered theirs, the tension seeming to deflate some.

Hand still resting on his shoulder, Sebastian pulled Silas around to face him. "Now then, down to business."

Four men with headlamps stood arrayed behind the man, flanked by two more on each side. Silas glanced over his shoulder, finding about the same package of hostiles, Gapinski and Torres guarded by five of them and Celeste standing now next to Chuke and three more goons.

Silas faced his brother, clenching his jaw and narrowing his eyes. "What business?"

Sebastian matched him. "We don't have time for this. Did you find it or didn't you?"

"I don't know what you think we're doing here. We were just readying ourselves for *salat al-fajr*."

"What the hell are you talking about?"

"It's morning prayers," Torres said from behind, "just before sunrise at dawn."

Silas smirked. That a girl.

Sebastian wasn't entertained. He took a step toward his brother, getting in his face now. "Where is the fragment?"

He took a step back and folded his arms. "Like I said, I don't know what you're talking about."

His brother held the stare, then took a step back himself, speaking something in Arabic to his men. One of them replied, which made one end of Sebastian's mouth curl upward. He looked over Silas's shoulder and nodded.

Someone approached from behind and placed a firm hand on his shoulder, spinning him around.

It was Chuke. Then he grabbed Silas's bottom jaw and squeezed, his cheeks being forced together with humiliation. The man got in his face, his breath reeking of fish and cabbage.

"Where is it, the final fragment of Constantine's confession? Found the well, we assume. And it looks like you were down inside. Like Sebastian said, we don't have time for this."

Silas wrenched himself from the man's grip, then rubbed

the pain out of his jaw. "What, got an important date, tough guy?"

"Company is what we'll have, and very soon, if you don't give us what we need."

Company? Who was he talking about? Other treasure hunters brought on by Braun and Rotberg, or the mystery sect of box-men tattoos? Perhaps Braun and Rotberg themselves?

Wasting no more time, Chuke yanked down the zipper to Silas's jacket.

And out fell the manila envelope.

Sebastian chuckled. He pushed past Silas and reached down to the floor, grabbing the evidence Silas needed to dismantle the conspiracy threatening the Church and disprove one of the more problematic accusations against the Christian faith.

He wanted to rip it from the man's hand, but he kept his cool. Best to let it play out. There was always a second chance in his line of work.

"Now, that wasn't so hard was it, big brother?" Sebastian said with a smirk. "Let's see what we have, then get the hell out of here. Bring them along."

Silas was shoved from behind, as were Celeste and Torres and Gapinski, who complained loudly. Sebastian led them back toward the entrance then paused, moonlight filtering in through the silvery glass dome at the center of the vast hall.

"Why don't we see what we have here..." He motioned his men with the headlamps toward his side then opened the envelope, removing the five fragments. "My, my, my. You've been a busy little bee, haven't you, Silas?"

"It was a community effort," he replied.

"I'm sure." The man shuffled through the parchment pieces, finding the final one they had just discovered.

His eyes got big and lusty. His mouth curled upward with satisfaction. "That settles it then. The final piece to Constantine's confession." He turned to Silas and glared. "And the Church's downfall."

Silas laughed. "I wouldn't be so sure about that. Just wait until you've read what the Emperor has to say about it all."

Sebastian's face fell, those dark eyes returning. "We'll see about that. Before we leave, how about we have ourselves a look-see at the last dying confession of our infamous Emperor Constantine."

He knelt on the ground and began arranging the pieces on the crimson carpet but was struggling to fit them together right.

Silas huffed. "Here, you're doing it wrong—"

A strong hand seized his arm when he tried bending to help.

"Get off of me!" he protested, looking to his brother for help.

He gave it, nodding the goon off and making room for Silas to help.

Kneeling next to his brother, Silas arranged the pieces as he had an hour before.

"We're missing the top portion, which Markus Braun has. But I've got it on my phone." He pulled it out slowly, by two fingers and without breaking eye contact, as if the cautious glance would breed trust.

The man didn't protest, waiting for him to retrieve what Zoe had sent over earlier. But before tapping over to the notes app, he made a detour, signaling Zoe at HQ in DC using a special emergency distress-call app.

Praying to the good Lord above he got a signal somehow to send the mayday.

"Ahh, here we go..." He finally brought what Braun had read a few days ago on the WeSolve video, pressing the volume button down to zero and hiding the app underneath. Then he gestured toward the reconstructed parchment, asking his brother: "May I? Or is your Latin up to snuff?"

Sebastian smirked. "I'd put it against yours any day of the week. But it would do us well to both take a crack at it. Together."

Silas nodded, his brother joining him as he readied his phone to finish the translation, typing it out as they went along and reading it aloud.

This is what it said.

CHAPTER 28

The confession of Emperor Caesar Flavius Constantinus, the Greatest, Pius, Felix, Augustus. Dictated by Titus, my imperial scribe, to be received as my last declaration on the threshold of death.

The Empire knows of my fondness for the Christian religion, how I liberated those who worship the man Jesus and sought the unity of the Church. But that is not the entire truth of the matter, for in him and through this ascendant religion was a new consciousness of human existence, instantiated in his life and emerging through his people across the Empire.

From all walks of life, people are encountering the infinite value bequeathed upon each person by nature of them bearing the image of their Creator. From plebeian to patrician, slave to free, male to female, the entirety of the Empire has encountered a strange new thing in the life of this man Jesus and his followers, the Christians, in Christ's Church. They are encountering a religious community unlike anything seen before, nay, even what the Empire itself has offered heretofore. Something personal and intimate, a connection to the divine apart from personal works and wholly through God becoming man.

I myself encountered this revelation on the battlefield, being wholly struck by the revelation of God's nearness and providential intervention in my schemes. This appearance of our Savior Jesus Christ to me personally and on the field of history more broadly has become known to all men.

Unlike other so-called revelations, this did not immediately make its appearance as a new religion, per se. Rather, and not in no small order, and not dwelling in some corner of the earth but across the entirety of the Empire, the Spirit of God himself helped birth it. For as Jesus himself instructed his disciples, "you receive power when the Holy Spirit has come upon you; and you will be my witnesses in Jerusalem, in all Judea and Samaria, and to the ends of the earth." And unto the ends of the earth it seems God is moving to reveal his heart of love and acceptance before all mankind, through His Spirit and through His Church, as well as through my own hand.

But there have been obstacles to this movement, primarily from a certain controversy surrounding a certain bishop from Africana. A scourge to some and brother to others, Bishop Arius has been a blessed comfort to me, instructing me in the ways of Christ at various times and confirming the essential tenets of the Christian faith, confessing what I myself came to confess, believing what I myself came to believe. Mainly, in one God, the Father Almighty, and in His Son the Lord Jesus Christ, who was begotten from Him before all ages, God the Word, by whom all things were made, whether things in heaven or on earth; that He came and took upon Him flesh, suffered and rose again, and ascended into heaven, whence He will again come to judge the quick and the dead; and also in the Holy Ghost, in the resurrection of the body, in the life to come, in the kingdom of heaven, and in one Catholic Church of God, established throughout the earth. This is my confession, and it is that which Arius had thus plainly spoken to me, and which I took at face value.

However, I understood that the origin of the controversy that emerged from the north of Africana, and what Alexander demanded of the priests, that they each testify to the opinion they maintained respecting a certain passage in Scripture concerning the divinity of the man Jesus, known as the Christ. Arius, for whom I shall have greater words below, inconsiderately insisted on what ought never to have been speculated about at all, or if pondered, should have been buried in profound silence. Hence, a dissension arose between two factions—Alexander and Arius—and fellowship was withdrawn. Consequently, the holy people of the Church itself were rent into diverse factions, no longer preserving the unity of the one body, of which I have felt a certain responsibility, having taken God's people under the shadow of my wings, like a nursing mother. Which is why I have intervened in the Church, seeking to build up the body of faith as if it were my own, responsible for its making.

And so I asked Alexander to show Arius a degree of consideration and to receive the advice which I gave, insisting that the cause of their differences had not been any of the leading doctrines or precepts of the Divine law of the Christian faith until that time of controversy, nor had any new heresy respecting the worship of God arisen among them in light of Arius' challenge to the manner in which Jesus was considered the Son of God. I insisted they were really of one and the same judgment, and so it was fitting for Alexander and Arius and the entirety of the holy people across the Church's spectrum to join in communion and fellowship at Nicaea. From my perspective, these controversies were small and very insignificant questions, the ones concerning the divinity of Jesus. Instead, what mattered was the profundity of the man's mission of love, teaching a profound depth to human dignity that had not existed before, and modeling the greatest extent of that love on the Roman cross through self-sacrifice. Thus, these divisions over doctrine, which had seemed needless, were in my opinion not merely unbecoming, but positively evil, that such should be the case.

There is only one faith, and one opinion about our religion, and the Divine commandment in all its parts imposes upon us all the duty of maintaining a spirit of peace and grace, in addition to truth and doctrine. I insisted they should not let the circumstance which had led to a slight difference between the two cause any division or *schism amongst them and the larger Church, since I believe it did not affect the validity of the whole. We are not all like-minded on every subject, nor is there such a thing as one universal disposition and judgment.*

I could not have been more wrong.

Having come to my senses, by the power and conviction of the Holy Ghost, I exhort all to withdraw with a good will from these temptations of the devil to neglect the good news that has been proclaimed to the world since the dawn of the Church, that which was handed on to all Christians from its dawn as of first importance: that Christ died for our sins in accordance with the scriptures, and that he was buried, and that he was raised on the third day in accordance with the scriptures, and that he appeared to Cephas, then to the twelve, and then to more than five hundred brothers and sisters at one time. And to this the necessity that Jesus is the reflection of God's glory and the exact imprint of God's very being, that he sustains all things by his powerful word, and that when he had made purification for sins, he sat down at the right hand of the Majesty on high.

Our great God and our common Savior has granted us all the same light of revelation. And as a steward of this faith, I sought to successfully bring my task to conclusion, under the direction of the Lord's providence, to be enabled, through my exhortations, diligence, and earnest warning, to recall his people to communion and fellowship around the unity of the faith.

It is true that religions and empires often rise together. Such was the case with the former ways of Roma. But it is equally true that religious creeds and practices can often be co-opted by civilization. That is the situation we find ourselves in the not too distant future, I'm afraid, a Church that is accommodating civilization and a faith this is being eaten alive by it! The same is true for the factions vying for control within itself, so many varying perspectives on what should or should not be held to be Christian belief, neglecting the once-for-all faith entrusted by Christ himself to God's holy people. So many different truths of the person and work of God and our Savior. Our religion must not merely align with the ideals of the society in which it finds itself. Its practices and beliefs cannot simply accomodate the general worldly sentiment or merely accommodate every whim and wind that blows.

Some would say that no new religion can easily arise within the lands that other religions have long been practiced, such as Roma. To survive, a religion must have a hierarchy, legal decrees, ordered practices, and, most important, consistency of doctrine. Thus, humbly I offer the following dogma as a means to foster and perpetuate that which we have hammered and honed the past two decades—and yet not merely by my own hand, but what the Church itself has established at its birth:

Although an angry God full of vengeance and spite might be preferable to a kind, loving one, that is not the case. As the Apostle John writes so eloquently: "For God so loved the world that he gave his only Son, so that everyone who believes in him may not perish but may have eternal life. Indeed, God did not send the Son into the world to condemn the world, but in order that the world might be saved through him." Thus, although we proclaim obedience to the teachings of Christ, it is not the manner in which we are saved. Salvation is through Christ, not Christianity; through the life, death and resurrection of Jesus, not of works lest anyone should boast. The only way to obtain the resurrection of the dead and life everlasting is through faith in his finished work on the cross.

Although fear of perpetual hellfire suffering could be used to keep people under our control, it is not necessary. For as John continues, "Those who believe in him are not condemned; but those who do not believe are condemned already, because they have not believed in the name of the only Son of God." Thus, it is not necessary to craft a list of sins in order to instill fear in people. However, may the Church continue to make clear that rejecting Christ is the surest path to rejecting God's forgiveness of sin and embracing the fires of hell! It is not merely that people cannot dwell with God unless they are *absolved of their sin through the Christian faith, as if mere intellectual assent to a set of dogmas was the cure. It's that God himself has extended his hand of friendship, offering the forgiveness of sins to all who seek it, resting in the death of Jesus as a ransom for sacrifice in personal faith.*

While other religions offer spiritual immortality and reincarnation, the blessed hope of Christ is the resurrection of the dead, as the Council reiterated and the Creed declares. Not a spiritual resurrection, but a physical one, where the soul is rebound to the body on the new earth, with Christ as King. This isn't something we create or define, but the scheme of Jesus Christ himself, who has been declared to be both Savior and Judge.

We must not tolerate even a whiff of false teaching. Although treason is a capital punishment, and one might be tempted to similarly deem heretics worthy of execution, know that the wrath of God is stored up for them instead! Nothing from their mouths can be tolerated. Let their deeds act as a clarion call to warn others against falling away. Instead, we must pay greater attention to what we have heard from the testimony of the Church, so that we do not drift away from it. It is unchanging, and the survival of the faith is not dependent upon keeping it relevant for the tickling ears of the masses.

Above all, dear brothers and sisters in the faith, remember the essence of Christianity is found in the words of our Lord, who when asked the greatest command he spoke thusly: "you shall love the Lord your God with all your heart, and with all your soul, and with all your mind, and with all your strength.' The second is this, 'You shall love your neighbor as yourself.' There is no other commandment greater than these." Let us rejoice with unity in these commands, being mindful to obey all of what Christ taught us and serving our neighbor in humility and love.

As I lay gasping for life, I am reminded of my greatest contribution to the world: putting to rest the dog Arius and unifying the true believers around the essence of Christianity. And so, with my last dying breath, I confess now before my baptism that which the Church itself confesses to be true:

We believe in one God, the Father Almighty, maker of all things visible and invisible; and in one Lord Jesus Christ, the Son of God, Light of Light, very God of very God, begotten, not made, being of one substance with the Father; by whom all things were made; Who for us men and for our salvation came down and was incarnate and was made man; He suffered and the third day he rose again, and ascended into heaven; from thence he shall come again to judge the quick and the dead. And in the Holy Ghost.

And whosoever shall say that there was a time when the Son of God was not, or that before he was begotten he was not, or that he was made of things that were not, or that he is of a different substance or essence from the Father or that he is a creature, or subject to change or conversion—all that so say, the Catholic and Apostolic Church anathematizes them!

This is what I believe, and I believe it is what makes me what I am: a child and friend of God in Christ. I did not create it, but rather it is what has created me anew. It is not the invention of any man, whether bishop or emperor; instead it is the very truth of God, gifted to the world through his Spirit and the Apostles.

In nomine patris et filii et spiritus sancti,

CHAPTER 29

Silas took a relieved breath even as his mind swam with the implications of what he had just read.

There it was in black and white. Or rather, black and faded brown parchment.

The confession of Emperor Caesar Flavius Constantinus, the Greatest, Pius, Felix, Augustus. The full measure of the code to his faith in all its glory...

Which was indeed just that. The Emperor confessing that he had been misguided about Arius and brushing off the threat he and his foreign theology posed to the Christian faith—to the *unity* of the Christian faith, both the Church's people and the Church's theological code, its doctrine and teachings.

But it was more than that. Because the man confessed the essential elements of the Christian faith. Confessed belief in them, in Jesus Christ for the forgiveness of his sins and the salvation of his soul! Confessing what the Church has confessed for seventeen hundred years.

The Emperor code...

The implications were astounding! Not least of which it would be the death knell for an entire cottage industry of academia that thrived on creating confusion around the founding of

Christianity and the rise of the Church. It would also slip the rug out from underneath all those blasted conspiracy theorists profiting off from the shoddy, shady academic flights of fancy at the heart of not only the West's bestseller lists, but also the ones saturating the internet and WeShare and now WeSolve.

Braun and Rotberg included.

And Silas would be the one to take them down, exposing them and their conspiracists for what they were.

Frauds.

"Would you look at that," Gapinski said, whistling with marvel. "The guy really did confess faith in Christ. How about that."

Torres snorted a laugh. "Yeah, that takes the cake, don't it? Pretty well settles the crazy conspiracy theories about Constantine creating Christianity."

"Right. Major bummer," Celeste chimed in. "Sort of blows your whole plot to obliterate the Church to smithereens, doesn't it, mate?"

Silas looked over at his brother.

Sebastian's nostrils were flaring, his mouth was hanging open, and he was heaving bitter breaths with eyes wide and face drained of color. Probably saw his life flashing before his eyes with what he was expected to accomplish by the upper echelons of Nous. And now look: The very thing the man sought in order to discredit the Christian faith actually made a pretty convincing case for its authenticity. For even the Roman Emperor confessed what the Christians have been confessing for nearly two millennia!

The man leaned toward the parchment fragments and ran a finger across the confession again, his lips moving and muttering to himself as if disbelieving the truth of it all.

Silas leaned back on his haunches, doing everything in his power to stifle a grin and not gloat. "I guess that settles it then."

His voice seemed to snap Sebastian out from his trance. He

narrowed his eyes and snapped his jaw close, color returning to his face with reddened rage. "It settles *nothing*," he growled, curling his lips upward with the faint memory of the demonic force that had emerged from him last fall.

Silas took a breath, knowing he needed to tread lightly. Sebastian's Nous agents were still holding his friends, Zarruq was still held hostage who knew where, and antagonizing his brother would do no one any good. He chose his words carefully.

"I get that this is a letdown for you, Sebastian. You expected what Braun and Rotberg expected: the mystery fragments to confirm what you all had suspected. That Constantine not only confessed to being on Arius's side, but also uttered his last dying breath, his last dying *confession* as a renunciation of all that he had helped create through summoning the bishops to Nicaea to craft the Church's code—Constantine's code, as some have suggested—him having a hand at crafting the essential beliefs and core doctrines that have sat at the heart of Christianity for nearly two millennia. Except it's the exact opposite."

He paused to take a breath and look for any hint of engagement from Sebastian. There was no interest, the man having returned to the fragments, muttering a confirming translation to himself.

He took that breath, then continued, "Look, I understand you have a complicated history with the Church and—"

Sebastian giggled with interruption before roaring: "*Complicated?* You call getting raped by a Vicar of Christ *complicated*?"

Silas cursed himself. This was not going at all as he had planned.

He swallowed and put out a staying, apologetic hand. "I'm sorry. That was a callous way to characterize your—" he choked back the 'r' word; he couldn't bring himself to voice the truth of it. Instead, he continued: "your abuse. And you have every reason to hate the Church for what happened to you. For your wicked, evil experience with the faith."

"But?" Sebastian bit back, face steely, eyes casting a burning glare.

Careful, Grey...

"But...you have to face the facts. I get you're out to destroy the faith that destroyed your life. We're on opposites sides on this one. But I also know you're a man of science, a man of reason, given your academic background at George Washington University before leaving for your crusade joining Nous." Silas pointed to the fragments. "It's all there, in black and white. Constantine's confession of faith in Christ. You can't deny it. And you can't go along with Braun's plan to discredit the Church, knowing what you've discovered."

Sebastian met his eyes, that steely stare unblinking, unrelenting. Silas didn't break it, mustering up the courage to confront the man with unwavering resolve. Not as his brother, but as the Order of Thaddeus Master going head to head with the Grand Master of Nous.

He knew it was a pipe dream, trying to convince the man's head of the facts when his heart was interested in anything but. He held out hope, however, that part of his brother still respected reason, and that it would prevail, as it once had.

Sebastian smirked, flaring his nostrils and grinning with wicked intent. "We shall see, big brother." Then he nodded to Chuke and stood. "They're coming with us. Let's go."

"Sebastian—" Silas was seized at the arm by one of his brother's Nous goons. He yanked it away, only for both arms to be seized. "Like hell we're going with you!"

"Get your cotton pickin' hands off me!" Gapinski growled.

Silas continued to resist, Gapinski and Torres and Celeste joining in the struggle, when something in the distance caught his attention.

A sound, faint at first but growing. Bassy and grumbly and thumping.

Surfacing a memory from his days in Iraq that made him recognize it in an instant.

Sebastian heard it too, pivoting back toward Silas and cocking his head to the side, eyes rising toward the ceiling with interest. "What do you suppose—"

A sudden explosion of fire and fury cut him off.

The dome above broke apart in flames, falling to the floor around in shattered pieces.

Silas dove for cover as an inflamed piece of jagged metal crashed a foot from where he had been sitting, glass raining down around and cutting him on the face and neck.

A *rat-a-tat-tat* of rifles amplified the assault, an angry volley of bullets slung this way and that.

But not from the Nous goons.

From above, a vortex of wind and thwapping chopper blades adding to the confusion.

Then there was the pitter patter of objects bouncing across that well-padded carpet Gapinski appreciated from before.

Three of them, continuing to bounce before rolling and coming to a stop.

Then exploding with a combined *BOOOOOMM!*

But no fallout.

Except for blinding light and defending sound.

Flashbangs!

Non-lethal explosive devices he had used a time or twelve in Iraq to temporarily disorient an enemy's senses while coming in hot and heavy to stomp out a cell of Republican Guard soldiers or arrest one of Donny Rumsfeld's deck of fifty-two most-wanted Iraqi playing cards. Producing a blinding flash of light of seven million candela and a headachingly loud "bang" of 170-plus decibels.

Silas rolled away from the brunt of the explosion, but was

instantly disoriented, his vision zapping down to nothing after the burst of light and ears ringing with a tuning-fork ting in the aftermath of the abrupt noise. The Nousati hired guns echoed his confusion, barking a jumble of Arabic and groping about.

He searched for Celeste, but she wasn't nearby. Or she was, but he couldn't tell. Same for Gapinski and Torres, the SEPIO agents getting lost in the chaos.

He staggered to his legs, bracing himself for what came next, catching a glimpse of ropes rippling down from the flaming maw that had been the dome of steel and glass.

And black-clad hostiles beginning to slip down below, firing as they descended from a chopper, blades whirling a wicked wind, the beating blades ratcheting up the mayhem.

Bad enough his brother had caught SEPIO by surprise, and with a platoon of men who managed to neutralize them in spades. Now this?

But who *this* was was the question.

An echoing reply fired from nearby, Sebastian's pals not taking the incoming fire lying down.

One of the Nousati who had been handling him shuddered from the incoming gunfire, his chest taking the brunt of it, no doubt protected from tactical armor. But then his head snapped back, and he crumpled to the floor, a line of blood spurting an arch into the already crimson carpet.

It was go time. Again.

And thrice over.

Wasting no time, Silas dove for the man's H&K and rolled behind a limestone pillar as the firefight continued, heating up with an unrelenting battery of rounds fired by more men descending from the fiery maw above, and as many men down below replying in equal measure before being slaughtered.

Celeste scrambled for him from the shadow of another limestone pillar, picking up the SIG lifted off her from the now-dead Nousati.

"Who the bloody hell is this do you suppose?" she asked, checking her weapon and putting it to good use.

She fired *one-two-three* shots at one of the men descending, catching him in the neck and sending him crashing into another a few feet from the floor. The two landed in a heaping pile until a Nousati hostile finished the job.

"Nice shot," Silas said. "Any sign of Gapinski and Torres?"

She chanced a glance, brightening and gesturing to the other side.

"There. Mirror limestone column at the other end of the hall."

"I see them now."

"What worries me more—"

Another *rat-a-tat-tat, rat-a-tat-tat* echoed from above, the mystery hostiles picking up the pace and pouring in now, fanning out as they dropped and setting up a menacing line of fire. The Nousati kept falling dead, half their numbers littering the carpet.

By his count, eight had made it down and were setting up behind a stone stairwell leading to a raised platform, four or five more still coming in from above.

"This is positively bedlam," Celeste mumbled. "A heavily financed mercenary outfit, that's for sure. A utility helicopter dropping in ten or twelve blokes, tossing flashbangs as cover, heavily armed and sporting—"

She was cut off by an explosion of limestone, bullets chewing the aged stone and sending them crouching lower for cover.

Again, who *this* was was still the question of the hour.

"Come on!" Silas said, grabbing her by the arm and leading her back behind another pillar as the fight raged between Nous and the mystery hostiles.

Zero clue who was winning. Zero clue who he was rooting for to win.

Except for SEPIO.

Which was a dicey proposition at that point.

Although, as the ancient proverb goes: The enemy of my enemy is my friend.

Speaking of which...

Silas spun around, bullets striking their newfound pillar and chewing the edges. But he didn't notice. He was straining for a look through the darkened hall painted in shadow and white light—rounding his pillar toward the others scattered about, looking for one thing, and one thing alone.

"Where's Sebastian?" he said in a panic, pivoting back around to the other side of their position.

"That's what I was going to say before the eruption of gunfire. What worries me more than the incoming blokes is where your bloomin' brother ran off to!"

Frustration mounting and panic growing at losing his brother—and in turn losing the fragments to Constantine's confession that could bolster the Church's reputation—he spun back toward the war and opened up the H&K on the hostiles. Without discrimination.

Celeste joined the fun as he downed one of the ISIS-wannabes from Sebastian's Nous outfit as well as the mystery jarheads who had come in all hot and heavy from above. She managed the same, evening the odds for both sides. As well as SEPIOs.

Angry *rat-a-tat-tats* from both directions sent them back behind their pillar. No doubt from both sides of the whack job equation.

But then something curious happened.

It all stopped. Just as quickly as it started, but with more of a whimper than the bang that launched it all to begin with. While the growling, whirling blades had left, and the grinding chew of assault rifles ceased, a quiet settled over the space, a bruising orange starting to bleed into the sky and down into the open wound above.

Which didn't bode well for Sebastian's Nousati hostiles.

Or the four SEPIO agents caught in the middle...

The silence hung, time along with it, until the entrance flew open with a deafening thud.

And Sebastian stumbled inside with a shout of injury. Chuke was close behind, bound and led by the newcomers.

Followed by another familiar man moving in long strides, an open collar, blue-checkered gingham shirt billowing in a light breeze, a leather fedora sitting atop a mane of salt-and-pepper hair, jaw set with concentrated purpose and a handlebar mustache.

Noland Rotberg.

Four of the mystery hostiles came up fast from behind, disarming Silas and Celeste before shoving them forward.

The man startled, shifting his gaze from Sebastian to the SEPIO pair, a wide smile playing across his face. "Well, lookie there. As I live and breathe!" The man shuffled farther into the hall, the dawn's rising light trailing him and seven other heavily armed men decked out in the same advanced gear as those who had dropped in from above.

Rotberg strolled over to Silas, one hand resting on his hips, the other lazily playing with one handlebar end of that annoying mustache, mouth widening into a grin now with the sort of toothy display of someone who just won a match.

"Fancy finding you here, *Professor*."

Silas clenched his jaw and narrowed his eyes, flexing his fingers into a fist until Celeste came up beside him and gently grabbed it.

He relaxed some at the gesture, taking a breath and squeezing her hand three times.

I. Love. You.

She did the same, adding one more before letting go.

I. Love. You. Too!

The pit growing in his stomach at the turn of things suddenly relaxed at her touch. And yet, all of it was unreal. Three forces standing off together. SEPIO, Nous, and Rotberg. Who, by every indication, was somehow involved in the mystery sect that had surfaced months ago when the authenticity of the Bible was on the line.

There they were. Three players on the bigger stage of history. This time showdowning over the authenticity of the Christian faith itself, with the reputation of the Church on the line.

With SEPIO and Nous now at the mercy of this new sect—and Rotberg, of all people.

Two of the newcomer hostiles grabbed Sebastian by the arms and raised him to his feet.

"I'll have you know," Sebastian crowed, "you're making a big mistake if you think taking me out is going to do you a lick of good."

Rotberg offered a nasally giggle. "Relax, partner." He turned to face Silas's brother. "Nobody's going to die. That is, unless you cooperate all gentleman like."

Sebastian scoffed. "Or else?"

The man grinned, those handlebars wiggling with delight. He pulled out a pistol from his waist. Mean thing with a long black barrel, almost cartoon-like in its length, with a polished wood handle. A revolver, and if Silas wasn't mistaken, a Smith & Wesson Model 29. The kind that achieved notoriety in the hands of Clint Eastwood in *Dirty Harry* but rarely saw the light of day now. Man sure liked his guns. First the Colt, now this?

Silas chuckled to himself and shook his head at the spectacle. Certainly suited the showboat. It also meant Rotberg meant business.

A second later, he was staring down the mouth of that cartoonish barrel, Celeste giving a startled yelp and Gapinski and Torres protesting before being restrained by the man's jarhead goons.

Rotberg cocked back the hammer and aimed it squarely between Silas's eyes.

"Or else," he said, "I'll blow your brother's cotton pickin' head off. Now where are the damn fragments? I'm guessing you have them. One of you does, at least."

A squeaky giggle escaped Sebastian before he composed himself, but not before another stifled chuckle slipped through his nose. "Apparently you're not too keen on our current relational arrangement, Silas and mine. Anyhow, I haven't the foggiest clue what you're talking about."

Another voice spoke up: "Are you being sure about that?"

Silas jolted at the sound and took in a startled breath.

No way...

Another man stepped forward, geared up in black padded armor and kevlar, a large H&K assault rifle slung over his back and helmet slung off somewhere on the carpet.

Markus Braun himself.

Sebastian's eyes went large, his mouth dropped before he snapped it shut, the color draining from his face. If Silas wasn't mistaken, the one thing his brother refused to show was written across every fiber of his complexion.

Fear.

Silas said, "Come to oversee the end of your little treasure hunt yourself, I see."

The man resembled his brother Hartwin, whom Silas had worked with a few months ago to verify and then debunk another scheme his twin Markus had cooked up.

Same scheme, different actors and chess pieces—with the Church squarely in its crosshairs.

An amused smile played across his face, and he crunched over to him across broken glass. "You are being Silas Grey, isn't that right? The professor I had hired to assist my brother with Gospel Zero, yes?"

Silas tried taking a step forward to meet the man, but a pair of hands wouldn't let him.

Keeping the boss alive, I get it. Probably why he stuck back long enough to make sure things were secure before revealing himself.

"That's right. And just like last time, I'll win."

Braun's face was steely, with the white light casting menacing shadows across his high, angular cheekbones and equine nose, lips flat and unmoving with shoulder-length chestnut hair falling to his shoulders slick with sweat from the hunt. He studied Silas for quite some time before breaking away. "We shall be seeing about that."

Braun sauntered over to Sebastian, mouth grinning widely. He unzipped Sebastian's jacket and retrieved the manila envelope.

He held it up. "I believe you were referring to these."

"You..." Sebastian growled, his throat catching before he continued: "You will not see the last of me. *Braun.*"

The man laughed but said nothing.

"Is it all there," Rotberg sounded from behind.

Braun sauntered past Silas and Celeste for his partner in crime —literally, in this case. He handed the envelope over to the man.

Rotberg gave another nasally, throaty, giddy laugh as he thumbed through the fragments. "Just what the doc ordered, as they say." He smiled and nodded. "He will be pleased."

He will be pleased? Who will be pleased?

Silas glanced at Celeste. She raised a brow and shrugged her shoulders, clearly not following either.

All of it was an interesting development. One Sebastian wouldn't live down. Whether because of his own wounded pride or because of Nous forces greater than himself who would surely take issue with his lapse in ability.

Silas tried feeling sorry for him, standing with hung head, mouth still agape with shock at the turn. Tried, but didn't. Not one bit. The guy had made his bed, then crapped in it something fierce with letting the mystery sect get the upper hand on him.

"Why don't we saddle up and move on out?" Rotberg said, striding toward the entrance. "I shouldn't think we should keep him waiting, Markus."

"No, we shan't." The man went with him, the two reaching the door.

Forceful hands came from behind, grabbing Silas's wrists. A fight-or-flight spike in adrenaline gave him fuel to spin around. He grunted and struggled with the man, but it was no use. Another jarhead came to assist, wrenching Silas's hands behind him.

Same for Celeste.

"Wait, where are you taking us?" Silas shouted after them.

Braun spun back around, his mouth finally rising with pleasure. "Why, to our leader."

"Your leader?" Celeste asked, glancing at Silas.

The man shrugged. "Everybody's gotta serve somebody, as they are saying."

Gapinski snorted a laugh. "Whether the Devil or the Lord, ehh?"

The man brightened. "Are you being a Dylan fan, too?"

"I thought you were the titular head of this outfit," Celeste interrupted, taking back hold of the conversation.

Braun laughed, a row of perfect white gleaming through parted lips. "Oh, no. I am being but a humble servant."

He turned to leave when Silas shouted after him, "What's his name? Who is he?"

"Come see for yourself." Rotberg said, nodding toward the jarheads, who seized Gapinski and Torres from across the way before a pair grabbed Celeste. Silas was next, his own arms getting seized.

Silas tensed, then struggled. "Get your hands off her!"

He broke free and went after the guard wrenching her arms behind her, pulling back a fist to let it swing into the side of his skull.

When he caught a fist himself to his right eye.

Stars and pain and dimming darkness instantly bloomed.

He stumbled back, disoriented and trying to steady himself when a pair of firm hands caught him and held him steady.

Then he caught sight of something even worse than Celeste being manhandled.

The silvery glint of a needle plunging into her neck.

Right before he felt the prick of a needle at his own.

And the world faded to black.

CHAPTER 30
JUNE 18. LOCATION UNKNOWN.

"Silas, you're such a pain in the ass sometimes, you know that?" Sebastian said at Silas's side, the two walking down a dirt road and sweating buckets under the high-noon sun made all the worse by a hundred-percent humidity.

And yes, for the record, he did know it. But what was he supposed to do? The way those bullies came after his family like that?

They continued trudging across the dirt road, Silas rubbing the ache from his jaw and his mouth tasting of pennies from the open cut still bleeding at the corner of his mouth.

"By the way," Sebastian went on, "how's the eye?"

Silas winced at the word, pain seeming to blossom at the site with the most damage at its mention. He shook it off, hanging his head higher as an M151 MUTT trundled past, dirt kicking up from behind the military utility tactical truck heading somewhere off base. Which meant they were nearing their on-base shack on the hunk of rock in the South Pacific.

"My eye's better than the other dude's," he said proudly. "I can tell you that much." Though he didn't quite believe it. The bozo did quite a number on his right eye, swelling it something fierce.

Then again, he did quite a number on the other guy, too.

The gang of bullies had come up on them as they were heading home from school, surrounding the newcomers and working hard to pick a fight. Had always been that way with them base hopping as kids, following Dad around in his role with the U.S. Army on assignments that lasted only a few years, having no one to lean on but themselves. As twins, they'd attracted their share of curiosity. Not identical, but a near resemblance but for the split in hair and eye color. Blond and blue for Sebastian, dark brown for both for Silas. And as kids of a single dad, rumors had a way of sparking to life and taking on a life of their own, even from eleven-year-old Army brats with nothing better to do.

"I still don't get why you had to go swing at the kid."

Silas stopped short, his brother nearly plowing into his backside. "What do you mean you don't get why I hit him? He insulted our mother, moron!"

"So what? She's dead. Been dead since bir—"

Silas shoved him hard in the chest, sending him stumbling backward and toppling to the ground.

"What d'you do that for?" Sebastian said, face twisting up with a mixture of surprise and anger. He leaped to his feet and got in Silas's face. Thought he was going to blacken his other eye, but he had more control than Silas.

"You always defend and protect what matters to you," Silas shouted, face hot with rage, whether from the moment or left over from earlier, he wasn't sure. "And family matters! Mom matters. No matter that she passed."

He took a calming breath and ran a hand across his close-cropped dark hair. Then backed down, hanging his head and giving it a shake, as if putting it back on right. But even that little motion made him wince again, pain blooming at his eye still swollen shut.

"Alright, alright!" Sebastian said, backing off himself and dusting off his backside. "Chill, would you? Let's get home before Dad does and get you cleaned up."

Silas nodded, and they headed back for home, the two brothers *nearly going to blows themselves before snapping back to normal like boys their age did.*

Always defend and protect what matters to you. Something Dad had taught him since he was young. Silas was the oldest of the pair by a minute or two, and he felt the oldest-son responsibility of taking that advice to heart. Whether for the dead Mom they never knew or Sebastian or any number of things he cared about and would go to the mat to defend and protect.

But what Dad would think about him getting into it with another boy—his commanding officer's son, no less—was something he wasn't quite sure about. He crossed himself at the thought, sending up a prayer to Jesus and Mary and Saint Pete, and any other saint who would listen to his plea for help!

They rounded their block, sandbags still lining the street from last week's flooding, and headed down toward the clapboard shack painted brown at the end—when the pounding of feet was heard from behind just under the grunting acceleration of another MUTT a few blocks over.

Came up fast, before Silas could turn to check it out, and a pair of hands shoved him hard at his back.

He stumbled forward, trying to catch his footing, but he fell into a muddy patch of road, the wet dirt tasting like chalk smearing down his face and getting in his mouth.

A cackling echoed across the road right before a scream stoked his fight-or-flight resolve.

Sebastian...

He spun to his back and caught his breath.

The bullies were back. And they had Sebastian, arms locked behind him by two oafs with the bozo he'd lit up with his hands earlier, taking swings at his brother's stomach and face.

His brother cried out from the blows, doubling over before his head swung back with a wicked uppercut to the face.

"Sebastian!" Silas shouted, but he couldn't move. The ground *began swallowing him whole, his hands bound behind him like quicksand and feet falling through as well.*

Another MUTT rumbled on by. He tried shouting for help, but it didn't stop. Kept right on rumbling by, as if it was completely oblivious to the fact his brother was being pummeled to his death.

And the ground was swallowing him farther and farther into his own!

He struggled against it with all his might, shouting for Sebastian again as the blows kept coming.

"Sebastian!"

But it was no use. He was a goner. And so was his brother.

"Sebastian!"

"Sebastian!" Silas shouted with a start, sitting up and heaving desperate breaths before wincing, his right eye blooming with pain and memory. He fell to the ground with an aching thud, his body covered with sweat.

He groaned at the fall and his eye, continuing to grope for breath and spinning around for Sebastian, but it was no use. His brother wasn't there. Neither was anyone else.

It was dark, and he was alone in a cell of some sort. Walls made of cut stone and bars of iron. No windows, a small wood frame with a sheet of plywood for a bed, garnished with a thin cloth sheet. The air clung to him with a stubborn subterranean coolness, the musty, humid air hanging with earth and mold and sour death. Reminded him of one of those eighteenth-century holding cells in the bowels of a castle or fortress, where pirates or political prisoners were held. Dripping water punctuated the mostly quiet space, outside the cell and down the corridor. Then a moan and cursing complaint.

Hope rose in his chest despite the fact he was held captive. Someone else was there!

But then the memory surfaced from what had happened just before darkness overcame him.

The glinting steel needle plunging into Celeste's neck. Then the painful prick of the same at the base of his own before being overcome by the fog of a damn-strong sedative.

And waking up in God only knew where.

He rushed to the bars and grasped them with both hands, shoving his face against the opening for a viewing but not making much headway. What he did see was a corridor stretching in both directions, with flat cut stone marked by streaking mildew staring him down across the way. He guessed there were at least three, maybe four more cells like his, sitting several stories below ground.

There it was again: a stronger thud and another moan, followed by a distant whisper.

"Hello," Silas chanced saying with a whispered rush. "Celeste? Torres?"

"Silas?" a voice called back farther down, groggy and high, accented by a Queen's English lilt he had come to adore the past two years.

"Celeste!" he said.

"What am I, chopped liver?" said another familiar voice from the other side of his cell. Grumbly and gruff and sitting inside a grizzly of a man.

"Matt!"

"I'm alive, too, if it matters," Torres complained from the other side, voice raw and tired.

Silas sighed with relief. His SEPIO crew lived on.

For now.

But what about Sebastian?

He chanced a quiet inquiry: "Baby brother? You there?"

Nothing.

"Yeah, about that..." Gapinski said, his paws shaking the bars of the cell next door and appearing from the corner of Silas's eye.

He leaned right, poking just enough of his face through to catch sight of the man. "What do you mean? What happened?"

"After the *idiotas* knocked you two out," Torres explained, "they slipped a black bag over his head and bound his hands and feet. Then they drugged his butt and bounced him out of there."

"The rest is as black as it was for you two," Gapinski added. "The bastards poked us with the same juju. So lights out for us three until now."

Silas closed his eyes and dipped his head against the bars. He'd tried to let his brother go emotionally the past year after it became clear they were aligning with two very different sides in a fight for the survival of the Church—or in Sebastian's case, its destruction. But he couldn't fully let go. *Wouldn't* fully let go. Even after the betrayals and Sebastian nearly killing Celeste in a murderous, demonic fit and his hell-bent mission to destroy the Christian faith.

Because it was like that memory back on that rock in the South Pacific that had stirred him with a start: You always defend what matters to you. And family matters. Even as fractured as it was between them two.

Lord Jesus Christ, Son of God, Sebastian better be alright...

A clanging shudder ricocheted through the cellblock, interrupting his prayer and snapping his head toward the sound.

Boots slapped against the stone with approach. A few of them, too. Then they came into view. Same black-clad hostiles that had assaulted them at the mosque. This time unmasked, olive faces hard and scarred, with dead dark eyes that meant nothing good.

A pair each took to the four cells housing the SEPIO agents, readying to open the doors and fish out the cargo inside.

With a klaxon clang, the doors shuddered open on command, and Silas's guests of honor approached—one with an outstretched pistol, the other ready to back him up with a menacing AK-47 slung around his shoulders.

Silas took a step back, calves knocking the small wood bed against the stone wall.

"What is this? Where are you taking us?"

The man threw a string of Arabic at him and pointed his pistol at his face. An older Beretta that did his heart somewhat good to see, but also felt ironic. Dying at the end of his choice weapon seemed about right.

But not today. Not when the conspiracy raging against the Church was unresolved. And not when his friends were still in harm's way.

Silas put his hands up and nodded, inching toward the man and ready to accede to his demands.

But then he stopped, the synapses of his brain sending a signal from one end to the other then back again in a matter of a split second, weighing his options and sizing up the whack job babbling on again and calculating the risk quotient—to him and his SEPIO agents.

There's a moment in every mission where the rubber meets the road. Often, there's more than one moment—as he found was typically the case with SEPIO. But there's that moment when the entire thing pivots around the choice made in that singular fraction of a spin around the sun that can make or break the mission outcome.

Silas sensed that particular pivot point was one of those moments.

So he dusted off a move that had served him more than once in Iraq to launch the whole thing. Those synapses in his brain firing off a neurological command to his arms and hands and fingers to relieve the poor soul of that older-model Beretta before he knew what was what—using one hand to jab up against his wrists in case of a misfire, and the other to swipe the Beretta in an alley-oop he thought was pretty magical, if he did say so himself.

Before Silas or the hostile knew it, the tables had turned,

and the one arm kept going once the Beretta was retrieved, thankfully without a firing incident. Silas spun the dude around in a pirouette, drawing the hostile's arm tight against his neck so quick that it dislocated just as Silas brought his shiny new pistol up to the man's temple.

Planned on leaving it there and taking the man as a hostage, though to be honest it wasn't much of a plan with seven more hostiles piled up just outside his cell without any knowledge how his other SEPIO pals would fare.

Instead, he shot the partner in the chest as he was raising his weapon. Which really wasn't a contest, since it's maddening to try and ready an assault rifle on the kind of dime Silas threw at the guy.

But the whole *one-two-three* punch completed the circuit he began just seconds ago when he flipped the switch and launched a whole new set of reactions and counterreactions he hoped would end in their release.

That was the hope anyway.

Silas finished putting his dog down with a single twist to the guy's neck.

Just as a scuffling and shuffling started up. Followed by growly grunting. Then angsty British slang was exchanged. Right before the *pop-pop-pops* started, and then another set. Which was followed up by a long, drawn-out *rat-a-tat-tat*.

Silas rushed out into the cellblock, ducking as one of those AKs was raised.

And the guy's head snapped back with a single *pop* from behind. Blood bloomed from his forehead as he slumped on two others who'd already been put to rest.

He spun around. Gapinski.

Score another for SEPIO.

"Get down!" yelled Torres.

Right before the wall exploded behind Gapinski's head, the

man having dropped to his haunches as Torres wrestled the offending weapon out from one of the hostiles.

Who she shot once, then two more times—the man flailing back on Silas. Who slammed him face down into the cold, hard stone floor.

He lost his old-school Beretta in the sudden turn. He scrambled after it as a woman cried out as another man struggled with grunting protests under her weight.

Silas crawled out from underneath and turned over just as the guy went limp, catching a glimpse of the perpetrator.

Celeste. Who else?

And it looked like that was the last of them.

It was over in a matter of twenty, maybe thirty seconds—which didn't surprise him in the least, considering the A-team SEPIO crew he had. Former MI6, IDF, and Marines makes for a pretty lethal dose of activating know-how.

All eight hostiles had either been killed or incapacitated, all of them dragged inside the cells for good measure.

SEPIO did it again.

But it still left one unresolved question.

What next?

CHAPTER 31

Silas caught his breath as he checked his Beretta over, finding the tank half empty. Or half full, depending how you looked at life. Either way, he was sending up a prayer of thanks.

"What the heck was that, chief?" Gapinski said, emerging from his cell after dealing with his hostiles, an AK-47 slung around his chest and another pistol shoved at his waist.

"Don't know," Silas said out of breath. "Improvising."

"Mind cluing us into your improvisational routine next time, love?" Celeste said, finishing her own clean-up work and shoving another old-school Beretta at her waist.

"Yes, darlin'."

"Now what?" Torres said, her own hostiles taken care of, an AK-47 of her own slung around her back.

Silas eyed his Beretta then frowned, comparing it to the others. It would have to do.

He said, "Now we get the heck out of Dodge."

"And where's that, exactly?"

"Castle Wolfenstein?" Gapinski said, eyeing the ceiling and walls, the pistol gripped in his hand now.

First things first...

He went to the one guy lying outside his cell and pulled back his wrist.

Nothing.

Which he expected, given the fact Sebastian had been nabbed as well.

He flipped the man over, seeing something peeking up behind his collar. Crouching, he pulled it down, confirming his suspicions.

"Box-men tattoo dudes..." Gapinski marveled.

"Well then," Celeste said. "Looks like we've found ourselves in the belly of the new beast on the block."

"Always something..."

Silas stood. Looked that way.

"Come on," he said, padding toward a steel door at the end.

It was closed. A small dirty window with a crack running from one corner to the other was all the visual beyond, but that was no use.

He came up fast, pressing his back against the cold cut stone at the knob with his weapon on taut arms, ready for anything.

Figuring surprise was in order after what just went down, he grasped the handle and pushed through, Beretta extended and moving in quick.

No one. Nothing.

Except for a chair and a small steel table with an array of monitors trained on their former cells and showing a bunch of lifeless hostiles inside.

Celeste walked over to a panel of buttons on the desk and pressed a large red one. A klaxon horn blared before the sound of gears and closing doors reverberated back from the cell block.

"I shouldn't think they'll be a bother for sometime," she said, eyeing the room. "But we better get to it. Can't imagine eight missing hostiles will go unnoticed for very long."

Torres said, "I guess we're armed well enough to take down whatever might be waiting for us beyond those doors."

"But we need to get our bearings," Silas said with frustration.

Then he caught sight of a safe underneath the desk. He crouched and examined it. Simple thing but locked tight with a key.

He aimed his Beretta at the keyhole, but Celeste put a staying hand on his shoulder.

"Best not, love," she said. "The cellblock pretty well contained the gunfire echo, but I'm not sure this room will hold it back from listening ears outside that door."

She was right. Best let it go.

"These might help." Torres dangled a key ring on an extended finger.

Silas grabbed them. "Where did you find these?"

"Swiped them from one of the whack jobs we put down. Thought they might come in handy."

"Naomi 'Sticky-Fingers' Torres," Gapinski said as Silas got to work on the locked safe. "Not your run-of-the-mill superhero name, but it works."

With a twisting *click*, he finally found the right key, the lock giving and Silas wrenching the key loose. He tossed the ring to the floor and threw open the door.

Then grinned with relieved satisfaction.

Retrieving not only their weapons but also their mobile phones.

He handed off the others to Celeste, who distributed them, while Silas powered up his unit. A few seconds later, it was active.

But no service.

Silas mumbled a curse under his breath, checking the emergency distress-call app he'd activated earlier before they were drugged in Urfa. At least it was still transmitting their distress, whenever the thing got back online.

Glancing around the tiny room, he noted the thick cut stone and the dank, damp air which reminded him of his childhood Falls Church basement. Several stories underground, surrounded by thick walls wasn't encouraging.

"I haven't got a signal," Celeste said, brow furrowed and holding the unit toward the ceiling like one of those old-school wireless commercials. "How are you faring?"

"No luck on my end, either."

"*Nada*," Torres said.

"Always something," Gapinski grumbled, shoving his device in a pocket.

"I just hope someone was paying attention at the switch before these went dark."

"Or else things could get interesting."

Silas said nothing, moving to the door and gripping his weapon for use. Unfortunately, this one was windowless. Which meant they were flying blind into the other side.

"On three?" Celeste asked, coming up to his side with her weapon at the ready.

Torres and Gapinski quickly fell into line, bringing their AK-47s around and aiming for the door.

"On three," he said.

"One. Two—"

Celeste swung open the door, revealing a dimly lit hallway looking similar to their cellblock.

Like some pirate outpost in the Caribbean or a Medieval castle dungeon, more mismatched cut stone walls and floors greeted them, cold and hard and hiding secrets long forgotten—or perhaps still ongoing. But where they might have expected torches bearing flapping flames in ornamental wall brackets, LED lights at the floors and recessed into the ceiling lit the way forward.

Air seemed less confining as well, no longer clinging to them in subterranean dankness. Perhaps filtered through a modern HVAC system. And no longer was there any sound of dripping water, just a quiet HVAC hum that seemed too good to be true.

Which meant it probably was.

Silas checked his weapon over and chambered a round, getting ready for anything.

"Where to?" Torres asked.

Gapinski pointed forward. "Follow the LED-lit road?"

"No other option, I reckon," Celeste said. "Let's push forward. Destiny is sure to meet us, one way or another."

Silas followed her lead on cautious feet, weapon extended and heaving steadying breaths as his heart strummed a mean beat in sync with each step.

"Oy, what's this?" she said, coming up to a closed door, a faint bluish glow falling on her face.

He joined her side, a dirty glass window on the outside of a strong steel door offering a view inside.

Similar cut stone stretched the length of a room the size of a small basketball court. Anchored to the floor were tanks as large as bathtubs, glowing the same blue that had fallen against Celeste's face. But inside...

Celeste gasped. "Are those—" She put a hand to her mouth.

They were indeed.

Men and women, old and young, of varying ethnicities, were completely submerged underwater. Tubes snaked out from their mouths and nose and out into ventilators anchored to the floor outside.

One stirred, his legs suddenly swaying and arms jolting.

The pair jumped back with a start. Celeste grabbed Silas's arm; Silas startled with renewed fright.

"Uhh, guys..." Gapinski sounded from behind.

"*Dios mío...*" Torres affirmed at his side.

Another door, similar steel with a window, stood on the

opposite wall.

Silas and Celeste joined them, thoroughly confused by what they saw.

Someone was seated in a chair. A sort of helmet was attached to their head, wires running out and up into the ceiling. Their back was to the door, the lights were dimmed low, and some psychedelic program was playing on a screen the size of a wall. Words and numbers and images flashed by in rapid succession, and thumping base was heard faintly from beyond the door.

"What is this place?" Gapinski asked, eyes darting up and down the hall and a shake in his voice betraying a sudden apprehension.

Silas shook his head. "Let's get out of here." He nodded just down the hall at a set of stairs leading toward that destiny Celeste mentioned. "Looks like the only way is up."

They padded toward the end, heads turning this way and that with expectation. For not only more weird nonsense straight out of *The X-Files,* but also more heavily armed men straight out of an ISIS training camp.

Neither came, thank the good Lord above.

Silas prayed he would steady their hand and show them his grace as they made their ascent through a winding staircase of familiar cut stone, the stairs twisting upward without stopping for several floors until they surfaced through a doorless entrance.

A warm hallway stretched before them, painted crimson with mahogany trim and closed doors lining the corridor, smelling oddly of faint incense with bright brass sconces shining the way, their orange glow refracted through crystal.

Looked about the farthest thing from Turkey they could find. Almost European, even. Which would mean they were down for the count for half a day, maybe more. It also made not a lick of sense. Then again, what from the past few days had?

"Talk about sensory whiplash," Gapinski said, coming from behind with his AK-47 raised and ready.

"You can say that again," Silas said. He headed toward a pair of darkly stained wood doors at the end.

Just as they opened and two men shoved through.

Without hesitating, Silas slung *one-two-three-four* bullets their way.

Two sank into one of the wood doors with a *thwap*. Another skipped across the crimson wall, sending chipped paint and plaster to the floor.

But the other slammed into the forehead of one hostile, his head snapping back and sinking fast.

The other opened fire with a menacing reply, faster than Silas expected and catching him off guard. But his SEPIO teammates were ready.

In an instant, the man was flailing backward with dramatic flair, his *rat-a-tat-tat* shots chewing across the floor as Silas danced out of the way and arching up the wall and ceiling until the man fell into a silent heap at the threshold of the door.

"Not bad, Hoss," Torres said. Gapinski pounded toward the man as Silas and Celeste made up the rear.

"I agree," Celeste said. "Although if the palace was still unaware of our dungeon escape, I reckon they're clued in now."

"Then we better hurry," Silas said. "Because we still don't know where the heck we are. And who knows what comes next."

He went to step over the dead hostiles when something caught his eye.

The glinting of light hitting him just so through a cracked door,

"Oy, Silas—" Celeste said in a hushed rush. But it was too late.

He pushed inside, then rushed farther into the room after what he saw.

It was a large study, with floor to ceiling bookcases stuffed full of aged tomes, a large unused fireplace with a pair of leather wingback chairs waiting to be used in front, a desk piled high with books and papers.

And, smack dab in the middle, a marble table with a golden cylinder resting on its side.

Silas rushed to it, his heart thumping with anticipation even as his head screamed for him to leave.

Could be a honey trap, meant to draw them in and finish the job. But no one came and no alarm sounded.

What he found made the risk worth it.

Six fragments of an ancient parchment, aligned at their proper tear point.

Silas instantly recognized them. Constantine's confession. All the pieces brought together.

Celeste rushed to his side, followed by Gapinski, who was spinning back toward the hallway with skepticism, and Torres, who had picked up the golden cylinder and confirmed it held a copy of the Nicene Creed.

"Thank you, Jesus..." Silas mumbled.

"What are the odds we stumble across this?" Torres asked.

"The Lord works in mysterious ways."

"*Dios mío*, have I ever witnessed the truth of that up close and personal working for you *amigos locos!*"

"And let's not try the good Lord's patience, ehh?" Gapinski said, motioning with his rifle toward the door.

Silas nodded, crossing himself before gathering the fragments and carefully stuffing them in his jacket. Torres shoved the cylinder at her back, and the SEPIO crew left in haste.

Another hallway beyond the downed hostiles stretched before them, same crimson painting and mahogany trim work as before with another door hiding its purpose at the end. Calm and vacant and a low HVAC hum, as well.

Too calm and too vacant for Silas's liking...

They padded toward the door at the end, which was smaller than the one they'd just blasted their way through. It also bore a frosted window.

Coming to it without incident, Silas peered through narrow strips of transparent glass rimming the opaque sections of the window to assess their options.

Not at all understanding what he was seeing.

Beyond the door lay a massive hall of the familiar cut stone stretching several stories high. Stained glass windows shone brightly and detailed frescoes with measured contrast and saturation depicted familiar biblical scenes painted on the ceiling.

If he wasn't mistaken, it was the great hall of some cathedral.

He shook his head, as if disbelieving his own eyes. It didn't make sense in the slightest.

"It looks like the Sistine Chapel out there," he mumbled.

"Saved by the Pope!" Gapinski said.

"Looks empty enough as well," Celeste said, peering through one of the other clear sections.

"But what the heck were we doing locked four stories below some cathedral?" Torres asked.

Good question. One he didn't have an answer for.

He went to push through when a hand held his arm.

Celeste said, "Are you sure?"

He frowned. "Not at all, but what choice do we have?"

She frowned as well but said nothing, letting go and gripping her pistol tighter.

Same for Gapinski and Torres, each readying their weapons for anything.

Silas readied his own Beretta. "Through the looking glass we go…"

Then he opened the door, taking a cautious step inside toward destiny.

CHAPTER 32

Through the looking glass, is right...

Silas went first, weapon held out on taut arms, followed by Celeste with Gapinski and Torres close behind, both of them pivoting back toward the hallway and backing up to protect their rear flank.

But soon, everyone was inside the vast hall, lowering their weapons at what they saw—and their guard.

First thing that struck Silas was the light, refracted off from thousands of crystals hanging from above a dome center, even forming parts of the pillar crowns holding the ceiling above. Combined with stained glass windows arrayed around the perimeter, they all focused and splintered the sunlight with brilliant high-definition refraction—casting reds and blues and greens, oranges and purples and yellows across the stone floor cleared of any benches or cushions or rugs. It was as if they had entered heaven itself, in all of its bright and colorful wonder.

Then there were the religious frescoes he had glimpsed earlier, depicting the range of biblical scenes. From the Garden of Eden to Abraham sacrificing Isaac on Mount Moriah, Moses parting the Red Sea to the birth of Jesus, his feeding of the five thousand miracle to his crucifixion.

But then it continued on with curiosity, with scenes depicting neither Christ's resurrection nor ascension, as one would expect in an ancient Christian cathedral. Silas knew in the pre-literate world, before believers had access and the ability to read the Scriptures themselves, ecclesiastical design was meant to teach the faith through images, which surely would have included the resurrection.

What was even more concerning were the other scenes, the frescos morphing into other less-familiar religious depictions that seemed out of place in what he had assumed was a place of Christian worship. If he wasn't mistaken, there was Muhammad's First Revelation, the event described in Islam where the prophet was visited by the angel Jibrīl and revealed to him the beginnings of what would later become the Qur'an. And then another: what looked like a familiar depiction of Siddhartha Gautama, Buddha, sitting cross-legged in a crimson sash, one hand raised with enlightenment.

But whatever the heck it was all about was lost on Silas.

The other thing he found interesting was the hall itself, its design: It wasn't built with a cruciform architecture in mind, as in Western churches, the common layout for a church built with Gothic architecture patterned after a Roman cross—with an east end containing an altar and decorated window, and west end containing a baptismal font, then the north and south transepts that acted as the "arms" of the cross with small side chapels and gathering rooms, and still more the crossing at the center, above which was often a tower or dome.

No, if Silas knew it right, this hall was a tetraconch, Greek for *four shells*, a religious building with four apses, one in each direction of equal size, patterned after a Greek cross and used in Byzantine cathedrals, sometimes even Muslim mosques. Doors stood open at each of the other three ends, leading into darkened corridors hiding ill intent. Thunder rumbled in the near distance, as if confirming the omen.

"It's like the Emerald City?" Gapinski marveled, spinning slowly and staring at the ceiling, weapon resting on his chest.

"You got that right, mate," Celeste said with the same curiosity.

A sudden dread seized Silas, his heart picking up pace and stomach tightening and brain blooming with instruction to get the heck out of there.

"Come on, let's—"

A sudden vibration seized the floor, the stone standing firm but something causing waves of perturbation to flow across it. But not from more thunder crashing above. Something mechanical.

Then with a resounding *slam*, one by one the doors at each of the four arms shut with purpose. And before they could react, gears ground in motion to lower heavy steel blast doors that thudded to the stone floor.

Silas's eyes went wide, and he heaved a breath like someone believing it was their last.

They were trapped, but for one open exit at the far end.

Except that wasn't true at all.

For stepping through it was a massive man with an eight-ball head, shoulders wide and wearing a *thawb*, the traditional garb of Arab men.

"Silas Grey..." the mystery man shouted, the tone and timbre of his lilt placing him somewhere in the part of the world they had been scouring the past few days. The Middle East or Asia Minor, perhaps even North Africa.

He was shrouded in shadows and followed by two familiar men Silas had come to loathe.

Markus Braun and Noland Rotberg.

The man with wide shoulders and hairless olive skin took another step forward, tattoos of symbols marking one side of his face, the man's sandals whispering across the stone floor beneath the plain, well-tailored *thawb*. He was also wearing a gray flowing outer cloak, draped around his shoulders and arms and down to the floor, crimson piping edging the *bisht* garment typically reserved for Middle Eastern royalty.

Or religious clergy.

Is that what this man was? Some sort of cleric, or Arabian prince, or—

The brilliant, refracting light stole his breath for a moment, the tattoo marking his face becoming clearer.

The box man.

A cubist interpretation with a boxy body and triangular legs, arms poking out from the shoulder with a triangle neck and a circular head bisected by a horizontal line through the center.

Silas's stomach sank at the sight, for he instinctively knew who this man was.

The boss. The man at the head of the new mystery sect he had first encountered at Sebastian's house almost two months ago.

He clenched his jaw and gripped his Beretta.

It's go time, Grey...

Silas took a step forward and raised his pistol, pointing it dead-center mass.

His SEPIO teammates hesitated at first, then fell in lockstep, chambering rounds and rustling their rifles around to face the challenge and raising pistols to match Silas's aim.

The man took a step forward, his mouth widening with gleaming white teeth before he threw his head back and laughed, a wicked sound coming from the depths of his belly. Full of haunting purpose and mocking intent, without any fear or hesitation or consequence.

"Impressive, Master Grey. I see your backbone is as sturdy as your head and hands, given all you have accomplished the past few months subverting my agenda."

Silas held steady. "I don't believe we've been introduced."

The man clucked and laughed again. "Where are my manners. Forgive me. I am Sha," he said lowly, taking another step forward, head dipping and eyes going dark. "Lord Mahdi and High Priest of the Church of the Theotites."

Silas's head swam at the revelation. The box-men were indeed another religious sect. Church of the Deities. Which made sense, given the nature of the tattoo they had glimpsed, where the Greek *'Theta'* letter served as the symbol's head—often used as a stand-in for *Theos*, the word for *God*. It had also been known to symbolize man, with him squarely at the center of the world, the eye of intelligence that understands all.

And here was the titular head, confirming what they had suspected. A religious sect committed to God as the human mind, the seat of intelligence, with the knowledge to be like the gods, as Satan had tempted humanity's first ancestors.

To be God themselves.

"I see your mind is working, Master Grey, Master of the Order of Thaddeus, defender and protector of the Church."

Silas startled at the reference, the man clearly well-versed in who he was and who he worked for.

"A lot in common, you and I have. Leaders of an ancient ecclesial order bent on shaping belief within the Church from the beginning of its inception. Two men in the same arena battling for the spiritual soul and intellectual mind and emotional heart of the faith."

What was he talking about? Did this character just put his religious order, Church of the Theotites, as he called it, on the same plane as the Order of Thaddeus? Making claim, even, to his mystery sect having some connection to Christianity?

Sha's eyes were bulging from their sockets now with crazed passion, like oversized yokes from a split hard-boiled egg, irises a curious shade of violet that looked haunting and seemed to glow in the refracted crystalline light. And that voice...something deep and garbly, almost Vader-like in its tone and timbre.

Silas didn't like it one bit, his heart hammering in his chest at all the possibilities of what came next.

He refocused his aim, raising his Beretta and focusing it on the man, wondering if he was truly going to follow through with killing him, this Sha character.

Murdering the man, really, in the name of protecting the true faith...

There was that laugh again. Sha took another step forward, one end of his mouth curling upward and holding up a bony finger before pointing toward Silas. "I don't think that would be wise, Master Grey, aiming for me like that..."

He suddenly snapped his fingers, the pad of the middle one slapping the ball of his thumb and echoing across the hall with surprising clarity.

Silas licked his lips and gripped his weapon tighter at the show, wondering what the man was playing at.

Rotberg and Braun withdrew back into the blackened void behind. Soon there was a commotion behind Sha, followed by shouts of protest and thudding and grunting before the pair reemerged.

Dragging two men inside.

Chuke, his hive of dreadlocks having come undone on one side, was thrown by Braun to the stone floor, the man falling with a thudding bounce at Sha's feet.

Rotberg did the same with another man.

Silas inhaled a sudden breath of panic, familiar blond hair caked to this one's head in a dark substance he could only assume was blood. The man stirred, pushing off the floor and raising his head.

Those eyes and cheekbones, that nose and mouth confirming what he knew to be true.

"Sebastian..." Silas whispered, his weapon lowering to his side with dread.

The mystery man chuckled. "You didn't strike me as a

family man, Master Grey. But it seems we should have ourselves a bit of a chat, wouldn't you say?"

He walked up to Silas's brother and slammed his boot into his back.

Sebastian collapsed and went still.

"Always something..." Gapinski mumbled behind before raising his weapon again. Torres followed, as did Celeste.

By Silas's count, it was four on four. Except they held all the firepower.

So what was his deal?

"Master Grey," the man echoed from the other side, "time to make a deal."

Silas laughed. "A deal?"

"Your brother for the fragments you stole from me. Again."

Apparently, the man had eyes at the back of his head! No matter. Except for his brother, they held all the cards.

"Looks like you've come to make a deal with nothing but words!" Silas shouted back. Who did this joker think he was? He was clearly outmatched and outgunned. Finally, the odds were in SEPIO's favor!

There was that chuckle again, dark and growly and from the belly. Right before he snapped his fingers a second time.

And that sudden vibration returned, seizing the floor with another round of flowing waves. Which was followed by another set of gears grinding in motion to raise those heavy steel blast doors, and the wooden ones set at each of the apses opening with a shudder.

Followed by men in the familiar black paramilitary getup, heads shaved and faces sporting a mirror image of Sha's cubist hominoid markings. All bearing menacing weapons that clearly meant business. Six men to a door, assault rifles aiming toward the center group.

Which meant more than five to one odds, something SEPIO had never faced and would surely lose against.

"Always something," Gapinski growled, backing up against Torres who had spun with her back to the man to face one of the other sextuplets while Celeste angled toward the other door opposite Silas.

Who stood facing Sha, unflinching and unmoving. Weapon still aimed for his head.

"Like I said," the man shouted. "I wouldn't do that if I were you. You may make your shot, but your friends will be cut down in an instant. And so will you, along with your brother."

Silas gripped the weapon tighter, licking his lips as the options ran through his head.

"While you deliberate, let me tell you a story," Sha said with interruption, widening his stance and folding his arms. "It's an ancient story, one I'm sure is quite familiar to a learned man such as yourself in these sorts of matters. It's the parable about blind men and a beast of unknown origin."

Panic and confusion began gripping Silas as the man began his retelling.

"One day," Sha began, "a group of blind men heard that a man traveling through town had stabled a strange animal in their village for the night. Out of curiosity, the men agreed that they must inspect and fully know this beast—and using the only means by which they could discern its features. By touch."

Silas certainly had heard the story, a common one from the spiritual-but-not-religious crowd who not only couldn't believe there was a God to begin with, but couldn't imagine there was only one way to the divine. They insisted there were multiple paths—multiple perspectives from all us blind men groping our way through our encounter with the elephant in the room. With God, or the Divine, or the Universe, or whatever.

Still aiming forward, he said curtly, "What's your point?"

"So the men sought the mystery beast," the man continued, ignoring his question. "When they found it, they groped about its various parts, for not one understood the beast entirely.

Only in its divided particularity did each man conceive of the animal. So they agreed to reveal to each other what it was that they had discerned individually, understanding that each perspective contributed to knowing the beast wholly."

"Silas, what's he playing at?" Celeste whispered from behind. "Any drunk freshman taking Comparative Religion 101 would spout such nonsense."

He shook his head, wondering the same thing.

"The first person," Sha went on, "described it as a snake, having found its trunk. Another grasped its ear and thought it a kind of fan. Still another felt its leg and said the beast was a tree. One fellow felt the beast's side, describing it as a wall. Another, who felt its tail, described it as a rope. And the last blind man, after feeling its tusks, insisted it was a spear."

Gapinski snorted from behind. "Sounds like the dude is drunk on some mad juju juice."

"*Si, muy loco...*" Torres agreed.

Sha took a breath, then grinned knowingly. "So there we are. Six different descriptions of the one elephant, coming from six different experiences."

"Stuff and nonsense is what this is," Celeste said, turning toward the man now.

"Ahh, Celeste Bourne, director of operations for Project SEPIO! She speaks, does she?"

Silas gave her a glance, his concern blooming at the mention of her name and position. Not to mention the Order's special-ops program. Who was this man? How did he know so much about the Order?

Sha continued, "Each man believed they understood the beast in its entirety based on their own personal experience, didn't they? In this case, an elephant. Although ignorant of the entire truth, each blind man assumed their personal truth matched their own limited description. And when they came together to share their revelation, not only did the men disagree over its nature, they squabbled about it—declaring the other bearers of revelation false, heretical, *anathema*!"

The man paused, crossing his arms with an impish grin. "Now, we enlightened ones know that an elephant isn't only tusks or legs. It isn't only a wiry tail or long trunk. It isn't just big ears or a rough wall-like body. No, the beast is all those things. The elephant is the whole of their revelation!"

"What the hell is your point?" Silas spat, growing irritated.

Sha laughed. "A man who gets to the point, you are! As you well know, as do I and others, each religion is like these blind men and our elephant is like the divine reality we understand to be God. Each religion has only a partial knowledge, only a limited experience with the divine reality, the ground of our being. Just like those blind men, all religions grasp mere parts of the one divine whole—all describing the same elephant, the same Absolute, just in different ways."

Then Sha took a step forward, edging in front of Sebastian who was stirring on the floor again. He said, "I myself have heard this parable spouted by some, but something about it has always troubled me."

"Oh, yeah, *hombre loco*," Torres said, now joining the conversation. "What's that?"

"Ah, and Naomi Torres. Ex-treasure hunter extraordinaire. A pleasure to make your acquaintance. Nice work on finding one of the original golden cylinders!"

Her eyes went wide, and she seemed to slink behind Silas.

"Now, where was I? Ah, yes, my problem with the parable. It is this: If the blind men were serious about the truth, why did they not just summon the traveling man to explain what he had brought? I mean, they were blind not deaf? Although they couldn't see the beast, they could still talk to the man. Simple enough, right? I'm sure the traveler would have gladly answered their burning question. *'It's an elephant,'* I can imagine him responding."

Silas's head was spinning now, not making sense of the man. But even more concerned that there was a ring of truth to what he was saying.

"I certainly would have had some questions if I were one of those blind men, groping around in the dark for an unknown beast. But I would have just walked up to the guy and asked!"

"What the hell is your point?" Silas exclaimed, wanting the man to get on with it.

"My point," he said, lowering his head and eyes drawing thin and voice growing dark, "is that a new caretaker has entered the world to share knowledge of the divine beast, joining hands with all the blind across the spiritual spectrum to offer a cohesive, unified revelation. From Jews—" he said, pointing at the fresco of Moses, "and Muslims and Buddhists —" he went on, pointing at the depictions of Muhammad and Buddha, "and yes, even Christians."

He ended with both hands raised, standing underneath the picture of Jesus feeding the five thousand. "Through the centuries, our brothers of the Way have been keen to tap into greater depths of divine knowledge, opening the faith into new realms of practice and belief. Just as Arius tried, but failed."

Celeste startled. "Arius was one of your bloomin' brothers?"

"And by brothers of the Way, you mean inside the true Church?" Silas asked, surprised at the ancient Christian name.

Sha smirked, folding his arms. "That is correct, Ms. Bourne. And what is the *true* Church, as you put it, Master Grey?"

"That which was affirmed at Nicaea. Nicene Christianity."

The man laughed, his cackle echoing from the heights of the crystalline dome. "Nicaea was a power play, nothing more. Meant to suppress and oppress the other voices within the Church, *our* voices that had been giving rise to a secret knowledge of the Spirit from the dawn of Jesus' prophetic ministry. It has been that way ever since, the dominant ecclesiastical voices suppressing the minority ones, stopping us from reimagining the faith for a new day—and in no small thanks to the Order, I might add. Just like it was seventeen hundred years ago. Speaking of which..."

Sha pointed and motioned with his hand. "The fragments."

"You are positively mad!" Celeste said, weapon lowered now and face twisted up. "You do know that the fragments actually make the exact opposite case, do you not? That from the outset there has been incredible unity to the faith. Even Emperor Constantine knew that, and confessed as much. It was Arius and his cronies and people like your Theotites or whoever the bloody hell they are who are responsible for trying to muddy the water."

"She's right," Silas said. "The fragments won't do you any good. They prove nothing to make your case. Or Braun's and Rotberg's case that the Church and the Christian faith was the creation of Constantine, pitting the political and dogmatic interests of those in power against the weaker voices." He paused, eyeing the two men who stood still behind Sha, adding: "Who I assume are with you?"

Sha just laughed. "Yes, well, everyone's got their minions. Besides, it would be a pity if those fragments got out, wouldn't it? And I'm sure I can work them to my advantage anyhow. I understand parts of them are rather vague about Constantine's position on the matter. I'm sure a little creativity would lend beautiful results."

He stepped back, motioning Rotberg to come forward and whispering an instruction. The man knelt at Sebastian's side. He stirred, moaning and muttering something as the man grabbed his hair, withdrawing a blade and pressing it against his exposed neck, drawing a line of blood.

"The fragments for the brother," Sha said.

Gapinski snorted a laugh from behind. "Give up our only leverage with two dozen barrels pointed at our asses? You crazy?"

"Boy has a point," Torres joined in. "How do we know you ain't pullin' our chain? That you won't finish what you started when you drugged us and dragged us to...wherever the heck this is?"

"You have my word," Sha said. "You may all go freely when you hand over Constantine's confession."

Silas's head ran hot with blood and confusion and indecision. What should he do?

Hand the fragments over to the newest spiritual whack job on the block bent on the Church's destruction, getting his brother back but also securing his enemy's release, only to wreak the same destruction with the same tone, just different timbre?

Or keep the fragments and fight like hell, ensuring Sebastian's death—or perhaps destroy them, then and there, which would probably end in the same result, including his and his friend's demise?

"Go on, then," Celeste said quietly from behind. "Let him have the bloomin' things. We verified they pose no threat to the Church. A pity we won't be able to leverage them for her defense, but so what. We'll live, and so will the faith."

Silas sighed with relief, thankful someone made the choice for him.

He turned back, that smirk on Sha's face almost changing his mind and infusing his veins with the gumption to stick it to him and fight to the death.

But he relented, withdrawing the broken pieces from his jacket and walking toward the man. He glanced at the platoon of spiritual soldiers arrayed at the four corners, ready to do the bidding of their master. Doubtful they'd make it out alive but not having any other choice.

He saw his brother lying prone on the cold, hard stone floor, the memory of that afternoon from that dream that had woken him with a start a few hours ago playing itself on repeat.

Always defend and protect what matters to you.

Even those who betray you time and time again?

He took a breath and nodded, making his choice by closing the length between him and Sha. Reaching him, he stretched out his arm to hand over the fragments.

When an alarm sounded, loud and clangy and urgent, the shrill echoing with ear-piercing indignation.

CHAPTER 33

There was a clap of thunder as if echoing the invasive explosion. Silas dropped the goods in the sudden confusion, the parchment pieces fluttering to the stone floor.

Sha's eyes shot open with recognition at the continued alarm before they narrowed and his head dipped with activating resolve.

The man knew things had changed. He knew why the alarm was sounding.

Help.

And Silas figured it was *his* help.

The SEPIO kind.

An explosion sent him stumbling to the ground. Sha fell back as well with surprise, tumbling over Sebastian who suddenly sprang to life with a roar. Whether from some hidden possession or from simple cunning at feigning incapacitation, it wasn't clear.

The Nous Master stumbled forward as another blast rocked the compound, coming to blows with Rotberg who was apparently still tasked with keeping their chief rival subdued.

Silas ignored them, his attention drawn to the drama at the other end.

And quite the drama it was.

The doors from where they had entered had been completely obliterated, the walls crumbled and remains smoldering. Bodies of the Theotite hostiles littered the ground like rag dolls tossed by a careless toddler. Some of the remaining ones at that wing had taken up positions against the forces pushing through, but it was no use.

Silas instantly recognized the SEPIO agents, the blue uniforms marked by crimson armbands offering a strong response and downing the hostiles one by one.

He spun around to find Gapinski ushering Celeste and Torres toward the entrance to join the newly arrived Order special-ops agents, the SEPIO trio taking care of the rest of the hostiles as their teammates continued their assault.

Which left the clusters of six men stationed at the other two apses, aside from Rotberg—who was still occupied with Sebastian—and Braun, who had fled.

So three to one now.

Much better odds.

And that wasn't even counting the help from the SEPIO new arrivals.

He hadn't seen anything like it, the impressive show of SEPIO force. Didn't even know the Order could offer such a muscular defense for the faith. Then again, he had only been Order Master for not even half a year.

The floor suddenly sparked with explosive violence, bullets striking up a chord along a line of the cut stone floor a few feet away.

Right before Sha slammed him in the back to the same floor.

Silas's forehead cracked against the stone, stars and darkness blooming. At least his nose held, blood not pouring down as it had in other such altercations. But dizziness overcame him, and he had trouble pushing himself to stand, collapsing again and cursing himself for his weakness.

But he managed to get to his knees, noticing his Beretta had skittered off to the side. He took to one leg, then shoved up to both, the battle continuing to rage around him.

He walked to the weapon and retrieved it. Then remembered.

The fragments!

Spinning around, he searched the floor for the parchment pieces.

Gone.

So was Sha.

His head was screaming now, a pounding county fair tilt-a-whirl that threatened to undo him.

Lord Jesus Christ, Son of God, keep me steady...

Silas managed, a surprising strength rising as he caught sight of his new enemy pushing past a pack of his men engaged in a firefight with SEPIO.

He let his own men take care of them while tearing after the only one who mattered, hiking his legs up and pumping his arms like he used to do it with the Rangers, bobbing and weaving through bombed-out city blocks, and then before that under Friday night lights on the well-manicured grass for the Falls Church Jaguars as lead quarterback.

He knew four years of summer training and then basic after that would come in handy one of those days.

Now was that day.

Catching up to the large man, Silas lunged for him. Returning the favor by slamming into his back and slamming him to the floor.

The fragments fell from the man's grip and scattered about near a wall that was now inflamed from the original blast stretching across the hall now.

Sha flipped to his back and kicked Silas as he reached for a piece, the jab to his backside toppling him back to the floor. And sending his Beretta sailing—again.

Not good...

The man sat up.

Only to find Silas kicking him from the floor squarely in the chest.

Sending his head slamming back against the cut stone.

Disoriented, Sha moaned and flailed about. Silas was about as spent from the exchange.

But the new enemy had been prepared with one final blow.

He grabbed a handful of the fragments within his reach and threw them against the flaming wall just over his shoulder.

Silas watched them tumble through the air, catching fire in the raging inferno and burning into nothingness in an instant.

"No!!" He ran for them to offer their salvation, but it was no use. They were gone.

Constantine's confession of his faith in Jesus Christ, and a worthy defense to support that faith, was lost to history.

A man crumpled a few feet away from a direct hit to his head, his weapon clattering to the stone floor. A dose of providential provision if he ever saw it!

Enraged at losing the fragments, he scrambled after it.

A hand grabbed his leg from behind, jerking him back with force. But he kicked it away, grunting as he pulled himself forward on his arms until he reached the rifle.

Gotchya...

Grinning, he snatched it and spun to his back.

Sha loomed over him before faltering his steps and kneeling with arms raised.

Silas leaped to his feet and aimed straight for the man's forehead, everything inside telling him to pull the trigger at that bald head that was stretching into a giggling grin.

"Do it!" Sha shouted. "But know this—the Theotites will

become more powerful than you can possibly imagine if I am martyred. Our kind have survived for centuries in the shadows and are primed for activating the masses to consume our knowledge of the spirit realm—channeling it for all to taste and see with enlightenment."

Silas gripped the rifle tighter, Sha's eyes closing with recognition and the moment drawing down to zero with his finger ready to pull.

But he didn't do it.

He couldn't do it.

He wouldn't take the man's life, not in this way. And no way would he make him a martyr for whatever wackadoodle spirituality he was peddling.

Sha snapped open his eyes, that grin having fallen into resigned death, only to be revived again with a smugness Silas had seen all too often on his own brother.

The man stood, fire consuming the wall behind him now and reaching up the dome and over. It would all come crashing down soon. And Silas prayed it was a metaphor for what would happen to the man's burgeoning spiritual empire.

But somehow he knew the fight was only just beginning. On yet another front.

Sha said nothing, grinning with a wink before fleeing through an open, unoccupied door.

Across the way, Silas saw Sebastian standing, taking aim with a weapon and firing off a shot into Rotberg who stood with arms raised, then another before taking off with Chuke through the doorway where he had been brought—disappearing into the blackened void clutching his arm but finding escape once again.

The least they could have done was thanked Silas and SEPIO for saving their asses.

A hand grabbed him from behind. He spun with an extended weapon.

Gapinski threw his hands up. "Whoa there, chief! It's me!"

Silas sighed and lowered his weapon. "What the heck are you doing?"

"Getting your butt out of here, that's what!"

Silas spun around, taking in the scene before him.

The vast, round hall was nearly consumed with fire now, the heat pressing in against him and billowing smoke suffocating. Looking around, it was clear the hostiles had either been killed or incapacitated, knocked out or tied up. Some of the Order's agents were also among those dead, bodies in those blue uniforms with red arm bands crumpled with the black-clad ones. Braun had fled the coup, and even Rotberg was missing just moments after being shot, though he couldn't be far with direct hits from Sebastian. SEPIO had come through. Big time!

But the others...

"Celeste!" he said in a panic, spinning back to Gapinski.

"Relax, lover boy. Greer brought her and Torres to the SEPIO bird waiting our extraction. I was sent to retrieve our fearless leader. Come on!"

Silas followed him through the original blast site that brought SEPIO into the complex in the first place, the sound of whirling blades competing with the rain pounding and thunder echoing overhead.

He hopped aboard the helicopter to find Bishop Zarruq strapped in—safe and sound.

"Victor!" Celeste said from behind as Silas climbed aboard, throwing his arms in relief around the man's neck as Gapinski and Torres huddled inside.

"You're safe," Silas said, voice choking and throat growing thick with emotion. "But how?"

"You can thank me for that."

It was Zoe, serving as wingman up front. She was hunched

over a computer and struggling to put her blue glasses back into place.

"Zoe! You came through," he shouted, grabbing her shoulder and shaking it with thanks.

"No, you came through!"

"What do you mean?"

"The emergency tracker app that you engaged on your mobile device."

That's right! He'd forgotten all about it since leaving the dungeon down below. Must have triggered the signal once they reached higher ground.

"The thing lit up SEPIO something crazy when an agent noticed the signal coming through. The guy didn't know what to make of it at first—something we're going to fix stat when we get back. We'd sent SEPIO agents to North Africa after Victor here, searching up and down the coast, but had no luck. Wasn't until you threw up that signal flair that we knew Nous was near—and the good bishop. So we assembled a team of operatives and sent them scrambling your way. Nabbed him not far from your last known location. And when you went dark, we figured you'd find a way to turn the beacon back on, and we'd be ready once it was reengaged for your own extraction. That was the hope anyway."

"You figured right. Way to go, Zoe! And, we owe you one. Big time!"

"And I also owe you, Master Grey," Zarruq said. "Although, I am not sure I am comfortable with the notion that your misfortune meant my rescue."

"I'm just glad you're safe, Victor," Silas said.

"A nice fat raise would be one way to show your appreciation," Zoe quipped, clacking away at her computer again.

He chuckled. "Let's discuss it back at the farm."

She looked back and smiled then got back to her work, leaving Silas to the scene outside.

But he didn't want to mess with it, didn't want to think about any of it anymore. Was completely spent now that it was all over.

"Let's get the heck out of here," he muttered, his face slick with rain whirling in his face surveying the damage from the helicopter and searching for any sign of his brother, but coming up empty.

"Sure thing, Master Grey," the pilot said.

The helicopter lifted, ascending high through plumes of smoke as flames struggled to consume the structure below in the deluge, the fire sizzling in protest and flapping for a surer footing as the blades whipped the world below into a frenzy.

Silas's heart rent at the thought Sebastian was burning to death down below.

Before burning for all eternity somewhere else...

He banished the thought, that horrid nightmare from the night rising to the surface and the maxim his father had taught him: Always defend and protect what matters to you.

Now his bowels were weakening at the truth of it all. He had helped defend and protect the Christian faith once again, saved it even. *That* certainly mattered. But at what cost?

His brother, dead? All the other terrorist whack jobs they'd taken out, bodies littered from Libya to Turkey to wherever they were? And that wasn't even counting the past missions from the past two years!

Silas sighed as they pulled away from the wreckage. Such was life in the Order of Thaddeus, he guessed. And as Order Master, no less.

The compound faded from view now, and the dark clouds overtook the flaming light. He took some small consolation that they had been able to more fully unmask the newest threat to the Christian faith, this Church of the Theotites outfit. What it all meant for the real Church he hadn't a clue, and he feared a new front was opening up in the assaults rising up against

Christianity, from within even, that would prove more threatening than even Nous had been.

Another pivot moment, with him at the helm now leading the charge.

Only time would tell.

CHAPTER 34
IZNIK, TURKEY. JUNE 19. ANNIVERSARY OF NICENE CREED.

I t was a bright, sunny day, all happy and warm. Just the way it should be celebrating what the Order of Thaddeus was celebrating.

The anniversary when Bishop Hosius, delegate to the Council of Nicaea, announced the Nicene Creed. That moment when the Church clarified her teaching about the person of Jesus Christ.

It wasn't that belief in Jesus' deity had been decided or created. It's clear from the Gospels and the letters written within decades of Christ's death that his earliest followers had *already* believed he was God, believed that he was the Son of God, second Person of the Trinity. Jesus himself equated himself with the God of Abraham, Isaac, and Jacob.

And they were celebrating it all where it had originally went down, in a church in the modern city of Iznik, the Hagia Sophia of Iznik as it is known, a Byzantine-era church originally constructed by Justinian I in the 6th century.

Silas sat listening to Bishop Zarruq's booming baritone voice, his heart warmed by the man's passionate articulation of God's love for the world, his desire for the communion of saints to make much of that love by sharing it, and the hope of eternal life. He and Celeste were arm in arm, joined by Gapinski and Torres and a hundred other ecclesiastical leaders from across the Christian spectrum, seated in makeshift wood pews that reminded Silas why he couldn't sit still for Mass as a boy. They were arrayed across a bright crimson carpet, dotted by gold and stripped by indigo, a majestic blue-and-gold patterned star anchoring the center.

The place was a bit stuffy in the cloistered ancient building of stone walls under exposed wood beams, the place smelling of wood and stone, the humidity pressing in against him. But he didn't care. His senses were alive, feeling and smelling and hearing and seeing, because he was alive. Which was about all he could ask for, given what SEPIO had gone through the past few months fighting to protect the faith. From threats inside and outside the Church.

He was certainly satisfied to make some headway on that front, and surely more would reveal itself in the coming months as SEPIO agents scoured the dark web and established contacts inside the new Church of the Theotites sect to gain a footing for information and insight, especially since its apparent leader suggested it had some historic connections within Christianity —whatever that meant.

Although now it meant Nous wasn't his only headache, nor his brother if he managed to survive. Now he had this Sha character to contend with, as well as Markus Braun with his network and ability to manipulate the masses and untold billions of dollars. Noland Rotberg was a showboat, but Silas now understood the man wasn't to be taken lightly. He had a brilliant mind, who understood Christianity and religion like few others in the world—not to mention a collection of fancy pistols he knew how to use. But a mind on a mission...that was a dangerous thing indeed.

Then there was the other issue: Silas was kicking himself for bungling Constantine's confession, that he'd allowed it to be destroyed—the fragments burning among the ruins. The Emperor's confession, his spiritual *code*, could have been used to further the faith.

Zarruq pounded the wood podium, apparently making an important point that had the effect of jolting Silas from his daydreaming. Celeste rested a hand on his leg and gently squeezed, three times.

I. Love. You.

Silas smiled and glanced at her, then replied with four squeezes of his own.

I. Love. You. Too.

She smiled back and winked, Zarruq pounding the podium again with passion and sending Silas to consider all that had happened.

Especially the frustration over losing the imperial confession relic. Sure, he had the digital photo he'd taken of the five fragments in the Urfa mosque, but that's wouldn't cut it. If only he had the real deal...

But should he be so frustrated? Should the Church need some confession by some dead emperor to further the faith? In many ways, what mattered more were the fruits of the Emperor's labor. His *theological* labor, even.

He smiled, shaking his head. "The emperor code..."

It was an apt description, given the theological gift the man Constantine had helped offer the Church, which had anchored the faith stretching back nearly seventeen hundred years.

Speaking of which...

A clapping arose, and Zarruq gestured toward Silas to come to the front. Time for his own remarks commemorating the occasion for the anniversary of the emperor code.

He rose from the pew and ascended three stairs to a makeshift dais, taking over the modest wood lectern Zarruq had been pounding with passion earlier. He grasped its side and stared out at the assembled, scanning the room of bishops and priests, pastors and professors who had come to honor the memory of the original gathering that had gifted the Church its code, reminding generation's of Christians what they believed.

He just wished he had an actual copy of Constantine's confession to show. Although, he did have something better…

After surveying the assembled crowd, catching an encouraging smile and nod from Celeste down front, he fixed his gaze on a camera that had been mounted straight ahead with a live feed to Facebook, WeShare, and other platforms to broadcast the Order's own message about the Nicene Creed.

Silas cleared his throat, then started: "There's this passage in the Holy Scriptures I'd like to draw our attention to this morning. 2 Kings 22 tells a story about a book that was missing for two generations. This was no ordinary book. It was vital to Israel's spiritual practices. And yet, even though this book was the foundation to their faith and life it was missing—for two generations!"

He could feel one end of his mouth curl upward, adrenaline coursing through him now as he stepped back into the role of professor—hopefully without sounding lecturey.

"Now, during the time the important book was missing, several kings ascended to the throne who introduced idolatry and pagan worship practices into Israel's spiritual life. Manasseh was one such king who built altars to Baal and worshiped the stars and moon and practiced witchcraft. His son Amon—like father like son—continued these practices for another few years until he was betrayed by his own advisors."

Silas paused, scanning the crowd again for effect, then continued: "You see the story of the lost book is much bigger than a story about a misplaced religious artifact. No, there's something deeper going on here: Israel forgot who they were as much as they lost a religious book. It wasn't until an eight-year-old boy came to the throne that things changed. King Josiah sought Yahweh with all his heart and purged the lands of idols and altars dedicated to pagan gods. During Josiah's reign, Israel found her story again. Literally! One day, the priest Hilkiah found the Book of the Law. What was this book, you ask?"

Silas paused with a grin, scanning the crowd for effect. "Most believe it was the Book of Deuteronomy, containing all the requirements for Yahweh's relationship with his people, specifically, the Shema—which goes like this: *'Hear, O Israel: The Lord our God, the Lord is one. Love the Lord your God with all your heart and with all your soul and with all your strength.'*"

He moved to the side, feeling a little like a country preacher working the room. "The Shema was the cornerstone to Israel's faith," he went on. "Yet for generations it was completely forgotten. No wonder Israel forgot who they were! Instead of loving and serving and believing in the one true God with all of their heart and soul and strength, they ran after false religious beliefs and gods. Israel's story was recovered *only* after the Book of the Law was recovered. Before they found it again, there was spiritual confusion."

Silas returned to the lectern, planting his hands on its sides as he caught a few in the audience checking their watches. Time to get to it.

"I've retold this ancient story because just like Israel, the Christian West has lost her way—forgotten the plot to our own Christian story, seeking to reimagine the faith for a new day even. And it's time to recover it. Where one generation in Israel found the lost Book of the Law, I believe a whole new generation needs to re-discover the central story to the Christian faith: God's Story, encapsulated in the Church's code, written nearly seventeen hundred years ago, which we are celebrating here today. And which is why we need this more than ever..."

He went to an easel that had been set up with a framed copy of the surviving Nicene Creed resting underneath a cloth. Grabbing one end of it, he slowly unveiled a gold frame before the full measure of the Church's code was seen.

A chorus of *oohs* and *ahhs* rippled across the room until some started standing for a better viewing.

Silas let the moment hang for a few minutes before continuing: "You know, growing up my dad told me to always defend and protect what matters."

He caught his breath, the memory of Sebastian from that nightmare surfacing, as well as the final glimpse of him fleeing into the darkened void. He said a prayer for him, asking the Lord to keep him safe, and save his soul.

Silas recovered, clearing his throat and resuming: "Always defend and protect what matters, he said. For me, that includes my faith. A faith contained in the words that make up beliefs countless believers across the centuries and continents have gone to the mat to defend and protect. Starting in Jerusalem, then in Judea and Samaria, later Antioch and Alexandria. On across North Africa to Ptolemais and Apollonia and Carthage, then back through Persia and India and Asia Major. Then back again through Asia Minor to Rome and Gaul and up to Britannia. Where eventually it saturated Europe and the Americas and every part of the world. Which exactly reflects the heart of God and the mission of our Savior. To invite everyone to find salvation from sin and the hope of eternal life in Christ."

Silas stepped back and took a breath, figuring he did enough damage for one morning. He raised his hands and grinned widely, channeling Gapinski's Southern Baptist Grandpappy preacher, saying: "Let us stand together, reciting what became of this creed, this theological code, that has guided the Church for two millennia."

Bishop Zarruq was first to his feet, followed by his SEPIO teammates. Then everyone rose, Catholics and Protestants and Orthodox believers, joining together in the unity of the faith.

Just as Emperor Constantine had wanted it.

Silas closed his eyes, and in one voice, the words echoing off the ancient stone walls and cedar timbers above, they recited:

We believe in one God,
the Father, the Almighty,
maker of heaven and earth,
of all that is, seen and unseen.

We believe in one Lord, Jesus Christ,
the only Son of God,
eternally begotten of the Father,
God from God, Light from Light,
true God from true God,
begotten, not made,
of one Being with the Father.
Through him all things were made.
For us and for our salvation
he came down from heaven:
by the power of the Holy Spirit
he became incarnate from the Virgin Mary,
and was made man.
For our sake he was crucified under Pontius Pilate;
he suffered death and was buried.
On the third day he rose again
in accordance with the Scriptures;
he ascended into heaven
and is seated at the right hand of the Father.
He will come again in glory to judge the living and the dead,
and his kingdom will have no end.

We believe in the Holy Spirit, the Lord, the giver of life,
who proceeds from the Father and the Son.
With the Father and the Son he is worshiped and glorified.
He has spoken through the Prophets.

We believe in one holy catholic and apostolic Church.
We acknowledge one baptism for the forgiveness of
  sins.
We look for the resurrection of the dead,
and the life of the world to come.
Amen.

Silas opened his eyes. A ray of sun sliced through a window high above, glinting off the gold framed copy of the Nicene Creed that had survived their ordeal. He smiled at the familiar sight of light hitting gold, reminding them of all they had gone through to secure this memory of the Church.

To secure the Church's code.

Always defend and protect what matters, Dad said.

Amen, indeed.

ENJOY THE EMPEROR CODE?

A big thanks for joining Silas Grey and the rest of SEPIO on their adventure saving the Church!

Enjoy the story? Here's what you can do next:

If you loved the book and have a moment to spare, **a short review is much appreciated.** Nothing fancy, just your honest take. Spreading the word is probably the #1 way you can help independent authors like me and help others enjoy the story.

If you're ready for another adventure, you can get a full-length novel in the series for free! All you have to do is join the insider's group to be notified of specials and new releases by going to this link: www.jabouma.com/free

You might also like my apocalyptic sci-fi thriller series, *Ichthus Chronicles.* Set 100 years in the future, the last remnant of Christianity is threatened from forces inside and outside the Church, written in the vein of the *Left Behind* series. Start the adventure today: www.jabouma.com/books/apostasy-rising-1

AUTHOR'S NOTE
THE HISTORY BEHIND THE STORY

In 2019, one of my favorite thriller authors and the inspiration behind my own stories, Steve Berry, published *The Malta Exchange*. The plot was intriguing, as he described it: *"The pope is dead. A conclave to select his replacement is about to begin. Cardinals are beginning to arrive at the Vatican, but one has fled Rome for Malta in search of a document that dates back to the 4th century and Constantine the Great."*

And yet the "document" was the typical yarn coming from people with a critical eye toward Christianity, rehashing well-worn tropes of early Church history with a dollop of bad historical revisionism on the side. Dan Brown is the more well-known of such writers who stunned the world with his "revelations" in *The Da Vinci Code*, making wild claims about key Christian beliefs, primarily the deity of Jesus Christ, as well as the Nicene Creed, Council of Nicaea, and of course Emperor Constantine.

So I thought I would do something about it by writing my own book! This is that book, which sought to shed a bit more light on the enigmatic emperor who did play a considerable role in the Church's rise, yet in ways far different from the postmodern lens of power plays and oppressed minority voices typical of such fiction. I also wanted to help people better understand how the central code of Christianity, the Nicene Creed, came about, as well as its central doctrine: the nature of Jesus Christ, and all the historical conflict clarifying the belief that had been central from the beginning.

As with all of my books, I like to add a note at the end with some thoughts and research that went into the story. I aim to definitely craft an entertainment-first tale, a story that's mostly about giving you a thrilling ride. But I also like to add a bit of insight and inspiration for faith. So, if you care to learn more about the foundation of this episode in the Order of Thaddeus, here is some of what I discovered that made its way into SEPIO's latest adventure.

Arius, the Council of Nicaea, and Jesus' Deity

I won't rehash what Bartholomew brought to the attention of the SEPIO agents in the Vatican Archives—the description of which was both thanks to Google Maps and my overactive imagination!—but all the quoted portions are from the historical record in the public domain, belonging to Arius, Eusebius, and Constantine himself. The main heresy the North African Bishop Arius perpetuated was the notion there was a time when the Son was not. Meaning: Jesus Christ, the Son of God and second Person of the Trinity, was created by God the Father, challenging the Church's teaching that Jesus is co-equal with the Father in power, glory, honor, authority, and Being.

Unfortunately, this codification in the Nicene Creed of Jesus' divine status along with the clarity to his nature at the Council of Nicaea has been twisted by the likes of Brown and Berry in popular culture. They peddle the lie that only since Nicaea has the Church started teaching and believing in the doctrine. This couldn't be further from the truth! The earliest of Christ's followers, which we see reflected in Scripture in addition to early post-Apostolic fathers, shows the Church equated Jesus with God, especially of the Hebrew Scriptures.

One of the more striking examples is in the Gospel of John, when the Jewish teachers were interrogating Jesus, accusing him of demonic possession:

> Jesus answered, "If I glorify myself, my glory is nothing. It is my Father who glorifies me, he of whom you say, 'He is our God,' though you do not know him. But I know him; if I would say that I do not know him, I would be a liar like you. But I do know him and I keep his word. Your ancestor Abraham rejoiced that he would see my day; he saw it and was glad." Then the Jews said to him, "You are not yet fifty years old, and have you seen Abraham?" Jesus said to them, "Very truly, I tell you, before Abraham was, I AM." (8:54–58)

In case you didn't catch it, I AM was how Yahweh described his own identity in Exodus when Moses asked the Lord who he should say sent him when he fetched the Israelites from slavery. The Book of Exodus reveals: "God said to Moses, 'I AM who I AM.' He said further, 'Thus you shall say to the Israelites, "I AM has sent me to you"'" (Exodus 4:14). Which means Jesus equated himself with the divine name revealed to the Israelites. No wonder the Jews wanted to stone him after that one!

Paul offers another example, writing in the First Letter of Paul to the Corinthians in a discourse on so-called gods:

> Indeed, even though there may be so-called gods in heaven or on earth—as in fact there are many gods and many lords—yet for us there is one God, the Father, from whom are all things and for whom we exist, and one Lord, Jesus Christ, through whom are all things and through whom we exist. (1 Corinthians 8:4–5)

Again, here Paul clearly says there is one true God, and Jesus is him! This is known in big churchy terms as christological monotheism, which is a fancy way of saying that Jesus' nature was equated with the one God of the universe. So the idea Christ's deity was invented in the 4th century, at a Church Council, and muscled by a pagan emperor is, to put it nicely, nonsense! And yet the myth continues to be perpetuated.

Much of the content in Noland Rotberg's monologue from the video found on WeSolve in chapter 7 on the subject reflects Brown's *The Da Vinci Code*, found in chapter 55 I changed the original in order to put the words in Rotberg's mouth while preserving the main line of argument in order to offer critical commentary of the myth. (If you haven't figured it out yet, Noland Rotberg, the new character I introduced in *Gospel Zero*, is an anagram for Robert Langdon, Brown's intrepid symbologist. Imitation is the best form of flattery, right?)

Constantine and Christianity

The relationship between Constantine and Christianity is an interesting one, which Silas and Celeste sort of hash out in chapter 14 on their way to search for one of the fragments in Istanbul. This complication has offered plenty of fodder for both conspiracists and detractors of Christianity, all suggesting the man used the Church for his own powerful ends while also muscling through particular doctrines and practices to create the religion we know of as Christianity.

(First: yes, the Emperor was originally buried in Istanbul and later moved, however it's unclear where his remains ended up. And yes, the sarcophagi outside the walls of the Istanbul Archaeology Museum are real, having been used for past Byzantine emperors and come from the now-vanished Church of the Holy Apostles. Even the non-red one of limestone bearing the Chi-Rho symbol of Constantine—which was too good to be true!)

One of the most enlightening books on the subject is Peter Leithart's *Defending Constantine*. He separates fact from fiction to paint a multi-faceted picture of the man, and his faith. Combined with Eusebius's account of the Emperor, *Life of Constantine*, which was a bit of a romanticized account (Although, I wouldn't blame him for such a bromance, given what the Church had endured for almost three hundred years before the Emperor gave Christianity a surer footing!), and Constantine's own *Oration of the Saints,* several themes emerge.

The first is unity. Part of this was practical and political, given divisions among the ascendant Christians could tear the Empire apart. But Leithart contends it was more a theological conviction, believing divisions displeased God and he would take vengeance out on not only the Church but Constantine himself. And this unity also bore itself out in mission, the universal mission of the Church to spread the gospel and renew the world. Constantine's desire for unity wasn't merely an emotional bond but a doctrinal one, expressing his joy to the bishops at the Council of Nicaea for being "united in one judgment, and that common spirit of peace and concord prevailing among you all, which it becomes you, as consecrated to the service of God, to commend to others." One judgement about one faith, centered around one Savior, Lord, and God: Jesus Christ. One quotation from *Oration* seemed to reveal this belief:

> While, therefore, it is natural for man occasionally to err, yet God is not the cause of human error. Hence it becomes all pious persons to render thanks to the Savior of all, first for our own individual security, and then for the happy posture of public affairs: at the same time intreating the favor of Christ with holy prayers and constant supplications, that he would continue to us our present blessings. For he is the invincible ally and protector of the righteous: he is the supreme judge of all things, the prince of immortality, the Giver of everlasting life. (*Orations*, Ch. 26)

I don't want to press the case too hard, because Celeste is right about Constantine's past as well, killing his own son from a previous marriage by poison and then boiling his wife in a bath. He also continued aspects of the Roman cult, consulting the Oracle of Apollo and referring to himself on occasion as the High Priest of Roman religion. However, he was a great blessing to the Church. Within a single generation, Christianity went from suffering its greatest persecution to enjoying its greatest privilege. His pledges through the Edict of Milan restored Christian freedom enjoyed before the Great Persecution, even going so far as to extend and enlarge those freedoms. He also launched a massive campaign to build churches across the Empire, giving the growing movement tangible places of worship, and afforded bishops protections from the state.

Perhaps Silas is right: We should conclude that Constantine was a Christian man, but one with deep flaws who at times used his faith as a political tool for maneuvering the Empire through tenuous times. Yes, he seemed to take his mission on earth to be more political than spiritual. However, he was the Emperor, and that doesn't mean he was not Christ's son or outside the grace of God. Considering all that the Lord used him to accomplish during the great upheaval almost seventeen hundred years ago, in addition to his own confession of Christ's deity and search for unity within the Church, it seems clear Christ was with him.

Chapters 23 and 24 contain a snapshot of some of Constantine's own writings and speeches from the public domain, edited slightly for clarity and length, concerning his faith and the Christian faith. Chapter 28, which is a compilation of the scattered pieces of Constantine's confession, somewhat mirrors chapter 62 from Berry's *The Malta Exchange* that inspired me to write this one as a way to offer critical commentary of his argument. My own chapter borrows some of the language from what the Emperor himself said to offer a decidedly different take on the man.

The Seedbed of Christianity

One of the more pernicious lies about the origins of Christianity is the suggestion that it was formed by white Roman Europeans. The truth of the matter is far different! It's a theme I began a bit in *Gospel Zero*, especially with the introduction of the Libyan Bishop Victor Zarruq (who will be sticking around a while), and continued in this book because the earliest decades and centuries were thoroughly African and Asian, which the ancient context included Palestine, Syria, Turkey, and Anatolia.

It is a faith contained in the words that make up the beliefs that countless believers across the centuries and continents have gone to the mat to defend and protect. Starting in Jerusalem, then in Judea and Samaria, later Antioch and Alexandria. On across North Africa to Ptolemais and Apollonia and Carthage, then back through Persia and India and Asia Major. Then back again through Asia Minor to Rome and Gaul and up to Britannia. Where eventually it saturated Europe and the Americas and every part of the world. It largely became a European religion after Christianity was decimated by invading Muslim Arabs across North Africa and around into Asia Minor, coming into Europe from both sides where it was nearly snuffed out. Something like 90% of churches and Christians were martyred across non-European lands, where the faith remained preserved in Europe only after Arab invaders were driven out—but that's the topic of another book (some of which was tackled in *Templars Rising*).

Reality is, Christianity has a far greater history in the African continent, especially in the north, than its Western or European expressions. From Egypt to Sudan and Ethiopia to Eritrea, from Libya to Tunisia and Algeria to Morocco—early African Christianity played a decisive role in the formation of the Church, both its culture and practices, but also its doctrine and teachings. What was later taught throughout Europe was originally shaped in Africa by such names as Tertullian, Cyprian, Athanasius, Augustine, and Cyril.

So I wanted to root this tale in those lands, beginning with the ruins of a basilica in Apollonia, a once thriving community of Christians whose ruins and history are accurately portrayed. The baptismal was my addition, along with the Chi-Rho insignia and buried golden cylinder, although who knows! The heretic Arius was also Libyan, and began teaching in those parts, with special help from the bishop of Ptolemais, so that was an added convenience for the story. Again, ruins in that city remain and were described according to photos from archaeological digs at the site.

Edessa had also been one of the centers of Christianity for centuries, rivaling Jerusalem and Ephesus early on, and then Antioch and Alexandria and Rome in later centuries. Despite the city having finally fallen under Muslim control through Arab conquest a millennium ago, one would have found a full-blooded Christian city, literally brimming with Christian churches and monasteries, numbering more than three hundred, according to one Arab geographer of the time. One of the primary mosques in the city was also built on the ruins of an ancient cathedral almost a thousand years ago, and apparently there is a stone well rumored to have housed the Shroud of Turin, a singular picture of which I found on the internet for research—but take it with a fictional grain of salt, as well as a hidden chamber with yet another Chi-Rho symbol, behind which hides a golden cylinder!

This story of non-European influence on the Church and Christian faith has been forgotten. This is unfortunate, and I hope to incorporate more of the global perspective and history of Christianity in future stories—because, frankly, I think the hope of the Church's future is with our Majority World brothers and sisters, so perhaps the Church's story will come full circle in the coming years!

(As an aside, my apocalyptic sci-fi series *Ichthus Chronicles* was largely created for this reason. It is set in a world 100 years from now where characters from outside the West are the main heroes, helping preserve the faith in a dystopian future on the edge of the End Times—including the relative of Victor Zarruq, his far distant grandson Alexander Zarruq!)

Research is an important part of my process for creating compelling stories that entertain, inform, and inspire. Here are a few resources I used to research the history behind Q source, the Muratorian Fragment, the Gnostic texts, and Christian forgeries:

- Bennet, William J. Tried By Fire. Nashville: Thomas Nelson, 2016. www.bouma.us/code1
- Leithart, Peter. Defending Constantine. Downers Grove, IL: IVP Academic, 2010. www.bouma.us/code2

- Oden, Thomas. *How Africa Shaped the Christian Mind*. Downers Grove, IL: IVP Academic, 2007. www.bouma.us/code3
- Oden, Thomas. *Early Libyan Christianity*. Downers Grove, IL: IVP Academic, 2011. www.bouma.us/code4

GET YOUR FREE THRILLER

Building a relationship with my readers is one of my all-time favorite joys of writing! Once in a while I like to send out a newsletter with giveaways, free stories, pre-release content, updates on new books, and other bits on my stories.

Join my insider's group for updates, giveaways, and your free novel—a full-length action-adventure story in my *Order of Thaddeus* thriller series. Just tell me where to send it.

Follow this link to subscribe:
www.jabouma.com/free

ALSO BY J. A. BOUMA

J. A. Bouma believes nobody should have to read bad religious fiction—whether it's cheesy plots with pat answers or misrepresentations of the Christian faith and the Bible. So he wants to do something about it by telling compelling, propulsive stories that thrill as much as inspire, while offering a dose of insight along the way.

Order of Thaddeus Action-Adventure Thriller Series

Holy Shroud • Book 1

The Thirteenth Apostle • Book 2

Hidden Covenant • Book 3

American God • Book 4

Grail of Power • Book 5

Templars Rising • Book 6

Rite of Darkness • Book 7

Gospel Zero • Book 8

The Emperor's Code • Book 9

Silas Grey Collection 1 (Books 1-3)

Silas Grey Collection 2 (Books 4-6)

Silas Grey Collection 3 (Books 7-9)

Ichthus Chronicles Sci-Fi Apocalyptic Series

Apostasy Rising / Season 1, Episode 1

Apostasy Rising / Season 1, Episode 2

Apostasy Rising / Season 1, Episode 3

Apostasy Rising / Season 1, Episode 4

Apostasy Rising / Full Season 1 (Episodes 1 to 4)

Apocalypse Rising / Season 2, Episode 1

Apocalypse Rising / Season 2, Episode 2

Apocalypse Rising / Season 2, Episode 3

Apocalypse Rising / Season 2, Episode 4

Apocalypse Rising / Full Season

Faith Reimagined **Spiritual Coming-of-Age Series**

A Reimagined Faith • Book 1

A Rediscovered Faith • Book 2

A Ruined Faith • Book 3 (2020)

A Resurrected Faith • Book 4 (2021)

Mill Creek Junction **Short Story Series**

Get all the latest short stories at: www.millcreekjunction.com

Find all of my latest book releases at: www.jabouma.com

ABOUT THE AUTHOR

J. A. Bouma believes nobody should have to read bad religious fiction--whether it's cheesy plots with pat answers or misrepresentations of the Christian faith and the Bible. So he wants to do something about it by telling compelling, propulsive stories that thrill as much as inspire, while offering a dose of insight along the way.

As a former congressional staffer and pastor, and award-nominated bestselling author of over forty religious fiction and nonfiction books, he blends a love for ideas and adventure, exploration and discovery, thrill and thought. With graduate degrees in Christian thought and the Bible, and armed with a voracious appetite for most mainstream genres, he tells stories you'll read with abandon and recommend with pride—exploring the tension of faith and doubt, spirituality and culture, belief and practice, and the gritty drama that is our collective pilgrim story.

When not putting fingers to keyboard, he loves vintage jazz vinyl, a glass of Malbec, and an epic read—preferably together. He lives in Grand Rapids with his wife, two kiddos, and rambunctious boxer-pug-terrier.

www.jabouma.com • jeremy@jabouma.com

Made in the USA
Monee, IL
22 June 2020